☑ P9-DCR-415

**Praise for *New York Times* bestselling author
RaeAnne Thayne**

"RaeAnne Thayne gets better with every book."
—Robyn Carr, #1 *New York Times* bestselling author

"RaeAnne Thayne is quickly becoming one of
my favorite authors…. Once you start reading,
you aren't going to be able to stop."
—*Fresh Fiction*

"This issue of the Cape Sanctuary series draws
the reader in from the first page to the gratifying
conclusion."
—*New York Journal of Books* on *The Sea Glass Cottage*

**Praise for *USA TODAY* bestselling author
Michelle Major**

"A fantastic mix of drama and romance, starring
a fragile, belligerent heroine and wounded hero.
The innuendos, banter and role-perfect nicknames
make it exceptional and genuine."
—*RT Book Reviews*
on *A Kiss on Crimson Ranch*, 4.5 stars

"A sweet start to a promising series, perfect for fans
of Debbie Macomber."
—*Publishers Weekly* (starred review)
on *The Magnolia Sisters*

RaeAnne Thayne finds inspiration in the beautiful northern Utah mountains, where the *New York Times* and *USA TODAY* bestselling author lives with her husband and three children. Her books have won numerous honors, including RITA® Award nominations from Romance Writers of America and a Career Achievement Award from *RT Book Reviews*. RaeAnne loves to hear from readers and can be contacted through her website, www.raeannethayne.com.

USA TODAY bestselling author **Michelle Major** loves stories of new beginnings, second chances and always with happily-ever-afters. An avid hiker and avoider of housework, she lives in the shadow of the Rocky Mountains with her husband, two teenagers and a menagerie of spoiled furbabies. Connect with her at www.michellemajor.com.

New York Times Bestselling Author

RaeAnne Thayne

SNOWED IN AT THE RANCH

Previously published as *Intimate Surrender*

**HARLEQUIN
BESTSELLING
AUTHOR
COLLECTION**

HARLEQUIN®
BESTSELLING
AUTHOR
COLLECTION

Recycling programs
for this product may
not exist in your area.

ISBN-13: 978-1-335-49836-6

Snowed In at the Ranch
First published as Intimate Surrender in 2004.
This edition published in 2022.
Copyright © 2004 by RaeAnne Thayne

A Kiss on Crimson Ranch
First published in 2014. This edition published in 2022.
Copyright © 2014 by Michelle Major

For questions and comments about the quality of this book,
please contact us at CustomerService@Harlequin.com.

Harlequin Enterprises ULC
22 Adelaide St. West, 41st Floor
Toronto, Ontario M5H 4E3, Canada
www.Harlequin.com

Printed in U.S.A.

CONTENTS

SNOWED IN
AT THE RANCH

RaeAnne Thayne

To Linda Kruger,
for unwavering support and encouragement.

Chapter 1

"We shouldn't go. It's not right to leave you here alone. Not with a storm coming on."

Margie Taylor's sturdy features creased with worry, and her weathered, capable hand fretted with the handle of her suitcase. With his typical stoicism, her husband, Clint, took it from her and stowed it behind the seat in their king-cab Ford pickup.

Katie Crosby managed a patient smile, just as if she and Margie hadn't just spent the last three hours circling this same argument more times than a green-broke horse at the end of a lead line. "Don't be silly," she said. "I'll be just fine. I can take care of myself for a few days and you said you'd made arrangements for Darwin Simmons to come over from the Bar S to feed and water the stock. I don't foresee any problems."

"Still, I don't feel good about leaving you. You know

we always try to be here when one of the family comes to Sweetwater."

"I know how seriously you and Clint take your responsibilities as caretakers of the ranch. You do a wonderful job here but you are certainly entitled to a private life, too."

Margie looked unconvinced and Katie squeezed her hand. "Your daughter needs you. It's her first baby and she's probably scared to death and needs her mother."

The bitter irony of her words didn't escape her, but Katie ignored the sudden pang in her chest. "You have to go to Idaho Falls," she went on. "I would feel just horrible if you missed seeing your new grandchild enter the world because of me."

"Weatherman says that storm is supposed to be a real doozy," Clint spoke up.

"Then you'd better hurry and get on your way so you aren't caught in it. I'll be fine, I promise."

"But what if you're stranded out here by yourself?" Margie asked, her forehead furrowed with worry.

"I won't mind, I promise. I came out from Portland looking for a little peace and quiet. I have plenty of books to read and the kitchen is fully stocked. I don't need anything else. As long as Darwin can take care of the stock, I'll be cozy and warm and snug as can be in the ranch house."

"I just don't feel right about this."

"Don't give me another thought. Just focus on Carly and that new grandbaby of yours."

Between her and Clint, they finally managed to herd Margie into the passenger seat of the truck, though she still looked worried.

Before they drove away, Clint rolled down the window. "If the power goes out, you'll have to start up the generator," he said gruffly. "Instructions are on the wall next to it."

"I'll be fine," she said for what seemed like the hundredth time. Through the open window she kissed him on the cheek, enjoying his blush. "Give the little darling a kiss for me, all right? Be safe."

He finally put the truck in gear and the four-wheel drive tires spit gravel as he headed down the long drive. Katie stood and watched them go while an unusually harsh wind for early March dug icy knuckles into her ribs inside her open canvas ranch coat. Despite her fleece hat, her head was freezing.

She should be used to this half-naked feeling after nearly three months without the heavy mane of hair she had always worn, but she still felt exposed with her new short, wispy hairstyle.

A few fluttery snowflakes settled on her skin and the canvas of her coat with deceptive gentleness. They might look lovely now, tiny swirling specks against the pale lavender twilight, but she knew a Wyoming winter storm could turn deadly with warp speed, even in March.

She had a feeling the weatherman was right about the storm. The air had a heavy, expectant quality to it, and thick dark clouds already concealed the tops of the mountains.

Katie filled her lungs with cold air that smelled of snow and lifted her face to the gossamer flakes.

She had always found peace out here and usually loved the view from the sprawling log-and-stone ranch house with its wide front porch and four gables along the steeply pitched roof. Even in winter, she could gaze for hours at the harsh and wild ring of snow-covered mountains that loomed over the ranch, the neat split-rail fences on either side of the driveway, the long row of bushy pine trees that formed a barrier from the endless Wyoming wind.

Try as she might, she knew she would find little comfort in the view this time. She was afraid peace would become a rare and elusive commodity in the coming months.

With a deep sigh, she reached a hand inside her coat and touched the tiny, barely noticeable bulge at her abdomen.

Just when, exactly, does a woman decide her life has spun completely and irrevocably out of her control? she wondered grimly.

Katie liked to think she was a fairly together kind of person. Sure, she had her problems. Who didn't? So what if her best friend Carrie compared her to a hermit crab with agoraphobia and her mother still thought she was a fat, homely thirteen-year-old with bad vision and a serious addiction to comfort food?

She might lack the grace and poise one might expect from an offspring of one of the Northwest's wealthiest families. But besides thick, gooey macaroni and cheese, Katie had always comforted herself with the immutable knowledge that she had something far more important than charm and beauty and a twenty-inch waist.

She was smart. Off-the-charts smart. She wasn't arrogant about it—it was just a fact of life, like her brown eyes, her streaky brown hair, the tiny heart-shaped mole just above her left eyebrow.

She might not have grace and poise, but she *had*

graduated summa cum laude from Stanford and become the vice president of research and development of one of the most powerful computer companies in the world. She knew her brother Trent relied on her logic and judgment at Crosby Systems and used her often as a sounding board.

So how, she wondered now as she gazed at the charcoal clouds gathering force, did she find herself in this predicament? Pregnant and alone and deep in the grip of a major panic attack?

Two days ago when her OB had confirmed the suspicion she hadn't even dared admit to herself, that panic had virtually paralyzed her. She had told herself the queasiness that had plagued her for several weeks must be some kind of lingering bug, had attributed her missed periods to stress and fatigue.

Hoping she only needed time away from the high stress of her life, she had come to the ranch, her own personal refuge, to recharge her batteries. After several weeks of telecommuting, the fatigue and the nausea hadn't abated. She returned to Portland for a meeting she couldn't miss and finally decided to see her doctor, who delivered the stunning news.

She had somehow driven in a numb haze to her condo and had sat in her living room all night long with the curtains drawn and the lights off.

The next morning she could think of nothing but returning to this haven where she had always felt such safety and solace. Maybe the clean mountain air would help her figure out how to cope with the atomic bomb that had just detonated in her neatly ordered life.

In the last few days, she'd had more time to get used to the idea that she was going to be a mother in a little over six months but she still didn't have the first idea how to chart out the rest of her life. She had always been one for blueprints and goals and lists, even as a little girl. So how was she supposed to pencil in an unplanned pregnancy at age twenty-eight, especially when her child's father didn't even know her real name?

She meant what she said to Margie. She was almost glad they had planned to leave for the birth of their new grandchild. As much as she loved the ranch caretakers, they tended to hover over her. Right now she desperately needed solitude—time to ponder and meditate and somehow shape an entirely new life plan for herself, one that included the tiny baby growing inside her.

One that certainly didn't include the child's father, no matter how much she might wish things could be different.

Kate shook off the foolish thought. A smart woman could never believe she and her baby's father would ever have more than the one incredible night they had shared.

An hour later she had just added another log to the fire in the massive river-rock fireplace of the great room and was settling onto the comfy couch with a mug of hot cocoa and a book she knew she wouldn't be able to concentrate on when she heard the bass rumble of a vehicle approaching.

What had Margie and Clint forgotten? she wondered. At this rate, they would find themselves stuck out here in the middle of the approaching blizzard.

A blast of cold air hit her as soon as she hurried to open the door for them. She shivered and saw that in the short time since she had stood in the driveway watching them leave, a half-inch of snow had fallen. The sun had slid behind the mountains and in the pale lavender twilight, she could make out a late-model SUV approaching the house.

Not Clint and Margie, then. Odd. They hadn't mentioned they were expecting anyone.

From the entryway, she watched a man climb out of the vehicle and had an impression of lean, muscular strength. She saw only dark wavy hair and a leather aviator jacket, then he turned to face her and the stoneware mug slipped from her clumsy fingers.

She reached for it just in time to keep the whole thing from gushing out all over the wood floor. Hot cocoa splashed her jeans but she barely registered it. She could focus on only one horrifying realization.

He had found her!

She couldn't seem to draw enough breath into her lungs as Peter Logan slammed the door to the SUV and stalked up the porch stairs. The blood rushed away from her oxygen-starved brain and she swayed, fighting a panicked urge to slam the door and shove the heavy hall table across it as a barricade against his anger. It took every ounce of concentration to keep her hands clenched tightly at her sides, not covering the tiny, barely there life growing inside her.

"Hello, Celeste." Her middle name came out more like a snarl.

Celeste. The name she'd used the night of the auction gala, when she'd kept her true identity a secret from him.

"Peter. Th-this is a surprise." She hated the stammer but couldn't seem to help it.

"I'll just bet it is."

She couldn't think what to say, could only stare at him as wild memories crowded through her mind of how that tight, angry mouth had once been tender and sensual, had once explored every inch of her skin.

"Are you going to stand there staring at me all night like I'm the Abominable Snowman come to call, or do you think you might condescend to let me inside?"

Did she have a choice? If she did, her vote would have been for locking him out on the porch rather than face a confrontation with him. But since she had a pretty good idea that a man like Peter Logan wouldn't let anything as inconsequential as a locked door keep him away, she had no choice but to surrender to the inevitable. She stepped aside.

"What are you doing here, Peter?"

"You mean how did I figure out who the hell you really were?"

Despite her best efforts at control, she shivered at the menace in his tone. "That, too."

"Don't you read the papers, sweetheart?"

She stared at him blankly. Across the vast room, she was oddly aware of a log breaking apart in the fireplace with a hiss and crackle. After a moment he yanked a folded newspaper from the inside pocket of his snow-flecked leather jacket and slapped it down on the narrow hall table next to her.

She eyed it like he'd just let loose a wolverine in the Sweetwater great room. Warily, her pulse skipping with sudden trepidation, Katie picked up the newspaper. It was a copy of the society page of *Portland Weekly,* the independent tabloid that delighted in poking fun at the city's movers and shakers.

Her gaze went to the photo first and her already

queasy stomach dipped. It was a photo of her and the man now standing before her, both of them in elegant evening wear. Her back—bared in a glittery emerald-colored designer gown she'd borrowed from her best friend—was to the camera, but anybody who saw the picture could clearly identify Peter Logan—and could see the two of them were locked in a passionate embrace.

She had seen it before. The newspaper had run the photo months ago as part of a feature spread of a bachelor auction and charity benefit for Children's Connection, a Portland adoption agency and fertility clinic. The caption had said only something about Peter being photographed in a hot kiss with a mystery woman. When they ran it the first time, she had seen it and thanked her very lucky stars that she hadn't been recognizable.

Apparently someone had figured it out. The headline above this photo read "Mystery Solved: Crosby, Logan scions put aside famous feud long enough for kiss."

Oh, no. She drew in a shaky breath. This was bad. Seriously bad. She read on.

> "We first brought you the juicy tidbit a few months ago that Logan Corporation CEO and oh-so-sexy bachelor Peter Logan was caught in a very heated embrace with a mysterious glamour-gal during a chi-chi gala for Children's Connection, a cause the Logan family notably supports. The two of them disappeared together soon after.
>
> At the time. Logan pointedly refused to answer questions about the object of his affections,

but after some digging, *Portland Weekly* has since learned his snuggle-honey was none other than Katherine Crosby. That's right, of *those* Crosbys—Logan rivals on and off the corporate battlefield.

Does their embrace signal an end to the famous feud? Are Portland's own versions of the Hatfield and McCoy clans really ready to kiss and make up?

Apparently at least two of them are.

Neither Logan nor Ms. Crosby were available for comment but we'll bring you more about this exciting development as soon as we find out more."

Her already queasy stomach dipped. Her mother was bound to hear about this; Katie had no doubt whatsoever about that. And when she did, Katie knew Sheila Crosby would rage and carry on for days, accusing her of everything from disloyalty to outright treason.

Just thinking about the inevitable scene made her shoulders sag with the exhaustion that never seemed far away these days.

"Nothing to say?" Peter finally asked when her silence dragged on.

"I've never been called a glamour-gal before. I don't believe it's as gratifying as I would have imagined."

His sculpted features darkened. "I dislike being made a fool of, Katherine."

"Kate," she murmured, regretting the glibness she tended to turn to during times of high stress. "Nearly everyone calls me Katie or Kate."

"Really, Celeste?" He asked in that same biting tone.

Oh, Katie. What a mess you're in, she thought. Pregnant with this man's baby, this overwhelming, powerful, *gorgeous* man who despised her and her family. If he hated her now, how would he react if he ever discovered the tiny secret she carried inside her?

The fragile threads of control seemed to slip a few more notches, but she flailed for them valiantly and faced him with what she hoped was cool aplomb.

Without waiting for the invitation she wasn't sure she could issue, he yanked off his jacket and tossed it over the rack of entwined elk antlers in the hallway then claimed one of the plump armchairs near the fire. She really had no choice but to follow him and perched on the edge of the sofa, trying not to let him see her nervousness.

"Okay, let's hear it. What's your game?"

"Game?"

"What are you playing at? What were you trying to achieve by your little masquerade?"

Of course he would want explanations from her, some justification for her deception. How could she possibly find the words for something she didn't even understand herself?

"Why didn't you tell me who you were?"

"I don't know that I have a good answer to that."

"Try." His voice was silk-sheathed steel.

She scrambled for some kind of explanation and finally came up with something she hoped sounded reasonable. It was part of the truth, just not all of it. "Katie Crosby is a fairly boring person," she said after a long moment. "All she ever thinks about is work. I suppose it was exciting being someone else for a few hours. Someone glamorous and adventurous and…

and desirable. I got carried away by the magic of the evening. Then, after we…kissed, I was afraid to tell you who I was. I knew you would be angry and it just seemed easier all around not to say anything."

Peter studied her. She chewed her bottom lip after she finished speaking, waiting for him to respond. He wondered how in the hell a woman could appear so sweet and innocent on the outside while inside she was nothing but a deceptive little snake.

He had never been so furious. It was taking every ounce of willpower he possessed not to rage and yell and throw a table or two through that huge wall of windows.

His blood should have had time to cool in the twenty-four hours since his assistant had warily shown him that damn newspaper and he'd finally learned the identity of the mystery lover who had obsessed him for months. It had taken him most of that time to use all his connections and finally run her to ground here at this Wyoming ranch in the middle of nowhere, another hour to have his plane readied and two more in the air between here and Portland.

The whole time he'd been behind the controls of his Gulfstream III, he had waited for his anger to fade, for the familiar cool reserve the world expected of him to take over. But throughout the flight, as now, his skin had been hot and itchy as this fury seethed through him.

This woman—this slender, delicate-looking woman with her short hair and big eyes, who looked like a teenager in stocking feet and faded jeans—had made a complete fool out of him. Every word out of her lush little lips had been a lie.

When he thought about how he had obsessed over her in the three months since she blew through his life, the energy he had wasted looking for her, he could barely think past his rage and self-disgust.

A Crosby.

Just the name left a sour taste in his mouth. What an idiot he had been to throw away years of family loyalty, of complete dedication to the Logan name and everything it stood for, all for a pretty face.

All right, more than pretty, he admitted. Even now, when she wore no makeup to set off those sculpted cheekbones and full lips and when she had dark circles under her eyes and her features were pale, his body instinctively reacted to her.

He wanted her, even knowing who she was, and the discovery infuriated him even more.

"This is about the super router we're developing, isn't it?" he asked.

She was a hell of an actress, he'd give her that much. If he didn't know better, he would almost believe that shock on her face was genuine. "What do you mean?" she asked.

"You went through my desk while I was asleep. Don't try to deny it. Find out anything interesting about the project?"

Color flared high on those cheekbones. "I don't know what you're talking about."

"Right. Now you're going to tell me you don't have any idea Logan is close to revolutionizing computer networking with our nano-peripheral-interface-router. And of course Crosby Systems, which coincidentally just released its own router-controller software, would have absolutely no interest in stealing the technology that would create the fastest networking system in the world. Come on, Crosby. You really think I'm dumb enough to fall for your lies twice?"

She gaped at him. "You think I was spying on you that night? That I was some kind of—of corporate Mata Hari, out for a little industrial espionage after I screw you into oblivion?"

"At this point, sweetheart, I wouldn't put anything past you."

"Because I'm a Crosby, right?"

That wounded belligerence in her voice grated down his spine like metal on metal. "Not *only* because you're a Crosby. Because you're also a lying, deceitful little—" He bit off the derogatory word just in time.

He was such an idiot. He hated to think about how his family would react to his abysmal lapse in judgment when they learned he'd been willing to risk the company's entire future for a roll in the sack. He had a feeling he would be lucky if his name was still on the door of the CEO's office at Logan. Hell, he'd be lucky if they even let him keep the name he'd been given as a six-year-old.

He never forgot how much he owed Terrence and Leslie Logan, how very blessed he had been to be adopted into their family two years after their own son had been kidnapped. If they hadn't rescued him from the Children's Connection orphanage, he hated thinking where he might have ended up. On the streets like his mother, probably, or in prison.

He owed them everything. His heart, his blood, his *soul*. When they read that damn tabloid article, he could just picture the disappointment in Terrence's eyes, the hurt in Leslie's. The knot in his stomach kinked a little tighter.

No. He had worked too hard for too long proving to his parents he was capable of running the Fortune 500 company they had built from the ground up. He refused to let a Crosby ruin everything, especially not this particular Crosby.

"Don't you think you're being a little paranoid, Peter?" she said now. "I never touched your desk."

Against his will, he had a vivid memory of her naked and flushed the second or third time they made love, her luscious skin glowing with perspiration and the soft little noises of arousal she made as he took her against the nearest surface, which at the time just happened to be the top of his antique walnut desk.

Throughout that incredible night of passion, there had scarcely been a corner of his loft they'd missed in their hunger for each other.

He raised an eyebrow but said nothing. He knew the instant her own memory clicked in. A rosy blush spilled over her cheeks and she dropped her gaze.

"Well, besides that time," she mumbled, looking so charmingly disconcerted he wondered how she could possibly be so deceitful.

"I've tried to think about what I might have had lying around about our NPIR project but I'm coming up empty. Why don't you refresh my memory? What did you find?"

"Nothing! I wasn't thinking about NPIRs or anything else computer related. I didn't go anywhere near your stupid desk, except that time with…you."

"Yet the note you left was written on my own personal stationery, which I just happen to keep in the top drawer of that stupid desk."

She stared at him for a long moment, then she drew a deep breath. When she spoke, her voice sounded weary. "What do you want, Peter? Why follow me out here to the middle of nowhere? You could have yelled at me over the phone."

He refused to let himself be sidetracked by how fragile she suddenly looked. "I want some answers. What did you learn about our project?"

"I didn't learn anything! I told you that. I never even gave work a thought that night. If you'll remember, you didn't give me time to think about much of anything but you."

They stared at each other for a moment and he remembered again the wild passion they had shared. Or at least he thought they'd shared it. Had it all been feigned on her part? All those long kisses, her sighs and moans, the way she acted as if she couldn't seem to get enough of him?

That was the part that he was finding most difficult to accept, he finally admitted to himself. He had been enthralled with her, completely entranced. He had wanted her with a fierce hunger unlike anything he'd ever known before.

While she had been as cold-blooded and calculating as an asp.

"Did your brother tell you to sleep with me?" he asked.

With a swift intake of breath, she stared at him, her brown eyes huge in her pale face. In any other woman, he might have almost believed she looked hurt. But he obviously couldn't trust anything his instincts told him about Katherine Crosby.

"That's insulting to Trent and to me. I shouldn't even justify it with a response but I will tell you that he knows nothing about this, about the two of us and that night. If he did, he would be livid."

Peter slapped the folded tabloid at her. "Hate to be the one to break it to you, sweetheart, but there's not a person in Portland who doesn't know by now."

She gazed at the paper for a moment, nibbling her lip again. "Okay so everyone might know we kissed. As for the rest of it, no one else has to know anything about that. We were both carried away by the champagne and the night and the whole thing. Matters never should have gone so far. We should both just forget it ever happened."

"You'd like that, wouldn't you?"

"Oh, you have no idea," she murmured.

At her words, another wave of anger washed over him. The intensity of it had him jumping to his feet and stalking to the fireplace. He hated that she could just dismiss the night they had spent together. *Forget it ever happened.* Right. As if he could just forget the most erotic night of his life.

He turned back to her. "A smart man never forgets his mistakes. And, sweetheart, this was one hell of a mistake."

"For both of us."

"The difference is, you knew exactly what you were doing—and who you were doing it with."

"That's right. I set out to seduce you from the moment I walked into that ballroom. It was a brilliant strategy, wouldn't you say? All I had to do was convince you to take me home with you, make love all night until you fell asleep, then comb through your office on the chance—slim to none though it was— that I might find some tiny snippet of information in your loft about your super-router that we could use at Crosby Systems. Right. You caught me. That's me, Katie Crosby, corporate spy. Trent sends his little sister out to sleep with all his business rivals."

"I wouldn't put anything past the Crosbys."

Something flashed in her dark eyes, something that looked like anger and hurt and maybe even a little sorrow. "Okay, that's enough," she snapped. "I would like you to leave now. I'm sure you don't want to spend another moment in the belly of the beast."

She rose as if to show him out but as soon as she stood, what little color remaining on her face drained out like wine spilling from a tipped glass and she swayed. Peter reached out instinctively to keep her from toppling over, then helped her back onto the couch.

"What's wrong? Are you ill?"

Her chin lifted. "What do you care?"

"I don't," he snapped. "Maybe I just happen to be fond of these particular boots and don't want you yakking all over them."

She glared at him. "Your precious boots are safe. I'm not going to *yak,* as you so charmingly put it. I stood up a little too soon but I'm perfectly fine now."

He only had to take one look at her to know she was lying, but then why should that surprise him? The woman wouldn't know the truth if it jumped up and bit her in the behind. With hollow eyes, her skin three shades past white and her mouth pinched like a shriveled apple left in the bottom of the bushel, she sat there and expected him to believe everything was fine.

"I didn't see signs of anybody else when I arrived. Who else is out here with you?"

She paused as if she didn't want to answer him, then she finally shrugged. "Usually the ranch foreman and his wife live in quarters at the rear of the house, but they're away for a few days."

"You're alone?"

"Not if you count two dogs, six barn cats, a dozen horses and two hundred head of cattle."

He studied her pale features again, suddenly chagrined at himself for bursting in on her, guns blazing. She might be a lying Crosby but she didn't look well at all.

Crosby or not, he didn't like the idea of her being out here alone. A thousand things could happen to an ill woman on her own at an isolated Wyoming ranch, especially with the storm percolating out there.

"If you're done yelling at me, I really would like you to leave now." Somehow she managed to inject regal condescension into her words, even with her pale features.

"I really think I should stay," he found himself saying.

Her eyes widened and he didn't miss the way her hand clenched over her stomach, as if just the idea of spending another moment with him was enough to make her insides churn.

"No. No, you shouldn't. The weather report said a nasty storm is heading this way. You'll want to fly back to Portland before it hits."

"It's already here. Can't you hear that wind? The

reports I heard before I landed said this area was due for at least two feet of snow. I won't be flying anywhere tonight."

"If you heard the storm reports before you left, why fly out here in such a rush? Acting on a whim like that hardly seems like typical behavior for the cold, ruthless CEO of Logan Corporation."

Nothing he had done since he'd seen her in that hotel ballroom had been typical behavior for him. He had seen the reports of an approaching storm in this area before he left Portland, but not even flying into the eye of a hurricane would have kept him grounded.

He had known he was foolish to leave but he had been so angry he hadn't cared about anything but running her to ground, after three long months of searching.

"It doesn't matter why I left," he answered. "I'm not going anywhere."

"I'm not in the mood for your macho posturing, Peter. I don't want or need you here."

"Fickle little thing, aren't you? Three months ago, you certainly wanted me around. If my memory serves—and believe me, it does—you couldn't get enough."

She glared at him, though he saw yet another blush heat those cheeks. "Which am I? Ruthless corporate spy or sex-crazed nymphomaniac?"

"Good question. One I would certainly like to know the answer to myself."

Before she could give voice to the heated response he could see brewing, a powerful gust of wind rattled the windowpanes and moaned under the eaves of the log ranch house.

The two lamps burning in the room flickered in unison then went out, pitching the room into darkness lit only by the fire's glow.

Chapter 2

"That settles it. I'm not going anywhere."

Even though the only light in the room came from the snapping flames in the fireplace, Katie could see the determination in Peter's eyes and she wanted to weep. Just when she thought she had hit absolute rock bottom in her life, somehow she managed to cartwheel down another few feet.

She suddenly wanted nothing in the world more than to curl up on that couch in front of the fireplace, wrap herself in her grandmother's wedding-ring quilt and sob.

What had she done to deserve this? Okay, maybe she hadn't been exactly forthcoming to Peter Logan three months earlier. In retrospect, she knew she should have told him her real name the moment he struck up a conversation with her, at the first sign of flirtation.

She wasn't sure why she had kept that important little detail to herself—maybe because she had been so shocked that the gorgeous and sought-after Peter Logan could actually be flirting with someone like her—boring, quiet Katie Crosby.

Who could blame any woman for being caught up in the magic of the evening? With a glamorous makeover, a new hairstyle, the designer clothes, she had *felt* like someone else. A stranger alluring enough to catch the interest of one of Portland's most wanted bachelors.

The champagne she had overindulged in hadn't helped any. She hadn't been thinking with a clear head but she did know she hadn't wanted the night to end. She also knew that the moment Peter found out her last name that flattering desire in his eyes would have changed to contempt and coldness faster than she could blink.

Okay, so she had perpetuated a tiny deception on the man by keeping her identity concealed. Was that really such a hideous crime that someone felt the need to take her calm, organized world and shake the dickens out of it as if she was stuck in some nightmarish live snow globe?

She thought things were bleak before when she was just pregnant and alone. Now she had the delightful added bonus of facing the reality that she was pregnant and alone and heartily despised by her baby's father.

The real hell of it was, seeing him again like this only served to remind her vividly of the heat and astonishing wonder of that night. Of kissing his hard mouth and touching those muscles underneath his clothes and burning only for him.

He hated her, she knew he did, but still she couldn't

control the way her insides trembled and sighed just seeing the firelight wash across those gorgeous, masculine features.

"Looks like we're in for a long night," he said abruptly and rose to his feet. "While you round up a flashlight and some candles, I'll go bring in some extra firewood."

Of course he would take charge, she thought. As Logan Corporation CEO, he was no doubt used to giving orders and having his minions obey without question. She should have been offended by his whole master-and-commander routine but she had to admit a tiny part of her wanted to let him throw his weight around a little, to let someone else carry the burdens of her worries for a while.

She sternly squashed the tempting impulse, ashamed of her weakness for even entertaining it for a second. "You don't need to do that. Clint loaded several days worth of wood on the back porch for me before he left. There's also a gas-fired generator out back that will juice up the appliances until the power kicks back on."

"You act as if you've been through this before."

"A few times. The power can be unreliable at best out here, especially during winter storms. I've had enough experience with outages that I should be perfectly fine. Believe me, you can head into town for the night with a completely clear conscience."

She might as well have been talking to the river rocks on the fireplace. His only answer was a raised eyebrow and a challenging stare.

Katie sighed. It was worth a try. The idea of spending even one night in such close quarters with Peter Logan was enough to send her into major panic mode.

He was staying, though, and she realized grimly

that no amount of arguing would change his mind. The same man who had the kindness as an eighteen-year-old college student to rescue a fat, awkward adolescent from the ugliness of her peers more than a decade earlier would never leave a woman alone out here in the middle of a blizzard.

"I don't suppose you know anything about generators, do you?" she asked. "I've seen Clint start it but never done it myself."

"Between the two of us, we should be able to figure it out, don't you think?"

Relieved that he seemed willing to put aside his animosity, even temporarily, she nodded. "Sure."

He cocked his head. "Are you sure you're up to it? You're still looking a little green around the edges. Maybe you should just take it easy and lie down here by the fire. I'm sure I can handle starting up a generator on my own."

She refused to let him see how very much she would like to do exactly that, just curl up on this couch and let him handle everything. Trying her best to conceal the greasy nausea writhing around in her stomach, she mustered a small smile.

"Don't worry about me." Using the fire's glow for illumination, she crossed the vast room to the hall storage closet. On the shelf near the door, just where she expected it, she found a large battery-powered lantern Clint and Margie kept available for exactly these kinds of emergencies. Wouldn't she love it if the engineers on her R & D team were half as efficient as the Sweetwater caretakers? she thought.

"This should help," she said to Peter. She led the way toward the utility porch off the kitchen. It seemed as if in just the few moments since the power had gone out, the temperature in the rooms away from the fireplace had dropped significantly. The Mexican tile floor in the kitchen was freezing, even through her thick wool socks.

All she could see outside the greenhouse window above the sink was thick blackness, but she could hear snow hurling against the logs and the wind moaning under the eaves.

It sounded lonely, mournful, and she shivered despite the sweater Ivy had sent her for Christmas from her new husband's country of Lantanya, where Max was king.

The lantern gave off enough light that Peter must have seen her reaction. "Everything okay? Do you need to sit down?"

She knew the concern in his voice was just the courtesy he would show anyone but she couldn't help being warmed by it. She had a feeling he wouldn't be so solicitous if he knew the secret she carried under that sweater, though.

"No. The cold just took me by surprise, that's all. The generator is this way."

With the lantern held out in front of her, she carefully navigated through the mudroom to the utility porch that housed the home's utilities—the furnace, water heater and the backup generator. The large room was vented with outside air for safety reasons and Katie found it even colder here than in the kitchen, so cold she could see her breath in the dim light she held in her hand.

"Any idea where to start?" Peter asked.

"Clint told me he left instructions." She held the lantern up higher and scanned the room.

"This what you were looking for?" Peter asked, plucking a clipboard from a nail near the generator. He handed it to her and she saw several laminated cards secured neatly to it.

"I'll say this for the man—he doesn't have much to say but he's an absolute genius at organization." Katie leafed through the cards until she found guidelines for the gas-fired generator, beneath a page detailing how to relight the pilot on the furnace and one for checking the heating oil level on the outside tank.

"Here we go." She studied the instructions, smiling a little at Clint's meticulousness. "This doesn't look bad."

She reached to replace the clipboard on the nail but misjudged the distance in the dim light and stumbled a little against the wall. The back of her hand scraped across the nail, hard enough to break the skin, and Katie couldn't contain a quick intake of breath.

"What's wrong?"

It was silly, she knew, but she suddenly didn't want Peter to know she was the world's biggest klutz. She might have been blessed with brains by some genetic quirk, but she had definitely been passed over when it came to grace and poise.

She had always been the most accident-prone of her siblings. If there was one thing worse than being fat and ugly in a family of beautiful people, it was being fat and ugly and clumsy.

Peter already thought she had some deadly disease. He didn't need to know about this.

"Um, nothing," she murmured, tucking her hand against her side. "I'm fine."

"You're lying." He sounded more resigned than angry, as if he expected nothing else. "You might as well tell me what happened."

Her hand throbbed wickedly and she could feel blood beginning to drip from it. She wouldn't be able to hide it from him for long and she suddenly felt foolish for trying. "Just a scratch. It's nothing."

"Let me see."

She recognized the CEO in his voice, that unmistakable note of command. Her father had it and now Trent shared it in spades. She had spent her entire life surrounded by powerful men, she suddenly realized. With all that experience, why wasn't she better at dealing with them?

With a weary sigh, she thrust out her hand. Peter took the lantern from her and set it on top of the furnace, then gripped her hand and tugged it under the circle of light.

"It doesn't look very deep," he decided after studying it for a few moments.

"I told you it was just a scratch."

"Still, you'll need to put something on it."

"Can it wait until we're finished here, Dr. Logan?"

"I hope your tetanus shot is up to date. That nail looked a little rusty."

Someone with her inherent klutziness would be foolish not to keep current with her shots. Her last tetanus booster had been the previous summer after an unfortunate encounter with a conch shell on her brother Danny's Hawaii retreat.

"Don't worry, you're not going to be trapped in the

middle of a blizzard with someone suffering from lock-jaw."

"Well, at least I've got that much going for me. I guess things really could be worse."

His dry tone surprised a laugh from her. Not much of one, she had to admit, but a laugh nonetheless.

He smiled in automatic response, his teeth gleaming in the artificial light. They stood close together under the pool of light spilling from the lantern. He still held her hand, and his fingers were warm and hard on her skin.

His gaze met hers for a moment and suddenly she could think of nothing except their night together, how they had laughed at nothing and kissed and laughed some more.

Everything inside her seemed to clench at the memory, a long, slow tightening of muscle and nerves. She saw something kindle in his eyes, something hot and wild and dangerous.

Before she realized it, she swayed a little toward him, then caught herself just in time. Horrified at her response, she wrenched her hand out of his grasp and stepped back so quickly she nearly stumbled again.

"We'd better get this thing fired up."

For a moment, he only stared at her with an odd look in his dark eyes—a combination of awareness and a baffled sort of anger. "Right," he finally muttered. "The wind sounds like it's kicking up a notch."

To her vast relief, he turned his attention to the generator. It was a little trickier than Clint's instructions had led her to believe, but soon they had it going and switched the power current over to the generator.

Despite the tension simmering through the room

and the pain still throbbing from her hand, she felt like Benjamin Franklin with his kite and his key when the lights flickered back on.

She grinned. "Bingo."

He gazed at her for a charged moment, that strange expression in his eyes again. She waited for him to say something but he continued to watch her, as if he couldn't quite figure her out.

She cleared her throat. "Would you like something to eat? Margie left a pot of beef stew on the stove for me that's probably still hot and she made fresh rolls this morning. It's probably not what you're used to, but she's a wonderful cook."

"Let's take care of that cut of yours first."

She absolutely did not want him touching her again, not when she couldn't stop remembering how his body had felt inside her, how his mouth had explored her skin.

"I've got it. You could add another log to the fire, though, and turn off any lights and nonessential electronics throughout the house. We'll need to conserve what generator power we have. Here, take the lantern. I've got another one in my bedroom."

He nodded and held out his hand. Their fingers brushed as they exchanged the light, and tiny sparks jumped between them. Just static electricity, she told herself.

They returned to the kitchen together, then split up as she headed for her bedroom suite. She left the overhead light on long enough to locate another battery-powered emergency lantern in her closet, switched it off and carried the lantern to the bathroom to get first-aid supplies.

While she rummaged through the medicine cabinet for a bandage and antibiotic ointment and washed the blood off her hand, she caught sight of her reflection in the mirror above the sink. She looked horrendous. Her hair was spiky and windblown from her time outside earlier and she hadn't bothered with makeup. Her eyes looked unnaturally huge in her pale face and her mouth had a pinched, sickly look to it.

No wonder Peter looked at her like he couldn't quite believe Katie Crosby and the glamorous Celeste could be the same person.

She could scarcely believe it herself. She had been playing a part that night, a thrilling masquerade. Stuck alone here with her, Peter would see the real her. The boring, sensible Kate who wore long underwear and read dry technical manuals and who would never dream of going home with a handsome man and making love all night long.

Well, okay, she dreamed about it, she admitted to herself with a long, honest look in the mirror. She dreamed about it every night and remembered in exquisitely painful detail how she had come alive for the first time in her life that night.

Perhaps it was best that he see her for the person she really was. Not glamorous, not glitzy. Just Katie. That night she had been Cinderella at the ball, dressed up in borrowed finery. It had been wonderful and magical dancing the night away with Prince Charming, but midnight had come and gone. There would be no glass slipper for her—but she had been left with a magical, wondrous gift.

She touched her abdomen. Could she keep the baby a secret from him in such close quarters? It was only for one night and then he would be gone again. She was only thirteen weeks along and wasn't really showing unless someone knew her well enough to recognize that the tiny swelling at her stomach hadn't been there a few weeks ago.

She would just have to make sure she stayed in baggy clothes so he wouldn't have that close a look.

The pesky morning sickness could be explained away by a lingering stomach bug, she hoped.

It would be a little tricky to pull it off, but what other choice did she have? She couldn't tell him. This was *her* baby. He might have unwittingly donated the sperm but that didn't make him a father. Bad enough that she deceived him by not telling him her name—she couldn't bind him forever to a Crosby because of a quirk of fate.

Besides, Peter Logan was not the father she wanted for her baby. He was far too much like her own father—completely consumed by his work. She knew what it was like to wait in vain for a few crumbs her busy, important father might scatter her way. She wouldn't do that to her own child. Better for her baby never to know a father than to suffer from inattention and indifference.

She could carry off the deception for one night, then they would go their separate ways and Peter would never have to know about the baby. She would invent an imaginary lover for the inevitable questions from her family and friends about her child's paternity—a man she had fallen hard for but who had been unattainable.

Not so very far from the truth, she thought grimly. In fact, too close for her own comfort.

With a weary sigh, she quickly brushed her hair and debated touching up her face with some of the makeup tricks Carrie Summers had shown her. In the end she decided against doing anything more than a quick brush of lipstick and a little blush on her cheeks so she didn't look so ghastly pale.

She returned to the gathering room to find that Peter had pulled a small table and two chairs near the fireplace and had set out two place settings. She nibbled her lip, fighting the urge to turn back around and hide out in her room for the rest of the night.

Dinner for two in a dimly lit room in front of a crackling fire looked entirely too romantic, too *intimate.*

He stood by one of the chairs waiting for her with a challenging kind of look in his eyes and she knew she couldn't be cowardly enough to run away. She squared her shoulders and sat down.

"I hope you don't mind me moving the furniture around a little," he said. "I figured this would be more comfortable than eating in a cold dining room."

"The dining room is rarely used anyway. When I stay here, I usually eat in the kitchen with the Taylors."

"Those are the caretakers?"

She nodded. "Their daughter is having her first baby. They've gone for moral support."

"I hope they made it through the storm."

"I'm sure they'll be fine. Clint's used to driving in this weather."

She returned to stirring her stew and the Herculean effort of swallowing the occasional bite.

"This is quite a place you've got here," Peter said.

"Somehow I never would have figured the Crosbys to go for rustic and isolated."

The faint note of derision in his voice raised her hackles. She wasn't sure if it was aimed at her family or at the ranch, both of which she loved dearly. Either way she didn't like it. A sharp retort formed in her throat but she squashed it. In the interest of peace, she should probably do her best to avoid needless bickering.

"My father bought it as a retreat several years ago when it seemed like everybody was moving west."

Like many of Jack Crosby's actions, Sweetwater had been purchased to please one of his many girlfriends, then had been forgotten as soon as her father moved on to more nubile pastures. But she decided that was old family business she didn't particularly need to share with Peter Logan.

"Does your family spend much time here together?" he asked.

She tried to remember when the Crosbys had last done anything together.

"We all came out for Christmas once right after Jack bought it," she remembered. "Trent and Ivy have been out to ski occasionally. Sweetwater is only about an hour from the Jackson Hole ski resorts."

He broke a roll in half and liberally spread some of Margie's strawberry preserves on it. "Is that why you're here? To ski?"

She wasn't sure quite how to answer that. She certainly couldn't tell him she had escaped to Sweetwater first because she'd been ill and then because she had been desperately in need of a safe haven, a sanctuary where she could come to terms with her pregnancy and figure out how she was going to map out the rest of her life after this unexpected detour.

"I'm not much of a skier," she finally said.

She would have preferred to leave it at that but he pressed on. "So why are you here?"

Katie fought the urge to gnash her teeth at what was beginning to feel like an interrogation. "I like it here. Of all my siblings, I probably spend the most time here. This is where I come when I need to relax and recharge. I love the mountains, even in the winter. I like the solitude of it and the slow, easy pace. I guess I just needed a break from the rain."

"So you decided howling winds and three feet of snow would be more to your liking?"

"It doesn't snow all the time," she muttered. She frowned suddenly, remembering something that had been puzzling her since he arrived. "How did you know how to find me, anyway? Only a few people knew I was coming."

"You know, it's amazing. The truth can open all kinds of doors. Maybe you ought to try it sometime."

Before she could control it, her breath caught as the jab poked under her skin. She deserved it, she acknowledged, especially with the secret she still kept from him, the one she knew she could never tell him. Knowing his contempt was warranted didn't make it any easier to take.

"Who told you?"

"I phoned your office. Once I gave your assistant my name and told her I needed to speak with you on an urgent matter, she was eager to help. She said you were staying at the family ranch and gave me the number here. From there, it was easy to connect the phone number to a location."

She should have known. If Peter hadn't been there, Katie would have groaned and banged her head against the back of her chair a few times. She loved her sixty-year-old assistant dearly but Lila Fitzgerald had a romantic streak as wide as the Columbia Gorge. She read the *Weekly* faithfully and must have seen the picture of them together at the bachelor auction.

Katie could just guess at the wild speculation that must have been running amok through Lila's feverish imagination when Peter had called looking for her.

What kind of gossip was raging around the water coolers at Crosby Systems about her and Peter Logan because of that blasted picture? There were already some on her team who thought she didn't have the experience or the know-how to lead the R & D division. What would her co-workers think when they saw a picture of her consorting with the man many considered to be the enemy?

What would her family think?

She already knew Sheila would be livid. She could only be grateful her mother was in Europe and wouldn't be returning for several weeks. What about Trent and Ivy and Danny? They wouldn't care so much that Peter was a Logan, but they would worry whether he had hurt her. And when she turned up pregnant, she knew they would wonder at the timing. She just had to hope she could brazen it out.

"I'm still not sure why you went to all the trouble to come out here. If you had the number, why couldn't we have had this delightful little reunion over the phone?"

Peter didn't have a rational answer to that. He only

knew that the moment he found out where she was, he'd known he would come after her. He'd used the excuse of finding out what she had learned about the super-router project, but the truth was he'd been consumed with the need to see her again, corporate spy or not.

He'd be damned before he told her that, though, and he opted to change the subject. "Are you going to eat this delicious stew or just push it around in the bowl?"

Color crept along her cheekbones but she still looked far too pale for him. "I'm not very hungry."

"Still feeling sick?"

Her gaze flashed to his, then back to the bowl of stew. "No. I'm fine."

He didn't want to worry about her. He wanted to wrap himself up in his well-deserved fury.

She had deceived him, had possibly stolen Logan secrets from him, jeopardizing a project that had been in the works for years. Maybe even jeopardizing his own future at Logan.

She was a *Crosby,* for hell's sake. That alone should have been enough to squash any softness he might be tempted to feel.

So why was he fighting the completely inappropriate urge to take care of her?

"Have you seen a doctor?" he asked abruptly.

That color spread until even her nose was pink. "It's just a—a bug. Nothing to worry about."

"Is it contagious?"

A corner of her lush mouth lifted at that, then settled back into solemn lines. "No. I can guarantee you won't catch this particular bug."

A particularly strong gust of wind rattled the big window, but the merry little fire put out plenty of heat.

Peter couldn't help wondering what they would be doing right now if circumstances had been different. If she wasn't ill, certainly, but also if he had never learned her true identity.

Two days ago he would have given everything he had to be right here with the woman who had haunted his dreams for three months. To be alone with Celeste in an isolated ranch house, snug and warm and enchanted, would have been a fantasy come true. They would have snuggled under a blanket and listened to the wind howl outside while they kissed and touched and made love a dozen times.

The reality of their situation was so far removed from that fantasy that he gave a humorless laugh.

"What?"

"Just wondering what your brother would say if he knew I was here," he improvised quickly.

"I'm old enough that I don't need to ask my brother's permission for much these days."

The depressing reality of their situation here made his voice sharper than he intended. "Do you bother to ask him which unwitting business rivals to seduce, or do you figure that out all on your own?"

He regretted the words and the end to their temporary détente as soon as they escaped, especially when he saw hurt flare in her brown eyes. Was the emotion real, he wondered, or was she just a damn good actress? Whatever the answer, he didn't like seeing her wounded.

Her chair scraped the wood floor and she pushed it back and rose, her expression now veiled. "I'm tired and I don't have the energy to trade barbs with you, so what do you say we call it a night?"

He opened his mouth to apologize for his cruelty then stopped himself just in time. He didn't have a damn thing to be sorry about. She was the one who had screwed him over.

"Sweetwater has six bedrooms suites," she went on. "Two on this floor and five upstairs. Each has clean linens and a wood stove or fireplace for warmth. I'm sure you're capable of starting your own fire, or you can sleep here on the couch if you would rather."

"Kate—" He wasn't sure what he was going to say. *Not* an apology, damn it. She cut him off anyway before he could form any kind of coherent sentence.

"Good night, Peter," she murmured in a voice every bit as cold as that bitch of a wind, then she picked up her bowl with its untouched stew and carried it to the kitchen.

Chapter 3

After her grand exit, Katie knew she had no choice but to hide here in her bedroom for the rest of the night.

It was too early to sleep, only about eight-thirty or so. She was tired enough, certainly—she was always tired these days—but even if she could manage to close her eyes, she had no doubt her mind would continue its wild race. She had a whole assortment of books to read, but none of them grabbed her interest. Why bother when she knew she wouldn't be able to concentrate on it anyway?

Surrendering to the inevitable, she pulled the quilt up to her chin and gazed into the flames and let her mind replay the night of the Children's Connection bachelor auction, one small slice of time that had altered the course of her life forever.

Stand up straight and smile. If you feel beautiful, the world will see you that way. Her best friend Carrie's advice rang in her ears as Katie stood outside the ballroom at the Portland Hilton.

Trouble was, she didn't feel beautiful. The borrowed dress was gorgeous and she liked the wispy supershort new haircut Carrie's stylist had given her, but she couldn't help feeling like a fraud.

This was a crazy idea, thinking a new look would change who she was inside, would somehow instantly transform her into someone glamorous and desirable.

Inside she still felt fat and dowdy and shy.

She would have been content to stay forever in the background. But then she received an e-mail from Stacy Cartier, an old friend at boarding school, who happened to mention she'd heard through the grapevine that another of their classmates Angelina Larson had come back to Portland for a visit and would be attending with her husband, Steve—who just happened to be Katie's ex-fiancé.

She hadn't seen Steve in years, not since she threw his ring at his head after she overheard him at a party laughing and joking with one of his friends about the little cash cow he was marrying.

She *had* been forty pounds overweight but she thought he loved her despite the extra weight and her propensity to feel most comfortable with her nose in a book. The realization that he was marrying her only for her family's money and connections had been a bitter betrayal she wasn't sure she had ever recovered from.

Though she never wanted to see him again, she was committed to attend this benefit auction. She had to be there but she suddenly couldn't bear to have Steve—or his wife, Angelina, who had tormented her mercilessly through their childhood—think she hadn't changed at all in the six years since she'd broken off the engagement. Hence the makeover, the haircut, the borrowed designer gown.

You look good, she reminded herself. *Better than you've ever looked in your life. Pretend you're beautiful and the world will see you that way.*

With one more deep breath for courage, Katie walked into the ballroom, festooned with magical twinkling lights and holiday greenery.

Maybe this was all for nothing, she thought. In this press of people, she likely wouldn't even run into Steve and Angelina. For a moment she stood there feeling lost, then she caught sight of her brother Trent talking to a group of people she didn't know.

She approached him, grabbing another flute of champagne from a passing waiter as she moved through the crowd. She stood behind him for a moment until he finished speaking, then tapped him on the shoulder when the group started to break up.

"What time do they start the bidding?" she asked. Trent was one of the bachelors up for bid; she had agreed to come in the first place only to give him moral support.

He turned at her words, a ready smile on his handsome features that slid away when he saw her. If she hadn't been so nervous about his reaction she would have laughed at the way his eyes widened and his jaw dropped.

"Katie?" he exclaimed. "What have you done to yourself? Where did you get that dress?"

The momentary delight she had taken at his stunned expression gave way to a flicker of annoyance. She hadn't expected him to put on his overprotective big brother act. Usually he reserved that for Ivy, since Katie seldom gave him any reason to worry.

"Carrie Summers. She has a whole closet full of designer clothes from her modeling days. Why? What's wrong with it?" she asked, when he continued to stare.

"Nothing, other than there isn't nearly enough of it." He cocked his head and took in all the changes she had made in the last few days. "You look incredible! You cut off all your hair. And where are your glasses? After all the years of Sheila's nagging, I can't believe you finally broke down and went for contacts."

Here's where things might get a little tricky, she thought. "I, um, had laser correction surgery earlier in the week. That's why I haven't been into the office. It was my Christmas present to myself."

Just as she feared, his commanding features tightened. "Surgery? You had *surgery* and you didn't bother to tell me? Why not? If you'd told me, I could have checked out the doctors and the facility, even researched the procedure. Hell, at the very least, I would have at least come with you to hold your hand."

That was exactly why she hadn't told him. He would take over like he always did and she would let him. She knew she relied too much on Trent. All of them did. Trent had basically raised all the Crosby children while Sheila was busy with her affairs and her position in society and Jack was busy building a business and carrying on plenty of affairs of his own.

She loved Trent deeply but after Ivy married a few months earlier, Katie realized perhaps she relied on him too much. She needed to stand on her own as Ivy had done, to find her own strength. The surgery was something she'd been thinking about for a long time and she wanted to do it alone. She didn't regret it for a second; she could see better now than she ever dreamed possible.

"I didn't want to bother you since I know how busy you've been with the super-router project."

He opened his mouth to argue—probably something about how he was never too busy for his little sister—but before he could utter a word, his name came over the loudspeaker.

"Will Mr. Trent Crosby approach the podium, please? Trent Crosby."

Katie turned and saw a woman she knew casually, Jenny Hall, giving the announcement.

Trent made a face. "Maybe I'll luck out and they're going to tell me they don't need to put me on the auction block after all."

She laughed. "You volunteered, buster. I think you're stuck."

He studied her for a moment. "You look good, Katie. If you can manage to fight off all the men who are going to be clamoring around you, save me a dance, okay?"

"Of course. Good luck."

She watched him go to the dais, then scanned the room looking for someone else she knew. The panic that had abated somewhat in Trent's presence bubbled back. This had to be the craziest idea she'd ever had, she thought again, nabbing her second—or was it third?—glass of champagne off a tray.

Whatever possessed her to think a little window dressing would cover her basic inadequacies? Her shyness, her social fumbling? She was one of those people who faded into the background and usually that was just the way she liked it.

It hadn't taken therapy for her to figure out it was a learned behavior, developed early when she discovered that if she could manage to avoid attention, Sheila's mercurial moods and sudden rages would rarely be aimed in her direction.

Trent wanted her here but she wished for once she could have said no to him. As much as she loved him, sometimes her older brother could be as forceful in his way as their father. She should have told him she couldn't come and stayed home in her little condo in Lake Oswego, where she was comfortable and boring and *safe*.

She should leave, she thought. Really, her obligation here was done. Trent needed moral support and she had given it. This whole idea was ridiculous. Childish. Even if she saw Steve Larson, he probably wouldn't care about any of this—the vision surgery, the blond highlights in her hair, the designer dress. He had the beautiful, though poisonous, Angelina on his arm.

She was about to set her glass on yet another tray carried by one of the ubiquitous waiters and make her escape when a tall man in an elegant black tuxedo approached her.

She recognized him instantly. Of course she knew who he was, since his younger self had starred in most of her adolescent fantasies—Peter Logan, oldest son of Terrence and Leslie Logan, and CEO of Crosby Systems' biggest competitor, Logan Corporation.

She waited for a spark of recognition, then the inevitable cold disdain once he realized she was one of the despised Crosbys. But all she could see in his eyes was frank male appreciation.

For her! Peter Logan was looking at shy, dowdy, plump Katie Crosby like he wanted to devour her from top to bottom.

No, not plump anymore, she reminded herself. After the debacle of her short-lived engagement, she had worked fiendishly hard to whip herself into shape. Instead of the comfort foods she had survived on since her lonely boarding school days, she began to eat a healthier diet and to exercise obsessively.

It took her three years of hard work but she hadn't been Steve Larson's cash cow for a long time, even if she still preferred dressing in baggy clothes and hiding behind thick glasses and long hair.

He smiled at her, then, before she realized what was happening, he gripped her arm and maneuvered her onto the dance floor. Despite her shock at his high-handedness, she couldn't help laughing. "Smooth. Very smooth. I see your reputation is not unfounded, Mr. Logan."

To her shock, her voice sounded sultry, smoky, like cognac trickling into a heavy crystal tumbler. Probably because she couldn't seem to breathe with him so close, with his expensive cologne filling her senses and his fingers entwined with hers.

"Ah, no fair. You know my name," he murmured, with what she almost thought looked like resignation in his eyes. She studied him for a moment, wondering at it. Perhaps the charmed life of a wealthy, successful bachelor wasn't as carefree as the world liked to believe.

"Peter Logan, CEO of Logan Corporation," she

murmured, her mind on the memory of another long-ago dance and an act of great kindness he had done for a fat, miserable fifteen-year-old girl at her first society event.

"What woman in Portland hasn't seen a picture of you in the society pages," she went on, "and longed to be magically transformed into the latest elegant creature at your side?"

Where did this sudden flirtatiousness come from? she wondered, stunned at herself. She didn't think she even knew *how* to flirt! She also hadn't realized this fantasy of dancing again with him had been lurking inside her all these years.

"Since you know who I am, it's only fair you tell me your name, then. And address and marital status while you're at it. Oh, and are you free tomorrow night?"

She laughed and opened her mouth to answer, then snapped it closed again. Suddenly she didn't want to tell him who she was. When she did—when he knew the woman in his arms was none other than Katherine Crosby—that warm, appreciative light would disappear and he would turn cold and angry.

Like the rest of his family, Peter Logan had no love for the Crosbys. She knew well the bitter history behind Portland's most famous feud. Once the two families had been neighbors—and if not precisely friends, at least more than passing acquaintances. Her older brother Danny had been best friends with Peter's parents' son, Robbie.

One day when she'd been little more than an infant, Robbie had been playing at their house, theoretically under the watchful eye of Sheila.

But with her typical selfish carelessness, Sheila had

paid little attention to the two boys. Sometime in the course of the day a stranger had approached them and Robbie had been kidnapped.

After an agonizing year of searching, a child's remains were found along a riverbank and were traced back to Robbie, allowing the Logans to at least have that much closure.

If Sheila had shown the tiniest ounce of remorse, Katie was sure that while Peter's parents might not have been able to forgive her mother for her inattention to the boys, Terrence and Leslie Logan likely would have kept their bitterness to themselves. But Katie's mother had tried to paint herself as the injured party, had blamed everyone for Robbie Logan's kidnapping except herself.

Over the years, the feud had taken on a life of its own. The Logans and the Crosbys were fierce competitors in business and cold as Alaskan tundra when they were forced to meet socially.

She had always grieved for the brother Peter never knew. But then, he had been adopted after Robbie's kidnapping. Perhaps if the events of that horrible day had never happened, the Logans wouldn't have had any interest in adopting a child.

"This is the first time I've made a woman forget her own name."

At Peter's remark, she realized he was still waiting for an answer. "I didn't forget," she murmured.

"Just trying to decide whether to share it with me, then?"

She mustered a smile. "Something like that."

"I'm completely harmless, I promise. Ask anyone."

"I'm not sure your business rivals would agree."

His shrug barely rippled the silk of his well-cut tux-edo. "That's their problem, isn't it?"

She didn't want this to end. Not yet. A beautiful woman in a glittery blue dress was singing a sultry version of an old Duke Ellington song, and Katie wanted to burn this memory into her mind.

"Celeste," she finally said, seizing on her middle name. "My name is Celeste."

"Aw, the French. *C'est magnifique.*" To her shock, he drew their clasped hands to his mouth and pressed his lips firmly to the first knuckle of her index finger. Heat sizzled through her and she couldn't believe she was actually here, in his arms.

Though Peter Logan had a reputation as a man who enjoyed the company of beautiful women, Katie never would have suspected him capable of this play-ful, single-minded pursuit. She knew him as a hard businessman, ruthless and aggressive about increasing his company's market share, no matter what it took.

She didn't know how to resist him like this. She couldn't think straight when he looked at her out of those deep brown eyes. Maybe if she had a clearer head, she could summon some kind of defense, but she had never had much tolerance for alcohol and she suddenly feared she'd had one too many glasses of champagne.

"I hope this isn't unforgivably rude but have we met before? You seem familiar."

A knot formed in her stomach as she waited for him to recognize her, but he only continued gazing at her features intently. How could she answer that? She fi-nally decided on the truth, or at least part of it. "Many years ago we danced together at another one of these society functions. I'm sure you wouldn't remember."

"I'm sorry. I should."

"Don't apologize. I've changed a great deal since then." The understatement of the century, she thought.

He twirled her around, his arms strong and commanding. He was a wonderful dancer, but she already knew that from the first time they had danced. And though she would never be graceful, she had to hope she had improved a little in thirteen years.

"Are you bidding tonight?" Peter asked. "If you are, let me give you a little advice. Stay away from my brother Eric. He's not worth what he'll end up costing you and will only end up breaking your heart."

She arched an eyebrow. "And I suppose you're going to tell me you would be the better bargain."

"I'm not up for bid this year. Eric is the only Logan on the auction block. I did my duty last year and ended up being purchased by Dorothea Aldridge. The woman in the purple turban over there."

Katie laughed. She didn't have to follow his gaze to know the woman in question. Dorothea's late husband left her a twelve-state restaurant chain. She had a passion for bridge, and she was old enough to be his great-grandmother. "What's the matter? Was she too much woman for you?"

He made a face. "I had to spend an entire Saturday playing cards and admiring photos of her grandchildren."

He paused, then added with a rueful smile. "You know, the really sad thing is, that Saturday with Dorothea was the most enjoyable date I've had in a long time."

She wasn't sure how to respond to that honest admission. She certainly couldn't tell him she hadn't been on a date in far longer than she wanted to think about.

"I'm not bidding," she finally said. "I'm only here as moral support to—" *My brother,* she started to say, but knew that would only raise questions she didn't want to answer. "A friend," she amended.

"A good friend?"

"Yes. Very good."

"Will this good friend—or anyone else, for that matter—mind that you're dancing with me?"

Trent would not be at all thrilled to see her dancing with Peter Logan. She was grateful they had moved to a darkened corner of the ballroom where they were out of the public eye. Maybe her brother would be too busy at the dais to notice them together. One could only hope.

"I can always tell him you kidnapped me before I knew what was happening," she murmured somewhat breathlessly when the last sultry notes of the jazz combo faded away.

"When a beautiful woman crosses my path, I'm not stupid enough to give her any chance to slip away."

Beautiful? Her? Awkward, pathetic Katie Crosby? Her heart did a little joyful dance in her chest and Katie decided if a typhoon swept through the Portland Hilton at exactly that moment, she would at least die a happy woman.

"I'm afraid that's just what I'm going to do. Slip away, I mean. I have to go find my…friend."

She had to admit, some small corner of her heart found his disappointed expression extremely gratifying. Maybe this idea to glam up for once wasn't so dumb after all, not if she could have this memory of dancing with him again after she faded once more into the background.

"I'd like to see you again somewhere a little less formal." He grabbed her hand before she could leave. "How can I reach you?"

She studied him as the crowd began gathering near the dais, trying to figure out how to answer that. She couldn't lie and tell him she wasn't interested in seeing him again. This was Peter Logan. No woman with a pulse would be able to honestly say she didn't want to see him again!

When she was younger, all the girls she knew had swooned over him, with his dark, slightly dangerous good looks and that intensity in his brown eyes. She had treasured the memory of that long-ago dance as one of the highlights of her adolescence.

What girl wouldn't have been thrilled to have him ride to her rescue like some gorgeous knight in shining armor, vanquishing all the dragons in his path—or in her case, Angelina Mitchell, now Larson, and some of her friends, who had cornered Katie during a benefit like this one and were mocking her relentlessly.

No, she couldn't tell him she didn't want to see him but she had to think of some evasion. Before she could, someone jostled her hard from behind. She would have fallen if Peter's arms hadn't come around her.

"Excuse me, dear," she heard a quavering voice say. "I'm terribly sorry. Are you all right?"

Katie turned to see who had bumped into her and found Dorothea Aldridge, purple turban and all.

"Dorothea?" Peter said. "Are you all right? You're looking a little pale."

She squinted at him. "Is that you, Peter Logan?"

"Yes. Is everything all right?"

"I'm just a little warm, dear. I was looking for a place to sit down and lost my balance. Too many people pushing and shoving for someone with a bad hip."

Katie realized everyone was heading toward the podium and she assumed the bachelor auction was about to begin.

"Let's find you a chair," Peter said. He offered his arm to Mrs. Aldridge and without prompting, Katie moved to the elderly woman's other side.

"Have we met, dear?" Dorothea asked as they made their way through the crowd to a row of chairs along the edge of the ballroom.

Only about a hundred times at various functions. Katie's stomach plummeted and she knew the game was up. She would have to identify herself and watch that exhilarating attraction in Peter's eyes fade to something else entirely.

"I—" She started to speak but Peter cut her off.

"This is Celeste," he said as he settled Mrs. Aldridge into a chair with a gentleness that did funny things to Katie's insides.

"How lovely to meet you," Dorothea said with a bleary-eyed smile. "And may I say, that's a lovely mink hat you're wearing. I have one just like it myself. My dear husband, Victor, gave it to me a few years before he passed. A little stuffy in here for fur, though, don't you think?"

Katie raised her eyebrows and fought the urge to run a hand over the head she knew perfectly well was bare.

"Where are your glasses, Dorothea?" Peter asked, laughter in his voice.

"Oh, I'm a silly old thing and left them up in my room."

"You're staying here?" he asked.

"Oh, yes. I do every year for the Children's Connection auction. I make a whole weekend out of it. It's the highlight of my year. Drat. I can't see who I'm bidding on. Since I heard you're not available this year, I had my eye on that brother of yours. Eric. He's quite the hottie, as my granddaughters would say. Peter, would you be a love and fetch my glasses for me? I think I left them on the bedside table."

"Of course."

"Oh, thank you! You're such a sweet boy. You always have been."

She said this with such sincerity that Katie had to bite her lip to keep from laughing. Peter Logan, sweet? She didn't hear that term bandied about much when it came to Peter. The man was a shark in the boardroom and everybody knew it.

He might have occasional bouts of kindness but otherwise he was hard and driven, completely focused on expanding the Logan empire.

"Now here's my room key," Mrs. Aldridge said. "I'm in suite 1460 and my glasses should be on the bedside table. Hurry now, before Eric and all the other good-looking fellows are gone."

"My feet are wings," Peter assured her with the smile that had fluttered the heart of more than one society matron, then headed out of the ballroom, tugging Katie along with him.

He was holding so tightly to her arm, she had no choice but to follow him. "I don't believe it takes both of us to fetch one pair of glasses," she exclaimed.

"I decided I'm not letting you go."

Ever? she wondered as a thrill shot through her. This was all pretend, she reminded herself. If he knew who she was, he would drop her arm so fast her head would spin.

"You're very used to getting your own way, aren't you?" she asked in the elevator.

His laugh was heartfelt and slid down her spine. "Do you have brothers or sisters, Celeste?"

"I... Yes. Both."

"Then you'll understand when I say that with two brothers and two sisters, I learned early to hang on tightly to anything I didn't particularly want to share."

"Should I be flattered that I'm apparently in the same category as a favorite toy, Mr. Logan?"

"No, you're not." He grinned. "You're much better than G.I. Joe and Stretch Armstrong combined."

She laughed. "I'm sure you wouldn't have thought so when you were ten."

"I don't know. I was a pretty smart kid."

He was, she knew. He had earned top grades at prep school and went on to graduate from Harvard with honors.

The elevator slid smoothly to a stop on the four-teenth floor before she could respond, and Peter led the way to room 1460.

The glasses weren't where Dorothea had claimed. All they found on the bedside table was a box of tissues and a pill keeper marked with the days of the week.

"Any ideas where to look?" Peter asked.

"The bathroom, maybe?"

He left her in the bedroom of the suite but returned a moment later. "No luck. We'd better hurry and find them or Dorothea might end up missing out on the bidding altogether."

"We certainly wouldn't want that."

Though she felt a little uncomfortable poking through someone else's hotel suite, she remembered what a dear Mrs. Aldridge was. If she enjoyed being in the company of younger men—and gave generously to the Children's Connection in the process—Katie didn't want to disappoint her.

After a few moments of fruitless searching, she glanced through the sliding doors toward the glittering city lights just beyond the small covered terrace.

It had been a lovely day, unusually mild for December. Perhaps Dorothea had decided to enjoy it while she awaited the big night. She slid open the doors and immediately saw a folded newspaper on the small table—along with a pair of glasses on a jeweled chain.

"I've got them," she called out, then was surprised when he answered her from the doorway.

"Good sleuthing. I never would have thought to look out here. Who's crazy enough to spend any time on the balcony of a hotel during a Portland December?"

"We're here, aren't we?" she said with a smile.

"That's different. We're doing a favor for a friend."

"And enjoying the view," she pointed out, gesturing to the glittering city lights below them. "I love looking at the city lights, especially with everything decorated for the holidays. It's gorgeous up here."

"Yes, it is," he said, his voice low, and Katie felt heat flood her face when she realized he wasn't looking at the view but at her.

"Um, we should be getting back, I suppose. Dorothea, er, Mrs. Aldridge, will be looking for these."

"I warned you I was an opportunist. When I find myself alone on a starlit balcony with a beautiful woman, I'd be a fool not to take advantage of it."

Before she realized what he intended, he leaned closer, then lowered his mouth to hers.

Peter Logan was kissing her! She could hardly believe it. It was an easy kiss, almost casual, the kind a man would give to a good friend. Later she thought maybe he only intended a quick buss but the moment their mouths collided, heat burned between them, like brilliant sunlight glimmering on the ocean, and they both lost control.

She wasn't aware of sliding her arms around his neck but she must have because somehow her fingers were in his thick hair, her achy breasts pressed tightly against him.

He groaned and deepened the kiss and she was vaguely aware of his hands, hot and firm, sliding down the bare skin of her back to press her closer to him. She could feel his arousal through the silk of his trousers and couldn't believe it. Peter Logan wanted her!

"You taste incredible," he murmured against her mouth. "I'll never drink champagne again without thinking of this moment."

She was afraid she wouldn't be able to ever *breathe* again without remembering this magical night. It would be forever burned into her consciousness.

She tightened her hold around his neck and kissed him fiercely with all the passion inside her.

She would have stayed there all night—Mrs. Aldridge's glasses be damned—but suddenly something odd registered in her dazed awareness, a bright flash of light.

She drew back slightly. "Did you see that?"

"What?" His voice sounded dazed and when he opened his eyes, they were dark and aroused and didn't stray from her face.

"Was that lightning?"

"It couldn't be. The sky is clear."

Katie realized now that must have been the moment the *Portland Weekly* photographer caught them kissing. He must have followed them from the ballroom and slipped out onto the public terrace next to them. At the time, she thought it must have been just a product of her overactive imagination—or the result of too little oxygen to her brain from Peter's kiss.

Whatever it was, the distraction reminded her of where they were, what she was doing—kissing a man who would hate her if he ever learned her name. "I… Mrs. Aldridge will be looking for her eyeglasses."

"Why don't we forget about the glasses and stay here for the rest of the night?"

"We can't do that. You promised you'd take them right back."

With a heavy sigh, he dropped his arms and stepped away from her. For the first time since coming out on the balcony, Katie felt chilled in the cold December air. She rubbed her bare arms.

"I'm a selfish bastard to keep you out here so long in that thin dress. Come on, let's go find Dorothea."

He held her hand on the elevator but they were joined by another couple and he didn't try to kiss her again.

She didn't want to go back inside the ballroom, Katie realized on the way back to the main floor.

For one thing, when Peter gave Mrs. Aldridge back her glasses, Katie knew the woman would recognize her immediately, makeover or not, and then Peter would know he had just spent several very heated moments with a Crosby in his arms.

For another, she wanted to remember this night just as it was. She didn't want to go inside the ballroom and have to make polite conversation when all she wanted to do was go home and hug her arms around herself and remember what it had been like to have Peter Logan want her!

Outside the ballroom, she scrambled to come up with an excuse for not accompanying him to Dorothea's side. "I need to find the ladies' room and repair my lipstick."

He looked reluctant to have her leave his side. "Will you meet me right back here, then, after I deliver these to Dorothea?"

She couldn't think of an excuse not to meet him so she simply nodded, fighting the urge to cross her fingers at the lie.

As soon as he went inside the ballroom, she hurried to the hotel's porte cochere, feeling again like Cinderella escaping the ball.

Unfortunately her pumpkin wasn't waiting for her. She couldn't see the Crosby driver Trent had sent for her in the row of limousines lined up outside and was forced to wait while the doorman paged him.

She wasn't able to escape so easily. Five moments later, her ride still hadn't appeared and her heart sank when she spied Peter hurrying through the lobby.

"You're leaving?" he asked when he reached her, disbelief and something else that sounded suspiciously like hurt in his voice.

She cleared her throat. "I was, ah, feeling a little

under the weather. I think I had a little too much champagne." That was at least true enough.

To her relief, he didn't question her claim. "Are you waiting for a taxi? My driver is right there. I'll drop you off."

"You can't want to leave the gala so early."

"Can't I?"

That sizzling heat was back in his eyes and she couldn't help feeling tremendously flattered. He would rather drive her home than stay at a benefit for his family's pet charity.

"I can't let you take me home. You have obligations here."

"No, I don't. I told you this year was my brother's turn. The only obligation I made was to show up and I did that. Now I'm free to leave."

She opened her mouth to argue with him just as she spied her driver pulling into the entrance in one of the Crosby Systems' limousines, complete with the discreet company logo on the side. When Peter saw her climb inside, he would figure out immediately who she was.

"Okay," she said quickly and headed toward the Logan limousine he'd gestured to earlier. "Let's go, then."

He followed her, looking a little disconcerted at her rapid about-face. He opened the door for her and she slid inside.

And sealed her fate.

Chapter 4

What time was it? Katie had no idea since she had unplugged her alarm clock to conserve power and her watch was somewhere jammed into her suitcase, but she assumed it was long after midnight.

The storm still raged outside, hurling snow at the windows and moaning under the eaves. The room was cool and she realized while she'd been lost in the past, she had let the fire burn down to embers.

She rose from the bed and threw another log on the glowing cinders, then stood in front of the fireplace watching the flames leap to consume new fuel with fierce, enthusiastic crackles.

Her hand went to her abdomen, to the tiny life she had only learned was growing there a few days before but already loved so dearly.

Oh, Katie, she thought with a sigh. *What a mess*

you've created, all because you got carried away by the magic of the night and caught up in your own lies.

In the limousine that night, Peter had asked where he could drop her. For the first time, she realized the trouble her spontaneity had gotten her into. What was she supposed to tell him? She couldn't very well give him her address in Lake Oswego. Though he likely had no idea where Katherine Crosby lived, her last name was on the mailbox of her town house.

"Can't we just drive for a while?"

"I thought you were feeling under the weather."

Caught in another lie. She grimaced and improvised quickly. "It must have been the crowds at the benefit. I'm fine now."

"Good," he said. His smile was just short of wolfish but it still sent sensual little shivers rippling down her spine.

He leaned forward to talk to the chauffeur. "Lou, it's a lovely night for a drive."

The driver, a man in his late fifties with a bushy salt-and-pepper mustache, smiled back at him. "It is indeed, Mr. Logan."

"The lady likes Christmas lights. Maybe you could show us some of the holiday decorations around town if you know of any particularly festive spots."

"I surely do," the driver said with a cheerful wink in the rearview mirror at Katie.

She lost track of time there in that limousine. They drove all over Portland talking and laughing and drinking champagne as the limousine driver took them to one brightly decorated spot after another.

With each sip of champagne, she felt her natural restraints melt away. When Peter raised the privacy barrier behind the chauffeur and kissed her again, all the heat from before on the balcony flared to life again. She had never known anything like that, had been outside of her head with desire, and she never wanted to stop.

She must have murmured something to that effect because in between more of those mind-numbing kisses he asked if she would go home with him. To her surprise, she heard herself eagerly agree.

They barely made it inside his vast loft before they were ripping clothes away and coming together in a fiery explosion. They had made love in every corner of his loft, she remembered now, flushing a little when she remembered her uninhibited response to him. Her breasts, now sensitive and achy from hormones, tingled at the memories flooding through her mind.

They had used protection every time but one, she remembered. She had slept a little and had awakened to find he had turned to her in his sleep. He awakened, poised to enter her. That time had been tender and slow and incredibly sensuous. And condomless, she remembered, although he had pulled out before his orgasm.

After he finally fell fully asleep, the enormity of what she had done hit her like a building crumbling around her head. She had slept with Peter Logan, not once but four times! It had been the most wonderful, magical night of her life.

And he didn't even know her name.

She had spent the last three months trying to forget, but the memory of that night was scored into her mind like circuits on a motherboard.

For a woman who had graduated summa cum laude from Stanford, it was remarkable how stupid she could be, she thought now as she gazed into the flames.

When she missed her first period, she hadn't really been surprised. She'd always had irregular periods, especially during times of stress. And even when it was regular, she had a longer than usual cycle. After she missed the second period, she started to become concerned but still it never even occurred to her that she might be pregnant until her breasts started to ache at even the slightest pressure and she started throwing up in the mornings.

This should be such a happy time. It was, she assured herself. She was excited about the challenge and joy of motherhood. But part of her yearned to have someone to share her excitement with.

She couldn't tell Peter, she thought again. If her resolve started to waver, she only had to look around her at this house her father had bought for one of his mistresses. Not because he thought his children would enjoy a ranch or because he wanted to spend time with them here, but for a woman. It was so typical of Jack.

Everything she knew about Peter told her he was cut from the same cloth. Maybe not the womanizing part, but his obsession would always be Logan Corporation. Something else would always come before his child, just as work and women had come first for her father.

She couldn't do that to her child. She *wouldn't*.

With a sigh, she returned to bed and pulled the quilt around her chin once more. She lay there for a long time, listening to the wind moan and trying not to want what she knew she could never have.

Peter awoke quickly, as he always did, his mind already racing with a dozen things requiring his attention. The board of directors meeting in a week, the paperwork for a new merger Logan was considering, the marketing plan for the super-router.

He was unlikely to accomplish any of those things while he was stuck here at some godforsaken Wyoming ranch house with the deceitful, manipulative Katherine Crosby, however.

He sighed and watched his breath puff out in a little cloud. In a *freezing* godforsaken ranch house, he amended. A gust of wind rattled the wide picture window that probably had a spectacular view under normal conditions. All he could see now in the pale early-morning light was snow. It was a virtual whiteout.

A glance at the huge river-rock fireplace in the gathering room showed him the fire was all but out. The temperature had dipped even colder in the night. Why hadn't the furnace clicked on, he wondered? Maybe the oil lines were frozen somehow or the pilot light had gone out. He would have to take a look at it this morning. What was the point of having a generator if they couldn't keep the furnace running?

For now he could at least work on the fire. He rose and selected a log from the supply next to the fireplace and tossed it onto the embers. He had to spend a few moments stoking it to get any sparks but after a moment the wood caught and began to burn merrily.

He didn't have time for this, he thought as he watched the flames. He had enough figurative fires of his own to tend to. Logan was at a critical point with this super-router, poised to make huge market gains. Besides that project, he had at least a dozen other items awaiting his attention.

He could only imagine what his family would say when he turned up missing. He had mentioned his destination to a few people, including his secretary, and had filed a flight plan, but he hadn't told his parents or any of his siblings. He didn't know if they would believe he could drop everything to chase after Katie Crosby.

Hell, he could hardly believe it himself. He had a reputation as someone who always kept a cool head, no matter the crisis. He had worked hard for that, had prided himself on his self-possession in tough circumstances. It was a skill he had picked up from his father, one necessary to run a huge company like Logan Corporation.

He wasn't exactly sure how he'd completely lost that cool head he was supposed to have. His brother Eric might take off after a woman on a whim like this but not Peter. Peter had spent his whole life trying to show he was responsible, dependable. He just wasn't the sort to let his emotions dictate his actions.

But he hadn't been himself since the moment his gaze met Katie's at the Children's Connection auction. It sounded corny when he tried to put it into words but that whole night seemed surreal, like something out of an incredibly erotic dream. Instant heat, complete enchantment.

What about her had affected him so strongly that night? She had been elegantly beautiful, but he had certainly dated his share of beautiful women. No, there was something more, something he still couldn't quite put his finger on.

Maybe it was that she hadn't seemed particularly impressed that he was one of the wealthiest, most powerful men in Portland. Or maybe it had been the way she seemed completely oblivious to her own appeal, or that soft, genuine smile of hers that had seemed fresh and almost innocent.

Whatever had mesmerized him, he still couldn't believe the spontaneous attraction between them. He enjoyed the company of women but that night had been different.

It had been a night of firsts for him—the first time he'd ever blown off a charity obligation, the first time he had ever driven around Portland with a woman just to look at Christmas lights, the first time he had ever taken a woman he had just met back to his apartment for an all-night session of lovemaking.

He hadn't intended to. It wasn't at all like him. When he'd offered her a ride home, all he'd been thinking about was flirting with her a little, finding out where she lived so he could make plans to see her again. Maybe stealing a kiss or two. But she had kissed him with such eager, wild abandon, he hadn't been able to think about anything but touching her, tasting her, coming inside her.

He blew out a breath. He had wanted Celeste—Katherine Crosby—with a fierceness he had never known before. Their lovemaking had been the most intense of his life, fiery and hot one moment, slow and sensual the next. Nothing in his experience had prepared him for that kind of stomach-clenching heat.

And then she disappeared.

He could still vividly recall the hard knot of betrayal that had lodged in his gut when he had awakened to find her gone. If it hadn't been for her soft perfume clinging to tangled sheets, and a polite note that could have been written by a stranger, he would have thought maybe it had all been some wild dream, the kind of thing he thought he'd outgrown when he left adolescence behind.

He had searched the loft for something she might have left behind, something that might help him trace her, but had found nothing. All that day he had paced his apartment, overwhelmed with the feeling that he had held something rare and precious in his hands for one fleeting second and then let it slip away.

That odd feeling of loss was the real reason he was so angry at her now, he acknowledged. He had been such a gullible fool. He had believed she had been as caught up in the magic of the night as he was, had wanted him just as fiercely as he had her, when she had only been using him as a pawn in this bitter feud between their families.

He hated thinking of the way he had missed her these three months. How could he miss a woman he had just met, one he didn't really even know? He hated remembering how for three long months, with no solid clue how to find her, he waited for her to contact him, looking for her as discreetly as possible.

That damn picture in the *Weekly* hadn't helped matters. How could he ask questions about the woman— like, oh, maybe her *name*—after the picture of them in a passionate embrace was plastered all over the paper?

In a million years, he never would have connected his Celeste to Katherine Crosby.

Since the moment he had seen the article identifying her the day before, he had been racking his brain trying to remember if they had ever met before the night of the gala. He had to think they must have bumped into each other at some function or other. Portland wasn't that big and, despite the infamous enmity between the families, the Crosbys and Logans moved in the same circles. How had he completely overlooked her?

He thought he remembered her as someone who tended to lurk in the background. He knew she was the vice president of research and development at Crosby Systems, but other than that, he thought maybe she was almost as reclusive as her brother, Danny, who was holed up on some island in Hawaii.

If someone had asked him a week ago about Katherine Crosby, he would have been hard-pressed to come up with a description, but he thought maybe she used to wear thick glasses and had long, bushy hair that all but hid her face. Had she been a little plump? Damn it, he couldn't remember. All he could picture was the lithe, sensual woman who had completely ensnared him the night of the gala.

And now here they were holed up together at some Wyoming ranch. Katherine Crosby, with her baggy sweater and her wool socks, hardly seemed like the elegant creature he had flirted with and danced with and kissed on a moonlit balcony. This woman was quiet, almost nervous around him.

She *should* be nervous, he thought. He couldn't remember ever being so furious at another human being before.

What was he going to do about it? He had no real evidence she had stolen anything from him that night. He couldn't press charges, even if he wanted to. He didn't. Bringing it all out into the open would only expose what a gullible idiot he'd been.

So what could he do? Nothing. Not one damn thing. The knowledge didn't sit well with him at all, not for a man used to seizing control of every situation.

He would have to wait out this storm for the next day or so, just until he could return to Portland and try to figure out just how much damage his stupid indiscretion had cost the company—and the family—he loved so dearly.

It irked him to lift a finger here to help a Crosby, but he wasn't any good at inactivity so he decided to take a look at the furnace while he waited for her to awaken.

He changed out of the sweats he'd slept in and into jeans and a sweater then headed for the utility room off the back porch where they had started the generator earlier.

The generator still hummed away. He checked the fuel level and saw the tank was still nearly full, so he turned his attention to the furnace. As he suspected, the pilot light had somehow gone out in the night, he soon discovered. It only took him a moment to relight it, and he was rewarded with the click and whir of the furnace coming to life.

That chore out of the way, he returned to the kitchen to put on some coffee. He was just pouring a cup when Katherine came in from her bedroom. She had changed into another pair of jeans, slightly less disreputable than the pair she'd been wearing the day before, and a Stanford sweatshirt.

"Good morning," she murmured, just enough sleepy huskiness in her voice to make him wonder what it would have been like to wake up with that sexy voice next to him.

"Have you looked outside yet?" he asked gruffly, angry at his instant response to her. "I don't think *good morning* really applies here."

She glanced out the kitchen window and grimaced. "It's freezing in here."

"Your pilot light on the furnace went out. I just lit it again. It should warm up in a minute."

Surprise flickered in her brown eyes. "Um, thank you. You've been busy this morning."

"Coffee's fresh if you'd like some."

She shook her head. "I'd better not. Thanks, though. I'll have some herbal tea."

She was riffling through the cupboards looking for it—and he was trying to figure out why she wouldn't have coffee when there had been clear longing in her voice—when he heard the low rumble of an approaching motor. A snowmobile, by the sound of it.

"That would be Darwin Simmons from the Bar S. He's taking care of the stock while Clint and Margie are gone."

A moment later the front doorbell rang. Katherine went to answer it and Peter followed her. She answered the door and he saw a heavily bundled figure in a thick snowmobile suit, only two blue eyes showing out of all the winter gear.

Katherine gestured the figure inside and Peter had the feeling he was much younger than he expected. That impression was confirmed when the figure removed his heavy wool face mask, revealing a teenager of no more than fourteen or fifteen.

Peter had an impression of wiry strength and the kind of competence that seemed bred into the bones of children raised on ranches.

"Joseph!" Katherine Crosby exclaimed. "I wasn't expecting you. Is your father outside?"

"No, ma'am. He's home. We lost part of the roof on

one of the hay sheds last night. Dad was working on it and slipped off."

"Oh, no!"

Peter wondered at the genuine distress he thought he saw on her features. He hardly would have expected her to be concerned for a neighbor to her family's hobby ranch, one she probably barely knew.

"Is he all right?" Katherine asked.

"No, ma'am," the boy said again. "Doc Harp met us at the clinic to X-ray it and she said his leg is broke in two places. He's got to stay off it for the next couple months. Dad was real worried about you over here, what with the Taylors gone and the storm and all, so he sent me to help out. Hope that's okay with you."

"No! No, it's not okay."

Peter narrowed his gaze. There was the spoiled rich bitch he would have expected. She didn't have to throw a tantrum about not getting her own way. Not when the kid was only trying to help. He was about to intervene when she went on quickly, surprising him again.

"With your father hurt, I'm sure you must be needed at home, aren't you? The Bar S is much bigger than Sweetwater."

"My dad said I'm to help you out. Feed and water the stock and so forth."

"You tell your father not to spend a minute worrying about me over here," she said. "You need to be with your family. I can take care of things here."

He paused, fingering his wool cap, worry on his young features. "A hay bale can be mighty heavy. No offense, Ms. Crosby, but are you sure a little thing like you can handle things here by yourself?"

"I'm hardly a little thing, Joseph," she said with

a laugh. "Anyway, I won't be by myself. This is my, um, my…"

Her voice trailed off and for some ridiculous reason, Peter found it amusing that she couldn't quite come up with a word to classify him.

"My friend, Peter Logan," she finally said. "He can help me."

He was further amused to find himself on the receiving end of a skeptical look from the kid, who undoubtedly figured he was some worthless city yuppie.

"You know anything about cattle, sir?" the boy asked.

He knew he liked his steaks medium-rare, but that was about it. He wasn't about to confess, though. "Enough," he lied. He gave a confident, take-charge kind of smile to set the kid's mind at rest. "We'll be just fine. Ms. Crosby's right. A man's got to look after his family first."

The boy still looked unconvinced, but Katie ushered him out the door so smoothly Peter didn't think he was even aware of it. "You go on home and help your mother and brother with your own livestock," she said. "If we run into trouble, we'll call you. I promise."

He was clearly torn between obeying his father and taking care of the many chores at the Bar S. Finally he nodded, though he still looked worried. "My dad said Mr. Taylor should have left a note in the tack room with instructions on how much to feed the horses and how much hay to take out to the cattle. You'll have to also make sure the trough heaters are working so the drinking water doesn't freeze."

Since the ranch caretaker was so organized that he left detailed notes about starting a generator, Peter wasn't at all surprised to learn he had left the same kind of clear instructions for watering and feeding the stock.

"We'll be fine," Katherine assured him again. "You tell your father not to worry a minute about us. Tell him to save his energy for healing that leg of his."

"I'll do that, ma'am."

With one last worried look, the boy disappeared once more inside his winter gear, mounted the snow-mobile at the bottom of the porch then roared off down the driveway.

"What now?" Peter asked when the throb of the sled's motor had faded to a distant roar.

She smiled, the first one she'd given him since his arrival the day before. "First we'd better find you something warmer than that leather jacket you came in. Then I guess we get to work."

She could do this.

Katie pulled on the warmest, thickest gloves she could find in the mudroom while she repeated the mantra to herself. She was a bright, healthy woman. She was strong, she was invincible, yada yada yada.

If she could keep from throwing up the half bagel she'd managed to choke down for breakfast, she just might make it through.

And if she could keep her mind away from the dangerous memory of how sleep-rumpled and sexy Peter Logan had looked that morning, she just might be able to control her chaotic hormones enough to keep her out of trouble.

You're already in a world of trouble, Katherine Celeste, a sly little voice in her head mocked.

But she didn't have to make things worse by doing

something utterly stupid like falling in love with him. She could only be relieved that Peter despised her so she wasn't tempted to complicate the mess by sleeping with him again.

She *was* relieved, she told herself. It was better this way. Once the storm cleared, he would return to Portland and leave her alone. He would likely want nothing more to do with her. And she could think of no reason for their paths to cross again.

She would be free to have her child alone and he would never know their single night of passion had left any legacy behind.

She drew in a shaky breath, fighting off the sudden depression that had settled on her shoulders, colder and heavier than even eighteen inches of snow. She had no choice, she reminded herself, and walked into the great room to face him.

Despite her lingering nausea and the ache in her heart, she had to laugh at the picture he made. The Portland gossip columnists would have a tough time believing the man zipping into brown insulated coveralls was the same sexy, urbane CEO they loved to write about, the one who consistently made it on to Portland's Top Ten Best-Dressed list.

Peter was a big man but Clint was huge, both tall and broad. His coveralls on Peter bagged in every direction.

He looked up at the sound of her laughter. "At least they're roomy," he said with a wry look.

Maybe it was a stress release from the tension still simmering between them, but her laughter seemed to bubble out like water from a geyser. "Look at it this way," she said. "If there are any half-frozen calves out there, we'll know just where to put them to warm them up."

"You can just forget that idea right now. I'm not sharing. Any half-frozen calves will just have to find their own heat source."

He finished zipping up the coveralls, watching her with an odd light in his eyes as her laughter faded. "Okay, I'm ready," he said. "Are you sure you're up to this? You're still looking a little peaked. I can probably take care of things on my own."

So much for that vaunted pregnancy glow, Katie thought. She looked horrid and she knew it perfectly well. She just had to keep him from figuring out why.

"I'm fine. Let's go," she muttered, and led the way out into the teeth of the storm.

Chapter 5

Once they were outside, she wasn't surprised when Peter took over the lead, bearing the full brunt of the wind that cut like jagged glass, even through all the layers. Despite her six-foot-tall moving windbreak, the storm still hurled swirling snowflakes at her like tiny, sharp stones that stung her eyes and lodged in every exposed nook.

Peter shortened his stride through the knee-high snowdrifts to match hers so she was better able to walk in his footsteps. She was grateful for his thoughtfulness. It was hard enough fighting the wind without having to blaze a path through the snow.

The three hundred feet from the house to the sturdy barn seemed to take an eternity to cross but at last they reached the door. Both of them worked another several moments clearing snow with their gloved hands away from the doorway so they could slide open the door.

By the time they made it inside, Katie was exhausted and queasy enough to fear the bagel would make a reappearance.

Peter pulled off his hat and gloves as Clint's two border collies greeted them with quick, well-mannered barks. He leaned down to pet one, shaking his head. "That storm is incredible. I've never seen anything like it!"

"Neither have I. I've been here a few times during storms but they were nothing like this. This is intense, even for western Wyoming. I can't believe it's March."

"Remind me to heed the weather forecast the next time I'm tempted to take off from Portland on a whim."

She wouldn't be around to remind him of anything, she thought with another pang. Back in the city, they would go their separate ways. He would return to the helm of Logan, probably still believing she stole company secrets. This interlude of theirs would probably add more fuel to the Logan-Crosby feud.

She hoped her baby never found out how much her father despised her mother.

"I suppose it's a good thing I did," Peter went on, scratching the other dog. "Come out here, I mean. You never could have handled this on your own."

She wasn't completely helpless. Really, she probably knew more about horses and cattle than he did from all the time she had spent out here. This further evidence of his poor opinion of her stung, she had to admit.

"I would have figured something out," she muttered.

He raised a skeptical eyebrow. "You would have

been in one hell of a bind on your own out here and we both know it."

She would have had a rough time of it alone, she had to admit, especially with the nausea so close to the surface and the fatigue weighing her down. To say she was glad he'd come to Sweetwater would have been a gross exaggeration, so she opted to change the subject.

"Let's find out what we have to do, shall we? Joseph said Clint left the instructions in the tack room, right over here."

Clint kept the barn in ruthless order. Just like the rest of his domain, it was clean and well organized— no clutter, no loose hay, no scattered tools. The tack room was used as the ranch office. A huge, scarred pine desk with a computer dominated the room, along with a couple of worn armchairs and one entire wall hung with saddles and bridles and leads. The smell of leather and horses was heavy in the room.

They found the note addressed to Darwin Simmons on a bulletin board behind the desk, sandwiched between an invoice from the feed and grain in Jackson and a list of phone numbers.

Katie tugged off her gloves to pull the note down. Peter stood behind her to peer over her shoulder, and she was suddenly intensely conscious of his nearness. Heat emanated from him in the cool room. He had taken time for a quick shower before bundling into the winter gear and she could smell clean soap and some indefinable scent uniquely Peter.

Pregnancy had definitely made her sense of smell more acute. The scent of him, familiar and erotic, instantly transported her to the night they spent together, reminding her of tasting every inch of his skin, of inhaling that scent as he kissed her, of lying in his arms and feeling safe and warm and *wanted.*

Oh, how she craved that again.

The intense hunger came out of nowhere and she drew in a sharp breath. What was the matter with her? Peter despised her and thought she had tricked him like some corporate Mata Hari into sleeping with her only so she could worm out Logan secrets.

She was foolish to even think about their night together. It would never happen again and wanting the impossible only wasted energy she couldn't afford to expend. Might as well wish for that storm out there to suddenly stop, she thought. She had as much chance of controlling her thoughts as she did of controlling the weather.

Where was she? She had lost her place, she realized with chagrin. Even worse, her body had instinctively leaned back toward his, drawn by his heat and the invisible ties that bound them inexorably together. She jerked upright just before she would have settled against him, just as if she had every right to snuggle there.

Had he noticed? she wondered. How could he have missed the motion? Embarrassed color flooded her face and her gaze flew to his. She found him watching her, a disconcerted expression in his eyes.

He cleared his throat and stepped away, putting space between them. "It all looks fairly self-explanatory," he said. "I'll take care of the cattle, you can feed and water the horses."

She didn't register his words for a few moments, still lost in her mortification. When she did, her spine straightened and she forgot all about being embarrassed.

"Forget it," she said sharply. "You take care of the horses and I'll see to the cattle."

Sweetwater's dozen horses could all be fed and watered from inside the barn, but the small herd of cattle were pastured out in the open, in the middle of the wind and swirling snow.

"I'm taking care of the cattle," he said, his voice leaving no room for arguments.

She didn't let his hard tone stop her. "It's my family's ranch. I won't ask you to go out into that storm again, just to help a Crosby."

A muscle worked in his jaw, as if he didn't like being reminded of her last name. "You didn't ask. I offered. No, I'm not offering, I'm insisting. Whether they're Crosby cattle or not, they still need to be fed."

"I can do it."

"You're a hell of a liar, *Celeste,* but even you won't be able to convince me you're able to haul a hundred-pound hay bale, not when I can tell you're still feeling under the weather."

She didn't like being reminded of how horrible she knew she must look—or the reason for it. "I would be doing everything myself if you hadn't come charging out to Sweetwater like some damn avenging angel. I can handle it. I'm tougher than I look."

"So am I. And if you want to see how tough I can really be, keep arguing."

She bristled. "Are you threatening me, Logan?"

He narrowed his gaze. "Damn right. Shut up or I'll lock you in this tack room until I'm done feeding all the cattle *and* the horses."

One look at his hard expression warned her he would make good on the threat. She blew out a frustrated breath but wasn't quite ready to give up. "You might run Logan with that iron fist of yours, but this ranch belongs to me and my family."

"I don't see anybody else here but you and me."

"Peter—"

"Give it up. You won't win this one." He headed for the door. "I'll meet you back here when I'm done."

"Take the dogs," she called out just before he went outside. "They'll help you find your way back to the barn with this poor visibility."

After he left with Luke and Millie in the lead, she fought a completely childish urge to throw something at the door behind him or at least to stomp her boot on the plank floor.

He was right. That was the hardest pill to swallow. She wanted to think she was capable and self-sufficient, but deep in her heart, she knew she would have been in a terrible bind without him here. She *couldn't* carry a hay bale by herself, even a few hundred feet to the fenceline of the vast pasture where the cattle grazed.

She knew she would have figured something out—maybe she could have rigged up one of the horses to help haul the hay bales out—but it would have taken her hours to do everything. In her current condition, she would have been completely exhausted.

Still, he didn't need to be so high-handed. Threatening to lock her in the tack room of her own ranch!

After a few more moments of fuming—and willing her morning sickness to subside—she sighed and rose from Clint's chair. If she didn't get off the south side of her pants, as Clint would say, Peter would finish his share of the workload before she did hers, even though he had the bigger job. And wouldn't she just hate that?

For the next hour, she cleaned out stalls and forked fresh straw and checked the water in each trough. She put out feed according to Clint's instructions and made sure the dogs had food and water in their snug little corner of the barn.

In the process, her nausea receded, to her vast relief. She even started to enjoy being among the horses. She saved her favorite for last, a bay with the prosaic name of Susan.

Katie loved the little mare and rode her whenever she stayed at the ranch. Susan wasn't the flashiest of horses on the ranch or the quickest or the strongest, but she was sturdy and dependable.

When she neared the horse's stall, Susan whinnied a greeting and edged close for her expected treat.

"I didn't bring you anything this time, sweetheart. I'm sorry."

Susan seemed quick to forgive. She nuzzled Katie's shoulder through the insulated coveralls. "Next time I'll bring you a goodie, I promise. I was just a little distracted this morning. Any woman would have been if she woke up with a gorgeous man in her kitchen—even a bossy, annoying one like Peter Logan."

Susan snorted and it sounded so much like the horse agreed with her that Katie couldn't help laughing.

Just as abruptly, her laughter faded. To her considerable dismay, she found herself sobbing instead. For the first time since discovering she was pregnant, Katie gave in to the jumbled emotions raging through her—anxiety and fear and dismay and joy.

Susan nickered and nudged her shoulder again, as if she wanted to give comfort, and Katie buried her face in the horse's warm neck. Where was all this emotion coming from? she wondered. It sneaked up on her out of nowhere, and she didn't know how to cope with it.

Not that she was ever much good at handling emotions, Katie thought. She had spent so much of her childhood trying to stay out of trouble that she suppressed the natural highs and lows every child learns to contend with. After her engagement ended so disastrously, she finally forced herself to see a therapist. Dr. Sikes helped her figure out that she turned to food to avoid facing the thick soup of emotions simmering inside her—the rage and rejection and loneliness.

Talking things out had helped her finally break the vicious cycle between what she ate and how she felt. It had worked with Dr. Sikes and maybe it would help her now.

Though she felt a little silly, she found herself now spilling the whole story of Peter and the charity gala to Susan, who listened with wide, compassionate eyes and only gave the occasional snort in response.

Ten minutes later she felt much better. She wiped at her eyes with the heavy sleeve of her coveralls, grateful beyond measure that Peter was tending to the cattle and hadn't caught her.

Though she knew it wasn't healthy to suppress her emotions completely, she also knew she couldn't afford to give in to them right now. Not with Peter here at Sweetwater, watching her every move. She couldn't give him any hint that she was pregnant. If he found out, he would be livid.

She had to be strong, as stoic as Clint, until Peter

left for Portland and she could figure out how to go on from here.

There was no question she was keeping her child. She loved her already, the tiny little life growing inside her. She didn't know how she could so fiercely love someone she hadn't known existed a week ago but she did know she was going to work hard to be a good mother.

Her own childhood had been terribly unhealthy, between Sheila's complete self-absorption and Jack's workaholic disinterest. But Katie was going to do everything in her power to give her own daughter a wonderful future, where her baby knew every moment of her life that she was loved.

That happy picture certainly didn't include Peter Logan. It couldn't possibly.

The wind still shrieked and howled when Peter finished with the cattle and returned to the barn. The two low-slung dogs led the way, leaping through snow drifts about as high as they were.

His muscles ached from the exertion of forking hay bales and fighting the storm, but he didn't mind. It was a pleasant kind of burn, the ache of knowing he had worked hard and earned each twinge.

He wasn't out of shape; he believed a tight, well-functioning body helped his mind work harder. He swam several dozen laps and ruthlessly lifted weights each morning. This was a different ache, though, one of knowing he had accomplished something more worthwhile than making it to the end of the pool in record time.

He caught the direction of his thoughts and gave a

rueful laugh. If he wasn't careful, he might find himself tempted to buy a ranch and move west. No, thanks. He would stick with his weights and his lap pool. His usual workout might lack this noble sense of purpose, but at least when he was done he could usually feel his toes and his eyelashes didn't freeze together.

Just in the hour or so since he'd left, more snow had piled up in front of the barn door and he had to shovel it away to swing the door open. The dogs were as eager as he for the warmth of the barn. They sidled through and immediately found their cozy spot.

He found Katherine nose to nose with one of the horses. She was still wearing her insulated coveralls but had removed her hat and her hair stuck out in little spikes.

"How did it go with the cattle?" she asked.

"Good. Your foreman runs a tight ship. Everything was right where he said it would be. I only had to fork the bales over the fence and the cattle came running."

"What about water?"

"There were a few spots of ice in the middle of the tank but the cattle seemed to be able to get enough water around the edges."

She frowned. "You said you saw some patches of ice? That's not right. The warmer should keep the water above freezing so there isn't any ice. Clint said he was a little concerned with that unit. I wonder if it's malfunctioning."

"They were still able to get to the water."

"Keeping a good water supply is vital to the cattle all year long but especially in winter. We'll have to keep an eye on it. It's solar powered but has a battery backup that should keep it juiced up even during the cloudiest of days."

She stepped away from the horse and he had his first full-on look at her since he had returned to the barn. Her eyes looked puffy and her nose was red.

"Is everything all right in here?"

She tilted her chin, a belligerent look in her eyes. "Just fine. Why wouldn't it be?"

He couldn't just come out and say she looked as if she'd been crying. In his experience, women didn't always appreciate that kind of information.

Besides, if she had been crying—something he found hard to reconcile with the sneaky manipulator he had decided she must be—he wasn't sure he wanted to know. It made her too human, too vulnerable.

Had he come on too strong before, bossing her around as he had? Too bad, he thought. He meant every word and would have had no compunction about locking her in the tack room while he cared for the stock.

If she was crying, it was probably because she hated being beholden to a Logan. Rather than go down that dangerous road—or any road that involved a woman's tears—he opted to change the subject.

"Nice horse. Is she yours?"

Katie gave him an odd look but seemed willing enough to travel the conversational side route. "Yes. Her name is Susan."

"And does Susan ever answer during your conversations?"

She flushed so brightly he had to wonder what she had been talking to the horse about. "No. That's why she's such a perfect conversationalist. Unlike some people," she added pointedly, "Susan doesn't pick at me

His mother never would have let them leave the house so young. She would have shriveled up and died without them. But Sheila Crosby was a far different woman than Leslie Logan.

On the other hand, with Sheila for a mother, maybe boarding school hadn't been such a bad thing.

He didn't like the compassion flickering through him. Why should he care if she had a lonely childhood? That didn't excuse the kind of woman she had become, one who could lie about her name and sleep with a business rival to pry out company secrets.

He didn't care, he told himself. He only wanted to find out more about her. Know thine enemy and all that.

"How long were you at boarding school?"

"Five years. I was admitted early to Stanford when I was sixteen and graduated with my masters at twenty-one. I've been at Crosby ever since."

"I understand your sister, Ivy, worked there, too, until her marriage to that Lantanyan royal."

"Yes. I talked her into coming to Crosby after the dot-com she worked for went bust. That's how she met Max," Katie went on. "She was in Lantanya managing the installation of one of our high-speed computer systems to link all their schools."

Her eyes lit up when she talked about her siblings, Peter thought. He wondered if she knew it.

She talked about her siblings with the same pride he talked about Eric and David and Jillian and Bridget.

He didn't like thinking they had this in common. It was far easier to dislike the whole Crosby clan when he viewed them as a bed of vipers, each willing to strike out at the other.

"Trent must have hated to lose another potential spy in his little network," he said, then instantly regretted the comment. It was petty and mean and all but extinguished that light in her eyes.

"Right. Technically, Ivy's staying on at Crosby to oversee the Lantanya project. But since she's busy with a new husband, her royal responsibilities and a baby on the way, she probably won't have time for much corporate espionage. I guess that means Trent is stuck with only me to do his dirty work."

"Well, you're good at what you do."

"If I need references for my next assignment, I'll be sure to come to you," she snapped.

He opened his mouth to snap back a retort, but before he could, the horse whinnied and shoved her nose into Katie's back, almost as if she didn't like her suddenly sharp tone.

Katie stumbled a little and would have fallen, but Peter instinctively stepped forward and caught her against him.

She was curvy and warm in his arms, a perfect fit, and like a match set to dry tinder, his body immediately reacted to her nearness just as it had done the night of the gala, as if three months and a world of bitterness didn't exist between them.

He would have released her as soon as she found her footing again but then she looked at him. An odd expression flitted across those huge, gorgeous brown eyes. He couldn't sort out all the emotions there, but if he didn't know better, he might have believed he saw longing and regret there.

He still wanted her. He didn't like it, but his body still yearned for her, still ached to touch her skin and kiss her mouth and fill his senses with her. Knowing she shared his hunger didn't make things any easier.

He had to kiss her. Just one kiss to see if the fire and intensity between them that night had been a fluke. He leaned forward, but just before his mouth met hers, he saw something else flare in her eyes, something that almost looked like fear.

What was she afraid of? Him? Impossible! Okay, maybe he'd groused and yelled a little since he showed up at Sweetwater. He might have come on a bit over-bearing with that whole locking her in the tack room bit but she had to know he would never hurt a woman, even a Crosby.

Despite what she had done to him, the irreparable harm she may have caused to his family and his posi-tion as CEO, he hated the idea that she might be afraid of him.

"Katie—"

He wasn't sure what he was going to say but she didn't give him a chance to finish the sentence. She jerked out of his arms and backed away until she al-most hit the stall's wooden railing.

"Since the animals are fed and watered, there's no reason to hang around here. I'm going back to the house."

Before he could argue, she rushed out of the barn, leaving him with the odd feeling that something sig-nificant had just happened between them—if he could only figure out what.

Chapter 6

"Will this damn storm ever stop?"

Katie glanced up from the mystery novel she had been pretending to read toward the spot where Peter stood at the wide picture window of the room, his fingers curled around the windowsill as he glowered out at the unrelenting snow.

"It can't snow forever," she murmured. "Spring eventually comes, even here in Wyoming."

"Very funny. I don't particularly care to be trapped here until the vernal equinox, thanks very much."

Every inch of him radiated tension, from the stiff set of his shoulders to the taut muscles of his jawline, and she regretted baiting him.

Peter Logan was obviously a man unused to inactivity. Since they had returned to the house from caring for the animals, he had been restless and edgy.

Of course, she hadn't been exactly serene, she admitted. After that scene in the barn when they had bickered and he had nearly kissed her, she had rushed back to the house, barely noticing the snowdrifts she struggled through. She hadn't even minded the relentless wind that whipped icy air and snow in a vicious mix. At least the cold helped cool her cheeks and her overheated senses.

How could she be foolish enough to crave his touch after everything between them? He despised her. She knew he did and yet she still hungered for him.

What a disaster it would have been if he had kissed her. She had been so afraid he would, terrified that she would respond to him as she had the night of the benefit and that his kiss would lead to more.

If she slept with him again, she wouldn't be able to keep the truth about the baby to herself. She would have told him everything, which would have been an unmitigated disaster.

Nothing happened, though. He had stopped just before he would have kissed her. She was glad, she told herself. That ache in her heart had only been the exertion of fighting the storm.

By the time she reached the house, she had her emotions firmly in control. He followed her a few moments later and she forced herself to pretend that scene in the barn never happened.

He seemed just as eager to forget it. While she reheated stew for their lunch, Peter took out a laptop from the luggage he'd retrieved out of his rental Jeep the night before and began working feverishly on it, his brow furrowed with concentration.

She had thought about retreating to her bedroom but

it seemed foolish and wasteful to keep two fires going just because of her own cowardice. The great room was large enough that they surely could both inhabit it without gnawing at each other's throats, so she had forced herself to curl up on a couch and pretend to read.

She should enjoy the chance to put her feet up for a few moments while she was temporarily nausea-free, she tried to tell herself.

After a few hours of activity at the computer during which he had picked up the phone at least a half-dozen times looking for a dial tone, only to slam it down with disgust when he remembered the phone was out, Peter must have finished as much as he could. He snapped the laptop shut and stalked to the window, where he had spent the last fifteen minutes glaring out at the storm beyond.

She was the hostess here, despite the fact that the role had been thrust on her against her will. She should at least try to alleviate his boredom.

"I'm sure the generator's got enough power that you could watch something on TV," she offered. "There's quite an extensive DVD collection. Everything from comedies to action-adventure to Westerns."

"I'm not much for movies or television. I like to watch a little basketball but that's about it."

"The ranch has a satellite system. You might have to sweep the snow out of the dish but you could probably find a game on."

"No, thanks."

"We could play a board game or something. Chess, cards, Monopoly. You probably love that one."

That idea obviously didn't appeal to him, either, judging by the surly look he sent her, so Katie figuratively threw up her hands. "Or you can keep pacing around the room like a caged grizzly. It's all the same to me. Stirring up all those molecules in the air must be helping the room stay a little warmer, at any rate."

Perversely, her annoyance seemed to cheer him up. He smiled and returned to the couch. "Getting on your nerves, am I?"

"You're not the most restful of companions." *In more ways than one,* she wanted to add, but swallowed the words.

"Sorry. My brother, Eric, in his more lyrical moments used to complain that I've got more energy than a one-armed monkey at a flea festival."

She laughed at the image. "My brother, Trent, is the same way. He always has to be busy doing something. I suppose it must be part of the whole CEO package."

He didn't look thrilled at the comparison to her brother, but Katie refused to feel guilty for bringing up what was obviously a touchy subject. She loved her brother dearly and wouldn't allow Peter's irrational dislike to prevent her from even bringing up Trent's name.

She waited for some kind of snide comment from him about Trent but he let the subject drop. Maybe he wanted a ceasefire as much as she did. She studied him, wondering about this complex, perplexing man who would give their child half its DNA.

What kind of a child had he been? she wondered. Had he been obedient or rebellious? Extroverted or withdrawn? She knew he had been a good student and she knew he could have moments of deep kindness but she suddenly wanted to know more.

Since they had nothing else to do, maybe they could manage to set aside their differences and have a real conversation, just so she could gain some insights into his personality. Maybe if she knew a little more about him, she could get some idea what traits he might pass on to their child.

"You're the oldest child, right?"

"The oldest *living* child," he said sharply.

Robbie again, she remembered, with her customary pang of sympathy for the Logans. As tragic as Robbie's kidnapping and death had been, she never forgot that although they had lost a son, in a very real way she had lost a brother that day, too. Danny had never stopped blaming himself for his best friend's disappearance, for not protecting him somehow.

Over the years, that guilt had manifested itself in horrible ways. In his teens, Danny had sought release in drugs and alcohol but had since turned his life around.

After he married, she thought maybe at last he could be happy. But that, too, had ended tragically when history grimly repeated itself and Danny's own son was kidnapped from a city park. His wife had been unable to bear the pain of losing her child and had killed herself, and Danny had retreated to his private island off the coast of Hawaii. No one seemed able to reach him. She tried as best she could but he was lost in his own hell outside her understanding.

Although she had visited him a few times, he seemed to prefer his solitude.

"Do you get along with your siblings?" she asked Peter.

He looked surprised at the question but finally nodded. "We're a very close family."

"There are five of you, right?"

"Right. I'm the oldest, then the twins, although my

parents didn't adopt them until they were five, after they'd had Eric and Bridget."

"That's right. I'd forgotten David and Jillian were adopted, too."

"Right."

"You were six when you were adopted by the Logans, weren't you? Do you remember anything of your life before you went to live with them?"

The sudden chill in his eyes at her question was far colder than anything Mother Nature could dish out. Despite the merry warmth from the fire, she shivered. Apparently she had crossed some intangible line by asking about his childhood. She wished she could yank back the question, but the words were already out there, hovering in the air.

"Forget I asked. I was simply making conversation but I can see now it was a presumptuous question. I apologize."

He was quiet for a moment longer, the silence broken only by the flames snapping in the hearth.

"I remember a little," he finally answered. "Not much of it good. I remember washing up in a dirty bus station sink once and sleeping at a shelter with some other kids. A bigger kid stole my toy airplane so I belted him. The woman who gave birth to me—I don't consider her my mother—was a heroin addict and a prostitute. She couldn't even take care of herself, forget about seeing to the needs of a kid. We were lucky to have a roof over our heads most nights."

Her heart twisted with sorrow for the little boy he must have been. Tears burned behind her eyelids and though she knew perfectly well he wouldn't welcome the gesture, she fought the urge to draw him against her for comfort.

"And your father?" she asked, then hoped he didn't notice the rough note in her voice.

"Don't know. I doubt she did, either." He shrugged. "I don't think about it much anymore. In every way that matters, my father is Terrence Logan and my mother is Leslie Logan."

"You were happy with them?"

"The day they adopted me from Children's Connection was the best day of my life. My first good memory is riding home with them from the orphanage, sitting wedged between them in the front seat of the car and feeling safe and warm for the first time in my life. I vowed that day that I would never do anything to disappoint them or make them regret picking me out of all the other kids at the orphanage."

Was that why he was so driven to succeed? she wondered. Why he was known as a completely focused, brilliant executive? When Terrence Logan retired, one of the Portland newspapers ran a big story about Peter taking over. She had always been fascinated with him and had read it with far more interest than she liked to admit.

In the story, she learned he had worked harder than she to get where he was. He was valedictorian of the exclusive private prep school he attended and also graduated magna cum laude from the Harvard School of Business. Like her, he had gone to work at his family's company right after graduation.

Where she preferred working behind the scenes in research and development, he seemed to have no problem being in the limelight. Through his tenure at

Logan, Peter had earned a reputation in the Portland business community as a fiercely loyal, dedicated, passionate CEO who gave everything to his work.

Was his dedication to the firm and his passion for the job just another way he tried to prove to Leslie and Terrence they hadn't made a mistake in adopting him?

She had a feeling he would deny it vigorously if she asked but something told her she was on the right track.

"I'm sure they're very proud of you," she said quietly. "You've been a good son to them."

"I've tried. I'm sure they've been disappointed in me a few times but they've always loved me anyway."

Would Terrence and Leslie be heartbroken if they ever found out Peter had fathered a grandchild they would never know? The thought jolted her. She had been thinking all along of the ramifications of keeping her pregnancy a secret from Peter but she hadn't given a thought to the concentric circle of people who would be affected by her decision.

By keeping the information from him, she suddenly realized she would also be depriving his family of the chance to know his child—and her child the chance to know his or her birthright.

She couldn't change her mind now, Katie thought. Though she might better understand Peter's single-minded passion to succeed now, that certainly didn't ameliorate it, by any means. She had grown up with a father who had the same focus, who saw nothing beyond his ambition and his ego and the women who fed it.

Peter Logan was too much like Jack Crosby for her to ever consider him good father material, though she knew he would rather wander naked out into that subzero storm than ever concede he might have anything in common with her father.

She wished suddenly that she'd never asked him about his childhood. She didn't want to picture a six-year-old boy with dark hair and brown eyes and a sweet smile vowing never to disappoint his new family. She also didn't need this guilt pinching at her when she thought of depriving Leslie and Terrence—who had lost so much already because of her family—the chance to know their grandchild.

She especially didn't want to feel this wary tenderness entwining around her heart.

Peter hadn't meant to tell her that whole bit about the day the Logans took him home. He never talked about it—hell, he didn't even think about it much. He meant what he'd said to her. In every way that mattered Terrence and Leslie were his parents. He loved them fiercely and never let himself forget how much he owed them.

He couldn't imagine how his life would have turned out if they hadn't adopted him. If he hadn't died early from malnutrition or one of the other many dangers he faced living on the street with a junkie and a whore for a mother, he didn't doubt that he would have spent his entire childhood either in the Children's Connection orphanage or in the foster-care system as a ward of the state.

Everything he had, all he had become, he owed to Leslie and Terrence, and he refused to lose sight of that.

They had never treated him any differently than their other children. They showered all of them—Eric and Bridget, their natural-born, and the adopted twins

David and Jillian—with the same steady love and attention. But even when he'd been just a kid, Peter had always been conscious of the debt he owed them.

While other teenage boys were experimenting with alcohol or trying to score with the head cheerleader, he was knuckling down at his studies or following his father around, trying to learn the ropes at Logan.

As he'd said to Katie, he knew there had been times he had been a disappointment to them, but overall he knew they were proud of the man he'd become.

That all might change, though. He didn't think they would be too crazy about the idea that he was here, trapped on a ranch with Katie Crosby—or about the circumstances that had led him here.

After all the bitterness between their families, he didn't want to think about how disappointed Leslie and Terrence would be when they saw that article in the *Weekly* and when they learned he may have compromised an important project because of his lust.

He had a feeling they also wouldn't be real thrilled to know how much he still burned for this particular Crosby.

Why was he so attracted to her? he wondered. He shouldn't be. She wasn't at all his usual type. She wasn't wearing makeup and her short, choppy hair was tousled. She still had circles under her eyes and she wore a baggy sweater, a pair of old jeans with frayed cuffs and thick wool socks the color of dryer lint.

But still he wanted her. All he could think about was the tight, lithe body underneath her clothes and the way she had responded in his arms with such fire and heat.

There was the real reason for his restlessness. Whenever he tried to concentrate on the shareholders report, all he could think about was how different things could have been between him and Katie.

If he never learned who she was—if he still thought she was the incredible, passionate Celeste—he would have given his left arm to find himself snowbound here alone with her.

He could have come up with at least a dozen ways to make love to her in every corner of this sprawling ranch house. Instead of this restless tension between them, they could be cuddling together under thick quilts, listening to the wind moan under the rafters and the snow tap against the glass. Or they could have curled up together in front of the fireplace with a bottle of wine.

The possibilities were limited only by his imagination and his stamina, and he had a feeling when it came to Katie Crosby he would have more than enough of both.

His body was only too willing to forget how angry he was about this whole mess, about her lies and even about her identity. His mind refused to capitulate, though.

It didn't help that he found her even more desirable here under these primitive conditions than with all the glitz and glamour of the charity benefit. She seemed more comfortable here, more natural.

Except for that moment in the barn when she had run away from him, she didn't even seem to mind his company.

"Why are you staring?" she asked him suddenly. His gaze met hers before he had a chance to mask the desire he knew was only too evident there. To his surprise, a blush crept from her throat to her cheekbones.

He didn't begin to understand this woman. He didn't

understand most women—he'd be the first to admit it. He enjoyed women, figured it was safe to say he loved everything about them. The way they smelled, the fancy things they did to their hair, the way they seemed incapable of visiting the ladies' room unless they went as a pack.

His brother, Eric, was the expert, the one who always knew just what to say and how to smile and where to touch. Eric had been charming women from the cradle.

To Peter, all women were a tantalizing, delicious mystery. But this one in particular had him baffled. How could she seduce him with such calculating cold-bloodedness, yet still blush at a look in his eyes?

It didn't make sense. *She* didn't make sense. He knew she slept with him that night to spy on their super-router project. Why else would she have lied to him about who she was, have kissed him on the balcony of Dorothea's hotel room and then again so eagerly in the limousine? Why would she have even climbed into that limo with him if she hadn't been planning all along to seduce him into taking her home?

Here, Katie seemed completely different. Softer, less sophisticated, maybe. She was someone he almost thought he could like under other circumstances.

"Peter?"

How long had he been staring at her with hunger in his eyes, he wondered, annoyed at himself.

"Why didn't you tell me who you were?" he asked suddenly and rose to his feet.

Her eyes widened at the question. As if she didn't like being at a height disadvantage, she rose, too, and stuck out that stubborn little chin. "I thought you already figured that out. It was all part of my devious plan. Isn't that what you think? You never would have slept with me if you had known I was Katherine Crosby."

"I'm not so sure of that," he muttered in a voice that should have been too low for her to hear.

She must have uncommonly good hearing, though. She stared at him. "What did you say?"

It was too late to back down, even if he wanted to. "I know exactly who you are now. So explain to me how I can still want you."

His words seemed to echo in the vast room. He would have let the matter drop, just left his imprudent admission to hover there between them, but he saw her pupils flare and saw her chest rise and fall in quick succession with her gasp.

Though he knew he would likely hate himself for it later, he couldn't resist tasting her, just one more time. Only once, he promised himself as he lowered his mouth to hers. Just a taste and then he would retreat back into his anger.

He could swear he felt the slow churn of blood through his veins and each rapid beat of his heart as he lowered his mouth to hers, swallowing another quick intake of her breath as their lips met.

Her mouth was soft, warm and just as delicious as he remembered. He wanted to taste every inch of it, to lick and probe and savor until she forgot even her own name.

Or at least until he forgot it.

He had missed this, the low burn of desire in his gut. He hadn't been with a woman since their night together three months ago. He hadn't even dated anyone, hadn't even been tempted to go out.

Even on New Year's Eve, he had gone alone to a party at a friend's house rather than summon the energy to ask anyone out when all he could think about was Celeste.

And here she was in his arms again, just as he had imagined hundreds of times, before he found out who she was. She fit against him just as perfectly as she had that night. Her body was curvy in all the right places. After that first moment when she stood motionless in his arms as though paralyzed by shock, her arms wrapped around him and she leaned into him. Her mouth softened under his and everything about her seemed to sigh.

He wanted to fill his senses with her. She smelled the same as she had that night, some kind of subtle floral scent that made him think of his mother's garden after an April rain.

He didn't know how long they kissed. He only knew he would have been happy to stand just like this for a week or two, with the wind howling at the window and the fire snapping in the grate. But when he lowered a hand to the small of her back to draw her closer, she seemed to snap back to her senses. Her eyes jerked open and she dropped her arms from around his neck and scrambled away as if she'd just found herself embracing a python.

If her uneven breathing was any indication, their embrace affected her as intensely as it did him. "What was that all about?" she asked, her voice thin, ragged.

"Isn't it obvious?"

She was quiet for a moment, then she shook her

head. "You're bored and restless. Inactivity is difficult for a man like you. I understand that and I'm sorry for it, but I won't help you pass the time this way. I *won't*. Not when it's obvious you despise me."

"I don't despise you."

Her laugh was harsh and disbelieving. "Right."

Why so much bitterness? he wondered. Her eyes were as bleak as the landscape outside the window.

"I don't."

It was the truth, he was startled to discover, but she didn't appear at all convinced. "I'm going to check on the fuel level on the generator and then see what I can round up for dinner."

And don't bother coming with me. She didn't add the words but he heard them loud and clear.

Chapter 7

The storm broke a few hours before dawn.

Though Katie should have been sleeping, oblivious to any change in weather at that ungodly hour, she had been lying awake in bed, the quilt snug around her chin as she gazed at the dying flames' sinuous dance and replayed their kiss.

She couldn't figure out why Peter had done it. He had seemed genuinely shocked when she accused him of merely trying to pass the time, kissing her out of boredom and restlessness.

But what other reason could there be?

He didn't like her and certainly didn't trust her. He had made that abundantly clear since he arrived at Sweetwater. He thought she had slept with him only to learn Logan Corporation secrets. So why kiss her until her bones melted? Until she was moaning and panting and closer than she cared to remember to begging for more?

She knew how dangerous it was to kiss him. Between her pregnancy and the trauma of seeing him again, her emotions were fragile, weak. She didn't like feeling vulnerable and exposed. She needed time and space to build her defenses against him but she'd had neither since his arrival.

Had it only been a day and a half? She couldn't believe it. Time seemed to stretch and thin. She felt as if she'd lived a lifetime in those thirty-six hours. Maybe because they had been together almost constantly since he swept into Sweetwater.

Even after that kiss, when she had wanted desperately to retreat to her room and hide away, she had forced herself to remain either in the kitchen or the great room.

After the dinner she had put together—well, the lasagna she had pulled out of the freezer and baked according to Margie's directions—she had even gone so far as to play a game with him. Monopoly. No big surprise, he won. She wasn't any better at empire building, she decided, than she was at forgetting how she had wanted to let him hold her forever.

Why had he kissed her? She had been up most of the night trying to figure it out but had come no closer to a solution when she suddenly registered a strange silence. It took her a moment to realize the mournful keening of the wind had stopped at last, leaving behind an unearthly quiet. She slipped from the bed and padded to the window.

The clouds had finally shifted and moonlight gleamed on the tiny fluttery snowflakes drifting slowly down. She found it hard to believe that the violence and rage of the storm could blow itself out and leave this tranquil scene, everything white-blue and still.

She watched it for a long time, trying to absorb some of that calm into her own psyche.

With the storm dying out, she knew Peter wouldn't be at Sweetwater much longer. It would probably take another day or so for the roads to be cleared and then he would be able to fly back to Portland.

She should be relieved, especially with the unbearable tension of the last evening after their kiss. When he was gone, she could at last find at the ranch what she had come for—peace.

She knew she should be praying for the roads to be cleared quickly so he could leave and she could come to terms with the changes her life was about to undergo.

But here in the quiet of her room in those grim hours before dawn, she could admit the truth. Her heart ached with a deep sense of loss whenever she thought about him returning to Portland. He would return to his world and she to hers. They might see each other at the rare social occasion but he would be cold and formal and distant.

She sighed as depression settled heavily on her shoulders. The wood floor was cold against her toes and she couldn't stifle a yawn. She knew she needed to sleep. She didn't know much about being pregnant except that pregnant women needed plenty of rest for the hard work of nurturing tiny developing bodies.

She threw another log on the fire then crawled into bed again, grateful her spot was still warm. After she pulled the quilt up to her chin, she pressed a hand to her abdomen.

"Good night," she whispered.

At least she didn't feel *completely* alone.

Hours later, Katie yawned, feeling the effects of too little sleep. She had managed three or four hours but they weren't nearly enough. If not for the cold whipping through her, keeping her senses as sharp as possible, she was afraid she would fall asleep in the saddle.

From atop Susan, the snow looked brilliant, so white her eyes burned even behind the sunglasses she had unearthed out of her luggage.

"How are you doing over there?" she called to Peter, riding next to her on a big roan gelding.

"Surprisingly well. And here I thought those riding lessons at Boy Scout camp twenty years ago would never come in handy."

She smiled at his wry tone. "You're doing great."

"Well, I haven't fallen off so I guess that's saying something."

With Luke and Millie following the horses' trail, Katie nudged Susan and the pack horse she led forward, following the fenceline around a copse of evergreen trees whose fringy branches sagged under the weight of the snow. The fence had acted as a windbreak, effectively containing much of the blowing snow behind posts wearing brilliant white top hats.

Though the horses still had to work hard to plunge through the deep snow, it wasn't anywhere near as high as the drifts on the other side of the fence.

She hoped this wasn't another fool's errand. After checking the huge round water trough closest to the barn while feeding the animals earlier, Peter had discovered the warmer she'd been worried about the day before had completely gone out sometime during the night, leaving a four-inch layer of ice.

They had managed to break it up with shovels and pitchforks but Katie knew with these frigid temperatures, she and Peter would have to come out several times a day and smash new ice as it formed unless they could figure something else out.

The cattle could eat snow for some of their necessary water but it wouldn't be enough, not with this cold.

There was an identical watering system on the distant side of the two-hundred-acre pasture and Katie had come up with the grand idea of switching its warmer with the broken unit until Clint returned and could figure out what had gone haywire.

She could have retrieved it by herself but Peter insisted on coming along. Probably afraid to let her out of his sight, she thought grumpily, just in case she had nefarious plans to slip more Logan Corporation secrets to someone in her vast and intricate spy network.

But if he thought she was some kind of evil corporate spy, why did he kiss her?

She was no closer to figuring that out than she'd been at 4:00 a.m. Her sigh fogged the air, even through her thick muffler.

"Everything okay?" he asked.

Peachy. Just peachy. I'm pregnant and exhausted and queasy and can't say a word about any of it. "There's the water tank." She changed the subject. "And look, no ice. At least something's working."

They both dismounted and hitched their horses to the fence keeping the cattle away from a small storage shed near the watering station.

"Since this one has plenty of water, why can't the

cattle just drink from here?" Peter asked as they walked to the tank.

"All the cattle have been sticking close to the barn since that's where they catch the gravy train. If we make them trudge all the way out here to drink, I'm afraid they'll burn up so many calories we'll have to put out even more feed to keep them warm enough. The colder the temperature, the more food the cattle need. Add this kind of extra exercise even for a few days and either they'll start losing bulk or the ranch will have to dig into its overhead to cover the cost of feed."

His mouth twisted into a half smile as he studied her. "I never would have taken Katherine Crosby for a cowgirl."

"I'm just full of surprises, aren't I?"

"I'm beginning to think so."

What did he mean by that? she wondered. She could feel a blush heat her skin and cleared her throat, unnerved by a strange light in his eyes. "We'd better figure this out so we can get out of the cold."

Like the one closer to the barn, the warming unit was solar powered and it took her a few moments to figure out how to take it apart. Give her a computer CPU and she could have it apart and back together in the blink of an eye, but cattle trough warming units weren't exactly in her line of expertise. Finally she managed to disconnect it from the solar cells.

Peter reached to take the floating unit from her. He carried it back to the trio of horses and helped her tie it down on the back of the pack horse.

"Is that it?" Peter asked. "Are we done here?"

"I think so—" she started to say, but her words were cut off by a whoosh as a deep shelf of snow slid off the steep roof of the storage shed—and directly onto Peter, standing below. Only his head was left sticking out of the pile of snow.

"Are you all right?" she gasped, rushing forward to help him.

"Dandy," he muttered. She could tell by his tone that he wasn't hurt, only disgruntled at being buried. In her relief, she finally took time to really look at him. The sight made her stop in her tracks and cover her mouth with a gloved hand, but she was too late to stop a giggle.

Oh, how she wished that dratted *Portland Weekly* photographer were here now! She would love a picture of the oh-so-correct Peter Logan standing in the middle of a cattle pasture like the abominable snowman, with snow covering him from head to toe.

"It's not funny," he growled. He shook his head vigorously, flinging snow in every direction.

"Oh, it is. I'm sorry, but if you could see yourself right now, you'd be laughing, too."

He glared at her. "I'm blaming you for this, Ms. Crosby. I should be safe and warm and hard at work in Portland right now. I left a million things undone, every single one of them far more important than rolling around in snow and cow manure, fixing your stupid trough warmer."

"I'm sorry," she said again, then laughed even harder at his offended dignity. Soon she was whooping uncontrollably. Every time she thought she had it contained he would dig himself out a little farther, pausing just long enough to send another glare her way, and she would start again.

He must think she was insane, she thought. If someone had laughed at her in the same situation, she likely would have been livid.

Though one corner of her mind knew she ought to be helping him, she couldn't seem to do anything but stand in the snow and laugh like some half-crazy hyena.

Maybe it was her lack of sleep or maybe the stress she'd been living with. But it felt wonderful to let go and laugh. She didn't want to stop.

If he could have kept his eyes off Katie, Peter might have been able to dig himself out and clear the snow off various parts of his person much faster. But even as the cold snow started to permeate his heavy clothing, he couldn't manage to look away.

She was so beautiful she took his breath away. She glowed out here. With her cheeks rosy and her nose pink from the cold, she shined brighter than the brilliant Wyoming sunshine glittering off the snow. He had never seen this side of her. She didn't look sophisticated or glamorous or even cool and remote as she'd been since he came to the ranch.

Out here, Katie looked young and lighthearted, and he was helpless to resist that infectious laugh.

"I guess I should probably help you," she gasped out between peals of laughter.

"Oh, don't mind me. I have no problem staying here until the snow melts."

That set her off again but she hurried over, still laughing, and began to scoop away the snow mound surrounding him.

"Here," she said after several moments of digging. "Let's see if I can tug you out of the rest of it now."

She gripped his hands and pulled with all her might. He felt his snowy cage give way and with the added force, he was able to pull his boots free and climb out.

All would have been well, but when Katie let go of his hands, the momentum of her tug carried her backward and with an "oomph" she landed on her rear end in the snow.

Under other circumstances, he would have hurried to help her up. But since she had found such unbridled amusement a few moments earlier at his expense, he found he couldn't resist taking whatever advantage he could find. He scooped up a huge armload of snow and with complete, ungentlemanly satisfaction, dumped it on her head.

She shrieked and sputtered, then stared at him with snow dripping off her hat and down her coat.

"I can't believe you just did that."

Neither could he, truth be told. Leslie would have been appalled at him for picking on a girl. But he had to admit, revenge—no matter how petty—had felt pretty damn good.

He shrugged. "You're right. Wearing all that snow does look funny from this angle."

With the sleeve of her coat, she wiped the snow off her face and her hat then narrowed her gaze at him. Her red nose spoiled the menace in her glare, as did the delight gleaming in her eyes.

"You know this means war, don't you, Logan?"

In one smooth motion, she scooped up a snowball then fired it straight at his chin with perfect aim. It splatted on his already freezing skin in an icy mess. Before he could even think about retaliating, she rushed around the other side of the shed.

"Oh, that's it," he said with menace in his voice. "You don't know who you're messing with."

She giggled again and peeked her head around the corner of the shed just long enough to throw a snowball that didn't even come close to hitting the mark.

"Ha. Missed me." He sounded like a third-grader on the playground but suddenly he didn't care. All his fury and stress of the last few days seemed to melt away in the pale sunshine.

Her next snowball hit him square on the chest, but he was ready for her. Before she could retreat to safety, he lobbed one back at her. It struck her collarbone with a satisfying plop and she shrieked and ducked her head.

For the next ten minutes they played like children in the snow, with the dogs barking around them and joining in the fun. He forgot about being CEO of a Fortune 500 company, forgot about the dignity and decorum he usually tried to achieve. All he could focus on was retaliation.

Had he ever engaged in a good old-fashioned snowball fight as a kid? He couldn't remember. He knew Terrence and Leslie had taken them all skiing several times to Mount Hood and they'd even spent a few vacations on the slopes of Utah, but he only remembered concentrating fiercely on trying to ski well enough to keep up with his father, not playing in the snow.

He couldn't remember the last time he enjoyed himself so much. Now it was even more fun because Katie wasn't afraid to talk smack, with a creativity that amazed him.

She insulted his aim. She laughed at his asymmetrical snowballs that usually fell apart before they could land anywhere. She ridiculed his sneak-attack strategy of skulking past the horses to try to surprise her around the other side of the shed—only to find her poised and waiting for him with a rapid volley.

She also had a wicked curve ball. His shots missed more often than not, but hers nearly always found their mark.

Finally he was laughing too hard to throw anymore. He pulled his hat off, stuck it on a stick and thrust it around the side of the shed. "Truce," he called out.

After a moment she peeked her head around, her gaze narrowed. "How do I know this isn't just a sneaky Logan trick, so I let down my guard just enough that you can hit me with a firestorm?"

He grinned at her. "I guess you'll just have to trust me."

She appeared to think it over, then she walked around the shed toward him. "Okay."

Now it was his turn to study her with suspicion. "Just like that? It can't be that easy."

She shrugged when she reached him. "My nose is frozen and whipping your wussy butt makes me hungry. I'm ready for lunch."

She looked so adorably cheeky that he laughed and tugged her hat down over her eyes. Then, before he could check the motion, he dipped his head and kissed her.

Despite the cold temperatures, her mouth was warm—incredibly, seductively warm—and more inviting than a blazing fire. As soon as he kissed her, he forgot the snow and the cold and the horses stamping and snorting to return to the barn. All he could think about was her.

"You taste so good," he murmured against her mouth. "I don't want to stop."

"We'll freeze to death."

"I'm not sure I'd mind."

At his low words, she seemed to relax even more. Entwining her arms around his neck, she kissed him back with an eagerness that made him instantly hard and aching.

He wanted to drag her back to the house and make love to her until neither of them could move. He wanted to touch her and taste her and come inside her while she cried out his name, just as she had done the night of the gala.

And he could do none of them.

He *would* do none of them.

Though it was just about the toughest thing he'd ever done, he wrenched his mouth away and rested his forehead against hers. All the reasons why he couldn't touch her rattled through his mind.

Didn't he ever learn? He had spent most of the night castigating himself for his weakness in kissing her the night before.

Frustrated desire sharpened his tone. "Why couldn't your name be Smith or Jones or Fletcher? Why did you have to be a damn Crosby?"

He hadn't meant to speak the words but they escaped to hover in the cold air like black, greasy crows.

With a harsh intake of breath, she jerked away from him, her eyes bruised and hurt. "I can't change who I am, Peter. And even if I could, I wouldn't. I love my family, warts and all."

His own hurt at being used by her prodded him on, urged him to slash and cut and make her bleed as he finally acknowledged he had bled when he learned of her betrayal.

"And you'll do anything for them, won't you? Even screw a Logan, just to help out the family business."

She paled as if he had slapped her. All the warmth and happiness that had lit up her face during their play in the snow leached away, leaving her icy cold, her eyes huge in her ashen face.

Without another word, she turned her back on him and yanked her horse's reins free of the fence, then mounted before he could even make his boots work to follow her.

I'm sorry. The words rang in his ears, over and over and over, but he refused to let them spill out.

"I'm sure you can find your way back. Just follow the fence line," she said, her voice cool and without inflection.

Susan took off with a canter. It wasn't until Katie and the horse were several hundred yards away that he realized she had left him to lead the pack horse with the tank warmer.

Even with pushing Susan much harder than was safe in the heavy snow, Katie didn't quite make it to the thick copse of trees before she finally gave in to the tears burning behind her eyelids.

They slid free, only to freeze instantly on her cheeks. How was it that she hadn't noticed the cold at all while she and Peter had been engaged in their fierce snowball battle but now she could think of nothing but how frozen she was, how her bones felt as brittle as new icicles?

Damn Peter Logan. *Damn* him.

How could he make her feel so warm and cherished one moment, then like a two-bit whore the next?

What did he want from her? He wanted to punish her for deceiving him. That much had been clear since he showed up at Sweetwater, all fire and fury. Were these sweet, sensual, torturous kisses just another form of punishment? Part of some exquisite revenge on his part?

He wanted to make her burn for him just as she had that night, make her think maybe they could somehow find some peace between them, and then slap her back down, again and again.

She couldn't bear it.

She was such a fool. His contempt shouldn't have the power to wound her so viciously. She knew it shouldn't and yet she couldn't deny the ache in her heart.

She sniffed and swiped at her eyes. She was coming to care for him entirely too much.

How could she have let things get to this point?

She had been halfway in love with him after that night and now she was afraid she had come too far to turn back.

No. She couldn't be in love with him. Just the thought horrified her. She would just use all her considerable powers of reason and intellect to convince herself otherwise. It was as simple as that.

He would go back to Portland, probably as early as the next day, and she would stay here at Sweetwater until she worked this ridiculous infatuation out of her system.

In her rush to put as much distance as possible between her and Peter, she was pushing Susan far too hard for conditions. She realized it suddenly and started to rein her in. But before the horse could slow her momentum, she stumbled over some thick brush hidden beneath the snow.

If she had been concentrating as she should have been, Katie might have been able to stay in the saddle. It was only a little stumble, after all. But she was distracted by her emotions.

Add to that her thick gloves that didn't grip the reins as well as usual and the bulky snow boots she wore in place of ropers and that little stumble was all it took for her to go flying off.

She came down hard on one leg, then lost her balance and collapsed face-first into the snow, and the breath left her in a whoosh.

Chapter 8

For several long seconds Katie tried frantically to suck oxygen into lungs that suddenly refused to function after the force of her fall. She lay in the snow, her chest pounding and her head spinning.

Oh, she hurt. She started to take an inventory of what pained her the most but gave up the overwhelming task. Despite the snow that cushioned her fall, every inch of her body complained loudly.

She wanted to curl up right here and just close her eyes for a moment, just long enough for the pain to subside and for her breathing to return to normal, but she knew she couldn't.

She had to force herself to move, not only because she didn't particularly care to freeze to death out here in the middle of nowhere, but also because she wasn't about to let Peter find her like this, bruised and shaken on the ground.

Susan nudged at her, her breath warm and her big brown eyes concerned. "I'm not mad," Katie murmured soothingly to the horse as soon as she could make her lungs work again. "It wasn't your fault. I know it wasn't. I never should have rushed you like that."

The horse whinnied softly as if to urge her to her feet. "I need to get up. I know. Give me a minute."

Susan stood placidly next to her, and after a moment Katie summoned the will to grab hold of a stirrup and try to pull herself up. She made it as far as her knees before blinding pain shot from her right ankle, the one she'd landed on.

She cried out and collapsed onto the snow again.

All she needed was a broken ankle. No, she thought when she realized she could still rotate it, it probably was just a sprain. It only seemed to hurt when she put weight on it.

But how was she going to mount without putting weight on her ankle? She would just have to push through the pain, she thought. The alternative was waiting here for Peter to find her.

She forced herself to her knees again. This time she didn't even make it to her feet before a vicious cramp hit her low in the abdomen. Katie gasped as hot waves radiated through her.

The baby!

In the initial shock from her fall and pain from the sprained ankle, she had completely forgotten about the tiny life inside her.

Another cramp hit her, stronger than the first, and she clutched at her abdomen and doubled over.

Oh, please, God, no! Panic flashed through her. She couldn't lose this baby. She *couldn't*.

She needed help. She needed to get out of this cold and find help right now!

Her breath came in little sobbing gasps as she cried and prayed at the same time, all the while she struggled to make it into the saddle. By sheer stubbornness, she managed to climb to her feet and stood on one foot, clinging to the pommel. Another cramp racked her.

Above her moan she heard dogs barking from behind her.

She turned and saw Luke and Millie approaching, with Peter behind them leading the pack horse.

"Oh, Peter. Help me!"

His eyes widened with shock as he took in her dishevelment and the panic she knew must be abundantly clear on her features.

He dismounted and rushed to her in one quick motion. "What happened? Are you all right?"

"Susan stumbled and I fell off. I need a doctor, Peter. It's urgent. You're going to have to leave the ranch and go for help."

He grabbed her arm. "What is it? Sit down. You shouldn't be moving around like that. You might have a spinal injury."

"I don't have a spinal injury. I need a doctor. Right now!"

Another wave of pain hit her and she clutched at her abdomen, moaning in distress. Oh, it hurt. Far, far worse than the physical pain was the guilt and self-loathing surging through her.

How could she have been foolish enough to risk her baby's life over hurt feelings and a stupid argument?

She should have been more careful.

She had no business even being up on a horse. Really, she shouldn't be here in Wyoming. If she cared about her child's safety, she would have been safe and warm in her quiet condo in Lake Oswego, not out here in the cold and snow and wind.

She sobbed again and Peter pulled her close. "You're scaring me, Katie. Tell me what's wrong. Where do you hurt? Do you think you might have internal injuries?"

She had to tell him. None of the reasons for keeping her pregnancy a secret mattered now, not when their child's life was at stake.

"I'm pregnant and I'm cramping. I don't want to lose this baby. Please, Peter. Help me!"

For several seconds Peter could only stare at her as her words seemed to echo in the cold, still air.

Pregnant? *Pregnant?*

He barely had time to register the concept before she was struggling frantically to mount her horse again.

A million questions poured through him, but he knew the most important thing now was taking care of her.

"Stop. You're going to fall again, Katie. Let me help you. Are you sure you can ride?"

"I don't have any other choice. It would take me too long to walk through the snow to the ranch house. And I don't think I could. I think I may have sprained my ankle."

He tried to figure out another way to get her back to the house but couldn't, so he carefully lifted her into the saddle. She clutched the reins as he led the way back, her face set against the pain and her breathing ragged.

The ride seemed to take forever and he couldn't concentrate on anything but seeing her safely settled. By the time they reached the ranch house, she was pale and trembling and he knew she was in pain.

"Hang on," he said in what he hoped was a reassuring tone. "We're almost there."

She didn't answer. Her eyes were huge, frightened. He rode all the way to the front porch and jumped from his horse and quickly tied the reins to a hitching post there. He reached up and pulled her from the horse and into his arms, then carried her into the house.

He carried her to the couch and lowered her gingerly. "What do you need me to do? Where can I go for help?"

"Check the phone first. Maybe service has been restored."

He lifted the receiver and the dial tone in his ear was the sweetest sound he'd ever heard. "It works. Should I call an ambulance?"

She appeared to think it over, then shook her head. "I doubt the roads out here in the rural areas have been plowed enough for one to make it through. Even with four-wheel drive, I don't know that we could make it to the clinic in Daniel."

"What can we do?"

"My friend, Laura Harp, is a doctor. She lives just a few ranches over and could probably make it to Sweetwater by snowmobile. I'll call her."

He handed the phone to Katie, who whipped off her gloves and punched in a number. While he stood by, hating his helplessness, she explained the situation to someone on the other end of the line.

"Yes, I'm sure. Thirteen weeks gestation, eleven weeks since conception," she murmured into the phone. He didn't miss the furtive look she sent in his direction.

He did a quick mental calculation back to their passionate night together before Christmas. The dates were definitely right, but he didn't need that extra proof to convince him the unbelievable truth his heart was already telling him.

The child she carried was his.

He had no doubt in his mind whatsoever. So many things made sense now. How stunned she had been to see him when he showed up at the ranch, her on-again, off-again sickness, the light-headedness, the secrets he had glimpsed several times in her eyes.

He wondered if she had had any intention at all of telling him. Somehow he didn't think so. He drew in a sharp breath at the idea that if she hadn't fallen and been forced to tell him, he might have spent his entire life never knowing he had fathered a child.

Later. He could think about all that later. Now he needed to do everything he could to help that child survive.

Katie hung up the phone. "She should be here within a half hour. Laura's a wonderful doctor. If anyone can save my baby, she can."

Though the questions crowding his mind begged to be asked, he knew this wasn't the time. "We need to get you into something dry."

"You're right," she said after a slight pause. "Would you mind helping me into my bedroom? I have a robe there I can put on."

"Of course," he answered, frustrated at her obvious reluctance to ask him for help, even in something as minor as this.

He scooped her from the couch and carried her down the hall to her bedroom. Through the tumult in his mind, he registered that her room was similar to his, decorated in mountain-lodge style with river rock and wood and natural colors.

He set her on the edge of a low trunk at the foot of the bed and knelt to pull her boots off first, then helped her out of her heavy insulated coveralls. She was wet clear through, and guilt swamped him as he remembered dumping snow on her. She was pregnant and he had just spent fifteen minutes throwing snowballs at her, for hell's sake.

"Thank you," she murmured. "If you'll just hand me that robe over the chair there, I believe I can handle it from here."

He complied then went to work building a fire in the stone fireplace. By the time the kindling caught, she had changed into her robe and started to hop from the chest to the bed.

"Damn it, Katie. Let me help."

Just as he moved to her side, she gasped again and clutched her stomach. He lifted her, struck by how fragile she felt in his arms, then tucked her into the bed.

"I'm so scared, Peter." Her voice sounded small, hollow.

"I know. I wish I could make it better."

He didn't know how to handle this powerless feeling. He wasn't used to it. In his world, he thrived on challenges but this was a force he could do nothing against. He wanted to make everything all right again, to ease her fear and her pain, and he hated that he couldn't.

She gripped his hand tightly. "I should have told you. I'm sorry."

The words surprised him and he didn't know how to respond. "We can talk about that later. Right now you just need to rest until the doctor gets here."

She nodded and even closed her eyes for a moment, her hand still gripping his. He watched her, not sure if she was sleeping.

A strange warmth started low in his chest, then pulsed through him. It took him a few moments to identify what he was feeling. When he realized it was tenderness, he wanted to drop her hand and get the hell out of there as fast as he could run. He forced himself to gently set her fingers onto the quilt instead.

She opened her eyes. "Please don't leave."

"I'm only going to see if the power has been restored along with the phone service. I'll be back, I promise."

She seemed satisfied with that and closed her eyes again.

A quick look at the power situation confirmed what he'd been hoping. They had electricity again. He shut off the generator and switched the household current back and was returning the bedroom when the doorbell rang.

The doctor. Hallelujah!

Laura Harp was at least sixty, petite and with short steel-gray hair and incongruously trendy tiny dark-rimmed glasses. She looked more like a librarian than a country doctor, until he looked into her vivid blue eyes and saw a mixture of warmth and concern and aeons of wisdom and experience he couldn't even begin to comprehend.

"That was quick."

"I've got a wicked-fast Polaris. Comes in real handy during weeks like this. It's the only way I've been able to get into the clinic since Thursday. You must be a friend of Katherine's."

He wouldn't go that far. But since he didn't know how else to characterize their relationship, he merely nodded. "Peter Logan."

Behind those glasses, her eyes widened with recognition. He could tell from her expression that she must be familiar with his name. He could only guess by her surprise that she must have heard about the infamous Logan-Crosby feud.

"Katie is lying down back here."

He led the way down the hall to the bedroom. Katie's eyelids fluttered open when he opened the door and her gaze immediately went to the small woman at his side.

"You're here," she breathed, with such palpable relief in her eyes that he felt large and male and out of place.

"I need to go take care of the horses and stable them. I'll, um, just get out of your way."

He escaped without giving either of them the chance to argue—not that he thought they would.

Outside, he filled his lungs with icy air, then let it out in a rush. At last he could come to terms with the stunning events of the last hour.

Pregnant.

If this Dr. Harp succeeded in saving the baby, he would be a father in a little over six months.

This was huge. Gigantic. So staggering, he couldn't

manage to work his mind around it. How could this have happened? Despite the fire and heat of that incredible night together, they had been scrupulously careful. He had used a condom every time.

Except one, he suddenly remembered. He had awakened sometime during the night, already aroused, and had been inside her before he was really conscious of it. He thought he had pulled out in time but obviously at least one little swimmer had hit the jackpot.

A baby.

A baby with Katherine *Crosby!*

What the hell was he supposed to do now? He stood there in the cold Wyoming air, gazing at the raw, snow-covered mountains, overwhelmed by the reality that his entire life was about to change.

Another man would probably think it best all around if Katie lost the baby.

He blew out a breath that clouded in the cold. Yeah, his life might be far less complicated if she miscarried but just the possibility filled him with a hard, spiny knot under his breastbone.

Kate already loved their unborn child. He had seen it in the hand she splayed protectively over her abdomen, in the fear in her eyes, in her frantic call for help.

Losing the baby would devastate her.

Despite everything—her deception that night and, really, in the weeks since when she should have told him about the baby—he didn't want to see her hurt.

What if he hadn't been here? If he hadn't been so determined to find her after he learned who she was and hadn't flown out from Portland despite the storm warning?

His blood ran cold thinking about it.

She would have been trapped out here for days, pregnant and alone, having to take care of all the stock by herself.

The horses, still hitched to the rail out front, stamped in the snow, and the little one, Susan, whinnied impatiently, dragging him from his thoughts.

"I'm coming, I'm coming." He grabbed their reins and started walking toward the barn, struck by how surreal this all seemed. His whole world had just shifted and he wasn't quite sure how to deal with it.

Three days earlier—hell, an *hour* earlier—he knew just who he was, what he wanted out of life.

He was Peter Logan, oldest child of Leslie and Terrence, brother to Eric and David and Jillian and Bridget. He was the young CEO of the Logan Corporation and brimmed over with vibrant, ambitious plans for moving the company forward.

Now, God willing, he was going to be a father.

And everything had changed.

"Isn't there something you can give me?" Katie asked after Laura had examined her. "Some pill that could stop the cramps?"

Laura squeezed her hand. "Not this early in the game, I'm afraid. I wish I had more to offer but the only thing I can prescribe at this point is plenty of rest. And don't discount the power of hope and prayers."

If hope and prayers were enough, she had more than enough of both to make all the difference. But Katie knew sometimes all the faith in the world couldn't defeat nature.

Still, she had to cling to that calm assurance in her friend's wise eyes.

"You're strong and healthy. I have high hopes you can keep the pregnancy if all goes well."

"Thank you." Katie tried to smile, but she had a feeling it was a little watery. Laura pressed a cool hand to her cheek, and the tears burning behind her eyes trickled out.

"Hey, now. What's this?" the doctor asked.

"I'm in such a mess, Laura."

"Ordinarily my policy is to mind my own business and stick to doctoring in matters like this, but we've been friends for a long time."

Despite the fear still heavy in her chest, Katie smiled at the memory. "Ever since you gave me six stitches in my hand after my ill-fated attempt at helping Clint string some barbed wire. I must have been all of, what, seventeen?"

"Right. You've been good business. Seems like every time you come out to the ranch I get to do a little doctoring. Since we're old friends and all, I guess that gives me the right to be a little nosy and bend my strict MYOB policy. I'll just come out and ask. Does the father know you're pregnant?"

"He does now," Katie muttered. "I had no choice but to tell him after I fell."

"Ah." Somehow Laura managed to inject that single syllable with an entire world full of understanding and sympathy. "The gorgeous Mr. Logan, then?"

Katie nodded, then bit her lip when it threatened to tremble. She swallowed her tears again and blew out a breath.

"It's a long story, Laura. One I'm afraid won't have a very happy ending. I haven't been precisely truthful with him from the beginning. I misled him and…

I didn't tell him about the baby. I doubt he'll ever be able to see past that."

Laura sat on the edge of the bed. "You might have made mistakes. You both might have, for all I know. But now is the time for both of you to put those differences behind you and concentrate on what's best for this baby of yours."

"I didn't want him to know."

"Here's your first parenting lesson. What you want or need doesn't really matter much anymore in the scheme of things. Your first and only priority is that baby. Whatever the circumstances, the two of you created a life together. It's up to you to do right by that little life."

"I'm going to be a terrible mother." The tears spilled free once more and trickled down her cheeks. "How can I be anything else? Just look at the kind of example I had!"

Laura handed her a tissue, then gathered her into her arms. "You'll be a wonderful mother. You have so much love inside you to give. You just have to trust yourself."

"I've already made so many mistakes."

"There's not a mother on earth who hasn't. It's a wonder I can even let my two boys out in public with all the mistakes I made. They're grown now and I'm still making mistakes with them. But you know, for all my shortcomings, they've turned out to be pretty decent people. So have you, despite your parents. You just need to trust yourself. You've always been much stronger than you've ever given yourself credit for."

Right now she felt like a weak and trembling child,

especially whenever she thought about the inevitable confrontation with Peter.

"Thank you," Katie murmured.

"Rest now. Stay off that sprain until you can put weight on it without pain. I'll call tomorrow to see how you're doing, but if you need me before then, I can be here in a heartbeat. You have your young man give me a call, all right?"

Katie nodded, though she wanted to protest that Peter was *not* her young man.

When it came right down to it, that was the entire problem.

Chapter 9

She awoke just after midnight.

With an anguished cry of alarm, she sat up and her hand automatically fluttered to her abdomen.

Peter jumped up from his chair by the fire, his heart pounding. "What is it? Another cramp?"

She frowned, as if not quite sure. After a moment she let out a breath and sagged against the pillows again. "No. I must have been dreaming."

"Not a good one, I'm guessing."

"No. It was horrible and so real. One of those dreams you try so hard to wake from."

He sat on the edge of the wide bed. "Want to tell me about it?"

Her fingers clutched the scalloped edge of the quilt she had pushed off in her sleep. "You'll think I'm crazy."

"Try me."

She closed her eyes. "I was riding Susan through thick trees and she stumbled. I fell off, just like today, but when I caught my breath, I found myself staring into the yellow eyes of a wolf. It was beautiful but terrifying at the same time. Silver with black fur around his face."

Her eyes opened and the remembered fear in them clutched his heart. "I can still see it when I close my eyes," she continued, "pacing back and forth. Pacing, endlessly pacing, until I thought I would scream."

She shuddered and pulled the blanket up to her shoulders. "Suddenly I had a baby in my arms. I'm not sure how it got there, but then the wolf started edging closer, so close I could feel the heat emanating from his fur and smell his breath. I knew, somehow I knew, he would try to wrench the baby away from me. Right before he lunged at me, I threw a snowball at him and he disappeared."

She grimaced. "Weird, isn't it? I knew you'd think I was crazy."

"I don't think you're crazy. You've had a rough day."

She looked around the room, at the dark windows. "What time is it?"

"Around midnight. How are you feeling?"

She touched her abdomen again, as if for reassurance. He wondered if she knew she slept that way, with one hand tucked under her cheek and the other curled around the tiny life growing inside her. All evening long he had watched her sleep as he tried to come to terms with the shock of finding out he was going to become a father.

"I'm fine. My ankle throbs but the rest of me seems okay."

"You slept through dinner. Are you hungry?"

Her brow furrowed as if she had to think about it. "I guess I am, a little," she said after a moment. "But you don't have to wait on me. I can find something."

"Don't even think about it," he said sternly. "I talked to Dr. Harp before she took off and she said she wants you on bed rest for at least the next few days. I'll fix you something."

"I don't want you to have to do that."

"Is there anyone else lurking around Sweetwater I don't know about who can feed you?"

"You know there's not."

"Right. A smart woman like you should know when she's all out of choices."

"Whoever said I was smart?" she muttered, looking so disgruntled he almost laughed.

He knew damn well she was brilliant. She had told him she'd been admitted to Stanford early and he knew she had graduated with honors.

He also knew enough about the inner workings at Crosby to know her brother Trent relied heavily on her brains and that she had revitalized research and development at the company under her tenure.

Brains and beauty. His baby could do a whole lot worse in a mother, he thought.

"Just give me a minute," he said.

When he returned fifteen minutes later with a tray, she was reading a pregnancy book with a photograph of a smiling baby on the cover. She set it down, coloring a little, he was charmed to see.

"I'm overwhelmed by all the things I never knew about pregnancy and childbirth. It's terrifying."

"Not nearly as frightening as what comes after the delivery," he pointed out.

"Don't think that hasn't been giving me nightmares, too."

She paused and her fingers clutched the edge of the quilt again, her expression a jumbled mix of emotions, determination in the forefront.

"Peter, I—"

"Omelettes taste like rubber school erasers when they're cold. For the baby's sake and for your own, you need to eat," he said, cutting her off. He knew what was coming. Yes, they would talk about her pregnancy and all the ramifications of it. They *had* to talk about it.

But he wasn't ready yet.

Though she looked as if she wanted to argue, he gave her his best don't-mess-with-me look and she finally turned that determination to the tray he set in front of her.

"This is delicious!" she exclaimed after a moment.

"You sound surprised."

"I don't know. I suppose I wouldn't have expected the Logan CEO to be a culinary whiz."

He laughed. "I'm far from that. Mom insisted each of us have at least one specialty in the kitchen. Since I've always been an early riser, I was relegated to breakfast food by default. Besides omelettes, I also make a wicked French toast."

He suddenly had the sobering realization that he knew relatively little about this woman who was pregnant with his child. "What about you? Do you like to cook?"

She took a sip of the juice he had included on the tray, then set the glass down at the same time she shrugged. "Too much. I also like to eat. That's why I used to be huge."

"I don't remember you as huge."

She studied him for several moments, her expression unreadable. "You don't remember me at all, do you?"

Again he tried to conjure up an image of her from before that night at the charity auction. He *should* remember her. Damn it, why couldn't he? "You used to have glasses and long, pretty hair, right?"

"And an extra forty pounds."

"I don't remember that part."

She rolled her eyes and laughed. "As if you would admit it, even if you did remember."

"We Logan men have never been dumb."

He paused and his smile slid away. "Although I certainly was three months ago. I should have recognized you. I'm sorry."

"Don't apologize. My own family barely knew me when I walked into the benefit. I've been hiding for a long time behind the image people expected to see when they looked at me."

What did people expect to see when they looked at her? he wondered. And what was she hiding from? He wanted to ask but he sensed she already regretted her comment.

"Why didn't you tell me who you were?" he asked instead.

He had posed the same question to her before, after he first arrived at Sweetwater, but she had brushed him off with some glib answer about being carried away by the glamour and excitement of pretending to be someone else for a while.

He hadn't bought it then. Now he didn't know what to believe.

She set her fork down next to her half-eaten omelette and let out a slow breath.

"I suppose I was shocked and flattered when you seemed interested," she admitted. "I've always been in the shadows, one of those women no one noticed. I didn't mind. I preferred it that way. But suddenly one of Portland's most eligible bachelors was flirting with me—*me,* fat, awkward Katie Crosby—and I didn't want it to end. I knew the moment you learned I was a Crosby you wouldn't be able to get away from me fast enough so I—I lied."

There was more to this story, he thought. Why had she gone home with him? He had learned enough about her since he arrived at the ranch that he had a feeling her actions that night had been as uncharacteristic for her as they'd been for him.

It had been far easier to accuse her of corporate thievery than to dig into his own psyche and ask himself why he had responded to her so instantly and so passionately—and why she had reacted to him the same way.

"And the baby?" he asked. "Were you ever going to tell me you were pregnant?"

He hadn't meant to ask the question, but somehow the words forced their way out.

She met his gaze for just a moment, her expression guarded, then gazed at the fire. "No," she finally said.

He was completely unprepared for the pain that pierced through him at her answer. "Why not?"

Her laugh was short, harsh. "A million reasons. You didn't even know my real name. I'm sorry but I couldn't quite figure out a good way to suddenly show up at your doorstep and say, 'Hey, remember me? Funny thing, my name isn't really Celeste, it's Katherine Crosby. Yes, of *those* Crosbys, the family you hate. Nice to meet you. Oh, and by the way, guess what? Great news! We're having a baby.'"

Without a pause Peter asked, "Didn't you think I had a right to know?"

Her gaze shifted to the fire. "I couldn't think about that, not with everything between us. I don't know, maybe I would have told you eventually, but to be honest, all I've been able to focus on for the last week has been my own shock. I haven't even had time to get used to the idea myself."

And yet he knew she already loved the child they had created together.

"So where do we go from here?" he asked.

"A baby was something neither of us ever expected. I don't know how or why it happened, not when we were so careful, but I do know I want this child, Peter. I don't expect anything from you. Tomorrow the roads should be clear enough for travel. You can go back to Portland and forget any of this ever happened."

A muscle clenched in his jaw. "You think I would just walk away from you and the baby? You must think I'm a real son of a bitch."

"I don't think that of you at all! I just don't want you to feel obligated to stick around and pretend to be happy about all of this. I know it's been a shock."

He wanted to laugh at the understatement but he could find very little humor in this whole thing.

He had thought of nothing but the future while he had sat by the fire watching her sleep. In that darkened room, he had gone over the very limited options available to them now that they had a child to consider and had come up with only one real solution.

"We should get married."

At his blunt words, her gaze flew to his and her mouth sagged open. She swallowed hard several times then shook her head vigorously. If she could have gotten out of bed, he had no doubt she would have stalked out of the room. "No. Absolutely not. Forget it!"

"Just like that? You're not even going to think about it?"

"What's to think about? As far as proposals go—if that's what you want to call that…proclamation—this one is both unnecessary and unwanted."

"I disagree."

He didn't see any other choice available to them. Wherever possible, a child needed both parents. He believed it fiercely. His parents would expect them to marry when they learned a child was involved.

He expected it.

Getting married was the right thing to do, and since that day the Logans had plucked him out of a bleak future and given him the world, he had spent his life always trying to do the right thing.

Katherine held her ground. "No. I am perfectly capable of raising my child by myself. I don't need you."

"Not *your* child," he said coolly. "*Our* child."

"You're the sperm donor. That's all."

He narrowed his gaze and refused to let her see how those words wounded him. "Is that why you seduced me that night? The old biological clock was ticking away and you decided you needed a warm, healthy male? What did you do, poke a few holes in one of the condoms and think I'd never find out?"

Even if he had believed his own words, the shock on her features would have told him how ludicrous that idea was.

"Of course not!" she exclaimed. "I *never* expected to end up pregnant from that night. This was as much a shock to me as it is to you! I didn't believe it myself. I denied it as long as possible until I could no longer avoid facing the truth. I never would have tricked you like that."

"And I'm supposed to believe you, *Celeste?*"

She flushed but met his gaze steadily. "All the more reason why your marriage offer is completely ridiculous. You don't like me or trust me. How are we supposed to base a marriage on that?"

"We'll just have to figure it out as we go along."

"We won't have to figure *anything* out because I'm not going to marry you!"

"This is my child, too. I intend to be part of his life."

"Or her life."

"Either way. I've got no preference."

"Fine. You can be involved. You don't have to marry me to do that. People find themselves in this situation all the time. They manage to work it out."

"To the satisfaction of no one involved," he pointed out, "especially not the child."

"You think a marriage between two people who barely know each other is the answer?"

"So we'll get to know each other. And then we'll get married."

* * *

Katie wanted to scream at his resolute tone. Of all the scenarios she had imagined for this conversation, this was a direction she absolutely never expected him to take. Marriage! Between a Crosby and a Logan. The idea was laughable.

This was no Romeo and Juliet. She wouldn't marry him. She *couldn't*. It would be disastrous all the way around. Her feelings for him were already too complicated, too intense. She wouldn't be able to bear trapping him in a loveless marriage.

She had seen the hell of her parents' marriage. The fierce fights, the cheating on both sides. They had stayed together far too long, not for the sake of the children—that novel idea never would have occurred to them—but because neither Jack nor Sheila wanted to be the one to cry uncle.

They must have loved each other at some point. She had to believe that. But by the time they divorced, that love had morphed into something ugly and bitter.

A marriage without even that foundation at the beginning didn't stand a chance—and an innocent child would be the one to suffer.

"No," she said almost frantically. "No. I won't do it."

Something of her distress must have shown on her features, in her tone, because Peter crossed the room, his expression concerned and faintly guilty. "Don't upset yourself about this right now. I'm sorry, I shouldn't have pushed you. You need to rest and take it easy, not argue with me. We have time to sort everything out."

Maybe they wouldn't have anything to sort out. The fear she had been holding at bay seeped through as she remembered just what challenges their child faced before entering the world. Maybe the pregnancy wouldn't survive and all this talk about marriage would be moot.

No. She wouldn't think like that. *You've always been much stronger than you've ever given yourself credit for,* Laura had said. She had to believe she could be strong for her baby—for *their* baby.

"Thank you for the omelette," she said to Peter. "Your mother would be proud."

"Of my cooking skills anyway," he said, just a shadow of bitterness in his voice. "I'll leave you to rest now. I'll be out on the couch. Call me if you need anything."

She nodded, then watched him carry the tray out of the room, wondering how it was that telling him about their child had left her feeling more alone than ever.

"No spotting at all and no cramping since yesterday afternoon, then?"

"Nothing," Katie answered Laura the next day when she stopped at the ranch before heading to the clinic. "I'm a little queasy but other than that, I feel great."

She had been too nauseated to even finish the French toast Peter prepared for her, though the few mouthfuls she'd been able to swallow had indeed tasted delicious, crispy and sweet and covered in cinnamon sugar.

"Most pregnant mothers have a hard time accepting it, but believe it or not, queasy can be a good sign," the doctor said. "Still, I'd like to hook up the Doppler here and listen to the baby's heartbeat."

"Can you do that this early?" Peter asked from where he stood by the window. The day before he had escaped to the barn while Laura was here but today he seemed reluctant to leave during her exam.

"We should be able to find it. You're thirteen weeks along, right?"

Katie nodded.

"Let's see what we've got, then."

Upon the doctor's instructions, Katie bared her midriff, chagrined at herself for feeling exposed with Peter in the room. The man had seen far more of her than her belly, she reminded herself. Still, that had been under far different circumstances. She couldn't help being a little uncomfortable in this intimate situation.

She forgot about her unease when Laura rubbed a small device over her abdomen. Immediately a loud pulsing filled the room.

"That's your heartbeat there," the doctor said, then passed the sensor across her skin again, pressing a little harder this time. After a moment the beats accelerated noticeably and Laura smiled widely. "And that's your baby's. You can tell because it's much faster than yours. It's a beautiful sound, isn't it?"

To Katie's deep embarrassment, tears began to glide down her cheeks. "Wonderful."

She was stunned when Peter crossed the room and sat beside her on the bed with an odd, stunned expression on his face. He placed his hand over hers and squeezed her fingers.

"Is the baby all right?" he asked Laura.

"I can't really tell without an ultrasound, but the heartbeat is strong and healthy, just the way I like them. You're not out of the woods yet, Katie my girl, but if you can make it to the second trimester—generally considered to be around fourteen weeks—the chance of miscarriage drops quite a bit. That's only another week for you."

"Is it safe for her to travel? Can I fly her home to Portland?"

Laura looked pensively at Katie. "That's a tricky one. Ordinarily I'd recommend at least a few days bed rest to give your body time to heal. That was a nasty fall and even if you weren't pregnant, I'd suggest taking it easy for a while. With that bum ankle, you could fall again, which wouldn't be good for you or the baby."

She put her equipment away in her bag. "When you're so close to the magic number of fourteen weeks, I guess I would err on the side of caution and suggest you lay low until then." She shrugged. "On the other hand, if it came down to a choice between staying out here by yourself or flying back to Portland, I'd have to go with Door Number Two."

Peter spoke up. "She's not by herself. I'll stay with her."

Katie swiped her eyes with the tissue the doctor handed her and stared at Peter, certain she must have misheard. "You can't take an entire week away from Logan to baby-sit me!"

"Why not?"

"Because you're—you're the CEO. Don't you have work? Mergers, meetings, that kind of thing?"

"I'm surrounded by excellent people. They can run things for a while without me, I'm sure. Don't worry, Crosby. The company won't fall apart in a week."

She couldn't believe he would consent to stay. He had already been stuck here for four days and she knew how restless he was to return to work. She wanted to tell him to go, to assure him she would be fine for a few days, even though she was so tempted to lean against him for a while.

"I can't ask you to do that," she said finally.

"You didn't. I'm offering. No, not offering, insisting."

Laura stood. "I'm going to wisely stay out of this and head over to the Bar S to check on Darwin's broken leg. Let me know how it all shakes out, though my money's on Mr. Logan here."

Katie thanked her friend for coming out to the ranch and bid her goodbye. She waited until Laura left before she turned on Peter. "You can't possibly stay another week."

"You would rather take on the world and come out swinging than admit when you're backed against a wall, wouldn't you? I'm staying, Katie. Deal with it. Anyway, with the phones back up, I can find plenty of work to do from here. Don't worry about me."

She didn't worry about him, she admitted. She worried about herself. Her emotions were already so vulnerable. She wanted desperately to lean on him for a while and she hated herself for it.

She was a strong, capable woman who could handle pregnancy on her own. But as he had said the night before, she was also smart enough to know when she was all out of choices.

Chapter 10

For a woman who had never been wooed before, resisting Peter Logan was proving an impossible task.

Like her brother Trent, Peter was a man used to getting what he wanted. Right now he seemed to want her—or at least the baby she carried. With the same single-minded purpose and determination that made him a formidable business opponent, the blasted man was doing everything he could to attain his goal.

He was charming, he was sweet, he was attentive. He brought her meals in bed and played games and watched old movies with her. Without a single murmur of complaint, he cared for the animals and made sure they had a steady supply of firewood.

He told her stories about growing up with the Logans—about family vacations and campouts in the backyard and playing basketball in the driveway.

him through the window as he threw a stick into the snow for Luke and Millie to chase.

She couldn't bear knowing she would have very few more of those memories. But this wasn't real life. They were suspended in a cheerful little bubble here, away from her family and his, away from the pressures of life in Portland. She couldn't pretend that just because they'd been able to live together well here at Sweetwater they could enjoy a happy marriage.

How could they, when he would be marrying her only out of that damn sense of responsibility he took so seriously? He didn't love her. A marriage in which only one person loved the other would be a nightmare of unimaginable pain.

No, she had to be strong and withstand his insidious assault on her willpower. The happily-ever-after she might secretly long for would never happen. She needed to accept that and prepare her heart for its inevitable fracture.

"What put that grim look on your face all of a sudden?" he asked. "Are you having a pain?"

She blinked away her depressing thoughts to find him watching her with concern in his dark eyes. "No. The baby is fine. I haven't had any pains since the day I fell."

"The ankle bugging you?"

"No. It's almost back to normal. I barely even notice when I put weight on it now."

"Then what is it?"

For a moment she debated how to answer him. When she couldn't come up with a plausible lie, she plunged ahead with the truth. "I've enjoyed these few days. I'm going to be sorry to see them end."

Oh, she shouldn't have admitted that, she thought when Peter raised an eyebrow, as if her confession surprised him as much as it did her.

"It doesn't have to end," he said. "Not if you marry me."

She shook her head in exasperation, though she could feel her heart splinter a little more around the edges. "I can't figure out if you're relentless or simply ruthless."

He grinned. "I'm both. You've played poker with me. Haven't you figured that out? You owe me something like eight hundred matchsticks by now, don't you?"

"Only because you cheat!"

"I prefer to think I'm innovative and think outside the box."

She laughed and tossed a pillow at him, grateful for the diversion from her melancholy. "I prefer to think you're a dirty rotten cheat who makes up his own rules."

"You're just sore because you never knew a pair of sixes automatically trumps every other possible hand. I'm telling you, it's the Holy Grail of five-card stud. Ask anyone."

"I can't believe you tried to pull that one. Or that you thought I was stupid enough to fall for it."

"Hey, a guy's got to try."

When he looked at her with that smile in his eyes, she almost thought maybe they could make a marriage work.

"How's the work going?" she asked.

"Surprisingly well. I'd forgotten what a little change in scenery can do for the creative juices. I've been able to accomplish more in just a couple hours a day here than I do putting in eighty-hour work weeks."

Despite his protestations that the company could run fine in his absence, she had to wonder what the other top brass at Logan thought about their CEO taking off to the wilds of Wyoming for a week.

She hadn't dared to ask him—or to ask if his family knew what he was doing here.

He hadn't been exactly inaccessible. Since the phones had been restored, she knew he e-mailed his staff regularly and had at least one lengthy phone conversation with his assistant each day. That interaction was minimal compared to what she knew her father would have been doing in the same situation.

Jack would have been a basket case. She remembered once he and Sheila had come to Switzerland for a parents' weekend at her boarding school—the only such event she could ever remember them attending—and her father had barely taken the phone away from his ear long enough to eat.

Peter was not her father. If she had learned anything these last few days it was that clear fact. She knew his work was important to him but it didn't seem to consume him.

He didn't seem to mind the interruption. After closing his laptop, he joined her on the couch and reached for her hand. That was another thing she had learned about Peter Logan during this time alone with him. He was more physically affectionate than she ever would have expected. He seemed to enjoy touching her, caressing her fingers, rubbing her shoulders, even kissing her casually on the cheek.

She wasn't used to it and didn't know quite how to

respond but she had to admit she found it both sweet and disarming.

"Speaking of innovation and outside-the-box ideas," he said, holding firm to her fingers, "I've been thinking about something."

She eyed him warily. "What?"

"Our families have wasted years and untold resources competing with each other. How much more successful would we both be if we could channel some of that negative energy into cooperating on certain projects?"

She stared at him, unable to believe the words were actually coming from him. The Crosbys and the Logans working together without the business world jerking to a complete standstill? Was it even possible?

"What kind of projects?" she asked.

"This super-router, for example. With your NPIC software system and the NPIR hardware we're developing, between Crosby and Logan we could create the fastest networking system the world has ever known. Both those components could of course be purchased separately but how much more effective would they be if we packaged them together? Made them one-hundred-percent compatible?"

"The industry wouldn't know what hit it." Her mind raced, imagining the possibilities. Trent had long talked about coming up with their own super-router hardware to complement the software they had put much of their design efforts into, but any project they started would be years behind Logan in development.

"You're not talking about a merger, right?"

"No. Just a cooperative agreement on this project.

And maybe if it was successful, we could look into working together on other projects down the line."

"It has potential," she admitted.

"I think it's brilliant."

She smiled at his arrogance, then sobered when she thought of all the ramifications to be considered, especially the single overriding concern. "Our families would never agree to work together. Not with all that's gone on between us."

"They might be more willing if we can find a way to bridge the gap between the Logans and the Crosbys. What better way to do that than if we married and gave them all a shared grandchild?" His thumb caressed her knuckle. "Marry me, Katie."

She stared at him, tempted beyond words. Oh, how she wanted to say yes. She closed her eyes, trying to draw courage from somewhere deep inside her to turn him down, even though she desperately wanted to agree.

"Peter, I—"

She didn't know exactly how she would have answered him. Whatever words hovered on her tongue were interrupted by the phone ringing.

They stared at each other for a moment, then with a sigh Peter reached for it, as nearly all the calls in the last three days had been for him.

"Hello?"

After a moment his features froze into an expression of acute dislike. "Yes. She's here. One moment, please."

He handed the cordless phone to Katie. She frowned, not sure what had put that icy look on his face, that chill in his voice.

With some degree of trepidation, she took it from

him. The moment she said hello, she understood. Her stomach dropped to her toes as her mother's smoky voice filled her ear.

"You have a man there? Why, Katie, you sly thing. Who is it? One of those boring computer nerds from work?"

With Sheila's animosity toward all things Logan, she certainly couldn't tell her mother Peter Logan was sitting on the couch with her. "No one," she murmured. "Um, just a friend."

"What friend? Anyone I know?"

"No, I don't believe so."

She had enough experience dealing with her mother to know she had to quickly deflect Sheila's attention to something else.

"Where are you? I thought you were staying in Tuscany until the end of the month."

To her relief, Sheila allowed herself to be sidetracked. "That was the plan but I was bored out of my mind after two days. The place was *horrible!* Absolutely ghastly. All anyone wanted to talk about was their food and their wine and how beautiful the countryside was."

Which meant that no one wanted to focus on Sheila's favorite topic—herself.

"If you ask me, one vineyard looks the same as the next. I mean, what's the big deal? It's a pile of dirt and straggly twigs. Clue in!"

Though she wanted to hang up, she knew the part she was expected to play to appease Sheila's narcissism.

"Did your friend return early with you?" Katie asked.

"Who? Gianni? He was as disappointing as Tuscany. I must tell you, he sadly misrepresented himself as some kind of rich Italian stallion. I guess one out of three wasn't bad; at least he was Italian. He just wanted to sponge off my money. I couldn't *wait* to get out of there. I left him in Milan and caught the first flight back."

Sheila paused only long enough to take a breath. "Speaking of hellholes, I don't know what you're doing in that primitive armpit but I need you to get back to Portland right now. You'll laugh about this, I'm sure, but there's the most ludicrous rumor going around that you were seen kissing *Peter Logan* at some event or other around Christmas."

She closed her eyes at the sheer loathing in her mother's voice when she said Peter's name. Here it comes, she thought. The confrontation she had been expecting. "Oh?"

"Yes! That brainless society reporter for the *Weekly* even ran a picture he claims is the two of you together in some steamy kiss. Can you believe that? I haven't seen the picture yet but Penelope Danner phoned me in Italy and told me all about it. You need to do damage control right away and have those idiots run a correction. As if you'd even be caught dead anywhere near that bastard!"

Katie's gaze fell on Peter, who had absently pulled her feet into his lap and was rubbing her toes through her thick socks. "Um, right."

"Besides, Peter Logan can have his pick of any woman in Portland. Why would he bother with you?"

Ah. She should have been expecting that one, too, but it still managed to slice at her self-confidence with brutal efficacy. "That's a very good question," she said quietly.

Sheila went on as if she hadn't heard her, which was probably true. "When will you be going back to Portland?"

"I'm not sure right now. Most likely by the end of the week." *And then wouldn't the you-know-what hit the fan?*

"Good. I need you to talk to your brother."

"Which one?"

"Who do you think? As if Danny has anything to do with anybody out in that isolation chamber of his. No, I'm talking about Trent, Mr. Holier-than-Thou, unnatural child. Ever since your father named him CEO, he thinks he can run the world. You're just about the only one he listens to. Maybe you can talk some sense into him. But you need to do it in person, not from that godforsaken ranch."

She sighed. "What did he do?"

"Nothing yet, but he'd like to. If Trent had his way, I'd be stuck in some retirement condo in Arizona wearing muumuus and watching game shows all day. He doesn't want me to have any fun. Now he's threatening to use his influence to have my country club membership yanked. Can you believe that?"

"What did you do to provoke him?"

"How do you know I did anything?" Sheila asked, affront in her voice.

Because I know you, she thought. *Because I have spent twenty-eight years being one of the many victims of your lies and manipulations and petty jealousies.*

She didn't say that, of course. "Trent rarely does anything without a good reason."

"I should have known you would take his side."

Of course, Katie wanted to say. *Why wouldn't I, when Trent has been more of a parent to me than either you or Jack combined?*

"I'm not taking any sides," she murmured. "I just wanted to know why Trent is angry with you."

"Because he's a tight-assed spoilsport, that's why. He's all bent out of shape because I found out some good dirt on the Logans' precious baby factory."

"Children's Connection?"

She regretted her instinctive question when Peter paused the foot rub, his interest sharpened. Oh, she was glad he couldn't hear Sheila's end of the conversation, especially with the venom in her mother's tone.

"It's pathetic the way the Logans throw money at that place, especially since it's nothing but a big joke. It's scandalous, that's what it is. A big fat scam. If Portland knew all the chaos surrounding that place, they would be outraged. First that Sanders baby was kidnapped and now there are rumors about a black-market baby ring operating out of the place. I even found out—I won't tell you how—that they can't even keep track of whose sperm they're giving whom."

A terrible sense of dread washed over her and she tried to avoid Peter's interested gaze. "What did you do?"

"I didn't have a chance to do anything before your brother blackmailed me to keep my mouth shut."

"What would you have done?" she asked impatiently.

"Nothing much. Just make a few phone calls to some friends in the media. Not those idiots at the *Weekly,* of course, who can't even get a photo caption right, but some of my other contacts. I would have loved to see the egg on that bitch Leslie Logan's face once the scandal broke, sending her precious clinic headed for the toilet. Can't you just see it?"

Katie closed her eyes. Nothing Sheila did should surprise her but this was vindictive, even for her. "But you didn't say anything." She prayed that was the case.

"No. Trent told me if so much as a whiff of rumor surfaced about the stupid clinic, he would make sure I never was invited to another society event. How did I raise such an ungrateful son?"

Again, a sharp rejoinder swelled in her throat. She wished she had the courage to let it out. *You didn't raise him,* she wanted to snap. *You made Trent raise himself and then he turned around and raised the rest of us while Jack was working and you were sleeping with half of Portland.*

As usual, she bit her tongue and Sheila went on without noticing her silence. "So now you understand why you need to get back to Portland ASAP so you can handle Trent for me."

"This is between you and Trent. I'm staying out of it. And I'm not sure when I'll return to Portland. Maybe never."

The idea held enormous appeal, she had to admit. Maybe she could hide away here forever to avoid the impending storm when her mother found out about the baby.

"What's gotten into you, Katherine Celeste?" Sheila asked.

"Fresh air does wonders for a person's sanity. Maybe you ought to try it some time," she couldn't resist adding.

Peter, shamelessly eavesdropping at the end of the

couch, made a strangled noise that sounded suspiciously like a laugh. It wasn't very loud but Sheila still heard it.

"Who's there with you? Is Jack there with that slut Toni Wells?"

Sheila despised her ex-husband's second wife, the trophy wife she had always dreaded would replace her.

"Of course not!" she replied.

"Then who is it?"

"A friend," she repeated.

"Why won't you tell me who it is?"

Katie let out a frustrated breath. "Look, I have to go."

"Don't hang up! You have to talk to Trent." Her voice took on a petulant note, like a spoiled child deprived of a favorite toy.

"No," Katie said firmly. "I won't let you put me in the middle. If you want him to change his mind, you talk to him. I'm sorry, Mother. I have to go."

"Why?"

She scrambled to come up with a believable excuse. "The, um, horses need to be fed." Out of old habit, she crossed her fingers at the lie, then flushed when she caught Peter's amused look.

"Doesn't your father have people to do that?"

Katie jerked her gaze away from that smile. "Y-yes, but they're not here right now so I need to feed the stock."

She could almost hear Sheila's shudder over the phone line, but before her mother could voice her disgust of anything associated with the ranch, Katie cut her off with a hurried farewell and quickly severed the connection.

She forced herself to take several deep, carefully measured breaths to settle her nerves, just as her therapist taught her. If she needed a reminder why she and Peter could never have a happily-ever-after, Sheila had just handed her a dandy.

She couldn't marry him. Any sweet, spun-sugar fantasies she might have been silly enough to entertain, even subconsciously, dissolved into nothing under the hard rain of reality.

If she succumbed to Peter's dogged pursuit, she would be dooming them both to a future of tension and stress. Sheila despised the Logans so fiercely, Katie couldn't even imagine how she could ever tell her mother she was marrying one.

If she did, she knew Sheila's hatred would fester and eventually bubble over, coating their lives with ugliness.

It wasn't fair, she wanted to cry. Why did an old bitterness have to ruin any chance she might have of finding happiness with the man she loved?

"Is she angry?" Peter asked.

Katie shoved down the regrets and met his gaze. "Not at me. Trent is the one in her sights this time."

"That surprises me."

"Why? She and Trent are always banging heads."

"I would have expected her to blow a gasket over that photograph."

She had completely forgotten! "Oh, that. She's been in Europe and hasn't seen it yet. She's heard rumors but of course thinks everyone must be grossly mistaken."

"Why?" he asked.

If she didn't know better, she would almost have thought the puzzled look on his face was genuine.

Could he really not see what was so obvious to her and to the rest of the world? Or did he just choose not to acknowledge it?

"We both know I'm not exactly the kind of woman you usually date. Portland's most gorgeous eligible bachelor and the Crosbys' fat, nerdy, ugly duckling of a daughter belong together about as much as champagne and corn dogs."

Chapter 11

Peter heard her words and the passion in them but didn't believe she could say them, at least with a straight face.

Ugly duckling? *Her?*

Didn't she ever look in the mirror and see the delicate features staring back at her? Those warm, expressive eyes, the elegant cheekbones, that sweetly bowed mouth that begged to be kissed?

He had been bowled over by her since that night at the charity gala, when she'd walked into the room, all grace and sophistication. From the first time she aimed that smile at him, he had been completely ensnared.

After the incredible passion they had shared, he hadn't wanted to look at another woman. He was completely obsessed with only one. His Celeste.

Not Celeste, he corrected himself. Celeste had been

a glamorous, shimmery mirage. Katie was flesh and blood, funny and stubborn and smart and real.

Even when he thought she had lied to him and deceived him, when he was sure she only slept with him to steal Logan secrets, he still hungered for her like a dying man who wants only one more moment of sunshine.

The last three days he had barely been able to take his eyes off her. She was so beautiful he couldn't look away. Knowing she was pregnant with his child filled him with awe, with wonder, with a terrifying tenderness.

He loved her.

The realization slammed into his gut like a prizefighter's uppercut. If he had been standing, he would have sagged against the ropes.

He loved Katherine Celeste Crosby.

All this time he had been trying to convince her they should marry for their child's sake. But he had only been using that as an excuse to bind her to him, he admitted now.

This couldn't be happening. He had his life carefully mapped out and he didn't have room for love in that plan—certainly not with Katie. What a mess. What a grade A, bona fide disaster.

"Peter? Are you all right?"

Katie looked concerned and even a little frightened, and he had no idea how long he had been standing there staring at her. He forced himself to smile with what he sincerely hoped was a casualness that belied his suddenly racing pulse.

"Everything's fine," he lied. "Just fine. I guess I'd better go check on the horses."

She frowned. "Because of what I said to my mother? I was just using that as an excuse to hang up the phone."

"I know you were but it's a good idea. I should still see how they're doing."

She looked unconvinced, probably because he had only come in from feeding them an hour before and they generally needed tending only once a day. He didn't care. He needed to get away *now*.

Without offering any other explanations he turned on his heel and hurried to the mudroom off the kitchen for the coveralls he used.

His thoughts a wild tangle, he fumbled to put them on and then his boots before he headed out into a frigid Wyoming afternoon.

The sky was a brilliant, cornea-scorching blue. He stood for a moment gazing at the mountains, wondering just what the hell he was supposed to do now.

If someone would have told him a week ago that he would be in love with a Crosby, he probably would have knocked their teeth out, but here he was. Somehow in the last few days her last name had ceased to matter to him. He still disliked some members of her family—her mother came immediately to mind—but he saw Katie as so much more than her name now. She was bright and funny and insightful.

The day before, she had offered a suggestion to a work dilemma he had been trying to solve long-distance and her answer had been right on the money.

These last few days had been a rare and peaceful interlude for him. He was always so busy with goals and objectives, with following the course he had charted for his life. He couldn't remember the last time he had taken time to sit and just *be*.

Being with Katie was balm to his soul. She calmed him and settled him and somehow quieted the strident voice in his head telling him he was never quite good enough.

He didn't want to lose her but he didn't see what other choice he had. Since the day he found out she was pregnant with his child, his one goal in life had been to convince her they should marry. He had done everything in his power to convince her. Now he could only be profoundly grateful for her stubbornness in continuing to refuse.

He still believed it was the decent, honorable thing to do. Intellectually he knew he should continue to press until she changed her mind. He wanted his child to have an intact home, a father and mother.

But he couldn't imagine any hell more exquisitely painful than being married to Katie when she didn't love him.

He would be miserable. What's more, he would no doubt make her miserable, as well.

What was he supposed to do? A man had an obligation to take care of his child. He believed that with all his heart. But how could he sentence himself to a loveless marriage when he wanted so much more?

"The baby's fine, then?" Katie asked Laura two days after her mother's phone call.

"As far as I can tell." The doctor smiled and returned her stethoscope to the weatherproof backpack full of medical supplies she had brought with her for the visit to Sweetwater.

"The heartbeat is strong and healthy," Laura went on, "and the baby's growth seems right on target for fourteen weeks. I've said it before, there are no guarantees when it comes to babies. But I've learned to trust my gut on these matters, and all my instincts are telling me you're past the danger zone of losing the pregnancy."

Katie let out the breath she'd been holding. Relief flooded through her like spring runoff, washing away the fear and worry she had carried around since the day of her fall. She wanted to hold her baby in her arms and whirl around the room.

Instead she contented herself with giving Laura a radiant smile. "Oh, thank you!"

Laura laughed. "Don't thank me. I didn't do anything. You're the one doing all the hard work here."

"I haven't done anything but lie around."

"That's just what you needed to be doing. Enjoy this chance to rest while you have it because once your little kiddo enters the picture, you'll forget you ever once had such a luxury as leisure time."

Laura's smile included Peter, sitting quietly in the armchair by the fireplace. "When do Clint and Margie return?" she asked.

"They called about an hour ago and said they should be here first thing in the morning," Katie said. "Their daughter caught the flu right after the delivery so they stayed until she was back on her feet."

"It's a good thing you had Mr. Logan here to help out while they were gone."

Katie managed a smile while inside some of her bleak mood returned. Peter *had* been a lifesaver, she admitted. But in the two day since Sheila called, things between them had changed.

He still cared for her just as diligently as before. He

still cooked for her and took care of the animals and watched over her. He still talked to her and read to her and watched old movies with her, but all with a new reserve between them.

He wasn't cold exactly, simply stiff and withdrawn, as if trying to maintain a safe distance between them.

For two days he had been kind and solicitous but all with that same polite detachment. And he hadn't said a single word in all that time about marriage.

Though she mourned his change of heart, she understood it and couldn't fault him for it.

He had only heard her part of the conversation with Sheila and missed out on most of the anti-Logan vitriol her mother had spewed. Nevertheless Katie was sure the one-sided snippets were enough to remind him of all the reasons they could never make a successful marriage.

She had seen the sudden panic flare in his eyes before he rushed outside on the flimsy excuse of taking care of livestock that certainly didn't need caring for.

She had known even then that he had changed his mind about marrying her. She tried to convince herself she was glad. Things surely would be easier between them if he dropped the ridiculous idea.

Wasn't she a contrary thing, though? Now that he stopped asking her, she could think of nothing she wanted more than to say yes.

"As far as I'm concerned," Laura went on, "you're cleared to return to Portland whenever you decide you're ready. Check in with your own obstetrician as soon as you get back. I'm sure she'll want to see you as soon as possible. But if you were my patient, I wouldn't put you on any other restrictions besides exercising normal caution. You're free to resume all your regular activities."

Oh, she didn't want to return to Portland and all the chaos that awaited her there. She dreaded facing her family with the news of her pregnancy. Her siblings would have mixed feelings about the baby, she knew. Ivy would be thrilled their babies would be born only months apart and Trent knew she longed for a child. But she knew both of them would worry about her having the child on her own.

Jack would probably show her his typical distracted indifference. And Sheila... Well, Sheila would go ballistic, especially when she learned who the father was, something Katie realized now she couldn't hide.

Her mother had called a half-dozen times since their conversation two days earlier but Katie chose not to answer when she saw the number flashing on the caller ID.

She just didn't think she was up to a confrontation with her mother yet, but she knew she couldn't put it off much longer.

She pushed away her dread to deal with later. For now she would focus on her overwhelming joy that all appeared to be well with her baby.

She squeezed Laura's hand. "Thank you for everything."

"You can thank me by letting me hold a bouncing, healthy baby in a few months."

"It's a deal." Katie smiled.

Laura kissed her cheek, then shrugged into her heavy parka. Before she could pick up her bulky pack, Peter beat her to it.

"Let me carry this out to your vehicle for you."

"I never turn down a handsome man." Laura winked at Katie, kissed her again and followed Peter outside.

She would love to have Laura deliver her baby, she thought as she watched them go out into the pale twilight. Not only was she a dear friend but Katie trusted her medical skills implicitly. If Laura didn't love the rural Wyoming lifestyle where she had raised her own family, she could have been practicing medicine anywhere in the world.

Could she manage it somehow? Katie wondered. Maybe Laura would consent to fly out to Portland for the birth or Katie could always return to Sweetwater and have the baby here. Laura's clinic wasn't set up for childbirth but perhaps they could go to the small hospital in Jackson Hole.

The idea appealed deeply and she vowed to talk it over with Peter. Whether he wanted to marry her or not, he had a say in all of this, she admitted to herself.

A few moments later Peter returned to the great room, his expression remote, as it had been since her mother's phone call. "If you're ready to go back to Portland, we can fly out together after the Taylors return in the morning."

She sighed, hating this distance between them. "I suppose I have to. If I don't return soon, Trent will come and yank me back."

His mouth tightened as if he disliked the mention of her brother. "I hope you're not planning to jump right back into the deep end. Despite Dr. Harp's ringing endorsement that everything should be fine, I think you need to take it easy now."

She raised an eyebrow at his dictatorial tone. "I have a job to do, a career I enjoy that I'm good at."

"I'm sure you do. But I know damn well how stressful R & D can be. The long hours at a computer, the constant pressure to come up with something new. I'm just suggesting you think about whether that's really the best environment for a pregnant woman. You have a baby to think about now."

In the last few days her abdomen had seemed to swell rapidly, as if the baby decided there was no reason to hide her presence anymore. Katie loved her new roundness, loved seeing the little mound and imagining the person inside.

"Believe me," she retorted, "I'm very well aware of that fact, Peter. But I'm not one of your employees that you can order around. You're not my boss or my husband or my father."

Before her mother's phone call, he probably would have come back with something about how he wanted to be her husband; she only had to say the word.

Instead his mouth tightened. "But I am the father of that child you're carrying. Whether you like it or not, that gives me certain responsibilities to make sure you don't wear yourself out during the pregnancy with unnecessary stress."

This concern was for his child, not for her. The knowledge made her heart ache, made her tone more combative than she intended. "Are you planning to monitor my time card?" she snapped.

His tone was just as cold. "Will I have to?"

Oh, she wanted to weep at the distance between them. This autocratic stranger was so different from the teasing, smiling man she had come to know in the days since her accident—the man she had come to love. She wanted him back!

"I know my limits. I don't intend to exceed them," she said quietly. "Contrary to the way I seem to act around you, I'm not completely lacking in common sense."

"I never said anything about your common sense or lack thereof. But you have a taxing, stressful position. I know how things go on the corporate level. You think you're only going to work a little late to tie up some loose ends and before you know it, the clock tolls midnight and you have to be back for a 6:00 a.m. conference call with Tokyo."

She knew that only too well. She had grown up watching it firsthand with her father. Before she had been sent to boarding school, she remembered sometimes going weeks without seeing Jack. He invariably left before she rose, no matter how early she set her alarm, and he returned home long after she went to bed.

She had to hope Peter would be different, for her baby's sake.

"It doesn't have to be that way. You said the other day you have good people who work for you. So do I. I fully intend to cede some of my duties to them during the pregnancy and talk to Trent about cutting both my hours and my responsibilities after the baby arrives."

"I'm sure he'll be just thrilled about that." Peter's voice dripped with sarcasm.

"He'll deal with it."

"You seem remarkably certain of that."

"He's my brother and he loves me."

His skeptical look made her ache again for all that lay between them. "He does," she said sharply. "Believe it or not, even we Crosbys are capable of loving each other."

"I never said you weren't."

You didn't have to say it, she started to say, but before she could open her mouth to utter her hot words, the strangest sensation tickled inside her—a flutter in her womb, like the tiny touch of butterfly wings whispering together.

She thought maybe she imagined it but then she felt it again, stronger this time, unmistakable.

The baby!

She froze and one hand flew to her mouth while the other covered the swell of her abdomen.

This was real!

She had a little life growing inside her, someone whose arms or legs—or both!—were flailing around right this minute. An incredible rush of emotion poured through her—shock and excitement and joy—and she couldn't hold back her tears.

"What is it?" Peter's voice was urgent, his brown eyes shadowed with concern. "Are you cramping again? Do I need to call Dr. Harp back?"

"No." The sound was halfway between a laugh and a sob. "I just felt the baby move."

He stared at her, thunderstruck. "Are you sure?"

"Yes. Absolutely." Those tiny butterfly wings quivered once more and Katie laughed out loud. "There she goes again."

He still looked shell-shocked. "Isn't it too early for that?"

"The books I've read say the fetus starts moving independently at around seven weeks but the first time the mother can detect it is usually between thirteen and eighteen weeks. I'm on the early side of that spread, I suppose. Maybe she's going to be a soccer player."

"Do you think—" He paused and cleared gruffness from his throat. "Could I feel it?"

"I don't know. It's very light, just a flicker really. But you could try," she offered.

She felt suddenly shy when he crossed the room to her but she hitched up her shirt. He placed one of those warm, strong hands on her abdomen and Katie was overwhelmed at the intimacy of standing here with him, sharing the sweetness of the moment.

"Is he moving?" Peter asked.

"A little. Not as much as before. She must be tired out. Can you feel anything."

He shook his head but seemed reluctant to remove his hand. Katie didn't mind. Even though he was only touching her abdomen, she felt embraced by him, almost cherished. Her heart brimmed over with love for him and for their child, and she tried fiercely to burn this moment into her memory.

"We spent one night together and now there's a little life in there." His voice was low, gruff and tugged at her heart. "It's amazing."

"I know. It's the most incredible thing that's ever happened to me."

He curled his hand over her abdomen as if he couldn't bear to let go and she leaned into his solid strength. She didn't want to move, didn't want to shatter this fragile, wonderful peace.

"I know this baby wasn't something you wanted," she said after a moment.

"It was unexpected, certainly, but not unwanted."

If she hadn't already been deeply in love with him at that moment, the sincerity of his words would have done the trick.

Peter seemed as reluctant as she to sever this fragile

connection between them. With his hand still warm on her skin, he moved to the plump sofa and pulled her onto his lap.

This wasn't bad, either, she decided. Not bad at all. She added another memory to her precious store.

"When I was about seven my father came home with a puppy," he said once they were settled. "Keep in mind, I had never said a word about getting one and had never even acknowledged to myself that I might like a pet until Dad showed up with the thing. From the moment I saw the little mutt, I adored him. Roscoe slept in my room until I went to college."

His words touched her, at the same time she grieved for a little boy she sensed had never felt completely secure in his parents' love.

"We're having a baby, not a puppy," she pointed out. "I wouldn't expect her to lick your hand or chew your slippers, at least not at first."

His laugh jostled her a little against his hard chest. "I know they're vastly different things but the principle's the same. I never knew how much I wanted a puppy until Dad brought Roscoe home."

He met her gaze with a tenderness in his eyes that stunned her. "And I never realized how much I wanted a child until I found out you were pregnant."

The tears burning behind her eyelids spilled out at his words. She sniffled, more in love with him than she ever believed possible.

At her tears, raw panic flickered across his features and his arms tightened around her. "Don't cry, Katie. Whatever I said, I'm sorry."

"It's the hormones," she lied, then decided she was tired of untruths between them. "Well, some of it's the hormones," she admitted. "Mostly I'm just so happy you want this baby as much as I do."

He was quiet for a long moment, an odd expression on his face. "Katie, I have to tell you something."

His voice sounded tight, almost nervous, and she suddenly didn't want to hear what he had to say. Whatever it was, it had to be something grim with that solemn look in his eyes.

"Later," she said. "Would you mind just kissing me for now?"

She didn't give him a chance to say no before she pressed her mouth to his.

He froze for one shocked second, his eyes wide, then he closed them and kissed her back with all the passion and heat that had been simmering between them for a week.

She didn't have the courage to tell him of her feelings but she could show him this way. Her arms held him close, her fingers entwining in his hair, as she poured into the kiss all the love she ached to give him.

They had kissed several times since he arrived at Sweetwater but every touch had been tarnished by the anger and tension simmering between them. For the first time since the night of the bachelor auction, she kissed him without reserve.

He groaned her name and pulled her closer, so close she could feel his erection jut against her hip. "You feel so good I could stay right here forever and do this."

"Okay," she murmured against his mouth. "But I think in three or four days we'd probably get hungry."

"By then the Taylors will be back. We can swallow mouthfuls of Margie's delicious stew between kisses."

Her laugh turned into a moan as he trailed kisses down

her throat. All she could think about were Laura's parting words, that she didn't need to restrict normal activities.

Did that mean they could they make love? she wondered, blood pulsing thickly through her veins. She wanted to, desperately. Her body cried out for his touch, for the heat and wonder they had found together for only that one night.

His mouth touched the high slope of one aching, sensitive breast through the open neck of her shirt and she gasped.

She couldn't bear it. She wanted him to touch her completely, to bare her skin and draw a taut, achy nipple into his mouth.

"I should stop," he murmured.

"Why?"

"Because if I keep torturing myself like this, I won't be *able* to stop."

"I don't want you to."

He groaned and his mouth found hers again in a kiss that scorched her clear to her toes.

Somewhere in the middle of another of those long, drugging kisses, she was vaguely aware of a noise that didn't belong, the squeak of the front door opening.

Before she could force her numbed brain cells to work so she could figure out how to extricate herself from his arms and see why the door would be opening, she heard a terrible sound.

A truly awful sound.

The most hideous sound she could imagine under the circumstances.

"What the hell is going on here?"

Her mother's voice rang through the room like metal grating on metal.

Chapter 12

Katie scrambled to her feet, terribly conscious of her tousled, just-been-kissed disarray. She was vaguely aware of Peter rising, as well, smoothing down the shirt her hands must have rearranged.

Oh, this was horrible!

"M-mother. This is a surprise. What are you doing here?"

Sheila's collagen-implanted lips curled into a snarl. "What is *he* doing here? This is the *friend* staying in this hellhole with you? Peter Logan?" Her voice rose on the last word until she was nearly screeching.

"Yes."

"Quite the cozy little love nest you have here. No wonder you wouldn't tell me the name of your mystery man."

Katie blew out a breath. "I knew you wouldn't be pleased."

Sheila's face started turning so purple her makeup took on a garish hue. "Not pleased? Not *pleased?* Have you completely lost your mind? I knew you were up to something—you've always been a terrible liar—so I decided to stop here on my way back to Portland. In my wildest dreams I never would have expected this!"

Sheila flung each word at her like wickedly sharp rocks, and Katie couldn't help flinching.

"What were you thinking? He's a *Logan.*" She said the word like the most vulgar of obscenities. "Or at least one of the adopted ones."

Peter's features had been without expression since Sheila barged into the house, but at this, his jaw clenched and his eyes darkened with anger. He stepped forward but Katie put a hand on his arm, begging him silently to let her handle it.

If he entered the fray, Sheila would annihilate him. She fought dirty and had no compunction about kicking below the belt.

"Mother, I can explain," Katie said lamely.

"I certainly hope so." Sheila stalked in and plopped onto the chair opposite the couch where they stood.

Katie didn't know where to start. She didn't want to tell her mother anything, not about the night of the gala and not about the days since. Somehow telling her mother would taint what had been the most wonderful time of her life.

Before she could catch hold of any of her wildly scrambling thoughts in order to offer some kind of coherent defense, Sheila's gaze landed on the stack of books on the coffee table between them.

"What is *this?*" She grabbed one and thrust it at Katie. *"Your Baby's First Nine Months?"*

She cringed. Oh, this was a nightmare. Worse than a nightmare. Katie closed her eyes, wishing she could retreat into her safe, invisible comfort zone. It was too late for that. She had walked out of that comfort zone forever the moment she let Carrie Summers talk her into a makeover.

"You want to tell me why you're reading pregnancy books?"

She opened her eyes and met her mother's gaze squarely. She refused to feel ashamed about her baby and she would do anything necessary to protect and defend this child. "The usual reason."

"You're *pregnant?*"

"Yes. About fourteen weeks along."

She had never seen her mother speechless but Sheila gaped for a full thirty seconds. All too soon, she found her voice. "He's the father? You got knocked up by Peter Logan?"

"This is not some version of *Rosemary's Baby*, Mother. He's not the devil incarnate." She wasn't sure where the sarcasm came from but it was too late to stow it back down.

"He might as well be!"

Sheila looked her up and down with more than her usual distaste and Katie burned under the perusal. "What were you thinking, Katherine? Are you truly that desperate for a man in your bed that you'll even sleep with a Logan?"

Though she wanted to stay calm and in control, Katie swayed a little from the attack. She brushed against Peter's chest and for the first time realized he was standing at her back.

At Sheila's words, though, he stepped forward, his eyes blazing. "That's enough," he snapped.

"I wondered if you were going to say anything or just stand there, you bastard. We both know damn well a man like you could never be attracted to Katie. What were you after, then? Crosby company secrets? Did she tell you any? I hope they were worth all you must have had to go through to get them."

Katie wanted to die. She wanted to curl up into a ball of humiliation and expire on the spot. The really sad thing was, she could have written the script for this conversation with her mother almost word for word, right down to Sheila's disbelief that someone like Peter Logan would ever be genuinely interested in her.

"Why not?" Peter asked.

Sheila looked baffled by his question. "What?"

"Why wouldn't I be attracted to Katie?"

Sheila arched one of her carefully waxed eyebrows. "I've seen the women you date. Katherine couldn't even be a bat girl in your league. She wears baggy clothes and she never does a thing with her makeup. She'd rather have her nose stuck in a book than have her nails done, and she wouldn't be able to tell a Dior from a Wang if her life depended on it. I love my daughter, Mr. Logan, but you have to admit, she's a mess."

Peter stared at her for several long moments, then shook his head, utter contempt in his eyes. "You are one first-rate bitch."

Sheila sputtered as if no one had ever called her that before, but Peter ignored her.

"Have you ever even looked at your daughter?" he asked.

"Of course I've looked at her. She's come a long way since college when she was fat and had hair like Cousin Itt. But she's not one of your slinky supermodels and she never will be."

Never in his life had he come so close to belting a woman. It was all he could do to keep his hands clenched at his sides, especially when he saw how pale Katie was.

Her hands were trembling and she looked mortified to have them fighting over her like this. He wanted to gather her close and kiss away all the pain he saw in her eyes.

He couldn't believe any mother would be so cruel to her own child. Mothers were supposed to think their children were the most beautiful creations on the planet. They were supposed to do anything they could to defend them from attacks like this one, not be the one doing the attacking.

How could Sheila be so blind about her daughter's loveliness?

Or was she?

Maybe she saw it clearly enough to feel threatened by it. The idea made sense. He had a feeling Sheila Crosby was just the kind of woman who would grind anybody she viewed as competition under the heels of her four-inch stilettos, even her own daughter.

"You're right, she'll never be a supermodel. She's too short." He smiled at Katie who gazed back at him with wide, confused eyes. "But with a few more inches, she could walk any runway in the world."

He laughed as Katie visibly shuddered at the image. He loved this woman. Loved her fiercely.

He turned back to Sheila. "The first time I saw Katie, I thought she was the most stunning thing I had ever seen. Since I've come to know her better, I've come to realize the woman inside is even more beautiful than what she shows to the world."

Sheila narrowed her gaze at him as if trying to figure out what game he was playing. It never would have occurred to her that he could be sincere, he realized, despising her fiercely.

How could she have raised someone as sweet and loving as Katie? he wondered, until he remembered Katie said her brother had basically raised her and her siblings.

Maybe he needed to rethink his animosity toward Trent Crosby. He had done a damn good job with his sister.

"If you ever looked closely at your daughter the way I do," he went on, "you would see a beautiful, smart, courageous woman any mother should be proud of."

He leaned forward until Sheila could look nowhere but at him. "If you ever really saw Kate through anything other than your own middle-aged narcissism and envy at anyone younger and prettier than you, you would also see a woman who could have any man she wants. For some incredible reason, she wanted me and that makes me the luckiest damn idiot in the world."

Sheila's features filled with a deep rage that aged her at least a dozen years. "Get out," she snarled.

During his little speech Katie hadn't taken her gaze from him. She looked stunned, so awed by his words that he wanted fiercely to kiss her. Wouldn't Sheila just love that?

Katie seemed to collect herself and turned back to Sheila. "Sweetwater isn't part of your divorce settlement, Mother. You can't order anybody around here."

"Then you kick him out! See if you can get that brain you're so damn proud of to work for five seconds and realize he's just using you to hurt Crosby Systems and the Crosby family."

"No. He's the father of my baby and he's asked me to marry him. I—I've decided I will."

She didn't look at him when she made her declaration—a good thing, he supposed, since he was sure someone had just shoved a bowling ball into his stomach.

"You're going to *marry* him?" Sheila looked as if she would spontaneously combust any second now.

Katie continued, "If he still wants me after he sees what kind of in-laws he'll be taking on."

Somehow Peter found his voice, though it sounded as if he'd swallowed a cubic yard of gravel. "He does."

She finally met his gaze, and the tentative smile in her eyes had him tumbling hard for her all over again.

"You've gone absolutely mental," Sheila shrieked. "Wait until the rest of the family hears about this. They're going to go through the roof!"

"No, they won't."

Katie blinked as a sweet assurance settled in her heart. She had been so worried about her family's reaction at learning of her pregnancy but she suddenly realized as she listened to her mother rant that Sheila was the only one in the family who would be angry.

A huge weight lifted from her shoulders and she suddenly couldn't wait to tell the world about the baby.

"Trent and Ivy will be thrilled for me. Danny will be, too. They love me and want the best for me, regardless of some silly feud we had nothing to do with. When they realize this is what I want, they'll accept it. Jack might bluster a little but I'm sure Toni will eventually make him come around."

"I never will!" her mother snarled. "You can be sure of that! If you marry this…bastard, to me you'll be one of them and so will the brat you're knocked up with."

"If I were you, I would choose my next words very carefully." Peter's voice was tungsten-hard, the threat unmistakable. As usual, Sheila didn't heed the warning signs.

"You're not me," she snapped. "You're a *Logan*. A filthy, lying, son-of-a-bitch Logan!"

"Stop right there." Katie stepped forward, her face hot from shame and embarrassment. "I'm sorry you feel that way. If you can't accept my child and be civil to Peter and his family, then I suppose we have nothing more to say to each other."

Her mother had never physically struck her but somehow Katie sensed that if Peter hadn't been standing beside her, she would have felt the sting of her mother's hand for the first time in her life. Instead Sheila stared at her for a long moment, then stomped out of the house, slamming the door so hard the windows quivered.

As soon as her mother left, Katie wanted to sink through the floor and disappear. Maybe if she were lucky, the force of that slamming door would collapse the roof in the next ten seconds, burying her in eight feet of snow so she wouldn't have to face Peter.

She had to settle for burying her face in her hands. "I'm so sorry," she murmured. "I'm afraid Sheila can be a little, um, difficult."

His laugh held deep amusement at her understatement. "I guess you could say that."

"I don't blame you for changing your mind about wanting to marry me, Peter. No matter what you said to my mother, you don't have to go through with it."

"I never changed my mind."

"Then why haven't you said a word about it for the last few days?"

He said nothing for so long she finally dropped her hands and squared her shoulders to face him. His mouth was tight and his eyes were dark with an unreadable expression, something deep and tender that sent butterflies somersaulting around her stomach.

"I meant what I said to your mother. I think you're a beautiful, smart, courageous woman. I didn't tell her everything, though."

He reached between them to clasp her fingers. The butterflies went into cartwheels and handsprings as her heart began to pump.

"No?" her voice sounded like a mouse's tiny squeak but he didn't appear to notice.

Peter shook his head. "I didn't tell her that night we spent together was the most incredible, magical night of my life. I didn't tell her how I searched for you for weeks and how empty and lonely my life seemed from the moment I woke alone in my bed until I found you again."

He was quiet again, then his gaze met hers. "I didn't tell her I fell in love that night."

For one brief moment, a brilliant, piercing joy washed through her, then she realized what he said and the joy quickly turned to ashes. "You fell in love with an illusion. Celeste wasn't real."

"She's part of you, whether you can see it or not."

Katie made a skeptical sound and Peter raised their entwined fingers and kissed the back of her hand. "She is. You're right, though, maybe I didn't know the real you after that single incredible night. But we've had more than that here and I've only fallen more deeply in love with you every day we've been together."

His kiss was sweet and tender and warmed all the cold, empty places inside of her. She clung to him, tears trickling down her cheeks.

"Blasted hormones," she mumbled through her tears. She had cried more the last week than she had her entire adult life.

"I hope those are happy tears," Peter murmured.

"They are. Oh, they are."

She kissed him with all the love and longing she had been saving for years. When he drew away several moments later, both of them were breathing raggedly and Peter's eyes were dazed, aroused.

He said only one word. "Wow."

She laughed even though those dratted tears continued to fall. He gently wiped one away with his thumb before it reached her cheek, then shook his head as if to clear it.

"I told your mother you could have your pick of any man in the world. Why did you pick me that night? I figured out a long time ago you weren't after Logan secrets. Why did you come home with me?"

Was that insecurity in his eyes? she wondered. Could he really not know how irresistible he was?

"You don't remember the first time we danced, do you? Not the night of the gala but long before then."

He shook his head, baffled.

"I do. Every second of it. I was fifteen years old and fat. Not chubby, fat. Sheila dressed me in ruffles and bows for my first big society event during one of my visits home and I looked hideous, with thick glasses and all those flounces."

She grimaced at the memory. "I felt even more miserable than I'm sure I looked. I didn't want to be there. I wanted to be home with a good book. Even boarding school would have been better."

Though he was confused, he didn't interrupt her story, curious where this was all going.

"I was an easy target for several girls who—who liked to pick on anyone more vulnerable than they were. We were standing in a corner of the ballroom and they started making fun of me, saying I looked like a giant pink birthday cake with all my flounces, which was nothing but the truth. I was trying my best not to let them see me cry but I was losing the battle. Then you came over."

He should remember. He *wanted* to remember but he'd been to so many of those kinds of functions, and this one just didn't stand out.

"You were eighteen and heading to college and all the girls were crazy about you."

She smiled a little. "You probably didn't know that, did you? As I remember, you were busy even then trying to follow in your father's footsteps. Anyway, Angelina Mitchell was the prettiest of the group and she preened a little, certain, I'm sure, that you were going to ask her to dance. But you didn't. You walked right up to me—shy, fat Katie Crosby!—and asked me in this deep, confident voice if I would do you the great honor of dancing with you."

He could feel himself flush, though he wasn't sure why. He still couldn't remember the event, maybe because he had often danced with wallflowers at country club functions or other society events. He had never had much interest in the popular girls. At least the wallflowers usually made halfway decent conversation and wanted to know more about him than what kind of car he drove.

He cleared the sudden gruffness from his voice. "I guess we danced, then?"

She nodded and he felt about a hundred miles tall at the stars in her eyes at the memory. "I know you were only being kind, rescuing me from what you must have figured out was the other girls' bullying, but it was the most romantic moment of my life. I think I fell in love with you that night."

His arms tightened around her and he closed his eyes, supremely grateful for a mother who drilled kindness and good manners into her sons.

"I haven't felt beautiful very often in my life," Katie went on. "That was the first time. The second time was the night of the charity gala. When you danced with me, I was fifteen years old again, in the arms of the most wonderful boy I'd ever met. I didn't want it to end. That's why I didn't tell you my name, because I wanted that night to last forever."

He shifted his hand to the swelling of her abdomen, to their child growing there. "In a way, I guess it has."

Her smile was radiant as she kissed him again. "That was the perfect thing to say," she murmured. "This baby is a gift. A precious way to help us always remember a wonderful, magical night. I love you, Peter. I loved you when I was fifteen and I love you a million times more now."

"When will you marry me?" he asked, when he could speak again through the emotions clogging his throat.

Doubts flickered in her eyes again. "Are you sure? You saw tonight what you might be in for. And what about your parents? They won't be thrilled about all this."

"When they get to know you, they'll love you as much as I do." It was true, he realized. His mom and Katie would bond instantly. His father might be a little harder to win over but he would be impressed by her brains and her business sense. Affection would soon follow. Terrence wouldn't be able to resist her.

"Marry me, Katie," he urged, his hand still on her abdomen. "Right now. Tonight. We can fly to Las Vegas and be married by midnight. I don't want to waste another moment."

She drew in a deep breath, then covered her hand with his, until they were both cradling the child growing there.

"All right." She gave him another one of those radiant smiles. "Let's go now. We have a new family dynasty to create."

One that would be built on joy and laughter and love.

Epilogue

"You look beautiful, Katie. I don't have to ask if Logan is making you happy. If the power suddenly went out in here, you would give off enough of a glow to light up the whole place."

Katie smiled at Trent, handsome and commanding in his tuxedo. "I'm happier than I've ever been in my life."

"Good. You deserve it. And I guess if Peter Logan is the one making you so happy, he can't be all bad."

Trent's bluster was mostly for show, she knew. Her brother and her new husband had actually gotten along remarkably well after she and Peter returned from their brief honeymoon. The two men were alike in far more ways than they were different.

As she and Trent twirled around the Hilton ballroom—where it all began, she thought with a smile—Katie gazed around at the crowd that had gathered to celebrate her marriage to Peter. Hundreds of people were here. Leslie Logan had thrown herself with enthusiasm into organizing the reception. She had invited not only all the Logan and Crosby employees but also employees at Portland General Hospital and Children's Connection, until the big room was filled to bursting.

Even the *Portland Weekly* society reporter was there. Katie had made a special point of making sure he received an invitation, since without that picture she and Peter wouldn't have found each other again.

Everyone she loved was in this room, she thought. Except Danny, who hadn't been able to leave his island retreat.

Her father was dancing with Toni. Ivy, glowing from pregnancy herself, was in the arms of her handsome king.

To her surprise, Sheila had even come, though under duress. She still wasn't at all pleased about her daughter marrying a Logan. But after Jack had surprised Katie by threatening to take Sheila back to court to reduce her alimony if she didn't support her daughter, Sheila seemed to resign herself to it.

She was coldly polite to Peter, but that was more than Katie ever expected.

Like a magnet finding north, her eyes turned automatically to her husband, currently smiling down at Dorothea Aldridge as they whirled around the room together.

She turned back to her brother. "Peter is wonderful. Every day I fall more in love with him."

Trent sighed. "You know, I envy you. I wish my own trip down the aisle had turned out as well as yours."

She hugged him, her heart aching for him even in the midst of her bubbling joy. She knew how much the failure of his marriage stung him. "I know. I do, too. But maybe the Crosby luck is finally changing. Ivy and Max are deliriously happy, just as Peter and I are. We both found love—maybe you and Danny will have your turn soon."

Trent looked skeptical but before he could reply, Peter whirled Mrs. Aldridge toward them and tapped Trent on the shoulder.

"Dorothea says now that I'm no longer available, dancing with me isn't nearly as much fun as it used to be. She's got this thing for bachelors. Since I told her you're the most eligible one I know, she decided she didn't want to waste her time dancing with an old married man like me and insisted we trade partners."

"We Crosbys are better dancers anyway." Trent smiled at Dorothea, who chuckled and allowed herself to be handed off to him. The two of them spun away, leaving Peter to take Katie into his arms.

"Smooth. Very smooth, Mr. Logan," she mimicked her words of that night months before.

He played along. "When a beautiful woman crosses my path, I'm not stupid enough to give her any chance to slip away."

"This woman doesn't want to slip away," she murmured. "She doesn't want to be anywhere but right here, in your arms."

He kissed her, and though it was chaste enough for the family crowd gathered in the ballroom, her insides still clenched with desire. Every time they touched, this same heat sparked between them.

She had to admit she'd been a little afraid the wild

passion between them after the charity gala had just been chance, a result of the romance of the night and maybe too much champagne. But any doubts she might have had on that score were quickly laid to rest on their honeymoon. She flushed, remembering.

If anything, their lovemaking had been better. Their shared love added a deep emotional intensity she never would have imagined.

She was warm suddenly from more than the exertion and the crowded ballroom. "I could use some water and fresh air."

With the solicitous care that constantly amazed her, he led her over to the bar and snagged a glass of ice water. "I'm sorry you can't have champagne," he said when he handed the water to her.

She made a wry face. "I'm not. It makes me do crazy things."

"I know. Believe me, I plan to keep that in mind after you have the baby."

His teasing leer made her laugh. "I don't need champagne when I'm around you. You're intoxicating enough."

At that, he had to stop and kiss her again. When he lifted his head, Katie felt someone watching them. She shifted her gaze from Peter's to find a dark-haired man watching them. He looked somehow familiar but she couldn't place him. She gave him a hesitant smile, a little unnerved by something in his expression.

He quickly looked away but not before she thought she saw confusion and naked pain in his eyes.

That was odd, she thought, but her attention was diverted when Leslie and Terrence approached them.

Peter kissed his mother on the cheek while Terrence threaded his arm through Katie's

"Everything is so lovely," Katie told Peter's mother. "You did a wonderful job with this reception."

"It's not every day that a mother's oldest son gets married." Leslie smiled at her. "And since we missed that part when the two of you rushed to Las Vegas, I wanted the reception to be spectacular."

That had been one of the biggest shocks of her marriage, Katie acknowledged. Peter had been right. Once they learned a child was on the way and realized their son loved her, Terrence and Leslie had welcomed her into their family—with hesitant arms at first, but their initial reserve had quickly melted. Already she was coming to care for them.

"Thank you. We'll remember this night for the rest of our lives."

Leslie smiled and reached for her hand. "You make a beautiful bride, Katie. My son is a lucky man."

She still wasn't sure she quite believed that—the beautiful part anyway—but after a week of marriage, she was beginning to see herself through different eyes. Maybe it was pregnancy, or maybe it came from being so deeply loved, but she had decided she wasn't the Crosby ugly duckling after all. She never had been. She had just preferred hiding in that invisible comfort zone.

Leaving it had been terrifying but so worth it, Katie thought, a sweet joy settling in her chest. Who would have believed the night of the bachelor charity auction that in a few months' time she would find herself married to the man she had loved since an act of kindness more than a decade ago, the man she loved more than she ever thought possible?

The baby moved, almost as if sensing her thoughts, and she smiled and touched a hand to her abdomen.

"How's he doing?" Peter asked. An ultrasound the day before had revealed their child was definitely a boy.

"Fine. I think he wants to dance."

Peter smiled. "We'd better oblige him, don't you think?"

Their baby would come into a loving home, Katie thought as her husband took her into his arms, to a mother and father who already adored him and each other.

She couldn't ask for anything more.

With an odd feeling of unreality, Everett Baker watched the newly married couple share a tender embrace then turn to smile at the groom's parents.

The Logans' oldest son and his bride.

His chest tightened and he couldn't seem to breathe in the stuffy ballroom. He felt odd, dizzy and a little nauseated as he watched them together. They looked so in love, so full of joy.

He should never have come. He didn't belong here with these happy, good, decent people. But when that invitation had arrived, as it had to all employees of Children's Connection, he had stared at a single line for hours.

Peter Logan, son of Leslie and Terrence Logan.

The line rang in his head like some horrible nursery rhyme, crowding everything else out until it was the only thing he could think about.

He hadn't been able to stay away but now that he was here, he knew coming had been a terrible mistake.

You're nothing, boy. Less than nothing.

He heard Lester Baker's voice in his head, as he did so often, and knew the man was right. Everett shouldn't be here. He didn't *deserve* to be here.

He jostled his way through the crowd and hurried out the door, away from all this laughter and dancing and painful happiness and into the darkness where he belonged.

* * * * *

A KISS
ON CRIMSON RANCH

Michelle Major

For Jackson.

I love you for your heart, your smile
and everything you are.

I'm so proud to be your mom.

Chapter 1

Sara Wells gripped the steering wheel of her ancient Toyota and tilted her chin. "Punch me," she said, and squeezed her eyes shut. "Right in the face. Go on, before I lose my nerve."

She heard movement next to her and braced herself, flinching when a soft hand stroked her cheek. "I'd never hit you, Sara, even if I wanted to. Which I don't."

Sara opened her eyes to gaze into the kind, guileless face of her best friend in the world, April Sommers. Her only friend. The friend whose entire life savings Sara had recently lost.

She swatted April's arm. "You should. I deserve it." A bead of sweat slid between her shoulder blades and she rolled down the window a crack. Her lungs stung as she inhaled the crisp alpine air. "How does anyone breathe around here?" she muttered. "I miss the L.A. smog."

"Go see the attorney. Stop avoiding reality."

"Reality Bites." She paused, then lifted a finger. "1994. Starring Ethan Hawke, Winona Ryder and a very green Ben Stiller. Who would have thought that of the three, Ben Stiller would end up the biggest star? Come on. *Little Fockers?* Are you kidding me?"

"You're doing it again."

Ignoring the soft admonishment, Sara leaned forward to gaze out the car's front window at the row of brightly colored Victorian stores lining Main Street. "Look at that. Warner Bros. couldn't have created a better Western set."

"This *is* the West."

Right.

Crimson, Colorado. Population 3,500 if the sign coming over the pass into town was accurate. Altitude 8,900 feet. Sara blamed the lack of air for her inability to catch her breath.

April rummaged in the sack at her feet. "Aren't you curious?" She offered Sara an apple. Sara held up a half-eaten Snickers in response.

"I gave up curious a long time ago." She stuffed the candy bar into her mouth. "Along with cigarettes, savage tans, men and chocolate." She swallowed. "Okay, scratch chocolate."

That resolution had fallen by the interstate about four hours into the thirteen-hour drive from Los Angeles. While Crimson was only thirty minutes down the road from the ritzy ski town of Aspen, it held as much appeal to Sara as a blistered big toe.

Sure, it was beautiful if you were one of those back-to-nature types who appreciated towering pines, glittering blue skies and breathtaking views. Sara was a city girl. A blanket of smog comforted her; horns blaring on the I-5 made her smile. In her world, ski boots were a fashion statement, not a cold-weather necessity.

She was out of her element.

Big-time.

"Go on." April leaned over and opened the driver's-side door. "The sooner you talk to the attorney, the quicker we'll be back on the road to La-La Land."

Sara's need to put Rocky Mountain Mayberry in her rearview mirror propelled her out of the car. She couldn't do that until she met with Jason Crenshaw, attorney-at-law, whose cryptic phone call two days earlier had started this unplanned road trip.

If nothing else, she hoped the money Crenshaw had for her would buy gas on the way back. And groceries. Sara could live on ramen noodles and snack cakes for weeks, but April was on a strict organic, vegan diet. Sara didn't understand eating food that looked like cat puke and tasted like sawdust, but she had no right to question April's choices. If it weren't for Sara, April would have plenty of money to spend on whatever she wanted. And rabbit food cost plenty of money.

She pulled her well-worn jeans jacket tight and squinted through a mini dust tornado as a gust of wind whipped along the town's main drag. Mid-May in Southern California and the temperature hovered at a balmy seventy degrees, but Crimson still had a bit of winter's chill to the air. The mountain peaks surrounding the town were covered in snow.

Sara didn't do snow.

She opened the pale turquoise door to the office of

Crenshaw and Associates and stepped in, lifting her knock-off Prada sunglasses to the top of her head.

The desk in the reception area sat vacant, large piles of paper stacked precariously high. "Hello?" she called in the general direction of the office door at the back of the lobby.

A chair creaked and through the door came a younger man who looked like he could have been Andy Griffith's rumpled but very handsome son. He peered at her over a pair of crooked reading glasses, wiping his hands on the paper napkin stuffed into his collared shirt.

Sara caught the whiff of barbecue and her stomach grumbled. No food envy, she reminded herself. Noodles were enough for her.

"Sorry, miss," the man said as he looked her over. "No soliciting. Try a couple doors down at the diner. Carol might have something left over from the lunch rush."

Sara felt her eyes widen a fraction. The guy thought she was a bum. Fantastic. She pulled at her spiky bangs. "I'm looking for Jester Crunchless," she said with a well-timed lip curl.

"I'm Jason Crenshaw." The man bristled. "And who might you be?"

"Sara Wells."

Immediately his posture relaxed. "Ms. Wells, of course." He pulled out the napkin as he studied her, revealing a tie decorated with rows of small snowboards. "You know, we watched *Just the Two of Us* religiously around here. You're different than I expected."

"I get that a lot."

"Right." He chuckled self-consciously. "You're a heck of a lady to track down."

"I'm here now."

"Of course," he repeated. "Why don't you step into my office?"

"Why don't you hand over the check?"

His brows drew together. "Excuse me?"

"On the phone you said *inheritance*." She reached into her purse. "I have ID right here. Let's get this over with."

"Were you close to your grandmother, Ms. Wells?"

"No." She could barely remember her grandmother. Sara's mother had burned a trail out of Crimson as soon as she could and had kept Sara far away from her estranged family.

"The heart attack was a shock. We're told she didn't suffer." He paused. "It's a loss for the whole town. Miss Trudy was the backbone of Crimson."

A sliver of something, a long-buried emotion, slipped across Sara's heart and she clamped it down quickly. Shaking her head, she made her voice flip. "It's tragic that she was your backbone and whatnot. I barely knew the woman. Can we talk about the money?"

Another pause. "There is no money." Crenshaw's tone took on a harsh edge. Harsh was Sara's home turf.

Sara matched his emotion. "Then why in the hell did I just drive all the way from California?"

He cleared his throat. "We discussed an inheritance on the phone, Ms. Wells. Not money, specifically." He turned to a rickety file cabinet and peered into the top drawer. "I have it right here."

Great. She and April had driven almost a thousand miles for an old piece of costume jewelry or something.

She mentally calculated if she could get to Denver on the fumes left in her gas tank.

He turned back to her and held out a set of keys. "There's some paperwork, for sure. We should talk to Josh about how he fits into the mix. He and Trudy had big plans for the place. But you look like you could use a rest. Go check it out. We can meet again tomorrow morning."

Tomorrow morning she'd be halfway to the Pacific Ocean. "What place?"

"Crimson Ranch," he told her. "Miss Trudy's property." He jingled the keys.

Sara's stomach lurched. "She left me a *property?*"

Before Crenshaw could answer, cool air tickled Sara's ponytail. She turned as her mother, Rosemarie Wells, glided in with bottle-blond hair piled high on top of her regal head. A man followed in her wake, indiscriminately middle-aged, slicked-back salt-and-pepper hair, slight paunch and cowboy boots that looked custom-made. Sara assumed he was the latest in her mother's long string of rich, powerful, jerk boyfriends.

Could this day get any worse?

Rose slanted Jason Crenshaw a dismissive glance then snapped her fingers at Sara. "We need to talk, Serena."

Sara's stomach lurched, but she focused on the attorney, snatching the keys out of his still-outstretched palm.

"May I help you?" he asked, his eyes a little dazed. Her mother had had that effect on men since Sara could remember. It had been at least two years since she'd seen her mother last, but Rose looked exactly the same as far as Sara could tell. Maybe with a few less wrinkles thanks to the wonders of modern plastic surgery.

"You can ignore her." Sara bit at a cuticle.

"Serena, stop that obnoxious behavior."

She nibbled harder. "This is kind of a coinkydink, Mom. You showing up now." Sara locked eyes with her mother. Rose knew about the will, she realized in an instant.

Her mother's gaze raked her. "You look like hell, Serena."

"Stop calling me that. My name is Sara." She narrowed her eyes but crossed her arms over her chest, suddenly conscious that she was wearing an ancient and not very supportive sports bra. "Sara Wells. The name you put on my birth certificate."

Her mother's large violet eyes rolled to the ceiling. "The name I had legally *changed* when you were eight."

"I changed it back and you know it." Sara took a step forward. "A monumental pain in the back end, by the way." She cocked her head to one side. "Although it's handy when collections comes calling."

Her mother's nose wrinkled. "I can help you with that, Serena."

"Sara."

Rose ignored her. "Richard wants to buy your grandmother's property." She tilted her head at the aging cowboy, who tipped his hat rim at Sara, Clint Eastwood style.

"I don't understand why Gran left it to me."

"To make things difficult for me, of course," Rose said with an exaggerated sigh. She dabbed at the corner of her eye. "Mothers are supposed to look out for their children, not keep them from their rightful inheritance."

Sara never could cry on cue. She envied her mother that.

"No matter. I know you've gotten yourself into another mess, Serena. A financial nightmare, really. We can fix that right now. Mr. Crenshaw, would you be so good as to draw up the paperwork?" She leveled a steely gaze at Sara. "I'm bailing you out again. Remember that."

Rose had never helped Sara out of anything—contract negotiations, come-ons from slimy casting directors, defamatory tabloid headlines, a career slowly swirling down the drain. The only times in Sara's life her mother had stepped in to *help* were when it benefited Rose at Sara's expense.

"I'm not selling."

"What?"

"Not yet. And not to you, Mother."

"Don't be ridiculous." Rose darted a worried glance toward the cowboy, whose hands fisted in front of his oversize belt buckle. "What choice do you have?"

"I'm not sure." Sara turned to the attorney. "Can you give me directions to the ranch?"

"I'll write them down," he said, and with obvious relief, disappeared into the back office.

"What kind of game are you playing?" Her mother pointed a French-tipped finger at Sara. "We both know you're desperate for money. You don't belong on that ranch." Rose's tone was laced with condescension. "She had no business leaving it to you."

Decades of anger boiled to the surface in Sara. "She did, and maybe if you'd look in the mirror beyond the fake boobs and Botox you'd see why. Maybe she wanted to keep it out of your hot little hands." She leaned closer. "Want to talk about that?"

Her mother recoiled for an instant, then straightened. "You don't have a choice."

"No." Sara's spine stiffened. "I didn't have a choice when I was eight and begged you not to take me on another round of auditions. I didn't have a choice when I was thirteen and I wanted to quit the show after the assistant director came on to me. I didn't have a choice at seventeen when you checked me into rehab for *exhaustion* because the publicity would help the fans see me as an adult."

"If you'd taken my advice, you wouldn't be in the position you are now. I had your best interest at heart. Always."

Sara laughed. Actually laughed out loud in her mother's face. The statement was that absurd. "You tell yourself whatever you need to make it through the day. We both know the truth. Here's the kicker. Right now I do have a choice." She gripped the keys hard in her fist. "Stay away from me, Mother. Stay off of my property or I'll have you hauled off to the local pokey."

"You wouldn't—"

Sara met her angry gaze. "Try me."

She flicked a gaze at Jason Crenshaw, who'd returned to the office's lobby. "I'll be in touch," she said and took the piece of paper he handed her. Without another glance at Rose, she reached for the door, but a large hand on her arm stopped her.

"You're making a big mistake here, missy," the aging Marlboro man told her, his voice a harsh rasp.

She shrugged out of his grasp. She'd been intimidated by far scarier men than this old coot. "What's new?" she asked, and pushed out into the too-clean mountain air.

Josh Travers took a deep breath, letting the fresh air clear his muddled head. He'd been doing trail maintenance on the hiking path behind the main house for over three hours, moving logs to reinforce the bridge across a stream that ran between the two properties. His knee had begun throbbing about forty-five minutes into the job. Now it felt like someone had lit a match to his leg. Josh could tolerate the physical pain. What almost killed him was the way the ache radiated into his brain, making him remember why he was stuck here working himself to the point of exhaustion on a cool spring morning.

What he'd lost and left behind. Voices whispering he'd never get it back. The pain was a constant reminder of his monumental fall—both literal and figurative.

He turned toward the house and, for the first time, noticed a silver sedan parked out front. He didn't recognize the car as any of the locals. He squinted and could just make out California plates.

Damn.

He thought of his daughter, Claire, alone in her bedroom, furiously texting friends from New York.

Double damn.

If his leg could have managed it, he'd have run. Instead, he walked as fast as his knee would allow, trying to hide his limp—just in case someone was watching. It was all he could do not to groan with every step.

By the time he burst through the back door, he was

panting and could feel sweat beading on his forehead. He stopped to catch his breath and heard the unfamiliar sound of laughter in the house. Claire's laughter.

He closed his eyes for a moment and let it wash over him, imagining that she was laughing at one of the lame jokes he regularly told to elicit a reaction. One he never got.

He stopped short in the doorway between the back hall and the kitchen. Claire's dark head bent forward into the refrigerator.

"How about cheese?" she asked. "Or yogurt?"

"Really, we're fine" a voice answered, and Josh's gaze switched like radar to the two women sitting on stools at the large island at the edge of the kitchen. One looked in her late thirties, two thick braids grazing her shoulders. She wore no makeup and might have a decent figure, but who could tell with the enormous tie-dye dress enveloping most of her body. She smiled at Claire and something about her made Josh relax a fraction.

His attention shifted to the other woman, and he sucked in another breath. She tapped painted black fingernails on the counter as her eyes darted around the room. Her long blond hair was pulled back in a high ponytail; streaks of—was that really fire-engine red?—framed her face. The same blazing color coated her mouth, making her lips look as plump as an overripe strawberry. He had a sudden urge to smear her perfect pout with his own mouth, as if the most important thing in the world was for him to know if it tasted as delicious as it looked.

His body tightened, and he realized with a start that his knee had company in the throbbing department.

No way.

Her lips parted, and he forced his gaze to her eyes. She stared back at him with an expression that said she knew just what he was thinking.

No how.

Her eyes were pale blue, a color made almost silver by the heavy liner that rimmed them. Her skin was unnaturally pale, and he wondered for a moment if she was into that vampire-zombie junk Claire had told him about. He wouldn't put anything past one of those Hollywood types.

"Josh, look who's here. Can you believe it?" Claire gushed. He studied his daughter, who'd spoken in primarily monotone grunts since she'd arrived at the ranch a month earlier, but now thrummed with excitement.

"Call me Dad. Not Josh," he told her.

"Whatever." She gave him one of her patented eye rolls. "It's Serena Wellens." Claire shot a glance at the women. "I mean Sara Wells. But you know who she is, right? A real-life star here in our kitchen."

"A real-life star?" Josh didn't subscribe to *Entertainment Weekly,* but he was pretty sure Sara Wells hadn't been considered a "real star" for close to a decade now. Josh eyed Sara, who wore a faded Led Zeppelin T-shirt and capri sweatpants that hugged her hips like…nope. That was not where he needed his thoughts to go.

Sara pushed back from the counter. "Your kitchen?" she asked, raising a brow. "That's not what Mr. Crapshoot told me."

"You saw Jason Crenshaw."

"Yep." She jangled a set of keys in front of her. "Looks like you've got a little 'splaining to do, Daddy-O."

Maybe he shouldn't have questioned the "star" bit.

What did he know about Hollywood and celebrities? If a former child actor who hadn't had a decent job in years wanted to consider herself a star, it was no business of his. He knew guys who hadn't gotten onto the back of a bull for decades, but their identity was still wrapped up in being a bull rider.

Not Josh, though.

He'd had his years in the ring. Made a pretty good living at it. Broken some records. Truth be told, it had been his whole life. The only thing he'd ever been a success at was bull riding. But the moment they'd wheeled him out of that last event in Amarillo, his kneecap smashed into a zillion bits, he'd known he was done. His world would never be the same. He walked away and never looked back. Hung up his Stetson and traded the Wranglers for a pair of Carhartts.

People had told him he had options. He could try announcing. Get hired on with a breeding operation. Coach young riders. That last one was the biggest laugh. Just the smell of the arena made Josh's fingers itch to wrap around a piece of leather. He could no sooner have a career on the periphery of riding than a drunk could tend bar night after night. Being that close to the action and not able to participate would kill him.

A couple of times in the hospital and during rehab, he'd almost wished the accident had done the job. His gaze flicked to Claire, who looked between Sara and him with a mix of confusion and worry on her delicate features. She looked like her mother. Both a blessing and a curse, if you asked him.

At the end of the day, she was the reason he'd made it this far after the accident. He wasn't going to let some two-bit tabloid diva mess with his plans.

He forced a smile and turned his attention back to Sara. "About that," he began.

He watched her sense the change in him and stiffen. *Charm, buddy. The groupies thought you had it. Let's see what you've still got.*

He stepped forward and held out a hand. "I'm Josh Travers."

She eyed his outstretched palm like he'd offered her a snake. "Why are you living in my house?"

"Her house?" Claire asked.

Josh turned to his daughter. "Maybe you could head up to your room for a bit?"

"You must be joking." Claire crossed her arms over her chest. "And miss this?"

He made his tone all business. "Now, Claire."

His daughter made a face. "Bite me, Josh. I'm not leaving."

He heard Sara muffle a laugh as he stared down the beautiful, belligerent thirteen-year-old who had every right to hate him as much as she did. He'd been a lousy dad. Almost as bad as his own father, which was quite an accomplishment. He didn't know how to deal with her anger or attitude. Did he play bad cop or go soft? He barely knew his daughter, and in the weeks she'd been living at the ranch, he hadn't made much progress on repairing their relationship. One of the laundry list of things he should feel guilty about.

"Fine." He turned to Sara, who smiled at him. At his expense. "Trudy and I were partners."

"Is that so?" She wiggled her eyebrows. "Very *The Graduate,* although you don't strike me as much of a Dustin Hoffman. And from what I remember, Gran was no Anne Bancroft."

Josh shook his head and glanced at the hippie lady. "What is she talking about?"

She gave him a sympathetic smile. "Sara likes movie analogies. Ignore it."

He wished he could ignore this entire situation.

"Dad, is this our house or what?" Claire asked.

He sighed. "Technically, it belonged to Trudy."

Sara jingled the keys again.

"And now to you," he admitted.

"Oh. My. God." Claire let out a muffled cry. "I have no home. Again." She whirled on Josh. "You told me we were going to stay here. I could paint my room. Are you going to send me off like Mom did? Who else is left to take me?"

"No, honey. We *are* going to stay here. I'll work it out. I'm not sending you anywhere."

She sniffled and Josh turned to Sara. "Your grandmother and I were opening a guest ranch. She owns the house, but I have the twenty-five acres surrounding it. We back up onto the National Forest so it's the perfect location for running tours. I've been here since the fall working on renovations and booking clients. Guests start arriving in a couple of weeks."

Sara looked from Claire to Josh, her gaze almost accusatory. "Does it make money?"

He tried to look confident. "It will. I've sunk everything I have into the place." *Everything I had left after medical bills,* he added silently. "Trudy was going to help for the first season. I planned to buy her out with my half of the profits."

"But now the house is mine."

Josh nodded. "I don't expect you to hang around.

I'll cover the mortgage. At the end of the summer, I can take the whole place off your hands."

"Why can't you buy it from me now?" Her gaze traveled around the large room.

"The bank wants to see that it's a viable business before they'll approve my loan. Trust me, it's a good plan. Trudy and I worked it out."

She looked him up and down. "Trudy isn't here anymore."

"I know," he agreed, feeling the familiar ache in his chest as he thought of the woman who'd been more of a mother to him than his own. He wondered how difficult Sara was going to make this for him. He'd known Trudy's granddaughter had inherited the house. Josh had gone directly from the funeral service to the bank to see if he had any options. He didn't. He needed time and a bang-up summer to make this work. Otherwise, he might as well burn his savings in a bonfire out back. There was no Plan B.

"What if I want to sell now?"

His gut tightened. "Rose got to you already."

"How do you know my mother?"

"She and her land-developer boyfriend have been here a couple of times. The guy wants to tear down the house and build luxury condos on the property. Make Crimson a suburb of Aspen. What an idiot."

Claire took a step forward. "Are you going to let us stay or should I start packing?" She eyed both Sara and Josh as she bit her lip. "Because all my stuff is folded and in drawers where I want it."

He heard the desperation in her voice, knew that despite her smart mouth, his daughter was hanging on by a short thread these days. As much as he didn't want to admit it, they had that much in common. He'd promised to take care of her, make up for his past mistakes. The ones he made with her and those he'd buried deeper than that. He needed this summer to do it.

"Claire, I told you—"

"I know what it's like to want a place to call home," Sara said quietly, her attention focused completely on Claire. Her eyes had gentled in a way that made his heartbeat race. For a moment, he wished she'd look at him with that soft gaze.

Claire blew out a pent-up breath and gave Sara a shy smile, not the sarcastic sneer she typically bestowed on him. His heart melted at both her innocence and how much she reminded him of another girl he'd once tried to protect.

Sara returned the smile and his pulse leaped to a full gallop. *Don't go there,* he reminded himself. Not with that one.

"Can you give your dad and me time to talk?" Sara asked. "To work things out? Maybe you could show April around." She pulled her friend forward. "She's into nature and stuff."

"Come on," April said. "Can we walk to the pond I saw on the way in?"

Claire nodded. "It's quicker to go out the back."

As she passed, Josh moved to give his daughter a hug. She shrugged away from his grasp. One step at a time. He'd seen her smile, even if it wasn't at him.

"Thanks," he said when the back door clicked. "I'm sure we can—"

"Cut the bull."

So much for the soft gaze.

She folded her arms across her chest. Josh forced himself to keep his eyes on her face.

"I don't want to hurt your kid, but I don't have time to play *Swiss Family Robinson* for the summer. I need money and I need it now. If you want to make a deal, what do you have to offer?"

His adrenaline from a moment ago turned to anger and frustration. "I put everything I had into buying the land and fixing up the place. I've paid for marketing, a website, direct mail. We've got a real chance of making this work." He raked his hands through his hair. "It has to work."

"I'm not about to…" She stopped and cocked her head.

"What? Not about to what?"

"Do you hear that?"

A sudden sound of pounding filled the air.

"That sounds like—"

He turned as Buster, his oversize bloodhound, charged down the hall, galloping toward the kitchen.

"Buster, sit." The dog slid across the hardwood floor and ran smack into Josh's legs, all enormous paws and wiggly bottom.

"Buster's harmless."

He looked back at Sara, now crouched on the butcher-block counter with wide eyes. "Keep that thing away from me."

He felt a momentary pang of sympathy for her obvious fear, then glanced at Buster and smiled. "Looks like I've got you right where I want you, Hollywood Barbie."

Chapter 2

So much for being cool, calm and in control.

"This isn't funny." Sara hated that her voice trembled.

Josh bent to rub the giant beast's belly. The dog was deep brown with a wide ring of black fur around the middle of its back. Its eyes were dark, at least what she could see under the wrinkles that covered its head. It yawned, displaying a mouth full of teeth and flopped onto the wood floor. One pancake-size ear flipped over his snout. Outstretched, it was nearly as long as she was.

"This is *Buster,*" Josh said with a laugh. "He wouldn't hurt a fly."

"That dog looks like he could eat me for breakfast."

"Lucky for you, it's nearly lunch."

"You are *so* not helping here."

"I like you better up there. You're not chewing me out."

"I wasn't chewing—" She stopped and met his gaze, now lit with humor. "You're living in my house."

"I explained that."

"I need to sell it."

"Sell it to me." He stepped closer. "At the end of the summer."

Fear had taken most of the fight out of her. "What am I supposed to do in the meantime?"

He held out a hand. "You could start by climbing off the counter."

She watched Buster, who'd begun to snore. "I don't like dogs."

Josh's low chuckle rumbled through her. "I never would have guessed."

She didn't move from the counter. "The fourth season of the show, I got a dog." She closed her eyes at the memory. "My character, Jenna, got a dog. It hated me on sight. The first day on set it bit me. Twice. I wanted to get rid of it, but the director's girlfriend was the dog trainer. She said it could sense my fear. That it was my fault the dog growled every time I came anywhere near it. Of course, the thing loved Amanda. Everyone loved Amanda."

"Who's Amanda?"

"Amanda Morrison."

"The movie star?"

"Highest-paid woman in Hollywood three years running. Back in the day, she was my sidekick on the show."

She expected a crack about how far the mighty had fallen. He asked, "How long was the dog around?"

"Lucky for me, the director was as big of a jerk with girlfriends as he was with me. By the end of the season, the dog was gone."

"Did it ever warm up to you?"

She shook her head. "I got faster at moving away after a scene. I never realized how much my fingers resemble bite-size sausages." She blew out a breath. "Animals and me, we don't mesh."

She looked away from the sleeping dog, surprised to find Josh standing next to her beside the kitchen island.

This close, she could see that his dark brown eyes were flecked with gold. A thin web of lines fanned out from the corner of them. He was tall, well over six feet, with broad shoulders that tapered into a muscled chest under his thin white T-shirt. Unlike most guys in Southern California, Josh didn't look like he'd gotten his shape with an expensive gym membership or fancy trainers. He'd clearly worked for it. Real sweat kind of work. He wasn't bulky, but solid. Although he wore faded cargo pants and gym shoes, he still gave off a definite cowboy Mr. Darcy air.

If Mr. Darcy had an unnervingly sexy shadow of stubble across his jaw, a small scar above his right eyebrow and a bit of a crook in his nose like he'd met the wrong end of a fist one too many times. A dangerous, bad boy Mr. Darcy.

It was one thing to slip on giving up chocolate; bad boys were quite another. She'd had enough of bad boys in her time. They swarmed L.A. like out-of-work actors.

His gaze caught hers, and it took her a moment to remember what she was doing in this house in the mountains, cowering on the kitchen counter.

He reached out a hand and she took it, still a little dazed. "It's not going to come after me?" she asked, throwing a sharp glance at the dog.

"I'll protect you," he answered, his tone so sincere it made her throat tighten. Among other parts of her body.

Off balance, she scrambled down, the heel of one shoe catching on the corner of a drawer and sending her against the hard wall of his chest. She stepped back as if he'd pinched her, but he didn't release her hand.

His calloused fingers ran the length of hers. "Nothing like sausages," he said with a wink.

She snatched her hand away and moved to the other side of the island, thinking the altitude was making her light-headed. Praying it was the altitude.

"Where's Claire's mother?" she asked. As she'd hoped, the spark went out of his eyes in an instant.

"She was having some problems—personal stuff— needed a little time to get herself back on track. So Claire's here with me."

"For how long?"

He shrugged. "As long as it takes. Why do you care?"

"I have experience with bad parents. It can mess with you if you're not careful."

"Are you careful, Sara?"

"I'm broke," she said by way of an answer. "Like I said before, I need the money from the sale of this house."

He hitched one hip onto the island. "You own the house, but it's only on a quarter-acre lot. I've got all the land surrounding it. Your part isn't going to be worth much without the land."

Crenshaw hadn't mentioned that. "Then why is my mother's latest boyfriend so hot for it?"

Josh took a moment to answer. "Basically, I'm hosed without the house. I can't run a guest ranch without a place to put the clients. If he gets you to sell to him now, I won't have an income stream this summer. And without money…"

"I know what happens without money."

"Right. Here's the deal. Assuming things go well when the season starts, I can pay you double the mortgage for the next three months. That should get you through until I can secure the loan."

"Why should I do it your way?"

He lifted one brow. "Because you're a kind and generous soul," he suggested.

She answered with a snort. "Is that the best you've got?"

"It will make your mother crazy mad."

"That's a little better."

"Listen, Sara. Your gran was one of the best. She was nice to me when I was a kid and a good friend since I got back. While I don't know the terms of her will, it doesn't surprise me that she left you the house. She loved this place and she talked about you a lot."

"I barely knew her."

He nodded. "One of her biggest regrets was that she didn't do more for you. Help you out when things got rough."

"Woulda, shoulda, coulda," Sara said, but turned away when her voice cracked. "You know, I spent a summer here right before the show got picked up."

"Trudy told me."

"It's funny. I don't remember a thing about that time."

"Look around the house...maybe it will come back to you. I'm going to find Claire. Whatever you decide, Sara, your grandmother did love you. You should know that."

She waited until his footsteps faded, then let her gaze wander after quickly checking that the dog remained sleeping on the floor.

The house was more an oversize log cabin, exposed beams running the length of the walls and across the ceiling. Their honey color gave the interior a cozy warmth in the late-afternoon sunlight. Across from the kitchen was a family room with high ceilings and a picture window that framed a million-dollar view of the craggy peaks surrounding the valley.

An overstuffed sectional and several leather armchairs sat in front of a wall of bookshelves with a large flat-screen TV in the center. Nothing looked the least bit familiar to her, and she wondered whether Josh had gotten the new gadgets or if her grandmother had been into cutting-edge electronics.

Did all of it belong to her, or would he strip the house if she sold? Maybe she should have spent a little more time with the attorney. Sara had been so angry when her mother had shown up that she clearly hadn't gotten the whole story about this place.

Couldn't anything be easy? she wondered as she made her way up to the second floor. She peeked her head into the first bedroom. Posters of pop stars and young actors lined the walls. A blue-and-purple comforter with peace signs covered the bed. Claire's room.

Next to that was a bathroom, and then came the

master bedroom. She stayed at the threshold, not wanting to venture into the room where Josh slept. Even from the doorway, she could smell the same scent he'd had today—a little woodsy, a little minty and totally male. She didn't want to be affected by his scent, by anything about a man who was entirely too rugged and rough for her taste.

She stepped quickly to the end of the hall. The final bedroom had soft yellow walls with lace-trimmed curtains, a four-poster bed and an antique dresser next to a dark wood ladder-back chair. She took a breath as she walked to the front of the dresser, skimming her fingers across the lace doily that covered the top. Framed photos lined one side, mostly her grandmother with people she didn't recognize, friends probably.

A few showed her mother as a girl, and in one she was a young woman carrying a baby: Sara. Sara was just a toddler in the photo and she smiled at the camera, one hand raised in a wave. Sara didn't remember a time before the endless rounds of auditions, cereal commercials and eventually prime-time celebrity. She'd been ten when *Just the Two of Us* first aired. The next seven years had been spent in a constant cycle of filming, promotions and off-season television movies.

It surprised her that her grandmother had none of her promo photos displayed. The only photos Rose had framed in their two-bedroom condo were publicity shots. Sara's hand trailed over a photo album that sat in front of the frames. She traced the jeweled beads that had been glued to the cover in the shape of her name. A sliver of memory trailed through her insides.

She sat down on the bed and flipped open the album. Her heart skipped a beat as she gazed at the first page.

It was a picture of her holding a giant ice-cream bar, mouth covered in chocolate, grinning wildly at the camera. In the next picture, she was on a trail, her blond hair pulled back in two pigtails and wearing an oversize cowboy hat. Her jaw dropped as she continued to turn the pages. Pictures of her feeding horses, a shot of her curled in a tight embrace with her grandmother. She read the caption below the photo: "Sara's first annual summer visit" written in Trudy's loping penmanship.

As she'd remembered, her mother had gotten a small part in a blockbuster Steven Spielberg movie that year. A part that had ended up on the cutting room floor. Shortly after that movie, Rose had switched her considerable energy to Sara's career. Which explained why first annual had quickly become one and only. Although Sara had no memory of this place, clearly she'd spent some happy times here.

And that was what her grandmother knew of her: Sara as a normal girl, before Rose had created Serena Wellens, deeming Sara too basic a name for the superstar she was destined to become. Even at the height of her fame, Sara had never identified herself as Serena. She'd been content with plain old Sara, although her mother had reminded her on a regular basis that freshfaced Saras were a dime a dozen in Hollywood.

She'd had to become someone else, someone more special than who she was.

Being Sara wasn't enough.

She sniffed as a tear fell onto the photo, then wiped at it with her thumb. Taking a deep breath, she stood. One thing she had in common with her more glamorous persona was that neither one of them did tears.

She placed the album back on the dresser and started down the hall, but her gaze caught on a poster on the far side of Claire's bedroom wall. It was a picture of Albert Einstein with a famous quote underneath.

Sara wasn't one for inspirational quotes. Actions spoke louder than words in her world. She didn't know any details of Josh and Claire's relationship, but it had been very clear that it wasn't good. As she looked around the bedroom, she wondered what would happen if they didn't get this summer together.

She shouldn't care. Neither of them were her business. A month ago when she'd landed back on the tabloid covers and lost her most recent waitressing job, she'd vowed to mind her own business. Take care of herself. She was number one.

But she'd seen something in Claire's eyes that she hadn't remembered feeling for way too long. Hope. Even as the girl had looked at Josh with anger and resentment, there'd been a spark of something that said *don't give up on me.* Josh didn't seem like a quitter, so maybe they'd have a chance. The chance Sara had never had for a normal life.

How could she take that away?

Her heart raced as she made a decision. She hurried down the stairs and out the back door before she came to her senses.

Josh, Claire and April were walking across the field behind the house. She waited until they got close. "Good news," she announced. "I'm staying."

Josh stopped dead in his tracks. "What do you mean *staying?*"

"Here. For the summer. I'll make sure you have a good season, and then sell it to you in September."

Claire did a little dance around him, making his head spin more than it already was. "That's so great," she gushed. "Now maybe this summer won't be as awful as I thought."

"Hey," he said, pulling her around to look at him. "You think it's going to be bad?"

She shrugged then wiggled out of his grasp. "Not as much as before."

He squeezed his eyes shut for a moment and counted to ten. When he looked at Sara again, she'd walked toward April and taken the other woman's hands in hers. "I know I messed up and I'm going to make it right for you. The cowboy here offered to pay me double the mortgage for the next three months. That should at least cover your expenses for the summer. If Ryan ever calls…"

He didn't bother to try to follow their conversation. "I said I'd pay you double to *leave*. Go back to California. Let me run things here. You'll get your money."

She shot him a dubious look. "Hell, no, partner. I'm sticking right here, and I'm going to make sure things go right."

"I've got it under control," he ground out.

"Oh, yeah? That kitchen looks pretty decked out. I'd guess my gran was going to do the cooking."

He nodded, not liking where this conversation was going.

"Best blueberry muffins ever," Claire added.

"And now?"

"I'm interviewing people," he admitted. "Do you cook?"

She rolled her eyes. "That's not my point."

"Which is?"

"You need help."

"Not from you, I don't."

"I could handle the kitchen," April offered quietly.

His gaze shot to April, who was looking at Sara.

"You don't have to do that," Sara told her. "You have a life."

April smiled. "I could use a little break, and I'm sure I can sublet the beach house for the summer."

"Is this because of losing the studio? You could teach some other place. Rent another space. You know your clients would follow you anywhere."

"That's the beautiful thing about yoga. I can take it anywhere, too." She gave Josh a hopeful smile. "I could even offer a few classes on the ranch. To start the morning, maybe."

Sara glared at him over April's shoulder, nodding vigorously. "That would be perfect," she said. "Your veggie burgers are the best. Josh, is there a Whole Foods anywhere around here?"

"A whole what?"

"They just opened one on the way to Aspen," Claire piped in. "But Dad only shops at the Red Creek Market."

April nodded. "It's important to support local businesses. I'll drive into town tomorrow morning and see what we can work out."

"When are the first guests arriving?" Sara asked no one in particular. "We'll need time to plan out the right menus. Do you have lists of food preferences and allergies? That sort of thing?"

"Hold on," Josh bellowed, raking his hands through his hair. "Hold on! No one is making veggie anything at my ranch. People book trips looking for action and adventure, not airy-fairy spa treatments and yoga classes. They want to fish and race ATVs, hike fourteeners and mountain bike the local trails. I'm the boss around here. I do the hiring. I make the plans. I'm the one—"

He looked at the three women, April's gaze a little hurt, Claire's eyes narrowed and Sara shaking her head just a bit as she chewed on her full lower lip.

"I'm the boss," he repeated quietly, willing it to be true.

"Don't be a hater," Claire mumbled.

"A what?" He rubbed his temples. "Never mind."

"You don't have a chef, do you?" Sara asked, her voice too knowing for his taste.

"I'm interviewing cooks."

"And who's planning all the so-called adventures?"

"I am."

"And leading the fun?"

Was it his imagination or did her gaze stray to his knee? "That's me, too. Got a problem?"

She took a step closer to him. Across the bridge of her nose, under who knew how many pounds of makeup, he could see the faint outline of freckles. Distracting freckles. Freckles he wanted to trace, wondering if her skin was as soft as it looked.

"Face it, cowboy," she said, bringing him back to the moment, "you need us."

"I don't need anyone."

He heard Claire snort.

"Jerk," Sara said under her breath.

A dull pounding started behind his left eye, matching the throbbing of his leg. "Fine. But this isn't the Ritz. If you're here, you work."

She tossed her streaked hair. "I've been working since I was eight years old."

He suppressed a growl. "Not the kind of work that involves a catered lunch."

"You think you know me so well."

"I know your type."

"We'll see about that." She gave his shoulder a hard flick. "I'll give it until Labor Day, Lone Ranger. If you can't get the bank loan approved by then, I'm taking the next best offer."

He studied her luminous blue eyes, their depths cold as an alpine stream. "Deal."

They glared at each other, and though he kept his eyes on her face, he noticed that her chest rose and fell unevenly and a soft pink flush rose to her cheeks. His own breath quickened, and without knowing why, he leaned in and enjoyed watching her big eyes widen.

The hippie chick clapped a few times, breaking the weighted silence. "If that's settled, we should think about planning. I'll start with dinner."

He forced his gaze from Sara's. "The local diner has decent takeout."

April laughed. "I'll cook tonight. Think of it as an official interview."

He nodded. "There are six smaller cabins on the property. Four of them are two bedrooms. You can have your pick."

"Can't they stay in the house with us?"

"No," Josh and Sara said in unison.

"Whatever," Claire mumbled.

Sara turned to his daughter. "Would you show me the other cabins?" She glanced warily at the thick pine forest that surrounded his land. "I want the one least likely to be invaded by critters."

Josh expected Claire to offer up one of the flip comebacks she gave him every time he asked for her help. To his surprise, she gave Sara a genuine smile. "Sure. Will you tell me about all the stars you know in Hollywood?"

A momentary cloud passed through Sara's eyes before she smiled brightly. "Oh, sweetie, I've got some stories for you."

Claire giggled. Actually giggled as she led Sara toward the row of cabins that sat in front of the small stream at the back of the property.

"Unbelievable," he said under his breath.

He heard April laugh again and whirled on her. "What?" he demanded. "What is so funny?"

She took a step back, palms up. "Nothing at all. Do you want to discuss menus while I check out the kitchen?"

Josh recognized a peace offering and was smart enough to take it. "Let's go," he said, and headed for the house.

Chapter 3

Sara glanced up from the computer in Crimson's small-town library. It had been three days since she and April had arrived in Colorado. Word spread fast that former starlet Serena Wellens was in town for the summer. A steady stream of locals had stopped by the ranch for neighborly visits. Of course the disappointment in meeting a once-upon-a-time celebrity in real life had been obvious from the comments she'd received.

"You looked taller on TV."

"You were so pretty when you were younger."

"Do you still talk to Amanda? Can you get her autograph?"

Her favorite had been from the town's mayor, who'd blurted, "I read you overdosed a year ago. I think I sent your gran flowers as a condolence."

It was a good thing the ego had been pummeled out of her years ago. Otherwise, the blatant disapproval might have done her in.

She watched a couple of teenage boys stare at her from behind the bookshelves at the far end of the room. She pulled off her headphones and winked in their direction. Her smile broadened as they ran away, books clattering to the floor in their wake.

"You enjoyed that a little too much."

She started at Josh's deep voice and swiveled her head to see him approach. Quickly, she clicked the mouse to minimize the screen and turned to block his view completely. "The picture-book section is on the other side," she said with a huff.

To her dismay, he gave her a knowing grin. "What-cha doin', Hollywood?" His lazy drawl made her insides twist in a way she didn't like.

She shrugged in response. "Checking out the gossip sites. A little Facebook. April's meeting with the owner at the market to arrange food deliveries to the ranch so I'm killing time."

He craned his neck to peer over her shoulder. "I think you looked me up on Google."

"You wish," she sputtered as a voice sounded through the headphones that she'd dropped to the desk.

"Josh Travers does it again. It's a new record and another amazing showing from bull riding's reigning king." Applause and cheers echoed in the background.

Heat rose to her cheeks as Josh arched a brow.

"Fine. I was curious. So what. Don't tell me you haven't looked me up, too."

"I wasn't sure which site I liked better—serena-wellensforever.com or sarawellsstinks.com."

"*Just the Two of Us* fans didn't love it when I changed my name. They thought they knew me when I was Serena. Like my name mattered."

"It mattered to you."

"Reigning king, huh?" she asked.

"That was a while back," he said with a smile, as if he knew she was changing the subject.

She studied him for a few moments. "I saw pictures of your accident."

His back stiffened. "Pictures exaggerate."

"The bull landed on top of you."

"They got him off quick."

"Does your knee still bother you?"

"Not really."

"Liar," she whispered. "Do you miss it?"

"Not really."

"Did you ever see that Jim Carrey movie *Liar, Liar* when he can only tell the truth?"

He scratched his jaw. "I don't think so."

"It's an interesting idea, don't you think? Even if he tried to tell a lie, it wouldn't come out of his mouth."

He just watched her.

"I'm kind of babbling."

"Yep."

He did that to her, she thought. He was such a presence. Big and broad and totally in his space—in her space. People in L.A. were always planning what came next, even if it was a trip to the mall. But Josh stayed in the moment no matter what he was doing. He kept busy, and to her eternal gratitude, she hadn't seen much of him other than watching him walk across the property early in the morning to take care of the horses, then catching glimpses of him throughout the day.

Yesterday, he'd spent most of his time on the roof of the largest cabin, replacing worn shingles. When the sun moved high overhead and the temperature rose with it, he'd taken off his shirt. Much to her dismay, Sara found herself staring out the window in the office far too often. It had been a while since she'd had a man in her life, but she figured she could get her wayward hormones under better control than that.

Here in the quiet intimacy of the library, those little buggers took flight again. With Josh standing in front of her, his faded T-shirt stretched over his chest and sculpted arms, she could imagine…

Nope.

She *did not* imagine. She'd given up her imagination when she'd abandoned her dreams, around the time she began filling in *waitress* under the occupation heading on paperwork.

This man was all that stood in the way of the possibility of reclaiming her life, or at the very least, creating a new one. The money from the sale would allow April and her to start over. The only view she'd let herself imagine was Josh Travers disappearing in her rearview mirror.

"So what *are* you doing here? Did they run out of *Playboy*s at the general store? I don't think the library has a subscription."

He shrugged then held out a book. The cover read *Talk To Your Teenager Without Losing Your Mind*.

"That's a mouthful."

"The librarian recommended it."

"It's nice that you're willing to read a parenting book."

"Claire hates me."

"She doesn't hate you," Sara argued as she stood and gathered her things.

"This morning after you and April left I asked her to help me feed the horses. You would have thought I was waterboarding her." He scrubbed a hand over his face. "I thought all girls loved horses."

"Not *all,*" she clarified.

"Thanks, I've got that now. One of the mares sniffed her and she freaked out. I laughed a little."

"You laughed at her?"

He smacked the heel of his hand to his forehead. "So shoot me. I didn't mean it. She threw a bucket of grain at me, screamed that she hated the ranch, she hated her mother and most of all she hated me. My dad would have whipped my butt if I'd thrown a fit like that."

"What did you do?"

"Nothing. She ran back to the house. I finished in the barn and came here."

Sara led the way out of the library and into the warm afternoon air. She glanced up at the bright blue sky, still surprised at how much this small mountain town resembled a movie set. "She doesn't hate you," she repeated.

"Did you hear anything I just said?" Josh asked, his face incredulous.

"She's a teenager. Hormones running rampant and in a new place with a parent she barely knows. Give her time."

He looked like he wanted to argue then took a breath. "Time. Right. When are you coming back?"

Sara checked her watch. "I'm supposed to meet April in a half hour."

"What's the deal with the two of you? She was willing to follow you to Crimson and seems happy to do her part at the ranch. That's quite the package deal."

"I don't know much about the rodeo circuit, but in Hollywood finding someone who truly cares is a rarity." Sara took a breath before continuing. "I met April about the time my career was starting to tank and my personal life was just as messed up. She stuck with me through the bad stuff, and I did the same with her when she had her own troubles. She doesn't belong in L.A. anymore. If a summer at the ranch can help her see that, all of this would be worth it. She deserves happiness more than anyone I know."

He studied her for several moments. She struggled not to fidget under his scrutiny. "You're a good friend," he said finally.

"Oh, I'm the bee's knees, and don't you forget it." She laughed, trying to ignore the intensity of his gaze. "I need to stop by that clothing store at the end of the block. My L.A. wardrobe doesn't really work here."

Josh took a long look at the outfit she wore today. A shapeless black-and-white-striped sweater dress over skintight black jeans that zipped from knee to ankle. Her shoes, Converse trainers, were at least more practical than the heeled boots she'd worn yesterday. Without the heels, she was pixie-size, and if it wasn't for the heavy makeup lining her eyes and dark wine-colored lipstick, she might have passed for a teenager herself.

A lock of neon hair slipped from her newsboy cap, and she tucked it behind her ear. Josh's gaze locked on the soft blond wisps at the base of her neck, and he was momentarily fascinated to imagine her natural honey color.

That was the kind of woman he was drawn to: natural, sweet and compliant. A woman who'd bake pies from scratch with strawberries fresh from the garden. The kind of woman he could grow old with, reveling in a normal, boring, run-of-the-mill Ozzie and Harriett life. Not a bitter, bossy, snappish former diva.

No attraction to that type.

Not at all.

He fell in step beside her.

"You mean Feathers and Threads?" Other than T-shirt shops and the fishing shop, which sold outdoor gear, that was the only women's clothing store in town.

"I prefer to think of it as Cowgirl Duds R Us."

He chuckled. "It's not bad. Do you think you could help me pick out something for Claire? Maybe a necklace or earrings?"

She slanted him a curious look.

"A peace offering. For this morning."

"Buying your way out of the doghouse?"

"Whatever it takes." They reached the end of the block. "I need to stop in at the fly shop first. I ordered vests and waders for the ranch."

She didn't slow her pace. "See you in a few."

He watched her walk away and couldn't help but notice that the way her hips swayed under the striped dress was all woman.

Damn.

The bells over the door of Feathers and Threads chimed as he walked in fifteen minutes later. He glanced around but didn't see Sara. Maybe she was in the dressing room.

"Hey, Rita," he called to the shop's owner, who stood behind the counter with a young salesgirl and a cluster of customers.

He'd brought Claire here when she'd first arrived in town. His daughter had taken one look at the racks and announced she'd be buying her clothes from the Hollister website. The morning after, he'd taken Rita to coffee as an apology for Claire's rudeness.

Too bad she'd read more into that than he'd meant. She'd all but suggested a quickie in the back room of the store. When he'd refused, she'd still found excuses to stop by the ranch several times, dropping off sparkly tops and hand-knit sweaters for Claire. To his relief, Claire had kept her snide comments to herself, and he'd been able to avoid Rita as much as possible. That was another reason he wanted to come in here at the same time as Sara—someone to distract Rita.

"Hi, Josh," she cooed. "Can I help you with something?"

"I'm picking up a gift for Claire. I'll look around."

"Let me know if you have questions," she answered and turned back to her conversation.

He silently congratulated himself and headed toward the jewelry case at the back of the store. Rita and her gaggle of customers laughed softly as he walked by. Snippets of conversation drifted his way.

"...rode hard and put away wet."

"No wonder she can't get work. Who'd want to see that on the big screen?"

"Is it just me or has she had her lips done?"

"Doesn't belong in Crimson, that's for sure."

Josh concentrated on the necklaces as unease skated around his chest. He glanced in the small mirror above the jewelry case and spotted Sara standing behind a sale rack.

As Josh turned toward the group of women, the conversation behind the counter continued, louder now. The women made no attempt to be discreet.

"I read she was into drugs for a while," one of the customers offered, bending forward so that Josh got too much of a view of her ample backside.

Eyes widened within the group. "Did you see track marks?"

"I can't get past those raccoon eyes," another woman said with a snicker.

"It looks like she hasn't seen the sun in years," Rita answered. "Maybe we should send her down to Nell's salon for a makeover."

Maybe you should shut your mouth, Josh thought. He glanced at Sara in the mirror, expecting to see steam rising from her ears. He was surprised she hadn't come out swinging already. Instead, he watched her swipe under her eyes and return a blouse to the rack, her hand shaking a bit.

"I wouldn't wish that hot mess on anyone," the younger salesgirl said, sending the other women into peals of laughter.

Josh felt his blood pressure rise along with the volume of giggles. He looked back to Sara, and her gaze met his in the mirror. For a single moment her eyes were unguarded and he saw pain, raw and real, in their depths. She blinked and shuttered them, turning the glare he'd come to know so well on him in full force. She shook her head slightly and backed away from the clothes rack.

Now, he thought. *Cut them down now.* She turned to a display of knit tops and picked one out at random. He watched her carry it to the front of the store. The women looked her up and down, not hiding their judgment and contempt.

"Just this," she said quietly, keeping her eyes forward. "You have some lovely things in the store."

"They all have security tags," Rita answered as she punched a few keys on the cash register.

"Of course."

Josh's temper hit the roof. How could Sara let that group of catty witches fillet her without defending herself? Where was the sarcastic, no-holds-barred woman he'd already come to expect? Hell, he hated to admit it, but he actually looked forward to their verbal sparring to break up the monotony of his day.

But this? This was total and complete bull. He grabbed two necklaces from the rack and stalked to the counter.

"What do you think of these?" he asked as he slammed them onto the glass top.

Rita jumped back an inch then pasted on a broad smile. "With Claire's gorgeous skin the turquoise will—"

"I'm not talking to you," he interrupted, unconcerned with how rude he sounded. "Which one, Sara?"

"The butterfly charm," she answered immediately. "The turquoise on the other one is dime-store quality."

"I beg your pardon?" Rita sputtered.

Sara didn't make eye contact with either of them, only dug in her purse for a wallet.

That a girl, Josh thought. *Just a little more.*

"Claire trusts your opinion," he continued conversationally. "I think she was sold the moment Gwyneth called to see what she should wear to her movie opening."

"Gwyneth Paltrow?" the salesgirl asked, her tone taking on a fraction of respect.

Sara's fingers tightened around her purse and she sliced a dead-meat look at him.

He forced a chuckle. "It's like Hollywood is one big sorority." He pointed to Sara. "Her phone is ringing every ten minutes. Julia needs to know where to find some kind of boots. Sandra's texting about a brand of fancy-pants jeans."

Rita raised an eyebrow at Sara. "And they're calling *you?*"

When Sara didn't answer, Josh spoke quickly, "Like you wouldn't believe."

Sara pulled out cash and handed it to Rita. "For the sweater." She didn't acknowledge Josh's comments or Rita's question.

Rita took the money, studying Sara. "I'm ordering for fall in a couple of weeks. Maybe you could stop by and take a look at the lines. We're not as exclusive as Aspen, but I still want to offer current trends. I'd appreciate a fresh opinion."

"Fresh?" Sara questioned. "As in fresh off heroin?" She yanked her sleeves above her elbows and held out her arms for inspection. "No track marks, ladies. Needles were never my thing."

Two of the women giggled nervously and backed away from the counter. After an awkward pause Rita said, "If you've got time, stop back later in the month."

Sara blew out a breath. "Give me a break," she mumbled, and left the store, leaving the bagged sweater and change Rita had placed on the counter.

Josh quickly paid for his necklace, grabbed Sara's

bag and followed her into the warming afternoon. He caught up with her half a block down the street.

"What happened in there?"

She rounded on him. "Why don't you tell me, Mr. Name Dropper?" She jabbed at his chest, her voice rising. "Since when are you an expert on celebrity fashion? Not one damn person has called my cell phone since I got here, famous or otherwise. And you know it."

"Excuse me for trying to help. Those women were out for blood, and you were about to open a vein for them."

"You should mind your own business," she countered.

"Who *are* you right now?" He took a deep breath, needing to clear his head. It didn't work. Not one bit. "All you've done since the minute you walked into my house—"

"My house."

"*The* house," he amended. "All you've done is bust my chops. If I look at you wrong, you read me the riot act, give me one of those snide remarks or smart comebacks you're so damn good at." He pointed in the direction of Rita's store. "You didn't say one word to those ladies in there."

She rolled her eyes. "You took care of it all on your own."

"Somebody had to. It was too painful to watch your slow death."

"Julia, Gwyneth? Even if I was in L.A., do you think one of those women would give me the time of day? They are A-list, Josh. I'm beyond Z. You have no idea what you're talking about."

"Rita didn't know that."

"*I* know it." She scrubbed her hands over her face. "I'm a has-been. A nobody. You don't get it. What those women dished out was nothing compared to what I hear every single day in California. At the grocery. The dry cleaners." She laughed without humor. "At least back in the day when I could afford dry cleaning. I've been a waitress now for the same number of years I was a paid actress. Do you know how many customers gave me career advice, hair tips, dissed my makeup, my boyfriends, all of it? Nothing was off-limits. I can take it, Josh. I don't need you to swoop in and rescue me."

"Excuse me for trying to help."

"I don't *want* help. This isn't *Pretty Woman* meets mountain town. I'm not Julia Roberts shopping on Rodeo Drive. You're not Richard Gere on the fire escape."

"Why do you do that?"

Her eyes narrowed. "Do what?"

"Throw out movie plots like they compare to what's happening. This is real life, Sara."

"I'm well aware."

He shook his head. "I thought you were a fighter."

"No," she said quietly. "I'm a survivor." With that, she turned and marched down the street away from him.

Chapter 4

Sara didn't say much on the drive from town, content to let April ramble about her meeting with the man who ran the local farm cooperative. She gazed at the tall pines that bordered the winding highway, continuing to be awed by her surroundings. The vivid colors, woodsy smells—the vast magnitude of every inch of this place.

She thought about Josh's "real life" comment. Sara knew real life. Real life was struggling to meet her rent every month, praying each time she used her debit card that her bank account wasn't overdrawn. She had to admit there was something about Crimson that felt—well, authentic. In L.A., life was about who you knew, where you could get a table, which plastic surgeon you frequented. She glanced in the rearview mirror, wondering for a moment about the last time she'd gone anywhere without full makeup. Her war paint, as she'd come to think of it.

Was it possible she could have a brief reprieve from battle in this small mountain community?

As Sara drove down the narrow driveway toward the ranch, she spotted a large black SUV parked in front of the main house.

"If that's my mother…" she muttered under her breath.

April patted her knee. "You can deal with your mother. You're a fighter."

The car almost swerved into the ditch. "Did you talk to Josh?" Sara accused her friend once she was back on the dirt road.

"No," April answered slowly, her dark eyes studying Sara. "What's going on with you two?"

"Nothing."

"I can feel the vibes. They aren't *nothing*."

"You're imagining it."

"He's hot."

"Go for it," Sara suggested. "Maybe he'd relax if he got a little something."

April chuckled. "You know that after my divorce I swore off men, at least until I've found someone who's worth the time and effort. So I don't *go for it* anymore. Besides, maybe *you* could relax if…"

"Not going there."

"We'll see."

"You think you know me so well."

"I've known you since you were fourteen."

The studio had hired April to be Sara's fitness coach when she'd put on a few pounds during puberty. Sara counted that decision as one of the few blessings from her years as a sitcom star. Without April's gentle guidance, Sara might have added "eating disorder" to her long list of personal issues.

Nine years older than Sara, April had quickly become Sara's soul sister and best friend. When April's stuntman husband left her a few years later during April's grueling battle with breast cancer, Sara had been more than willing to see her friend through months of chemotherapy and radiation treatments and the nasty divorce that resulted.

Neither woman had been lucky in the relationship department—another fact that, despite their different outlooks on life, bonded them deeply.

"You only think you know me. I'm a mystery wrapped in a puzzle clothed in an enigma," Sara told her friend with a wry smile.

"Right."

Sara parked the car next to the SUV. "Are you trying to distract me from the probability of another scene with *Mommie Dearest?*"

"Is it working?" April asked, reaching for the door handle.

Sara grabbed her arm. "Have I told you today how sorry I am you're in this predicament with me?"

April shrugged. "Things happen for a reason."

"Don't go all *Sliding Doors* on me. The reason your savings account was wiped out and you lost the yoga studio is because I'm a gullible idiot, a loser and the worst friend in the world. We're stuck in high-altitude Pleasantville for the summer, thanks to me."

"Sara…" April began, her tone gentle.

Sara thumped her head against the steering wheel. "Maybe I was wrong to agree to Josh's plan for the summer. If I sold to Mom's latest sugar daddy we could be back in California next week."

"Back to what?"

"Our lives."

"Neither of our lives was that great to begin with, and you know it. Besides, what about Josh and Claire?"

"Not my problem."

"I guess that's true," April admitted. She pushed open the passenger door. "But we're not going to get anywhere sitting in this car. If you want to hear your mom out, that's your decision. You have to take control of this situation."

"Lucky me," Sara answered, and started toward the house.

Sara walked through the front door, waiting for the scent of White Diamonds, the perfume her mother had worn for decades to hit her. She smelled nothing.

She turned the corner from the foyer and stopped so suddenly that April knocked into the back of her. She stood perfectly still for one moment, then launched herself across the family room at the man who stood on the other side of the couch.

"I'm going to kill you," she yelled, reaching out to wrap her fingers around his neck.

Strong arms pulled her away and she was enveloped in a different scent—one that even in her anger still had an effect on her insides. "Settle down," Josh whispered in her ear.

"Let me go," she said on a hiss of breath. She fought, and his arms clamped around her, pressing her against the solid wall of his chest. After a minute she stopped struggling. "Let me go," she repeated. "I'm not going to hurt him."

Slowly, Josh loosened his hold on her. For the briefest second, Sara fought the urge to snuggle back into the warmth that radiated off his soft denim shirt, to bury her face into the crook of his neck and simply breathe.

She stepped away, needing to break their invisible connection, and straightened the hem of her long shirt. "You've got a lot of nerve showing up here, Ryan. Unless you've got my money and April's, too, you can crawl back under the rock you came from."

"Hi, Sara." Ryan Thompson, her onetime business partner and long-ago ex-boyfriend flashed a sheepish smile. "I came to apologize." He held out his hands, palms up. "To beg your forgiveness. Go ahead, attack me if you want. I deserve it. Whatever it takes to put this behind us."

Sara felt her temper building but kept her voice steady. "What it will take is you handing me a check for two hundred thousand dollars. The money it will take to repay April for losing the studio."

Ryan looked past her to April. "Do you, at least, forgive me, April? You understand, right?"

"I understand *you,* Ryan" came April's taut response.

His brows furrowed and he turned his attention to Sara again. "I messed up. I'm sorry. I'm going to make it better."

"By writing a check?"

He sighed. "You know I can't do that."

Sara knew a lot about Ryan Thompson. They'd met when she was nineteen.

Her career had stalled; audiences did not want to see another childhood star grow into a bona fide actor. She'd had a couple of box office flops, lost roles in several Lifetime movies to former cast members of *90210* and could barely get casting directors to meet with her for even supporting roles. She'd briefly thought of applying to college until her mother had informed her that with the quality of on-set tutoring she'd received, she'd been lucky to get her GED.

Her mother, who was still managing her at the time, had come up with the brilliant idea of sending Sara to rehab for undisclosed reasons.

Although the closest she'd come to an addiction was a great affinity for Reese's cups, Sara had been legitimately exhausted for months and welcomed a break from the Hollywood rat race.

Rose thought the publicity would make people see Sara as an adult, and if they didn't get specific about an addiction, the backlash would be manageable. The whole Drew Barrymore comeback—maybe even a book deal.

It hadn't worked. At all. She'd been blacklisted by every major studio, and her stalled career had gone down the toilet completely. But she'd loved her time at the secluded facility, morning meditation classes and long walks through the desert trails. On one of those solitary walks, she'd met Ryan, a hot young director who'd blown a huge wad of his last project's budget on his gambling addiction. The producers had sent him to the Next Steps treatment facility for a month-long program. As far as Sara could tell, he was the only other patient at the center not half crazed with withdrawal symptoms or buying drugs from the cleaning crew.

They'd been fast friends and had even tried a romance for about a millisecond. Ryan was prettier than Brad Pitt in *Thelma and Louise* and higher maintenance than a full-blown diva. He loved women, could flirt the pants off the Pope's sister and was as good at monogamy as he was at staying away from the blackjack table.

They'd remained close, and while he'd had a couple of critical and box office hits, Ryan continued to be a master of self-sabotage, finding it impossible to resist the lure of Las Vegas's shiny lights.

He'd been clean a year and a half when he'd approached Sara about forming a production company together. She was at the end of her rope with bad waitressing jobs and potential projects falling through. He presented a well-thought-out business plan, complete with spreadsheets, a list of potential investors and a movie script that had *award* written all over it. One with a lead role that made Sara literally salivate with need.

She'd agreed, and for months they'd hit the pavement, calling and setting up meetings to try to make this new dream a reality. After one of the major investors backed out, Sara'd complained to April, who'd offered to take a second mortgage on her yoga studio and give the money to Sara. April had a solid client list of California high rollers and had even been offered her own DVD series working alongside one starlet yoga devotee.

At first Sara had resisted her friend's offer, but April was confident in Sara's ability to make the production company a success. April was the only person who knew that Sara had been taking classes part-time at UCLA and was close to earning a business degree.

She and April planned on franchising the studio, and April's particular brand of yoga and one hit movie could help finance the expansion. Sara saw her chance to create a career away from Hollywood that would both fulfill her and give her the respect she craved.

That was before Ryan fell off the wagon again, blowing all their money on a weekend in Vegas. In less than a month, Sara had lost her savings, her apartment, her latest job and almost her friendship with April.

Now Ryan stood in front of her, offering to *make it better*. She'd trusted him once and wouldn't make that mistake again.

"If you can't write a check, how could you possibly make anything all right again?"

"The financing is almost set. I've got a new director interested. One who wants you for the lead. He's in Aspen for a few weeks. I just need to get hold of his people and set up a meeting with the two of you." His eyes shifted to April. "I'll get your money back. All of it."

Sara shook her head. "No way. We're done, Ryan. I don't trust you. I don't want to work with you. I don't want you anywhere near me."

"Sara, please," he pleaded, his voice a soft caress just short of a whine.

"She said no, bud." Josh had been so quiet where he stood a few feet behind her, she'd almost forgotten he was there.

Almost.

"I wasn't talking to you, Roy Rogers."

Sara saw Josh's fists bunch at his sides. "Well, I'm talking to you," he said, and took a step forward.

She put up a hand. "It's okay, Josh."

She'd been friends with Ryan long enough to know the pain and regret in his eyes were real. She wouldn't admit it, but it got to her. That was Sara's problem. She was a sucker for lost causes. Having been one for so many years, she could smell desperation on a person like some people could sniff out a good barbecue.

"I'm sorry," Ryan said again.

"You didn't even call. I had to find out from your assistant."

"I went straight from the casino to another stint in rehab." He offered a sheepish smile. "I'm a little more self-aware now, at least."

"Some good it did me."

"Give me a chance, Sara."

She blew out a breath and tried to ignore Josh seething next to her. "Fine. Call me if you get a meeting."

Ryan gave her a bright smile. "That's great. I'll—"

"In the meantime, you can help out around the ranch. Aspen's not that far and I know you have time on your hands. There's lots to do before the guests arrive."

"Hell, no." Josh sliced the air with one hand. "He's a lazy, no-good, designer-jeans-wearing wimp, and he's not touching anything in my house."

Sara whirled on him. "As I remember, this is *my* house."

"You know what I mean."

"I do," she said with a sniff. "And I don't like it." She turned to Ryan. "You'll work, Ryan. And not as in making reservations. The real thing. Start paying off your debt."

The frown he gave her said he wanted to argue but knew he didn't have a leg to stand on. "Sure. I'll do it. This is a guest ranch, right? What do you need? Someone to charm the clients. A wine sommelier, perhaps?"

She grinned. "A prep cook."

"A what?"

"Someone to help April in the kitchen."

April coughed loudly. "No, no, no. I don't need him, don't want him, won't have him."

Sara studied her friend. April was the kindest person she'd ever met. She didn't have a bad word to say about anyone. She'd give the coat off her back to a complete stranger. She'd expected April to take on Ryan like another one her charity cases. After all, April had been taking care of Sara for close to a decade. April's typically peaches-and-cream complexion had gone almost beet-red, and her chest rose and fell in frustrated huffs as she glared at Ryan.

He'd cost April her business and most of her savings, but even when Sara'd first shared the awful news, April had taken it in stride. She never lost her temper or got ruffled.

Until now.

She waited for Ryan to turn on his almost irresistible charm, offer April one of his trademark lines, smooth talk her into agreeing. Instead, he looked at Josh.

"Could you use a hand with maintenance?"

Josh shook his head.

"Grass to cut?"

"Nope."

"Horse droppings to scoop?"

"Nothing."

Ryan's squeezed shut his eyes. "I can't be completely useless. I'm done with useless."

Sara threw a sharp glance in April's direction. "Come on," she mouthed silently.

April growled low in her throat. "You can help. But you'll do what I say, which mainly involves staying out of my way."

To Sara's surprise, Ryan nodded, then stepped forward and wrapped her in a tight hug. "I *am* sorry."

"Make it better with April," Sara whispered.

"She hates me."

"Do you blame her?"

"I'm a good guy. With a little problem."

"Ryan."

"I need to get back to Aspen today." He leaned back and scrubbed his hand over his face. "But I'll be back and I'll try."

Sara glanced to where April stood, but her friend was gone. "Try hard," she told Ryan. "April deserves to be happy."

He ran a finger across her cheek. "We all do."

"If you say so," she answered. They both knew she didn't mean it.

Josh watched Ryan head toward the front door. His plan had seemed so simple a few months ago. Move back to his small hometown and make a new life on this secluded property. Work at the ranch would give both he and Claire the home and stability he needed. He'd be able to forget his past, the pain of his accident and losing his career—the only thing he'd ever cared about in his life.

With enough hard work, he'd be so exhausted he wouldn't miss the smell of the arena, would stop aching for the feel of a thousand-pound bull beneath him and the adrenaline rush that came with those seconds in the ring.

With enough patience, his daughter would stop looking at him like he was the enemy.

Now he had three California misfits crowding his space. Josh didn't do people and their problems. He had friends, sure. Other bull riders who were like him, happy to spend time drinking beer and watching old footage. Once guys left the ring and made homes and families for themselves, he usually lost touch. He was a loner and liked it that way. No complications.

The woman who walked over to the picture window at the far end of the family room was the biggest complication he'd ever met. She complicated his life. What happened to his insides when he watched her was a problem he sure didn't need.

He took a few steps toward her, not close enough to smell the scent that always surrounded her—some strange mix of honey and cinnamon—sweet with a bit of kick. But close enough that she couldn't *not* be aware of him. He wanted her to notice him as much as he did her.

"Do you two have a thing going?" he asked casually.

She looked over her shoulder at him. "You mean Ryan?"

"Who else?"

"Does it matter?"

A muscle ticked at the side of his jaw. "Stop answering my questions with questions." He hooked his thumbs into his belt loops. "My thirteen-year-old daughter is right down the hall from him. I don't want her waking up to any moaning and groaning next door."

One side of her mouth kicked up. "What if Ryan's at my cabin?"

He fought the urge to growl. "I don't need a soap opera played out in front of the clients."

She turned to him fully. "I don't do soap operas." Her eyes narrowed. "What makes you think I'm a moaner?"

Only the fact he'd spent the past three nights imagining the sounds she'd make when she was in his arms, under him, wrapped around him.

He took a step closer, so near that her subtle scent surrounded him and he could feel her breath against his jaw. His fingers reached out and pushed a wayward lock of streaked hair behind her ear. He'd only meant to touch her that little bit, but she turned her cheek, ever so slightly, into his palm. Her warm skin tempted him, called to his inner need. It wasn't a fight he could possibly win.

He brought his other hand up to cradle her face, tracing the edge of her lips with a calloused thumb. Her eyes remained glued to his mouth, and as he came nearer they drifted closed.

The desire to kiss her raced through him like a runaway train, almost knocking him back with its speed and strength. He needed to know if she tasted as sweet as she smelled, if her mouth was as soft as her skin. This prickly, snappish woman who played it so tough on the outside had sparked something in him he'd never felt before. Because he had a feeling that on the inside she was soft and warm. He craved knowing that side of her.

Josh tried to pull away, but he'd never been much

for self-preservation instincts. This moment was no different.

She made a noise somewhere between a sigh and a moan.

He was a goner.

"I knew it," he whispered against her mouth.

"Why are you still talking?" she asked, her eyes dark with the same desire he knew was reflected in his.

He pressed his lips to hers. Although he'd known she'd taste amazing, he wasn't prepared for his body's reaction to her. Electricity charged through him as he brushed his tongue across the seam of her lips. He forced himself to keep the kiss gentle when what he wanted was to wrap his arms around her and carry her to his bedroom.

"I don't want to do this," she said on a ragged breath.

He stilled. "Do you want me to stop?"

"Lord help me, no." Her arms twined around his neck, drawing him closer.

What a hypocrite, to complain that his daughter might catch wind of her and Ryan when Josh was ready to get naked in front of an oversize window.

The window. Claire. The thought of Claire seeing him play tonsil hockey with Sara made him pull away from her.

"What's the matter?"

He rested his forehead on hers and drew in several steadying breaths. "Everything. This summer is about Claire. About starting over with her. A second chance."

"Second chances," she said, her voice impossibly quiet. "I get that." The next moment she pushed hard on his chest. "You know what you are, Lone Ranger?"

He shook his head as she started past him, wondering how she could go from soft and pliant to prickly in less time than he could stay on the meanest bull. "What's that, Hollywood Barbie?"

"A tease."

Fighting words. She'd probably chosen them purposely to break the spell between them, but he couldn't let it go. He grabbed her wrist and swung her around to face him. "You'd better take that back. Now."

She shook free of his grasp. "You won't let anyone in and you'll throw out any excuse in the book so you don't have to." Her eyes glinted, daring him to argue.

His gaze locked on hers, and he let her see how much he craved her. Her breath caught. She took a small step back.

"Do you want in, Sara? Really?"

She looked at a point past his shoulder for a few moments, and when her eyes finally found his, she shook her head. "I want out. Out of Colorado. Out of debt. Out of owing people."

The right answer for both of them, Josh knew, but a sliver of pain sliced across his chest. He wasn't the kind of man women took a chance on. He had nothing to offer except a wild night between the sheets and a wave in the morning.

Even if she didn't know it, he could tell Sara needed a man who would stick.

Joe Hollywood upstairs wasn't it, but neither was Josh.

"It's better this way," she told him. "No complications."

Right.

She tapped her fingers against her jaw as if deep in

thought. "I don't like you that much anyway," she said finally. "You're not my type."

"Could you stop waving red flags in front of me?" He dug his hands deep into his pockets to keep from reaching out to her again. Every time she made some kind of ridiculous comment, he itched to prove her wrong. Over and over again.

As if sensing his intentions, she took another step away. "Sorry. No red flags. I have some voice mails to return, so I'll see you later. Or not. Probably not."

"Are we still in good shape?"

Her brow arched.

"Bookings," he clarified. "Guests. Good shape with actually making money this summer." He hadn't wanted to turn the office side of the ranch over to her, but as the start of the season got closer, it became harder to balance the preparations on the property with the work involved in making reservations and talking to potential customers. Sara had insisted that customer service was her strong suit, and despite her sassy attitude with him, so far she'd been a whiz. In less than a week, she'd organized the jumble of paperwork in the office, confirmed their current reservations and followed up with a half-dozen prospective clients.

The best part was that Josh's cell phone, where he'd had the office calls forwarded, had stopped ringing every ten minutes. He'd actually been able to get a lot of projects done. He felt almost ready for guests to arrive.

"We're in better than good shape. I just confirmed a family reunion for six nights at the end of June. There's only one weekend in July still open and August is full." She studied him. "You did an excellent job with the marketing. I guess there was a write-up in *Sunset* magazine recommending the ranch. That's quite a bit of publicity."

He shrugged. "I know an editor there."

She leaned in closer. "Must be an ex-girlfriend because you're blushing."

"I don't blush."

That elicited a full-blown laugh. "If you say so."

The sound of her laughter flowed through him. He grinned back at her. The moment grew quiet again, just the two of them watching each other. The heat in his cheeks took a nosedive south.

She blinked and her lips thinned. "I'm going to the office now."

"Gotcha."

"Don't follow me."

He tipped his head. "Wouldn't dream of it."

She headed for the other side of the house and the two rooms he'd converted to central operations with a little too much speed for a natural gait.

It looked as if she was running away.

Good. Maybe that would save them both.

Chapter 5

The crash from the floor above made Sara jump out of her seat. She rubbed her eyes and bent to retrieve the stack of papers that had spilled off the desk.

After spending the past few days buried in the office or driving back and forth to town for supplies before the first guests arrived, her eyes felt like sandpaper and her back ached. The time sequestered away from everyone was necessary, she told both herself and April, who'd brought trays of food into the office at regular intervals. For the most part, April had kept her opinion to herself, only dropping one or two pointed questions about the real reason Sara was in self-induced isolation.

Sara wasn't ready to admit she was avoiding anyone in particular. Definitely not Josh. Or Ryan, with his continuous stream of apologies and the puppy-dog eyes he kept shooting her.

Another loud thud came from upstairs, this one actually shaking the framed pictures on the office walls. It had to be Ryan, Sara thought with an accompanying curse. He must know she was working, and she guessed this was his ploy for her attention. She'd convinced herself it wasn't going to work until the telltale clatter of glass breaking reverberated through the ceiling.

She muttered another curse and stalked up the stairs. As she made her way down the hall, the sound of muffled crying came from behind one of the closed doors. Claire's room.

Sara knocked softly, then peeked in when no one answered.

"Claire, are you okay?"

Claire sat on the floor at the foot of the bed, her head resting against knees drawn tight to her chest. "Go away," she whispered, her voice clearly pained.

Good idea, Sara thought. That was exactly what she wanted to do, retreat back to her own office and not get involved in one more person's life. Her gaze caught on the nightstand that had been knocked on its side. That explained the crash. Next to the broken lamp was a framed photo, broken glass surrounding it. Claire smiled from the picture, cradled in the arms of a woman—a drop-dead gorgeous woman—who seemed vaguely familiar.

Sara stepped into the room for a closer look. She recognized Jennifer Holmes, international supermodel. In the past decade, Jennifer had graced the covers of countless fashion magazines and several Victoria's Secret catalogs.

"Is this your mother?" she asked, carefully lifting the frame from the carpet. "She's beautiful." She found a wastebasket beside the dresser and dumped the pieces of glass into it.

"I hate her," Claire mumbled. "She doesn't care about me at all."

"From this picture, she looks like she does."

"Duh." Claire lifted her tearstained face. "She's a supermodel. She can make herself look however she wants for a camera. That isn't real."

Sara knew there could be a big difference between what the camera showed and reality. "What makes you think she doesn't care? Tell me what's real, Claire."

The girl stared at her for several seconds, mouth pressed tight together. Then her eyes filled with tears. "What's real is that she's on some yacht in France with her new rock-star boyfriend. She told me she was getting help. For her drinking and stuff. She's supposed to be putting her life back together so I can live with her again." Claire sucked in a ragged breath, her words spilling forth like the tears that ran down her face. "And she's not. She won't. She doesn't care."

"Maybe she's—"

"I saw it on a gossip website. Pictures of her in a bikini with a guy's hand on her butt. I called her cell phone. She tried to tell me she was at the rehab place." Claire stood and flopped onto the bed. "*After* I saw the website. She's a liar. I asked her if I could come to where she was and she said no. She needs a break." Claire hiccupped and swiped at her cheeks. "A break from *me*."

Sara's heart melted. "Claire, I'm sorry—"

"I hate it here. I don't know anyone. I don't have any friends. Dad act likes we're going to do all this bonding, but he's always working. He barely says two words to me when he's around. It's like he doesn't know what to talk about." She shook her head. "How can I be so bad that neither of my parents want to be around me?"

"Oh, honey." Sara sat down next to the bed and wrapped one arm around the girl's shaking shoulder. Claire stayed stiff and then, with a sigh, sank against Sara.

"It's me," she repeated.

"It's absolutely not you." Sara gave Claire's arm a gentle squeeze. "I know for a fact that your dad loves you very much. He works so hard so he can make the ranch into a home for the two of you."

"It's not going to be much of home when you sell it," Claire said miserably.

Touché, Sara thought with a mental groan. "Whatever happens," she answered without addressing Claire's comment, "he wants to be with you. He's trying to do what's best because of you."

"He doesn't even like to be around me."

Sara squeezed her eyes shut, thinking of the love, longing and confusion in Josh's eyes when he looked at his daughter. "How long did your dad ride bulls?"

"I don't know. Forever," Claire mumbled. "I think since he was like seventeen or something."

"That's only a few years older than you. And how old was he when you were born?"

"Eighteen. My mom was, too."

"Yeah, well. Take it from someone who knows— young parents don't always know what they're doing. Your dad is trying. That has to count for something."

"Was your mom young when you were born?"

"Nineteen." Claire sniffed, and Sara dug in her pocket for a tissue. "Here, use this."

Claire blew hard then said, "She's really pretty. Your mom. She came to the ranch a few weeks ago. Tried to kick Dad and me out."

"That sounds like Mom."

"Are you close with her?"

Sara laughed softly. "Not exactly. You're changing the subject."

"I'm good at that." Claire shifted away from Sara and smiled a little.

"Me, too." Sara reached out a finger and ran it along Claire's cheek. "Have you talked to your dad about how hard it's been here for you?"

Claire shook her head. "I can't."

Sara watched her without answering.

"I don't want to make it a big deal. I guess it's not that bad," Claire said with a sigh. "I mean, I like the mountains. And how the air smells. Like it's..."

"So clean it almost hurts," Sara finished.

"Exactly." Claire picked at an invisible spot on her jeans. "And Brandon's okay."

"The kid who helps your dad in the barn?"

"He's fifteen. His family owns the property across the highway. He's kind of nice."

"And cute."

Claire looked up, pink coloring her cheeks as she met Sara's gaze. "Do you think so?"

"He's got those great big blue eyes, right?"

Claire sighed. "And that smile. He'll actually talk to me. But he's got a girlfriend, I think."

"You can still hang out when he's here. Just friends. I bet your dad would love an extra hand in the barn."

"I don't know anything about horses."

"Just like he doesn't know anything about what

teenage girls are into. It's up to you, but I know your dad does care about you. He wants you around. That counts for something. Maybe if you seemed interested in something he knew about, it could help with that bonding you mentioned."

"I wouldn't be in the way?"

Sara smiled. "April and I get in the way. Ryan is always in the way. You're the one Josh wants around."

"I think he wants you around, too," Claire said softly, then asked, "Is Ryan your boyfriend?"

"Absolutely not."

"Do you have a boyfriend?"

"Nope."

"Do you want one?"

Josh's face came to mind, and Sara tried to ignore the shiver that curled through her belly at the thought of his mouth on hers. "I've given up on men."

Claire studied her, looking suddenly older than her thirteen years. "Aren't you a little young for that?"

"I'm twenty-eight. That's like one-foot-in-the-grave time in Hollywood."

Claire nodded as if she understood. "My mom turned thirty-one last year. That's when she started to freak out. Party more. She gets Botox and some other wacky stuff." Claire stood and looked in the mirror above the dresser, pinching two fingers to the bridge of her nose. "She said I could have my nose done as a sweet sixteen gift. That'll be cool. I might look a little more like her and she'll…"

Sara turned Claire to face her. "Listen to me. You are perfect the way you are. Plastic surgery isn't going to change your relationship with your mother."

"You don't know—"

"I do know. I spent years jumping through hoops to win my mother's approval. Guess what? Never happened. Maybe it never will. I hope it does for you, Claire. I hope your mom gets healthy and realizes how precious you are to her. Until then, I know your dad loves you. Even if he isn't great at showing you how much."

"I just want to fit in here," Claire said miserably, her green eyes, so like Josh's, welling again.

"I know, sweetie."

"Would you take me shopping sometime?" Claire asked. "None of my clothes are right for Colorado, you know?"

Sara thought about the women in Feathers and Floss. "Are you looking for Wranglers and studded belt buckles?"

"No." Claire laughed. "Just clothes to hang out in. If you don't have time, I understand."

Sara gave her a quick hug. "I have time. How about before the weekend? I'll drive us down to Denver. We can make it a girls' day out. Go to lunch. Get our nails done."

"Really?"

"Of course, I may only be able to afford one sock, but we'll do our best."

"Dad has money. I could ask if we can use his credit card."

Sara almost choked from laughing so hard. "I bet he'd love that." She pushed the hair off Claire's innocent face. "I pay my own way. But, heck, yeah, we'll get his card for you. A shopping trip is one thing dads are always good for."

"Was your dad good for that kind of stuff?"

Sara's father had been a nameless stuntman on one of her mother's B movies. An on-set fling for Rose, who hadn't even told him she was pregnant and had never shared his identity with Sara.

"I don't know my father."

"Oh. I guess it's good that Josh wants me to live with him anyway."

"He doesn't like it when you call him Josh."

Claire grinned. "I know."

"How much did you see him before this summer?"

"A couple of times a year when he had time off from the tour. He'd come to my school and take me out to dinner. He sent me presents from the road. Lots of stuffed animals and things like that. I'd never been to the rodeo until…" Claire wrapped her arms tight around her chest. "The accident was my fault. Did you know that?"

Sara had read a half-dozen articles about the horrific accident that had ended Josh's career. It still made her sick to her stomach to think about the images she'd seen on YouTube. But none of the reports had mentioned Claire. "Why do you say that?"

"I was there." Claire scrunched up her face. "Mom was having a bad time. It was winter break and she was stuck with me. She found out there was an event a few days before Christmas and flew us both down there. I think she wanted to dump me with him for the holidays. She didn't tell him we were coming. Right before he came out of the gate, he looked up and saw me. It broke his concentration." Claire drew in a shaky breath. "They let the bull go right at that moment and…" Her voice broke off as she shook her head. "The whole arena was silent when it happened. I thought he was dead. The bull was so big and it landed right on him."

"Claire." Sara drew the girl into another tight hug. Sara had been through some bad stuff as a kid, but this poor girl gave her a run for her money in the bad-childhood department.

"They took him to the hospital straight from the event. I didn't see him again until he showed up on the last day of spring semester." Claire wiped her cheek against Sara's sleeve. "If I hadn't been there, he'd still be riding."

"It wasn't your fault," Sara whispered against the girl's head. "It was a terrible accident. But not your fault. Not your fault."

"But I—"

"Have you and your dad talked about what happened?"

Claire didn't answer.

"I'm sure he doesn't blame you."

"He should."

"You need to talk to him."

"No," Claire whispered. "I don't want to hear him tell me I ruined his life."

Josh sagged onto the wall outside his daughter's bedroom and swallowed against the bile that rose in his throat. He'd come to find her minutes ago but stopped short when he'd heard her conversation with Sara.

He didn't blame Claire for the accident. His break in concentration was his own fault. He'd been riding bulls long enough to know his focus should be zeroed in on the thousand pounds of angry animal between his legs. But when he'd seen Claire, he'd been thrown. Literally and figuratively.

Apparently, they'd both paid a price for his lapse in focus.

In his mind, he'd hoped she hadn't seen much or understood how bad it had been. Hoped her mother would whisk her away before she realized how serious it was. Jennifer had probably been too tipsy to understand the extent of the damage. But not Claire.

He had a hazy memory of trying to smile even as he felt his leg shatter, thinking that if his daughter could see him he didn't want to frighten her. He hadn't wanted her to know how scared he had been. Even now, that thought kept him rooted to his spot in the hall when his heart knew he should be the one with his arms around her, comforting and soothing her.

He'd waited until he could hide his injury before he'd come to see her, thinking that would be easier for both of them. Since he'd brought her to the ranch, sometimes he'd catch her staring at his right knee, especially toward the end of the day when exhaustion and overuse made it more difficult to hide his slight limp.

He wanted to be strong for her, not weak and half-broken. Bending forward, he rubbed at his leg, willing the pain to go away. He straightened and thumped on the wall as he walked to the end of the hall. "Claire," he called, coming back toward her room. "Are you up here?"

He made some more noise before poking his head in her room. She sat on the edge of the bed with Sara next to her. While she smiled at him, her eyes were red and puffy from her tears. "Hey, Dad," she said cheerfully, a sure sign that things were very wrong.

Sara watched him as if his face gave away the fact that he'd been eavesdropping. Impossible, he thought, but kept his gaze on Claire. "It's a gorgeous day," he said to his daughter. "I thought we could take an ATV up to Bitter Creek Pass, check on the trails and maybe have lunch."

Her smile faded. "I don't think so."

He took a breath and made his tone light. "Come on. It'll be fun. Just you and me and a ton of horsepower."

She scrunched up her nose. "Those things are so loud and they go really fast."

"That's supposed to be the fun part," he said, trying not to sound frustrated.

He let his eyes drift to Sara, who looked at him with a hint of sympathetic smile. "Can I come, too?" she asked.

As much as his body ached to be near Sara, part of him was angry his daughter had confided her pain to someone besides him. And he wanted her to know it. "There's only room for two on the ATVs, Hollywood."

"Einstein in a Stetson, aren't you? Thanks for pointing that out. I was thinking I'd have my own four-wheeler."

Her attitude made him grin despite himself. "You think you can handle it?"

She matched his smile. "Oh, yeah. I can handle it."

Claire cleared her throat, and Sara turned that million-watt grin on his daughter. "What do you say? I bet I can beat you and your old man to the top of the pass."

"He's knows a lot about ATVs."

Sara tossed her hair. "I'm not scared of his ego."

Claire gave a tiny giggle. "We're going to kick your butt," she said quietly.

"Oh, smack talk," Sara said with a loud laugh. "Guess the cowboy isn't the only one in the Travers family with a healthy ego. I love it. I'll help April pack a lunch while you two get the equipment ready."

Claire popped up off the bed and took two steps before Josh saw her realize her part of the deal. She slowed, dragging one bare foot across the carpet. "I guess that would be okay."

Josh didn't wait for her to change her mind. "Let's go, then," he said, hoping he sounded enthusiastic and not as scared as he was to mess up this chance with her. "We'll make sure Sara gets the slow one," he added in a stage whisper.

"Dad, that's not fair." Claire wiggled a finger at him.

"Right. Sorry."

"I mean, we're going to beat her bad enough as it is." Claire's eyes danced as she grinned at him and his heart skipped a beat. Her smile was so like his sister, Beth's. A smile he missed like he missed riding.

"You bet we are," he agreed, and motioned her to lead him out the door.

As she walked past, he met Sara's gaze. She arched a brow.

"Thank you," he mouthed.

Instead of the sassy comeback he expected, she only nodded and shooed him after Claire.

Chapter 6

"Get her!" Claire yelled in his ear over the roar of the four-wheeler's motor. "She's killing us."

Josh smiled as he hit the gas. He watched Sara's jeans stretch tight across her perfect bottom as she leaned into a turn on the narrow trail. He couldn't muster one bit of temper at getting his butt kicked by Hollywood Barbie. He was simply having too much fun racing up the mountain with his daughter's laughter filling him and her small arms wrapped around his waist as though she was totally comfortable in the moment. As though she trusted him.

He pushed hard on the throttle because the one thing Claire trusted him to do right now was catch up to Sara.

This day was another revelation about Sara. He'd expected her to be hesitant and unsure on the ATV, since she said she'd never ridden one before. But after a few minutes of instruction and warm-up, she took off on the dirt road that led from the property to the forest service trail as though she'd spent her life on the mountain.

Between the pain in his leg and Claire's extra weight behind him, it had taken Josh longer to find his groove. By that time, Sara was at least three hundred yards ahead of them.

She looked back over her shoulder, and her grin widened, hair escaping its ponytail under the helmet to whirl around her neck. He felt something unfamiliar around his stomach as he followed her, the powerful ATV vibrating under him, and realized it was happiness—an emotion he hadn't experienced in far too long.

Most of his last two years on the PBR tour had been spent defending his title and reputation from a new crop of upstarts willing to risk life and limb for a steady paycheck and an adrenaline rush. Green kids, the same as Josh had been when he'd first gone pro, with nothing to hold him down or back in his quest for fame and what little fortune there was to be had in the arena. Years on the back of a bull had taken its toll on his mind and body. He still felt the repercussions as he maneuvered around a fallen log, his back screaming as his knee throbbed.

"We're gaining on her," Claire yelled in his ear. "Go, Dad, go! You can do it!"

A surge of power coursed through him. Who needed Advil when he had his daughter's confidence?

"Hold on tight," he answered, and took a sharp left onto a single-track trail invisible to anyone unfamiliar with this mountain.

They sped along rocks and exposed roots. Hundred-year-old pine trees rose on either side of the trail, the smell of the woods thick and warm on this beautiful afternoon. It reminded him of all the reasons he'd come here with his daughter, why he believed—with enough time and patience—this place could heal them both.

Claire let out a delighted screech and Josh's smile spread. "Almost there."

He made another turn and the forest cleared. They raced into a high country meadow, bathed in sunlight. The Rocky Mountain peaks towered in the background, their tips still covered in snow. At this altitude, Josh still felt a slight chill to the air as he slowed the ATV in the middle of the clearing.

Claire hopped off and looked around. "We did it," she screamed.

At the same moment, Sara's four-wheeler came into view. She stood up from her seat as she got closer, shock and amusement clear on her face.

Skidding to a stop in front of them, she cut the engine and sank back onto the machine, gasping for breath. "How in the world did you beat me?" she asked with a laugh.

"Shortcut," he answered simply.

Claire danced a circle around Sara's ATV. "We won, we won," she chanted, and did a complicated series of dance moves that made Josh smile.

"Nice work." Sara gave Josh a small nod as she climbed off the machine. "You did good."

Another surprise.

Josh didn't often encounter good sportsmanship, so he expected at least a little pouting or fuss. Nothing. It was like she didn't care a bit about winning. For so long Josh had been focused on competing it was hard to change gears and enjoy something just for the fun of it.

Sara seemed to appreciate his daughter's buoyant mood as much as he did. Claire wrapped her arms around her. "That was awesome!"

"It sure was." She released Claire after a long hug, and Josh watched her take in the scene in front of them. She sucked in a breath. "Wow. This is amazing."

"Yes, it is," Josh agreed, but continued to watch her.

Sensation rippled across Sara's stomach as she felt his gaze. She was careful not to look at him, afraid of what she'd see in his stormy sea eyes and what her own might reveal. She prided herself on staying in control of her emotions, and had the hard-won walls around her heart to prove it. But she'd left that self-possession somewhere on the mountain and needed a few moments to regain it.

She turned a circle to see the full meadow view, then took another deep breath and closed her eyes. Her whole body tingled from the excitement of the ride. Yep, she told herself, it was an adrenaline rush and nothing more. Not her reaction to Josh.

Not at all.

It had been years since she'd let herself go all out like she had on the mountain. She'd left the world and its troubles behind and simply felt free.

When was the last time she'd truly felt free? She honestly couldn't answer that question.

Still not trusting her emotions, she busied herself removing a backpack from the rack of the ATV. "I've got sandwiches and drinks here," she called over her shoulder.

"I'm spreading the blanket," Claire answered from the middle of the meadow.

"Is everything okay?"

Josh's voice so close to her made Sara practically leap out of her skin. "Good gravy," she said, thumping her heart with one hand. "Sneak up on a person much?"

"Avoid eye contact much?" he countered.

Sara knew a challenge when she heard it but didn't rise to the bait. "I'm trying to help out, you know, get your kid fed."

He spun her around to look at him and lifted her sunglasses onto her head. Her eyelids fluttered shut as his finger traced her eyelashes. "You left off the heavy makeup today. It's nice."

She batted at his hand. "I should have known you'd be a sucker for plain Janes. Trust me, I won't tempt you again."

"There is nothing plain about you, Hollywood." His voice was a caress that made her insides warm and gooey. She swayed just a little. "Besides which, you tempt me each and every time I lay eyes on you. Now, tell me what's going on."

"Nothing," she said, an obvious lie. "I'm just a little light-headed, probably the altitude. Food will help."

"This is why I want the ranch to work."

She stared at him. "To make people sick?"

His mouth twitched but his eyes remained serious. "To take them out of their comfort zone," he said, dropping his arms to spread his hands wide. "These mountains change people. Inspire them. Make them see the world and their place in it in a different light. Sometimes there's no other way."

She nodded, although she didn't know if he was

talking generally or about her in particular. Either way, she understood down to her soul what he meant.

"I want to do that for the people coming here. When someone books a trip with us, it's not like heading to Disney World or Fort Lauderdale at spring break. It means something. To them. To me."

"I get it," she answered automatically, taken aback at his emotion.

"Do you? Do you understand how precious these mountains are? How few truly wild places there are left in this country? I want to celebrate that, help people appreciate it."

"A cowboy environmentalist?" Her lame attempt to lighten the moment fell flat.

He shook his head in clear frustration. "Do you think your mother's fast-talking boyfriend is going to give a rat's behind about the beauty of this place when he builds his luxury condos?"

"Rich people can have breakthroughs, too, you know."

"Not with what he has planned. Have you seen them? The plans?"

"No."

"He's going to level the trees that surround your grandmother's house. Put in a competition-size swimming pool under a huge bubble. Sure, he'll have a couple miles of paved trails—wouldn't want to scuff your running shoes on actual dirt."

"He's not going to demolish the entire forest," she argued.

"It changes things, Sara. Crimson is special. We don't need another Aspen-type playground for the rich and famous. Can't you see that?"

She did see it, but the knowledge left her in a precarious position. "What I see is that I need money and Richard Hamish has it. I haven't sold yet. You still have time, the entire season, to line up financing. But if not, you know what I have to do."

He crossed his arms over his chest. "Spoken like a true Californian."

"Was that the reason you let me come today, to prove some kind of point?" Despite her rising anger, her heart hammered in her chest anticipating his answer.

He stared at her, then sighed and said, "No. I wanted you to see this because it's amazing and breathtaking. I thought you'd like it. Both you and Claire." Reaching out, his thumb trailed across the skin exposed above the collar of her V-neck sweatshirt. "I wanted you here."

She itched for a fight, a reason to funnel her traitorous emotions into anger. She needed to pull away, from this man and his daughter, from the house that her grandmother had loved. The place that, despite her best efforts, Sara had quickly come to consider home. The honesty of his response and the warmth in his gaze melted away her defenses, and she felt herself more drawn to him than ever.

Her hand lifted to his, her fingers rubbing his calloused palm. "Let's focus on that, okay? Just for now. Can you do that? We'll have lunch, make Claire happy and deal with the rest later."

Her own version of a peace offering.

He lifted her fingers to his mouth and rubbed his lips across her knuckles. Butterflies flitted along her spine in response. "Later," he murmured.

Somehow she didn't think he was talking about their problems.

Which scared her even more.

* * *

Sara left Josh and Claire in the equipment garage two hours later and brought the backpacks into the kitchen to clean up. The afternoon had been perfect, relaxed and easy, with dad and daughter actually having a real conversation about Claire's homesickness for her old friends. Josh had suggested setting up Skype on the office computer so Claire could stay in touch, which had made Claire happy.

Neither had brought up Claire's mother or her dubious summer activities. The question remained what would happen once school started. But that was another issue to deal with later. And not hers, she reminded herself.

She couldn't quite wipe the grin off her face and was relieved April didn't seem to be around to ask questions about the afternoon. She bent forward to put the leftover apples back into the fridge.

"You're avoiding me."

At the sound of the voice, Sara jumped, banging her head on the top of the refrigerator. "Then take a hint, Ryan," she said, rubbing the bump.

"We need to talk." He stood, one hip hitched up on the counter, wearing a wrinkled polo shirt, cargo shorts and flip-flops.

"I don't think so." She pointed at his feet. "What kind of help can you be on a ranch wearing those?"

"I had a meeting in Aspen earlier." He raised a brow. "Besides, I saw you take off with Josh. Looks like I'm not the only one playing hooky today."

She blew out a breath. "He wanted to take Claire for a ride. It made her more comfortable if I came, too."

"You're still as much of an addict as me, Sara."

"I was in that rehab center for publicity and you know it. I am *not* an addict."

"I'm not talking drugs or alcohol. People and their problems. You're addicted to fixing other people's issues. Makes it easier to ignore your own."

"You're crazy."

"Tell me why you're here."

"Because this house belongs to me now," she said, holding tight to the refrigerator door handle but unsure why she needed the support. "I can make more money from a successful season than a bust."

"And what will you do then?"

"Repay April the money that you gambled away. Finally start the yoga center she wants."

"Her dream. Her problem."

"She's my friend, Ryan. The only one who's stuck with me all these years. And I want to run a business. I want to *do* something. Something real. Can't you get that?"

"Read for the part. That's real. Do you really think you can go back to L.A. and run an exercise studio? Cater to whatever star of the week flounces through the front door looking to use yoga as a front for her latest eating disorder?"

Her eyes narrowed. "It would sure beat waiting tables and clearing up their plates of barely touched food."

"You're an actress, Sara. It's in your blood. You have something to prove still. I know it. Don't give up on your dream."

"Acting wasn't my dream, Ryan. That one belonged to my mother." It was true, but so was his comment about Sara having something to prove. She hated that her career had fizzled so publicly. If she'd been able to walk away on her own terms, with some of her pride intact…well, maybe that would have made a difference. She didn't know. What could she do about it now? Read for a part and open herself up to more ridicule? She'd swallowed loads of that in the past and wasn't sure she could stomach any more.

"Your mother's here right now."

Her gaze flicked to Ryan's face. He looked guilty and sheepish. "Why?" she said on a growl.

"To help you. Sell this place to her boyfriend. He tells me he made you a pretty good offer."

"It's not worth what he plans to do to this place. It was my grandmother's house, Ryan. Her home. I may not have known her well, but I have to respect what she built here. I can't let it be destroyed without at least trying to save it."

Her mind strayed to the photo album on the dresser upstairs and the genuine smile on her eight-year-old face sitting on that porch swing. She thought about the pure joy she'd felt racing through the forest earlier, the way the mountain peaks felt like they cradled this valley and the peace it brought her. A feeling she hadn't known for years, if ever.

Ryan's voice broke through her reverie. "He wants the property, Sara. He's going to get it one way or another."

"Not from me." Sara didn't have much to hold on to in her life, but that feeling of peace was worth fighting for. She wouldn't give it up. She glanced at the doorway to the family room. "Is she waiting?"

"In the office."

She released her death grip on the refrigerator, flexing her cramped fingers. "Put some decent shoes on and go find April. Whatever she's doing, I'm sure she can use some help."

Ryan's full mouth twisted. "She doesn't like me."

"Do you blame her?"

"I'm a cad. That's my deal. But women still like me. They can't help themselves. She's different."

Sara stifled a laugh. "I can't believe you just said that line out loud. This isn't the nineteenth century. *I'm a cad.* So what? You can't flirt and charm your way out of what you did to April. This time you may have to actually work at making things better." She paused. "Trust me, Ryan. It's worth it."

He scrubbed his hand over his face. "Fine. You deal with your mother. I'll face the wrath of the hippie princess."

"You're so brave." Sara patted his cheek as she passed him.

He held on to her wrist. "I really am sorry, Sara."

"I know. Now go make it better." She slipped from his grasp and walked out of the kitchen, hesitating at the doorway to the office.

Go make it better.

Could she take her own advice? Was it possible to make better all the things that were wrong in her relationship with her mother? Did she even want to try? Since her career had gotten so far off track, Sara hadn't seen Rose often. She'd quickly tired of the never-ending litany of advice and criticism. Without the spotlight, Sara didn't have much to offer her mother. Rose was a stage mother in the worst sense of the word—Sara could give Lindsay Lohan or Brooke Shields a definite run for their money in the bad-mama department.

As awful and contentious as their relationship had become, some part of Sara still craved her mother's approval. That knowledge upset her more than anything. The fact that Rose could still send her into a tailspin with a well-chosen dig or subtle jab ate at her self-confidence before either of them spoke a word.

Laughter rang down to where she stood. Not her mother's voice. Claire. Sara took the steps two at a time but slowed in the hallway outside Claire's bedroom.

"That's right, dear," she heard her mother say. "Look over your shoulder. Just the hint of a smile. Make them want more of you."

Sara's stomach lurched. She'd listened to that same litany of advice for years. Before every Hollywood event, premier or even trip to the mall Rose had coached her on what to wear and how to carry herself. According to Rose, being an actress was a 24/7 occupation. Sara had never been allowed to be truly off. Even now she'd catch herself doing an unconscious hair toss when someone recognized her. Maybe the training had served her well, she thought, as it was the one thing that had made her hold her head high in the face of many moments of ridicule.

But that had nothing to do with Claire.

"What are you doing?" she asked, bracing one hand against the door frame.

Claire beamed at her. "Auntie Rose is giving me lessons on how to be a star." The girl breathed the word *star* with such reverence it made Sara's teeth hurt.

"Auntie Rose?" She flashed a pointed glance at her mother.

"Do you know who Claire's mother is?" Rose asked by way of an answer.

Sara nodded and tried not to roll her eyes.

"Jennifer Holmes, the supermodel," she answered anyway. "The girl has an *in*. You know how much that can help, Sara. How my fame opened doors for you."

Give me a break, Sara thought to herself. "Claire doesn't need doors opened for her, Mom. She's thirteen."

"I know it's a late start." Rose walked around the desk and stood next to Claire, running one finger along her cheek. "But look at her bone structure. She was meant to be on screen. The camera will love her. I have a friend over at Disney. They're always looking for the next big thing." She tipped Claire's face to hers. "You could be it. Can you sing?"

"I think so," Claire said, looking dazed.

"Mom! Stop." Sara stepped forward and pulled Claire away from Rose. "She has a life here. A good, normal life. She's not going to California or anywhere with you. Leave her alone."

"Just because you crashed and burned…" her mother began.

At the same time Claire asked, "Don't you think I'm good enough?"

Sara squeezed her eyes shut and tried to block out the sharp stab of pain Rose's words caused. She focused on Claire. "Honey, of course you'd be amazing. That's not the point. It isn't all fun and glamour. It's not a good place sometimes. There are a lot of bad people in show business." She threw a glare at Rose. "People who only care about themselves."

"Maybe it would give me something in common with my mom. If I was famous she might come be with me instead of…" Her voice trailed off and she swiped under her eyes.

"Oh, Claire." Sara enveloped in her in a tight hug. "Why are you doing this?" she asked her mother over Claire's shoulder.

Rose smiled sweetly. "I came here today to talk to you about this house. Richard wants to stay in Colorado until you decide to sell. I need a something to keep me busy. Claire is a lovely girl. Maybe she's it."

Sara's throat tightened. "Leave her alone, Mom."

"You know how to get rid of me," Rose said softly, and tapped the corner of the bed where a stack of paperwork sat. "Are you ready to sign?"

Chapter 7

Sara swallowed against the lump of regret balled in her throat. She'd spent years avoiding Rose, and now she wanted nothing more than to get rid of her mother. But not at the expense of her grandmother's dream. Selling would be simple and give her the money she desperately needed to repay April and get her own second chance.

Yet what would it cost her soul?

She'd given up on so much in her life, compromised her hopes and values to make life easier. She was done running from the hard stuff or letting other people bully her. If nothing else, being in Colorado had made her see that she could live life on her own terms. She had something to contribute. Her mother wasn't going to rob her of that so soon.

"I'm not selling, Mom. Not now. Not to Richard."

Rose's delicately arched eyebrows lifted. "Well, then—"

"And you're not spending any more time here. I want you to leave."

"This was my childhood home, Sara." Rose dabbed at the corner of one eye.

"You hated it here. Counted the moments until you could leave. I know the story by heart, so don't try to change it."

Her mother's eyes narrowed briefly. "You always were an ungrateful child," she said on a huff of breath. "Because of me you had every opportunity to succeed."

"Because of you I didn't have a childhood."

"Don't be dramatic, Serena."

"I quit being dramatic years ago, Mother. Now I'm trying for normal."

"Normal is boring."

"I'll take that, too."

Rose made a sound somewhere between a sigh and a growl. She wrapped one arm around Claire's small shoulders. "I'm so looking forward to getting to know you better, dear," she said, and flashed a smile at Sara. "I'll make a few calls to agents this week, then see if I can find a decent photographer to do some head shots of you. I bet the camera will love you the way it does your mother."

"That would be great."

Sara opened her mouth to argue but before she could get a word out, Josh appeared next to her. "There won't be any photographers or agents for my daughter, Ms. Wells." His voice was controlled, but Sara could see a muscle tick in his jaw.

Her mother's smile broadened. "Mr. Travers, how

nice of you to join us. Have you been listening from the hallway?"

"Long enough to know this discussion is finished, ma'am. And I'd appreciate if you'd stop filling my daughter's head with your celebrity mumbo-jumbo."

"She has star potential," Rose cooed.

"I believe Sara asked you to leave."

"Daddy, don't be rude," Claire said, crossing her arms across her chest. "Sara's mom wants to help me."

"You don't need her kind of help."

Tears welled in Claire's wide eyes. "You don't understand anything," she yelled, and tore past Josh, her angry footfalls echoing from the stairs.

Rose pressed her soft pink lips together. "Well, that's unfortunate. How do you think her mother would feel about a chance at Claire making it in the big time?"

Josh felt his blood turn from boiling to ice-cold. He knew exactly how Jennifer would feel—thrilled about an opportunity to meet bigger Hollywood A-listers and score better drugs. While Claire's mother was still one of the most beautiful women in the world, she'd lately gotten more press for her partying than her photo spreads. She'd even lost her contract as the face of one of the big cosmetic companies because of her extracurricular activities.

The only saving grace was that the further she spiraled out of control, the less Jennifer took an interest in Claire. Josh planned to go back to court and file for sole custody once the ranch was stable and profitable. He didn't figure Jen would fight him, but that would change if she thought Claire was useful to her.

He took a step toward Rose. "Stay away from my

daughter and out of my family's business," he commanded, not trying to hide his anger.

To her credit, the older woman didn't flinch. "It's too bad you're building your business in a house that should rightfully belong to me." She tapped one finger against her mouth, a slight smile playing at her lips. "Claire really is lovely. Plus she has a budding flair for the dramatic. I like that in a girl."

Sara moved in front of him before he could wrap his hands around Rose's birdlike throat. "Enough, Mother. The house belongs to me. I'm telling you to leave. Now."

Rose backed away, palms up. "I can take a hint, honey. But I'll be back. One way or another, mark my words."

"This isn't *The Terminator,* Mom." Sara leaned in and said softly, "Are you so desperate to keep your boyfriend that you'll stoop this low this to get what you want? I always thought you had a replacement guy waiting in the wings. I guess things get tougher as you age. How sad."

Josh watched Rose's perfectly bronzed cheeks turn a deep shade of pink. "I don't know what I did to deserve such an awful daughter," she said with a sputter. "I gave up everything for you and this is how you repay me? You were a horrible, colicky baby and a demanding child. You couldn't even make something of the career I practically gift wrapped for you. Does it make you happy to watch your own mother struggle when we both know you could help me if you wanted to? You make me sick."

He saw Sara's sharp intake of breath as Rose stormed past them both, slamming the door shut in her wake.

"Okay, then," Sara whispered after several moments, her back still to him. "That was fun and a great trip down memory lane." She said the last with a laugh that caught in her throat and turned into a strangled sob.

Josh reached for her and slowly turned her so she was facing him. His gut twisted at the tears that filled her eyes. "I'm sorry," he told her. "You don't deserve that."

She shook her head. "I'm the one who's sorry. That she's giving you so much trouble. For ideas she may have put into Claire's head." She swiped her hands across her face. "I'll do whatever it takes to make sure she doesn't corrupt Claire, Josh. She's an amazing girl. I know you only want what's best for her."

He trailed a thumb across a stray tear that ran down her cheek. "Even if I'm an idiot about knowing how to talk to my own daughter?"

She sniffed. "All men are idiots sometimes." Holding up her fingertips, she cringed. "I can't cry anymore. My makeup is going to run all over the place."

He wrapped his hands around hers. "Why do you wear so much makeup anyway? You don't need it." As soon as the words were out, he regretted them. Jeez, maybe he should ask her if she was pregnant next or say her thighs were fat. He really was an idiot.

She stared at him for what seemed like minutes as he braced himself for an explosion. Instead, she said softly, "It makes me feel protected—like armor. People see the goop and not me. I like it that way."

The brutal honesty of her words contrasted with the stark vulnerability in her eyes. His breath caught and his cold, hard heart melted. She leveled him. He bent forward and dropped a soft kiss on each of her eyelids.

Up close she smelled like cinnamon and honey, sweet and spicy at the same time.

"I see you," he whispered against her forehead.

"That's a James Cameron line," she answered, her voice not quite even. Her hands pressed against his chest as she pressed into him. "From *Avatar*."

He smiled and brushed his mouth across hers. "You know a lot of movies."

"Uh-huh."

"And you talk too much."

"Probably. I think it's because—"

He covered her mouth with his, ran his tongue along the seam of her lips until she opened for him. Everything about her drew him closer. He savored the feel of her in his arms. His hands trailed up and down along her back, played with the soft strands of her hair. Her whole body pressed into him, and for a moment he tried to hide the evidence of his desire. Then she moaned into his mouth and he lost all coherent thought.

She pulled his shirt out of his waistband, and her long fingers were cool on his skin. "Good lord," he muttered as what was left of his brain cells took the fast train south.

He tugged at the top of her shirt and trailed kisses from her jaw down her neck and across her collarbone. Just as he moved aside her bra strap, a horn honked from the driveway below. He bolted upright. The horn blared again, this time followed by a chorus of loud whooping and slamming doors.

"Travers, where the hell are you? Let's get this party started, man!" a deep voice called.

Josh met Sara's gaze, knew his eyes were as hazy as hers. He stepped away and cursed under his breath, dug the heel of his hand into his forehead, willing his brain to start functioning again.

"Who is that?" she asked, her voice shaky as she readjusted her shirt.

He cursed again. "Our first guests."

"Your friends from the rodeo? I thought they weren't coming until next week."

"Sounds like they're early."

She blew out a breath. "Right. We can do this. I'll find April and have her whip up something for dinner. Most of the things on the itinerary can be moved up to the next few days. I'll make calls once everyone is settled. Ryan can at least put sheets on a few beds." She turned toward the door, all business.

He tugged on her arm, pulling her back against him, and wrapped his arms around her. "Are you okay?" he asked, his lips just grazing her ear.

"No, I'm freaking out. These are the first paying guests. Things have to be perfect."

"As long as we have cold beer and lots of food, they'll be fine. I mean, are *you* okay?"

She stiffened in his arms and he held her tighter. "I'm fine. I'm sorry about my mother. I'll try to control her better."

"You're not responsible for your mom. She shouldn't have said what she did to you. It will work out in the end. I'm not giving up." He paused then asked, "Are we okay?"

She wiggled until he released her. "There is no *we*, Josh."

Irritation bubbled in him. "That's funny, because I don't think I was kissing myself just now."

She threw him an eye roll over her shoulder. Her big

blue eyes held none of the spark he'd seen earlier. She'd been so relaxed on the mountain, more of whom he believed she truly was. Not the guarded, fragile woman who stood before him now. "We were both upset. No big deal. It was a kiss, not a marriage proposal."

Her attitude got under his skin and he couldn't help baiting her. "Are you looking for a marriage proposal, Sara?"

"Not from you, cowboy," she answered with a scoff, but her shoulders tensed even more.

He wanted to grab her, kiss her until she was once again soft and pliant in his arms. The horn honked for a third time and he heard a loud knocking at the front door.

Sara smoothed her fingers over her shirtfront. "Go greet your buddies. I'll get everyone moving."

"This conversation isn't finished," he told her as he headed for the stairs.

"My end of it is," he heard her say under her breath.

He smiled despite his frustration, wondering how the fact that she always had to get in the last word could be so endearing to him. He shook his head, making a mental note to start thinking with his brain rather than other parts of his anatomy.

Sara came through the back door of the main house an hour later. Music streamed into the kitchen as April appeared from the family room, two empty platters in her hand.

"You'd think those guys hadn't eaten in months," she grumbled. But Sara noticed her grin and the light in her eyes. April was at her best when she could take care of people.

"I've got the two big cabins made up. That should hold everyone. Do you need anything?"

"I've got another batch of wings ready to come out and a vat of queso dip almost heated. I'll need to run to the grocery tomorrow. We should at least make it through breakfast."

Sara glanced at the spotless counters. "Can I help clean up?"

April gave her a knowing look. "Go introduce yourself. They're rowdy but seem nice enough. Four guys and one girlfriend. Her name is Brandy. She's a looker in that farm-fresh way."

Sara took a tube of deep plum lipstick from her jeans pocket and applied a liberal layer to her mouth. "I don't want to interrupt."

"It's a party in there," April countered. "The more the merrier."

"Has he told them who I am?"

April's smile turned gentle. "I don't think so. It's not a big deal, you know. Maybe they won't recognize you."

"How old is Brandy?"

"Early twenties."

"Unless she was raised without a TV in the house, she'll know me."

"It doesn't matter."

"It doesn't matter in L.A. Much. I can blend in a little in the land of falling stars. Especially with a new crop of beautiful losers coming through every year. But here it's just me—the only big fat failure for miles."

April took a pot holder and opened the oven to pull out a baking sheet of wings. They smelled delicious.

"Did you ever consider you might be the only one who believes you're a failure?"

"My mom thinks I'm a failure," Sara said with a shrug.

"Your mom is a witch."

Sara snorted. April didn't call people names. Ever. "Whoa, there, lady. Them's fightin' words."

"Bring it," April said as she dumped the wings into an oversize basket. Her hands free, she turned and hugged Sara. "I'll take down your mother and the broom she rode in on."

"You're a Buddhist."

"I'll make an exception for her. And you. Go out there for a few minutes. Have fun tonight, Sara. You deserve it."

"What would I do without you?" Sara gave her friend one last squeeze and walked into the family room.

Josh and his four friends sat on the sofas and chairs surrounding the coffee table, filling the large room with their presence. Three of the men looked around Josh's age. The last one was so young he seemed barely out of puberty, despite having the broadest build in the group. Two were clearly brothers, both blond, tall and lanky. The third had a thick head of midnight-black hair and deep brown skin. The young one reached for another handful of chips, a shock of red hair falling over one eye. As a whole, they were tough, rangy and utterly male. Something Sara was unused to in Hollywood.

"It's enough testosterone to choke you," a voice said close to her ear.

Sara turned to see a young woman standing at her

side who was as "farm fresh" as April had described. Her light brown hair was pulled back in a plastic clip and cascaded in healthy, unprocessed waves to the middle of her back. She wore little makeup other than a hint of lip gloss, and her soft denim shirt was tucked into a pair of high-waisted jeans. Actual Wranglers, if Sara guessed right.

"You must be Brandy," she said and held out her hand. "I'm—"

"Serena Wellens," the woman finished, her eyes widening.

"I go by Sara now. Sara Wells is my real name."

Brandy pumped Sara's hand at fever pace. "I loved *Just the Two of Us.* My sister and I lived for Tuesday nights."

"Thanks," Sara said weakly, her stomach beginning to churn. She braced herself for the questions about her career, her fall from stardom, her stint in rehab. She waited for criticism to cloud Brandy's gaze.

Her eyes clear, Brandy glanced around the room. "Josh said this house belonged to your grandmother."

That was it? Where was the third degree she was so used to from people she met in L.A.? She answered, "I didn't know her well, but she left it to me when she passed."

"It's a great setup and really nice of you to help Josh make it work this summer. Having a place of his own for Claire means the world to him."

Her mother's refrain from her childhood filled Sara's mind: "the world doesn't revolve around you." Based on life in Crimson, that might really be the case. Maybe outside the dysfunctional Hollywood bubble, people didn't care about her past. She wanted to keep the conversation away from her personal life so she asked, "Do you know Josh well?"

"Those four are like brothers." Brandy nodded. "Manny and Josh started the circuit at the same time. Noah and Dave are the only ones related by blood, ten months apart. Irish twins, if you know what I mean? Noah doesn't actually ride. He does search and rescue up here in the mountains, but he's an honorary member of this crew. I've been dating Dave, the older one, for about five years."

"You don't look old enough for that."

"We met when I was sixteen at a county fair in Indiana. My dad's a big-time doctor so it about killed him that I had it bad for a bull rider. He'd expected me to follow in his med school footsteps. But I graduated high school and got a job at a preschool so I could have summers off to be with Dave."

"How'd your dad take that?"

"He was on fire for a while, but in his heart he wants me to be happy. He learned to live with it. You know how it goes."

Sara only wished that were true.

"We're getting married this fall." Brandy held out her left hand where a small diamond ring glittered on her finger.

"Congratulations. I hope you have a great life together. What about the baby-faced redhead?"

Brandy smiled. "That's Bryson. He's new this year and the guys have taken him under their wing. He was dying to meet Josh so came with us to the ranch. I'm sorry if getting here early made extra work for you."

"It's no biggie." Sara watched Josh throw back his

head and laugh at something Manny said. "He seems happy tonight."

"He seems happy *here*," Brandy corrected. "We weren't sure whether he'd recover from the accident."

Sara turned her attention more fully to the other woman. "I didn't realize his injuries were life threatening."

"The physical part was bad, but the worst part was losing his career and the life he'd known. He took it hard. If it wasn't for having to get things together for Claire, I'm not sure he would have made it."

Sara had assumed Josh's leg and the surgeries he'd endured to fix it had been the worst of his struggles. She knew a thing or two about losing a career and the emotional damage it could inflict. She hadn't considered she and Josh might have that in common.

"I'll introduce you." Brandy walked forward into the room, clearly expecting Sara to follow.

"You all need a chance to catch up," Sara said, suddenly feeling out of place in her low-slung jeans, tight T-shirt and heavily made-up face. Even the streaks in her hair made her feel like an outsider. It was one thing to wear her carefully crafted mask in California, but these people were real. She felt like a huge phony.

"Come on." Brandy's smile was open and friendly. "They know me too well to be on their best behavior. Without backup, I'll be stuck judging burping contests, or worse."

Sara couldn't help but return Brandy's smile. "For a few minutes, I guess."

"Hey, y'all," Brandy announced over the music. "This is Sara. She's keeping Josh's tight buns out of trouble this summer. And she's taking care of all you yahoos while we're here. Try not to make her regret the hospitality."

Sara felt a blush rise to her cheeks as the attention turned to her. That and the mention of Josh's buns. Good gravy.

All four men jumped to attention. "Nice to meetcha," Dave said, coming around the coffee table to shake Sara's hand before draping a long arm across Brandy's shoulders. "Thanks for taking us in early."

"No wonder you look so dang happy," Noah told Josh as he came to stand in front of Sara. "You are the prettiest thing I've seen in ages," he said to her, making her color deepen. She put out her hand but he swatted it away, instead grabbing her up in a bear hug and twirling her in a fast circle.

"Put her down," Josh ordered.

"Oh, darlin', you smell so good. Sweet as my mama's apple pie." He nuzzled his face into Sara's neck. She heard Josh growl behind him.

"I mean it, Noah. Enough."

Manny stepped in front of Josh. *"Señorita,"* he crooned, pulling Sara away from Noah's tight embrace. "You make us crazy hombres act even more loco." He took her hand, but instead of shaking it, brushed his lips across her knuckles.

"You've got to be kidding me," Josh grumbled.

"Wow," Sara whispered. She hadn't experienced anything like this in years. To be the center of attention for these men was strange and exhilarating, like the first time she'd flipped through channels and watched herself on TV. She felt strangely exposed, but not in a bad way like she had so many times in L.A.—still safe, although not quite herself. It gave her a dizzy sort of feeling.

"You guys are funny," she said with a giggle, then cupped her hand over her mouth. Sara was not a giggler by nature.

Manny released her hand as Noah stepped forward. "I feel like I know you from somewhere. Do you have a twin sister?"

Sara's shook her head as her grin evaporated. *Here it comes,* she thought.

He paused and wiggled his eyebrows. "Then you must be the most beautiful girl in the world," he said to a chorus of groans from the rest of the group.

Josh gave him a quick thump on the head. "Knock it off, bozo."

"Who died and made you boss of me?" Noah countered, his good-ole-boy ease replaced with six feet of tall, angry man. Josh's shoulders stiffened.

"It's okay," Sara said, stepping between the two.

"Not to me," Josh answered. It felt like all the air whooshed out of the room at the intensity of his tone.

Noah studied Josh. "Is there something you're not telling us? You guys have a fling going on here?"

"No," Sara and Josh answered at once. Josh continued, "I don't want things complicated while you're here."

"Uncomplicated," Dave said, giving Noah a soft elbow to the back. "That's us."

"Dinner," April announced in the ensuing silence.

As quick as that, the mood changed again. "I'm starving," Noah said, heading for the dining room.

"With service like this, we may never leave," Manny agreed with a wink at Sara as he passed.

When everyone else had left, Sara turned to Josh. "I know they're just joking with all of the compliments. Trying to be nice."

"Those guys don't do nice." He scrubbed one hand across his face.

She put her fingers on his arm, shocked at the tension in his corded muscles. "What's the problem?"

"Is Noah your type?"

"What?" The question took her aback.

"At first I thought it was Ryan, the slick Hollywood bit. But maybe you'd like slumming with a bad boy. Tell me, which way is it going to go?"

Sara sucked in a breath. "You are way out of line, Josh. My idea was to spend the night holed up in my cabin. Alone. But April convinced me to come out here to meet your friends. It was hard as hell since I was sure they'd give me the same once-over I get every day in L.A. then make a big deal about who I used to be. But you know what? Those guys were nice. And sweet. And funny. I don't get that a lot and would appreciate if you'd stop raining on my parade with your bad attitude."

She whirled away but he held her wrist. She wouldn't turn around but felt his heat against her back. "I'm sorry," he said finally.

"Fine. Now let go."

He didn't release her. "You deserve someone nice, sweet and funny. You deserve someone whole. I hope you find that man. Even if it's one of those guys. Any of them would be lucky to have you."

She looked over her shoulder and her breath caught at the stark pain in his eyes. "What do you mean *whole?*"

He dropped her arm. "Never mind. Let's go eat." He moved past her without another word.

As he walked from the room, her gaze caught on the slight limp in his gait that became more pronounced at the end of a long day. She couldn't answer for herself, but she was certain he didn't deserve the self-inflicted solitude he seemed to carry as his burden. He'd had everything in his life taken from him. Not the slow unraveling that marked her failure, but one instant that stole his future and challenged a reputation he'd built for years.

At least she knew that she could go back to acting if given the chance. His days on the back of a bull were done. She couldn't imagine the strength it had taken him to move on, to start over on the ranch and with Claire. How could he think he was anything less than whole? His strength of character was deeper than most of the men she'd known combined.

The question remained: What did she want in a man? Her eyes roved over his strong body as he disappeared around the corner, a shiver dancing along her spine. It had been years since she'd considered dating after a string of relationships with would-be actors had left her hollow inside.

Josh was 100 percent real man. As she followed him into the dining room, the thought crossed her mind that she might not even be up for the challenge that he held.

Once again, she reminded herself it was a good thing she was only on the ranch for the summer. For any number of reasons.

Chapter 8

Josh sat through dinner with a chip on his shoulder and a pit in his stomach that prevented him from enjoying any of the delicious food April had prepared. Not so for his friends, who dug into heaping dishes of enchiladas and all the trimmings with the gusto of a pack of NFL linebackers.

What ate at his gut even more was the way Noah and Manny continued to flirt with Sara right in front of his face. Her rich, musical laughter filled the dining room as she immediately slid into the rhythm of their close circle as if she'd been a part of it for years.

That got him, too, because she was so different from any of the girls he'd met on the circuit. The ones he'd known his buddies to date throughout the years. The "buckle bunnies," as they were called, were a special brand of groupies, and it was rare to find a true love, like Dave and Brandy, when you were on the road in cheap motels and seedy diners for weeks at a time.

He took another pull on his beer and groaned inwardly when he heard the front door slam shut. One more complication for his evening.

"Daddy? Sara? Whose truck is that in the driveway?"

Claire came into the dining room, and out of the corner of his eye, Josh saw Bryson sit up straighter.

Down boy, Josh thought to himself, giving a mental eye roll at how much he sounded like an old geezer.

He got out of his chair to stand next to Claire. "Claire, I think you've met Dave and Brandy. The guy who looks like his twin is his little brother, Noah. That's Manny at the end of the table and Bryson next to him. Everyone, this is my daughter, Claire." He pointed a finger in Bryson's direction. "Off-limits," he ordered, placing a protective arm around Claire's shoulders.

"Dad," Claire said with a groan, "don't embarrass me."

"Hi, sweetie," Brandy crooned. "It's so good to see you again."

"Hey." Claire gave a small wave and shifted uncomfortably next to him. "I'll just go up to my room."

He wondered what could be wrong with Claire. There wasn't a more welcoming group than this bunch, but he got the sense that Claire was ready to bolt. Sara stood before Josh could answer. Her eyes met his for a brief second before she turned to Claire. "Did you have a good time with your friend?"

"Sure, I guess."

"Come and sit next to me. We can be newbies to this group together."

After a little push from Josh, Claire shuffled toward Sara and sank into the empty chair next to her.

Noah took up the conversation without a beat. "Did you hear about the last event?" he asked Josh.

"I don't get a lot of bull-riding news out here," Josh said without emotion. "And that's the way I—"

"It was awesome, man. I rode Big Mabel and after six seconds she really let loose. I hung on like never before, legs back and chin down just like you taught me. You wouldn't believe the high. I was in the zone like never before. You have no idea."

"I have an idea," Josh grumbled as he took his seat again.

"Five thousand dollars, dude. The biggest purse this season and it was all mine."

Manny leaned over and thumped Noah on the head. "Shut up, amigo."

"No, it's fine." Josh took another drink of his beer. "I want to hear everything." He turned to Bryson. "How's your first season going?"

Sara rubbed her hand along Claire's back as she kept one eye on Josh. "Are we still going shopping this weekend?" she asked quietly.

"Sure."

"What's wrong, honey?"

"Do you think they blame me for what happened to Dad? I mean, maybe they hate me. It was my fault he—"

"Stop," Sara said, hoping to soothe the young girl before Josh noticed her distress. "What happened to your dad wasn't your fault. We've been over this. These are his friends. I think he'd want you to enjoy tonight, not to beat yourself up."

"You're right." Claire smiled, although it looked more like a grimace.

Sara laughed softly. "That's a start." She grabbed the plate of brownies April had brought out a few minutes earlier. "Let me share something I've learned over the years. Chocolate is often the best medicine."

Claire's smile turned genuine. "I like that philosophy."

With Claire happily nibbling on the brownie, Sara turned her attention back to Josh. His full focus was on Bryson as he nodded at something the young bull rider said. To a casual observer he'd looked relaxed, but Sara noticed the tension that radiated from his jawline down through his shoulders. His fingers gripped the beer bottle with a white-knuckled grasp.

It must be so difficult for him to listen to stories from a new crop of bull riders. She knew what it was like to have failure tap you on the shoulder and ask for advice in the form of a new generation of rising stars.

Sara stood without thinking. "How about a game of charades?" Everyone at the table looked at her like she'd grown a horn. "You know, the game?" she clarified.

Continued silence and stares. Finally Dave cleared his throat. "Cowboys don't usually play parlor games, darlin'."

Of course not. Sara felt color creep into her cheeks once again. She glanced at Josh, who'd finally loosened his grip on the beer bottle. Too bad for the cowboys, she thought. If it could keep these guys distracted and give Josh a little breathing room, she'd push them into it one way or another.

She leaned over the table toward Dave. "What's the matter? Afraid of being beat by a girl?"

Brandy gave a quiet snort of laughter. "I'm on Sara's team," she announced.

"Women against men," April added as she came into the room. "Perfect."

Josh pushed away from the table. "I don't think—"

Sara made squawking noises and flapped her elbows.

Josh's eyes widened. "Are you calling me a chicken?"

Sara smiled broadly. "If the feathers fit."

"Come on, boys," Josh ordered. "Into the family room. These ladies are begging to be trounced."

"Charades," Dave mumbled, but stood without argument. "This has to be a first."

"Should I come, too?" Claire asked.

"It wouldn't be a girls' team without you," Sara told her, meeting Josh's gaze for a brief second. She thought she saw gratitude and maybe a little relief before his mask snapped into place.

"Let's do this." He hustled the other bull riders out of the dining room, grumbling all the way.

Sara didn't make it back to her cabin until close to eleven, way past her bedtime with the early-morning hours on the ranch. She'd helped April clean up in the kitchen after Brandy and Claire had gone to bed, leaving the guys to relive old stories around the fire pit on the side patio.

To her surprise, Ryan had seemed to find his place in the overtestosteroned group, happily sharing stories of which Hollywood starlets had what body parts surgically enhanced.

She smiled to herself at the stories she could tell if she wanted, then jumped at a noise from the trees next to her front door.

"Heart-attack central over here," she squeaked as Josh stepped out of the darkness.

"Sorry." He didn't look sorry. He looked big and gorgeous in his soft flannel shirt, faded jeans and boots. A light was on in her cabin, its glow illuminating the front step enough for her to see him clearly.

Late-night stubble shadowed his jaw, defining it even more and making her wonder how that roughness would feel across her skin. She quickly pulled her mind away from that train of thought. No good could come from there.

"Expecting someone else?" he asked.

"Yogi Bear?" she answered, still trying to catch her breath. "Or Grizzly Adams, maybe?"

One corner of his mouth hitched up, matching the catch in her throat. "Noah likes you."

"I got the impression Noah likes anyone with breasts and a pulse."

That drew a laugh from him. "Probably. The question is, do you like him?"

Something in his tone of voice put her on edge. "I don't think that's any of your business." She took a step toward her door but he blocked the path.

"It is if you're going to mix business with pleasure."

She eyed him for a moment then swallowed, too tired to play games or even put up a fight. "I'm not interested in Noah."

He watched her.

"Or Manny. Or Bryson."

He continued to stare.

She huffed out a breath. "I'm not after your friends. Why do I feel like there's still a problem?"

He blinked several times then mumbled, "Thank you."

"I'm having trouble following you."

"For tonight. You made Claire feel comfortable, and I have a feeling you suggested the stupid game to do the same for me."

"Everyone had fun playing the game," she said, letting a little temper seep into her voice. "I was just keeping the guests entertained. I'm sure you can handle your own feelings."

"You're right—it wasn't stupid. We did have fun. Because of you."

The cool night air licked across her bare arms and goose bumps tickled her skin in its wake. She took another deep breath, hoping the scent of the surrounding mountains would calm her. Josh's gaze fell to her chest, which had the exact opposite effect on her jumbled emotions.

His eyes squeezed shut. "I don't know how to do this."

"Do what?"

"Want you so badly and not act on it."

She knew that feeling. "There are a lot of reasons we shouldn't be together."

He nodded but said, "Tell me why I shouldn't kiss you right now."

Every shred of rational thought dissolved from her brain. Without meaning to, she swayed a tiny bit closer to him. "I don't want to."

"You don't want to kiss me?"

"I don't want to give you a reason not to," she said on a shaky laugh.

He laced his fingers with hers and tugged her closer. With his other hand he cupped the back of her head, bringing her mouth against his. Like before, his kiss mesmerized her. Her defenses, her protective walls—everything inside her loosened and traveled south to parts of her body that hadn't been lit up for years. Those bits were glowing now as he claimed her, pulling her against him and deepening the kiss.

A shiver ran across her back and he wrapped his arms tightly around her. She snuggled into the heat that radiated from his body, losing herself in his spicy scent.

Tugging at the hem of her T-shirt, his warm hands pressed against her skin for several minutes before his fingers worked at her bra strap. *Yes, yes, yes,* her reawakened senses shouted in her head. At the same time, a trickle of unease danced across her conscience.

Darned conscience.

She didn't do casual flings. That was one of the few standards she'd held true to, both in and out of the spotlight. L.A. was filled with relationships built on nothing more than mutual attraction and soul-crushing loneliness. Sara hadn't given her body or her heart in a moment of weakness in the past. She wasn't going to let her hormones take over now. She knew how badly that could play out in the morning, and she wouldn't risk her pride, no matter how good it felt.

The silent snap of her bra opening brought her fully to her right mind.

"Stop." She wasn't sure if she'd said the word out loud until Josh's hands stilled on her waist.

He buried his face in the side of her neck. "Is this

what you call a dramatic pause?" he asked, his voice ragged.

"We shouldn't do this."

"I hope you mean we should take it inside your cabin instead."

Sara gave him a small push and he immediately moved back. "I mean, the two of us is a bad idea for a lot of reasons."

"If I'd known you'd actually muster an argument, I'm not sure I would have asked the question."

"What do you want out of this summer, Josh?"

He tilted his head, massaged his thumb and index finger above his eyes. "Money," he answered simply.

"Is that all?"

"Give me a break on the twenty questions, Sara. My brain isn't firing on all cylinders right now." He sighed. "I want a future for Claire and me. I want this ranch to feel like home for her."

She nodded and tried not to admit that the truth in his words stung. She was used to not being a priority to anyone, even herself. But it still hurt to hear it out loud. "It's about Claire for you. For me it's about a second chance of a different kind."

In a way, things had been easier in California. The day-to-day struggle to make ends meet had left her little time to ponder the sad state of the rest of her life. Now that she had that time, it was up to her to protect herself. No one else was going to.

She liked to believe that her grandma would have fought for Sara if her mother hadn't made sure they never returned to Crimson. Maybe her grandmother would have been the positive role model Sara had so desperately needed.

She wanted to think that was why Gran had left her the house. An olive branch of sorts. Sara had no intention of letting it go to waste.

"I want the money and the fresh start it will give me. I'm going to get it one way or another. Even if that means…"

The lingering heat in his eyes went instantly frosty. "Even if that means crushing my future to guarantee your own."

"I want both of us to get what we want. I really do. But at the end of the summer, that might not be possible. I'm going to sell this house. I hope it's to you. I'm working to make sure that happens. But getting involved is a complication I'm not willing to risk."

"And that's what this is? A complication?"

"I don't know. I think so."

"What about Claire?"

"I'd never hurt Claire. You know that."

"She feels close to you. It will break her heart if you throw us over."

"That's not fair, Josh. Whatever happens, I've been honest about my intentions. I'm not going to mess with you and Claire."

"Why does it feel like you already are?"

His anger felt like a slap in the face.

"You don't understand."

"Explain it to me, then." Frustration radiated off him, hitting her like rolling waves.

She opened her mouth but couldn't think of how to tell him how scared she was. How frightened her feelings for him and his daughter made her.

As she'd done so often in her life, she took the

coward's way out. "It's late. We're both tired. You should go."

"That's what you want?"

No, no, no. "Yes." She stepped aside to let him pass.

He moved past her, but at the last moment, swept her into his arms and claimed her mouth in a kiss she felt all the way to her toes. When he finally released her, she stumbled back against the door of the cabin, her knees as wobbly as a newborn foal.

He didn't look any more in control than she did, but his voice was steady as he told her, "You think too much, Hollywood," before turning and disappearing back into the darkness.

Chapter 9

Josh finished wiping down the last ATV and leaned back against the machine's front tire. Massaging his fingers against his leg, he thought about how happy everyone had looked coming back from last night's sunset ride.

The weather had been perfect for the past three days and his friends had taken full advantage, spending as much time as possible hiking, biking and fishing on the mountain. Yesterday afternoon, they'd ridden the four-wheelers up to the old mining town on the other side of the peak. He'd even convinced Claire to come along.

Things were exactly the way he'd pictured them for the summer. Except for watching Noah and Manny continue to flirt with Sara while Bryson made cow eyes at his daughter. That wasn't part of the plan.

Neither was the way his knee throbbed after several days of constant action.

The door to the equipment barn squeaked. "Josh, are you in here?"

Josh straightened as Dave shuffled into the barn. "I'm just cleaning things up a bit."

"That ride was killer today. The views from the top are definitely worth the price of admission."

"Yep." Josh rubbed the towel across the seat of one ATV. "Brandy seemed happy."

Dave snorted. "She's happy anytime I let her drive. That woman has the heaviest lead foot in history."

"I'm glad it's working out with the two of you."

"Me, too." His friend studied him. "Sara's pretty great."

"It's business, Dave. Nothing more."

"You don't look at her like it's business."

Josh flipped the towel onto the workbench and turned. "She's going to sell the house at the end of the summer and head back to L.A. If I can't get the bank to finance me, there's a decent chance all my work will have been for nothing."

"Really?" Dave whistled under his breath. "She seems happy here. Not a Hollywood type. Have you thought about asking her to stay?"

"Why would I do that?"

"Because you're crazy about her."

"That'll pass."

"How long have I known you, Josh? More than ten years, right? We started the circuit the same season. I remember how bad things got with Jen, how hard you tried to make it work."

"Not hard enough."

"Sara isn't your ex-wife."

"Thanks for the insight. But I'm making a life for Claire. One that will keep her safe and out of trouble."

Dave's eyes widened a fraction. "This is about your sister," he whispered.

"Don't go there."

Dave ignored the warning in Josh's voice. "You'd been gone three years when Beth died. The car accident was stupid and tragic but not your fault."

"I should have been there for her," Josh argued, shaking his head. "I knew how bad things were between my parents, what kind of hell that house was to live in every day. I could take out my anger in the ring, but she didn't have that option. If I'd been around to help, maybe she wouldn't have been drinking that night. Maybe she'd have been strong enough to not get in that car."

"Not your fault," Dave repeated.

"It doesn't matter." Josh opened the barn door, letting bright light flood the sawdust floor. He stepped into the warmth and took a deep breath. "I have a chance to make things right for Claire. I'm not going to blow it."

"Part of Claire being happy is you being happy. Sara does that. Everyone can see it except you. Your daughter is a teenager. She needs a woman in her life who isn't as messed up as her mother. You don't have to do it alone."

Josh let his eyes drift closed. He'd done things alone for so long he wasn't sure if he knew another way. He saw how much Claire was drawn to Sara. More often than not he'd find her curled in the overstuffed chair in the office while Sara was on the computer.

At first he hadn't wanted his daughter to have anything to do with Hollywood Barbie. As time went on, he could see Sara's influence on Claire's behavior in good ways. Claire seemed less sullen and moody. Hell, she'd even smiled at him a couple of times—a big improvement over the start of the summer. He'd felt the change, hard as it was to admit, in himself, as well. Something about Sara gave a lift to his heart. Her unflagging energy and upbeat spirit drew him out of the fog that had become a constant in his life since the accident.

Could it be something more? She said she was leaving at the end of the summer, but he knew she was happy on the ranch. She also said she didn't do casual relationships. If he offered her something more, he might have a chance of changing her mind about the future.

Sara and Claire were leaving this morning to go shopping in Denver. He checked his watch and pulled off his work gloves, tossing them to Dave.

"Can you guys handle a day on your own?"

Dave nodded. "The plan was fishing, and Noah can get us to the best water."

"Then do me a favor and close up the barn. I've got someplace I need to be."

Sara stepped out of her cabin at the sound of a horn honking. *Not more unannounced guests,* she thought, then stopped at the sight of Josh's enormous black truck idling in front of her.

Claire opened the door and scrambled into the backseat. "Dad's coming with us," she called over her shoulder. "He's got his credit card. Woo-hoo!"

"Don't get too crazy," Josh told his daughter, then patted the seat next to him. "Are you ready?" he called to Sara.

To spend three hours next to him in the front seat? No way, no how.

"Sure." She walked toward the truck. "What made you decide to spend your afternoon shopping?"

He looked at her through aviator glasses so dark she couldn't see his eyes. "I have a couple of parts to pick up from a mechanic in north Denver. Thought we could stop by on the way to Cherry Creek."

Sara's stomach gave a lurch at the mention of the up-scale shopping area. She was bound to be recognized, which had seemed bad enough with Claire, but to add Josh to the mix was almost too much. She had no control over the things complete strangers were willing to say to her, most of them embarrassing.

She hesitated, then hoisted herself into the truck. She could handle whatever came her way, she told herself. This summer was about taking back her power, and dealing with public attention was part of that.

She glanced in the backseat, where Claire had already popped in a pair of earbuds. She gave Sara a thumbs-up and returned to mouthing the lyrics of the song from her iPod.

Buckling her seat belt, Sara turned to Josh. "I think we're set."

He continued to watch her, then lowered his glasses to the tip of his nose. "You're not wearing makeup again."

He'd noticed. Damn. Sara had put her hair in a long braid and applied just a touch of mascara and gloss, hoping to blend in more with the other shoppers and

avoid recognition. She forced a casual smile. "I am, just
not as much. Thought I'd give my skin a rest. A little
detox for the pores, you know. I think…"

Josh's hand on her wrist stopped her nervous babble.
"You look beautiful," he said softly, rubbing his thumb
across her knuckles.

"Oh" was all she could manage. She looked down
at his fingers the way she might eye a rattlesnake on
the trail. Without thinking, she snatched her hand away
and dug through her purse for her own sunglasses.

He gave a deep chuckle and switched the truck into
gear. "Is country music okay?"

"Fine." Anything to fill the charged silence.

He swung onto the road and turned on the radio,
drumming his fingers on the console in time with a
song.

Sara kept her gaze focused on the scenery rolling by
and soon lost herself in the beauty of the mountains.
Driving in from California, she'd been so consumed
with what she'd find that she'd given little thought to
the jagged peaks that framed the interstate. Now she
had time to take in the mountains that had been carved
out to create this road through them. She thought about
the hours of work it must have taken—the blood, sweat
and tears of the men who built it. Her own life felt even
more insignificant in comparison.

"It's humbling, isn't it?" Josh asked, as if reading
her thoughts.

Sara blinked several times. "How did you know
that's what I was thinking about?"

He pointed toward the front window. "It's hard not
to, driving through here. The majesty of this place
takes my breath away every time."

Sara nodded. "That's exactly right. It makes me feel so small. But in a good way. Like nature is protecting us with its very mass. The things that make me feel little in my life don't seem to matter when I'm faced with this type of beauty."

"I feel the same way," Josh answered, his voice so soft she barely heard him.

Sara felt the warmth of his glance and squirmed a bit in the seat. What happened to his anger from before? Anger was clear-cut, no questions. Not like the feelings his kindness produced in her.

"Are the guys having a good time?" she asked, hoping for an easier subject.

He smiled. "The best. Everything you planned is perfect."

A little zing tripped along her spine. "The questionnaire helps narrow down their interests. Your friends were easy. Anything loud, with lots of adrenaline."

"When does the next group come in?"

"This weekend, only one day between them and your crew. It's the family reunion. Age range from toddlers to the patriarch in his seventies."

"The old man who wants to catch a trout with his great-grandson as part of his bucket list?" Josh laughed. "No pressure on me."

"You have a gift for leading the groups, Josh. Everything will be fine."

"I hope it's enough to make it work."

She sighed. "Me, too," she answered, unsure if she was talking about the ranch or her life.

They talked easily the rest of the drive, about his life on the tour and the places he'd seen in his travels. The way he described them, those seconds in the ring reminded her of the way she felt the moment a director called, "Action," the spotlight on her with adrenaline pumping. While a scene wasn't life-or-death high stakes the way a ride on a thousand-pound animal could be, it had the same emotional letdown when it was over.

Talking to Josh made her remember how much she'd loved the actual acting part of her job if she could leave behind the baggage that crowded her life.

By the time they got to the shopping area, Sara felt relaxed. Claire's excitement about the boutiques that lined the streets was contagious to the point that she'd almost forgotten her trepidation about a public outing.

Josh dropped them along the block that looked the most interesting to Claire and went to park. Sara followed Claire into a store and to a rack of colorful sundresses near the front.

"I love this," Claire said on an excited breath, holding up a low-cut V-neck sundress with a deep back.

Sara stifled a laugh at what Josh would think of that choice. She thumbed through the dresses and pulled out two with a more modest neckline. "I think one of these would be perfect."

Claire hesitated, then put the first dress back. "The blue one is pretty."

Sara's sigh of relief was interrupted by a voice behind her. "Let me know if I can be of any help," a saleslady purred. "We're having a great summer sale on all dresses in the store."

Sara turned and met the woman's critical gaze with a bright smile. "Thanks. Are the dressing rooms in the back?"

To her surprise, the woman returned her smile. "Yes. Can I take those dresses for you?"

"The blue one," Sara answered, and released the breath she hadn't realized she was holding. Okay. That went well. One stranger down, dozens of others to go. She hated feeling so nervous and out of sorts, especially when Josh was along to watch her squirm.

Claire's squealing caught her attention.

"This one," the young girl said on a rapturous breath. Sara's grin broadened at the soft pink fabric draped across Claire's arm.

"It's beautiful," she agreed.

"What's beautiful?" Josh asked at her shoulder.

"Dad, look at this dress. I love, love, love it."

"Try it on then. Let's see how it fits."

Claire practically ran toward the dressing room. "Be right back," she called over her shoulder.

"I don't get women and shopping."

Sara turned to Josh, who looked more than uncomfortable standing between racks of feminine clothes. He adjusted the bill of his baseball cap lower on his face.

Sara studied the color that crept up his neck. "Are you blushing?" she asked, and followed his gaze. "At a mannequin wearing a bra and panties?"

"I don't blush," he argued, adjusting his cap again. "And I like to see a real woman wearing a bra and panties." His gaze raked her. "I'd like to see you in a bra and panties." He paused, then added softly, "Or out of them."

She swayed forward a fraction as her southern hemisphere revved to life. Glancing over her shoulder to make sure no one else had heard him, she pointed a finger at him. "You can't say that here. Your daughter's in the dressing room."

"I know where she is, and I can say whatever I want." His big shoulders shrugged. "I've got to think of something interesting to keep me going today. You need a distraction, too. You're wound like a top."

"I am not." She followed his gaze and quickly let go of the wad of fabric bunched in her hand, placing the dress back on its hanger and smoothing her hand over it. "What happened to your attitude from the other night?"

A Cheshire grin spread across his face. "I got a better one."

"I'm not sure this is any better. We agreed nothing will happen between us."

"You agreed." He took a step toward her, his hand brushing her bare arm. "I might buy you something to model later for me."

Sara coughed and sputtered at his brazen words. "I don't need you to buy me anything, and I'm not anyone's model."

Josh winked. "That's more like it. I like you all full of spunk."

"Okay, I'm ready," Claire called from the back of the store.

Sara narrowed her eyes as Josh walked toward the dressing rooms but couldn't quite stop herself from smiling.

He did that to her.

Their easy banter felt strangely right, and her whole body tingled at the message in his eyes when he looked at her. His attitude might be joking but his energy was intensely serious.

As she followed the sound of Claire's voice, the saleslady grabbed her arm and pulled her behind a bathing suit display. "Just a minute," she whispered, her head bobbing over the shelves to make sure they couldn't be heard. "I need to ask you something."

Here it comes, Sara thought, tension curling tight in her chest once again.

"Is that Josh Travers?" the woman asked, her eyes bright with expectation. "Are you with *the* Josh Travers?"

Sara blinked and looked over her shoulder. He had to have put the woman up to this. "*The* Josh Travers?"

The saleslady nodded. "He's the retired PBR champ, right?"

Sara racked her brain. "Professional Bull Riders," she said, almost to herself. "Yep, that's him."

"I knew it." The woman patted her chest. "He's even hotter in person than on TV."

Sara felt her jaw drop. "Are you for real?"

"Ever since they put the tour on cable, my husband's been addicted. He grew up down in Calhan, so even though we're in the big city he's a cowboy at heart. He likes me to watch, too—makes him feel like I get him."

She leaned closer and squeezed Sara's arm. "Let me tell you, it's no chore sitting on the couch watching those gorgeous boys do their thing. Josh Travers was the best of the best. It does my heart good to see him getting around, looking so happy and in love."

Sara's mouth dropped farther. "In love? Oh, no. We work together. We're here with his daughter."

"Whatever you say," the saleswoman said with a knowing smile. "You look like a nice girl."

"Sara, where are you?" Claire's voice came from the back of the store.

"Let's see how that young lady did with her choices." The saleswoman pulled a stunned Sara toward the dressing room. All that worry and someone recognized her as Josh's girlfriend?

Unbelievable.

The rest of the afternoon was just as surreal. Sara noticed several people staring and a few pointing at her as they meandered up the tree-lined streets. Each time it happened, Josh gave her hand a gentle squeeze, told a bad joke or generally teased her to distraction.

Claire did her best to put a generous dent into Josh's credit balance, growing happier with each store they entered. Sara felt the same way but for a different reason. Away from the looming tension about the fate of the ranch, she and Josh relaxed into an easy camaraderie that made hope bubble in Sara. She hadn't felt the sensation in years: the possibility of a normal life.

She floated along on that feeling until they stopped for dinner at a quaint bistro at the edge of the shopping district.

The young man at the host desk informed them that without a reservation, the wait for a table would be over an hour. Claire gave a sigh of disappointment, as the cozy restaurant had been her first choice.

As Sara turned to scan the street for nearby options, a gray-haired woman approached her from the sidewalk. "Are you Serena Wellens? The one who used to be a movie star?"

Sara sucked in a breath, unused to hearing her failure phrased quite that way. She forced a smile. "I guess you could say I used to be Serena Wellens. And yes, I was an actress. I go by Sara now."

She waited for the criticism to come—as it always did. It was human nature, Sara thought. People loved to sit in judgment of others' lives. The explosion of the internet and media outlets made it easy to feel like you had insight into someone else's business, no matter how untrue so much of what was published could be.

Josh's warm hand pressed against the small of her back, reminding her to take a calming breath. "Is everything okay here?" he asked.

Claire came to stand beside her, grabbing hold of Sara's hand. "Let's find another place," she said, and gave Sara a small tug.

Sara glanced at Claire and leaned against Josh ever so slightly. *He and Claire have my back,* she thought. *They literally have my back.* One thing about being in L.A. that she'd hated was the feeling of being alone against the world, as though she had no one but herself to depend on. She'd never been her own best defense. April had been there, but in the past few years had gone through so many of her own troubles, Sara hadn't wanted to be a burden with her own insignificant worries.

Still she stood transfixed by the stranger in front of her, like a deer in headlights. "We should go," she whispered.

"Wait." The woman took a step forward and Josh moved even closer. "I have to thank you first. My daughter, she's in college now, but when she was younger her father and I got divorced. It was messy and she was caught in the cross fire."

"I'm sorry," Sara responded automatically.

"Jessica, that's my daughter, closed off emotionally. She'd barely even look at me. But she loved your show. So every week we'd watch together. It was the only time she'd let me sit next to her. We'd talk during commercials. I swear *Just the Two of Us* saved our relationship." The woman dabbed at her eyes. "I'm sure that sounds stupid to you but it's the truth."

Sara reached out and took the woman's hand. "It doesn't sound stupid. I'm flattered that you told me."

"So thank you. We've been following Amanda's career since the show ended. Not hard since she's everywhere these days."

"She's had an amazing career," Sara agreed woodenly.

"When are you going to make your comeback? You were a much better actress than she was on the show. I'm sure that hasn't changed."

"My life has gone in a different direction."

The woman let out a bark of laughter. "I read the tabloids but I don't believe half of it. It'll happen when you're ready. You have a natural gift. Always have."

Emotions clogged Sara's throat. "Thank you again," she whispered.

The maître d' from the restaurant peeked around Josh. "Ms. Wellens?" he asked. "The manager has found a table for you."

"I'll let you get on with your evening," the woman said, and with a last squeeze of Sara's arm, scuttled down the sidewalk.

Sara met Josh's questioning gaze. "That was different, even for me," she said, trying to make her tone casual.

He gave her a knowing nod. "Looks like Serena got us a table."

"She's good for something, at least."

Chapter 10

Josh rubbed his hand over his face and gave a weary look around yet another store filled with racks of women's clothes. How many different shops had he been into today? More than in the past ten years if he had to guess. After eating, Claire had led them from one end of the ritzy neighborhood to the other.

She'd promised this would be the last one, and Josh couldn't be finished soon enough. His knee ached, his head pounded and all he wanted was to get out of the city and up into the mountains again. Sara had gamely kept up with Claire's boundless energy, but even she'd begun to wilt a little as she'd followed his daughter back to the fitting rooms.

He'd also noticed that in the whole day, Sara hadn't purchased one thing for herself. All of her attention remained focused on Claire's needs. He knew Claire had never had that with her own mother, and it made his heart open to Sara all the more.

"I'm not sure that's your size," a voice said next to him.

Sara stood just to the side of a rack of dresses, eyeing him with a smile.

He looked down at the soft fabric he clutched to his chest, then held up the dress. "It would look good on you," he said softly.

Her eyes sparked, whether with humor or temper he couldn't tell. "Today isn't about me."

"You haven't seen anything you want?"

"Doesn't matter." She sighed. "I don't have the money for new clothes."

He ignored the way his gut tightened at her comment. "I thought maybe Colorado wasn't trendy enough for you."

"What do you know about trendy?"

"More than I ever wanted to after today." He held the dress out. "Try it on," he coaxed, suddenly wanting to see her in something other than her chosen uniform of jeans and shapeless T-shirts.

"No point," she answered, but he thought he saw a sliver of longing in her gaze. Josh knew all about longing these days. Although he found it hard to believe, Sara had almost as many walls built up as he did. Right now, he wanted to crash through each and every one of them.

"You're right, though," he told her. "It doesn't matter what you wear. The bottom line is you're beautiful."

She took a step toward him and reached for the dress. "I'm not sure—"

"What do you think?"

He and Sara turned as Claire came from the back of the store. Josh felt his eyes widen. "I think you have thirty seconds to take that off and put on a decent outfit."

Sara's mouth dropped open as her gaze traveled up and down Claire. The saleswoman who'd followed Claire from the dressing room quickly backed away as Sara shot her a glare.

His daughter wore a skintight, black lace concoction that revealed more skin than it covered. Suddenly, he saw her not as his little girl but as a woman, one who was quickly going to rival her supermodel mother in the looks department. He had a visceral need to polish a shotgun or move to Tibet. Anything to avoid what the next few years held for him as a father.

"That's not the dress we'd picked," Sara said carefully.

Claire did a quick twirl, and he realized the dress was practically backless. He growled low under his breath. "No. Way."

"Dad," Claire whined, her bright smile turning to a pout. "Don't be a stick-in-the-mud. I saw Mom wearing something like this in a magazine last month. I want to have something she'll like when I go to visit her before school starts."

"You don't have a trip planned to see your mother," Josh argued. "And you're not going anywhere in that dress."

Claire's tiny hands came to rest on her hips. "I want to see her. I texted this morning and asked when she'd be back in New York. I could fly out next month if it works for her."

"What did she answer?"

Claire's mouth thinned, and she didn't meet his gaze. "She hasn't responded yet. But she will. You know how Mom does things last minute. I want to be ready."

"You aren't going to 'fly out' to be with her. We're spending the summer in Colorado."

Claire shook her head. "You can't stop me."

"The hell I can't," he shot back.

"You're not the boss of me."

"I'm your father and you'll do as I say."

"She's my mom. You can't keep me from her."

He couldn't think straight with Claire in that dress, looking so grown-up and out of his control. He had to keep her safe. He'd do anything, say anything to make sure she stayed with him. "I'm not keeping you from her," he yelled. "She doesn't want—"

He broke off, knowing the words were a mistake as soon as he said them.

"Me," Claire finished on a sob. "You think she doesn't want me."

He watched his daughter's eyes fill with tears and cursed himself for being the biggest idiot on the planet. "Claire, I didn't mean—"

She shook her head. "You're wrong," she said quietly, the pain in her gaze cutting a deep hole in his heart. "I hate you. Mom is going to take me back. I know she will." She turned and ran for the fitting room, silence filling the small store.

He took a step forward, but Sara put a hand on his arm. "She needs some time."

"I can't let her be with Jennifer. Too many bad things could happen."

Sara shook her head. "Then don't push her away."

She was right, but that only fueled his frustration more. "What do you know about protecting the people you love? From what you've told me, April is the only friend you have and you lost her entire life savings. If you and your mother hadn't put thoughts of another world in Claire's head, we wouldn't be here today. She'd be on the ranch. She'd be safe." His hands balled into hard fists. "Only I can keep her safe."

Sara sucked in a breath as if he'd slapped her. He waited for her to argue, to fight back. His words were untrue, but he'd baited her on purpose. He needed a good fight right now, a way to get rid of the fear crawling through every pore, making him feel weak and defenseless.

Instead, she looked away. "I'm going to get Claire. Pull the truck out front. I think this day is done."

"Sara," he called out as she walked away. She shook her head and kept moving, leaving Josh alone. His gaze dropped to the dress he held, a wrinkled, balled-up mess in his hands.

A lot like his life right now.

Sara followed Claire into the kitchen at the ranch three hours later. Three of the longest hours of her recent life. She was on edge down to her teeth after the tense ride back from Denver.

Claire had spent the entire time with her earbuds shoved in her ears, heaving dramatic sighs from the backseat as she furiously texted on her phone. Josh had turned the music loud, not the lulling country tunes from the morning but a pounding heavy-metal station that had only served to intensify Sara's headache.

She'd leaned her head against the cool window glass

and tried to tune out everything around her. It was a trick she'd learned as a girl on set, the ability to ignore the world and crawl into her own internal life.

But with Josh's hulking presence next to her, it felt like all her other senses became more attuned to him when she closed her eyes. His clean, male scent. The hot tension curling from him. She could even sense the pattern of his breathing and wasn't surprised when she opened her eyes to see that his chest rose and fell at the same rate hers did.

Although the words he'd spoken were the truth, he'd hurt her feelings. Still, she wanted to reach out and comfort him. He was a bumbling bull in a china shop when it came to Claire, but at least he cared. That was more than Sara had ever gotten from either of her parents, and she knew how much it mattered.

She also knew, because April continually reminded her, that she was a sucker for lost causes. Maybe it was because her secret dream had always been that someone would care enough to rescue her. She gave the best parts of herself to people who couldn't return the emotion. Part of her fresh start, her second chance, had been the opportunity to finally take care of herself. To make herself whole and right so she could move forward with her dreams. If she let herself get too involved with Josh and Claire, all her careful plans could slip through her fingers.

She might, once again, be left with nothing.

Regardless, she couldn't stand to see either of them in this kind of pain.

"He didn't mean to hurt you," she said to Claire's back as the girl grabbed a bottle of water from the refrigerator.

April walked in from the family room. "How was the shopping trip? Do I get a fashion show tonight?"

Claire slammed shut the fridge door and whirled. "I'd like to burn every single piece of clothing my jerk of a dad bought today." She swiped at her cheeks, her desperate gaze swinging between Sara and April. "He's wrong, you know. My mom loves me. She's busy, but she loves me."

"I know, honey," Sara answered. "He knows it, too. You scared him in that dress."

"I looked scary?" Claire's voice rose to a squeak.

Sara pressed her palm to the girl's face, smoothing away a tear. "You looked gorgeous and grown-up. That's the scariest thing a father can face. It makes them a little crazy."

"A crazy jerk," Claire mumbled.

A door slammed at the front of the house. Claire looked around wildly. "I don't want to see his friends tonight. I don't want to see anyone."

Sara glanced at April. "Are you making dinner?"

"Everyone is going into town. Ryan made reservations."

"Ryan is entertaining a group of cowboys?"

April nodded. "He stopped by earlier, looking for you. He's adamant that you be there, too. For moral support."

"I'm staying here if Claire wants company."

April stepped forward. "I'll keep Claire company." She smiled. "I made chicken soup and an apple crisp earlier. I happen to know there's a Jane Austen marathon tonight. *Emma* and *Sense and Sensibility,* two of my favorites. Does that sound okay, Claire?"

The girl nodded then gave a tiny hiccup. "I'm going

to take a shower. I'll be down when everyone else is gone."

She gave Sara a quick hug. "I had a good time with *you*. Sorry Dad ruined it for both of us."

"I enjoyed the day, no matter what."

"I'll get fresh towels for you," April said, and took Claire's hand, leading her up the back stairs.

Sara braced her hands on the counter and leaned forward, dropping her head to stretch out some of the tension in her neck.

"Now I ruined the whole day?"

She looked up as Josh filled the doorway leading to the front hall. His broad shoulders looked as tense as hers felt.

"You need to apologize," she answered.

"To Claire or to you?" He crossed his arms over his chest, his dark eyes unreadable in the shadows of the soft evening light.

"I'm not important here." She straightened, wiping an imaginary crumb from the counter. "Your daughter is."

"You're important to me," he said quietly.

"Don't do that, Josh."

"Do what?"

"Care."

He took a step forward at the same moment the back door of the house burst open.

"Come on, you two," Ryan said. "I've got the masses corralled into the Suburban. We need to make it to town before the poor vehicle implodes from the force of all that testosterone."

Sara saw his eyebrows raise as he studied both Josh

and her. "Whatever's going on here can only be helped by a drink and some food. Let's go."

Before she could argue, Ryan took her hand and pulled her out into the night.

Josh emptied his second beer and set it on the table. He looked down to where Sara sat, Manny and Noah on either side of her. He made eye contact with the waitress and lifted his finger to order another round.

"Rough day with the girls?" Dave asked from his seat next to him.

"I'd rather spend an hour in the ring with the orneriest bull you can find than another minute shopping."

"Amen to that," his friend agreed. "But I sure do like the results."

Josh followed Dave's gaze to where Brandy did a quick two-step with young Bryson on the dance floor. She wore a short skirt and a colorful blouse that flowed as she spun to the music. "How do you two make it look so easy?" he grumbled.

"I'm smarter than you," his friend told him sagely. "I keep my mouth shut unless I'm giving her a compliment."

Josh's laugh turned into a coughing fit as Noah leaned in close to whisper in Sara's ear.

He started to stand but Dave cuffed him on the shoulder. "He's doing it to get a rise out of you."

"Looks more like he's trying to get a rise out of himself."

"It's freaking him out being in town again, but we wanted to make sure you were doing okay. Neither of us planned on ever coming back to Crimson until we heard you'd settled here."

"Wasn't my plan either, but I'm going to make it work."

"Have you seen Logan and Jake recently?"

Josh took a breath at the mention of his two brothers. "Jake was here for Mom's funeral a couple of years ago. We both stayed less than twenty-four hours. Long enough to hire someone to clear out the old house and get it on the market. He flew off to whatever country needed doctors again after that. Logan…well, he couldn't exactly get away at the time."

"I'm sorry, man. About a lot of things."

Josh did stand now. He wasn't ready for this conversation. "I'm going to stretch my legs while doing my best to ignore your brother."

He got his beer at the bar and tried not to watch his two so-called friends flirting with Sara. It wasn't any business of his what she did with her time, but it still grated on his nerves.

His eyes strayed to the woman next to him, or at least to her hands, which were busily building some sort of structure out of a pile of matchbooks. "That's quite a building you've got there," he said, focusing all his wayward attention on the intricate display.

The woman jumped three feet in the air at his words, the house of matchbooks crumbling onto the bar.

"Sorry," he said with a wince. "Looks like that took some time."

He saw color rise to her pale cheeks. She turned and gave him an embarrassed smile. "It's a silly pastime." Her light brown hair was pulled back into a tight bun at the back of her head. She began stacking the little cardboard boxes into neat rows. "You're Josh Travers, right?"

He nodded. "Have we met?"

She shook her head. "No, but my husband grew up here, so he's mentioned you." She glanced over her shoulder. "He told me Serena Wellens is staying with you for the summer."

"Her name is Sara Wells now," Josh said, his protective instinct kicking in. "Who is your husband?"

The woman closed her eyes for a moment as if she'd said too much. Just then a firm hand clasped Josh on the shoulder. "Travers, it's been a while. How's it hangin'?"

Josh turned to see Craig Wilder, one of his least favorite people in all of Crimson, Colorado. Craig had been an insufferable prig as a kid. His family was the wealthiest in town, and they'd made sure everyone else knew it. Craig had had no time for any of the Travers kids, who were way below him on the social totem pole. Since Josh had come back, not much had changed. He knew Craig had become mayor last year, and he'd heard rumors that he'd bought the election. But Josh hadn't had a conversation with him for years, and he didn't want to start now.

One more reason he kept to himself out on the ranch.

"It's hanging fine," he said through clenched teeth.

"I see you met my wife, Olivia." Craig glanced at the woman. "Seriously, you aren't making those stupid houses again, are you, Liv?"

"No," she mumbled, and gave Josh an apologetic smile.

"I'm going to head back to the table," Josh said quickly. "Dave and Noah are at the ranch this week."

Craig stepped in front of him. "I hear Serena Wellens is there, too."

"She prefers Sara Wells," Olivia interjected.

Craig shot his wife a silencing glare. "You may have heard that in addition to my duties as mayor, I bought the old community-center building in town. I feel as though it's my civic duty to bring some culture back to Crimson. There are plenty of people who'd drive over from Aspen with the right incentive."

Josh took a slow pull on his beer. "You think Sara is the right incentive?"

"A D-list celebrity," Craig said with a chuckle, "is better than no celebrity at all."

Without thinking, Josh reached out and grabbed the other man by his shirtfront, pulling him close enough to see the whites of his eyes. "You're not using Sara for anything, Wilder. Don't talk to her. Don't even look at her. You were a slimeball when we were young, and I don't see that much has changed."

Craig fidgeted. then narrowed his eyes. "You're going to need the support of this town and the visitors' center to draw people to your ranch. Don't forget that."

Olivia stood and smiled at Josh. "I volunteer at the visitors' center. I'll make sure you get whatever publicity you need, Mr. Travers."

"Shut it, Liv," Craig said on a hiss of breath.

"I'll wait for you in the car," she answered, and turned away.

Josh released Craig and stared as he stomped off after his wife. He couldn't imagine all the things wrong in that marriage, but he'd meant what he said. He wouldn't let anyone use Sara for her fame. She deserved much more than that.

His eyes tracked to where she sat at the table. A man he didn't recognize sat next to her now, with Ryan standing between them, his face alight with excitement. The other man was clearly another Hollywood type. A shaggy beard covered his jaw, but his button-down shirt looked like some sort of expensive fabric. and a heavy gold Rolex flashed on his wrist.

Crimson had seen its share of wealth and fame. The town's close proximity to Aspen drew enough moneyed tourists to keep the town thriving. He'd been able to ignore them growing up and hoped that wouldn't change. The who's who wasn't the crowd he hoped to attract to the ranch—his ideal guests were people who'd appreciate the beauty and majesty of the mountains as much as he did. People who wanted a true Colorado vacation experience. But money was money, and he'd take what he could get if it meant having enough savings to buy the ranch at the end of the summer.

Watching Sara smile at Ryan and the other man made him wonder what she truly wanted. He was only guessing at the things that made her happy.

He had trouble believing all she cared about was selling her grandmother's house. Already she was an important part of his daughter's life and had captured a big part of his heart, even if he didn't want to admit it. But he couldn't blame her for wanting to reclaim her life on her own terms. He only hoped he could convince her there was room enough in it for him.

Chapter 11

Sara twirled the stem of the wineglass between her fingertips as she looked up at the stars dotting the Colorado night sky. It was well past midnight, but she wasn't the least bit tired.

She'd feigned a yawn when the group had gotten back from town, needing to be alone to sort out her thoughts. Her emotions were a jumble, and something about sitting under the vast expanse of stars calmed her frazzled nerves.

Footsteps echoed across the flagstone path that led from her small porch to the main house. She half expected Ryan to seek her out and thought about retreating into her cabin, unwilling to submit to his relentless pressure any more tonight.

But the way the hairs on her neck pricked as the figure drew closer made her think of beating a retreat for an entirely different reason. Instead. she remained rooted in her chair as Josh's tall figure came clearly into view.

"I saw your light on," he said simply as he hoisted one hip onto her front porch rail. Buster trotted forward out of the darkness, sniffed at her leg and plopped onto the ground.

"I couldn't sleep yet," she answered. "I have a lot on my mind."

He glanced up at the sky above them. "This is as good a place as any to work things out."

Her mouth curved into an unwilling smile at how succinctly he'd guessed her reason for being outside tonight. Still, she shivered as a sudden breeze whipped up from the creek bed behind the property.

"Your grandma loved that robe," he said as she cinched the belt of it tighter.

"I found it in her bedroom." She smoothed her fingers across the soft folds of chenille and cotton. "I hope you don't mind that I took it."

He waited until she met his gaze. "Everything in that house belongs to you, Sara. Don't forget that."

"It doesn't feel like mine." She shook her head. "You and Claire belong here, Josh."

"If I don't push her away." He repeated her words from earlier.

"Like you said, what do I know about making relationships work?" She tried to laugh but it caught in her throat. She wanted to muster the righteous anger she'd felt earlier but didn't have the energy or inclination for it.

"I'm sorry," he said softly. "I didn't mean that." He stood, walking to the edge of the porch. "It scares the hell out of me to think of Claire with her mother. Jennifer wouldn't know a maternal instinct if it bit her on the nose. Claire was an easy little girl, quiet and bent on pleasing whomever she was with at the time. Jennifer could send her off to school then shuttle her around on breaks, parading her in front of the media for a photo op before pawning her off on nannies or lackeys or whoever was available at the time. She let me have Claire more as she got older and had needs of her own. Now that Claire's on the verge of becoming a woman, I'm afraid Jen will treat her as a young protégé, using Claire to get into clubs or entice men." He ran a hand through his hair. "If I'm not there to protect her, there's no telling what could happen."

"Claire has a good head on her shoulders." Sara didn't know how to assuage his fears. "You've raised an amazing daughter and you have to trust she'll make the right decisions."

"I can't," he whispered miserably. "The stakes are too high. If I let her go…"

"You don't know—"

He whirled around. "I do know, Sara. My sister died in a car accident because I left her behind. I didn't take care of Beth, and I'm not going to make the same mistake with Claire."

She stood, wanting to reach out to him. For the first time she saw the stark pain his strength hid so well. Now it made sense to her. It was in the hard line of his jaw, the square set of his broad shoulders, the sharp pull of a mouth she knew to be soft as a butterfly kiss. All of that hid the pain and guilt he felt over his sister's death.

She knew what it was like to hide your true self

so thoroughly that you almost believed the mask you wore was real. She knew the emotional risk involved in revealing the wound behind it.

"Tell me," she whispered.

He turned away again.

For a moment she thought he'd leap off the porch and disappear into the black night. When he didn't move, she came slowly toward him, wrapping her arms around his strong middle. Her cheek pressed against the back of his denim jacket. She breathed in his scent as she willed away the tension pouring off him. Willed him not to leave.

After a moment, his warm hands enveloped hers and he took a deep, shuddering breath. His muscles remained tight but he stayed with her. That was enough for now.

"Tell me," she said again. "Please."

"My father was a mean drunk," he began. "My mom, she both loved and feared him. I'm not sure which one made her stay. In the end, it didn't really matter. There were four of us kids. My brother Jake is two years older than me. When I was four, the twins were born. Beth and my other brother, Logan. My mom did what she could to keep us in line. My dad worked construction, mainly over in Aspen. The more time he spent building mansions for rich people, the more bitter he became about our tiny, run-down farmhouse. And the more bitter he became, the more he drank. Then…"

Sara laced her fingers in his. "What happened?"

"It's not an uncommon story in the mountains. As beautiful as it is up here, it's isolating, especially in the winter. Especially when there's not much work or a man can't hold a job because he's too tempted by the bottle. When we were young, my mom tried to keep us away from him when he was in a mood. That didn't always work with three boys underfoot. Beth was the only one of us he ever seemed to care about. She was shy and quiet. A hell of a lot easier to be around than the rest of us."

He squeezed her hands. "As soon as Jake and I got big enough to fight back, Dad left us alone. He'd take out that anger on Mom when we weren't around. She'd hide the bruises, but we knew. She never sent him away or thought of leaving. Said he needed her too much. More than we needed a decent life.

"Jake got a college scholarship and never looked back. I started on the circuit soon after. I sent money back to Mom when I could. Jake and I both did. But without us in the house to temper his behavior, Dad got even worse. Beth was so quiet, and Logan was a scrawny, sickly kid back then. Mom eventually kicked the jerk out, but it was too late. Beth and Logan were running wild. Beth had an older boyfriend. One night there was an accident. Beth and a group of friends had been drinking—the boyfriend was driving drunk. He hit an elk crossing the highway and..."

Sara wrapped her arms tighter around Josh's waist as he spoke. The anguish and guilt were clear in his tone.

"It wasn't your fault," she whispered.

"I left her here. I left both of them here. I was so intent on getting out, I deserted them. The twins weren't like Jake and me. They needed someone to protect them." He paused to drag in a miserable breath. "I should have protected them. If I'd been here..."

Sara unlaced her fingers from his and scooted

around to stand in front of him. She took his face in her hands and tipped it down so he had to look her in the eyes. The pain she saw there tore at her heart. "That's why you want to keep Claire away from her mother."

"Claire was the same age as Beth when I left. I can't take the chance that something in my daughter could change. What if something happens and I'm not around to make it okay?"

"You should explain that to Claire." Sara drew her fingers through the soft hair along Josh's neck, wanting to relax some of his tension. "Right now she thinks you want to squash her fun. If she understood the reasons why you're protective of her, it might help."

"How can I admit that to her? I'm supposed to be the dad, the one with all the answers."

"You're the dad who loves her with your whole heart. That doesn't always mean you have the answers." Unable to resist, she reached on tiptoe and kissed the corner of his mouth. "You're human, Josh. Not a superhero. You know that, right?"

"If my injury has taught me anything, it's that I'm all too human."

"Human is good," she whispered. "Flesh and blood makes things more interesting."

His eyes darkened as a slow smile broke across his face.

"What did I say?"

"Flesh."

"And blood," she offered.

"Right now, I'm focused on the flesh." He drew his palms up her arms and across the front of the soft robe, rubbing his thumbs against her exposed collarbone. "Yours in particular."

As much as his touch made her skin tingle, she shook her head. "Will you talk to Claire?"

"Will you kiss me again if I say yes?"

"One doesn't have anything to do with the other," she argued, but leaned into him just the tiniest bit.

"I know," he agreed. "Yes, I'll talk to Claire."

She nodded. "You do look a little like a superhero, you know. Like you could handle the weight of the world because you're so strong and tough."

"You're talking movies again. You must be nervous."

She huffed out a breath. "I'm not nervous."

His eyebrows lifted in disbelief. "Anxious, then?" He lowered his head and touched his lips to the curve of her neck. "Or excited?"

He traced a path of kisses along her jaw, then whispered in her ear, "Wondering what it will be like between us?" His teeth grazed her earlobe gently.

Goose bumps rose along her heated skin. "We agreed this was a bad idea."

"I didn't agree to that." His fingers undid the knot of the robe's sash, then moved under the tank top she wore, massaging her back.

Her eyes drifted closed from the pleasure of his touch. She felt each of her arguments fade away in the riptide of desire building throughout her body. It was dangerous, she knew, because she felt more for this man than simple physical attraction. He'd wound his way into her heart with his quiet strength and deep commitment to doing the right thing. Sara hadn't had a lot of experience with men who were truly good, and she found it to be a heady thing and not easy to resist.

"I want you, Sara. From the moment you walked

through the door, I've wanted you." His mouth moved to hers and she felt the smile on his lips. "If I were a superhero, the type who could fly and leap over tall buildings, you'd be my one weakness."

"Did you just make a movie reference for me?" She melted against him a bit more.

"Officially, it was a comic book reference, but you can interpret it any way you want. *If* it means you'll invite me in."

"Come in, Josh," she said as a sigh against his mouth.

A groan of pleasure escaped his lips as he lifted her into his arms and turned for the cabin.

She wrapped her legs around his lean waist as they all but crashed through the front door. His kisses became hotter and more demanding, drawing from her a need she hadn't known she could feel. Pleasure and passion banked inside her for years bubbled to the surface demanding a release.

Josh slammed shut the door then pressed her into it, balancing her weight with his own body as his tongue swept between her lips, mingling with hers in a dance that made her body ache with longing for him.

"Bedroom," he said on a moan.

"Can't wait," she answered, frantic to touch and be touched by him in this moment. Not wanting to delay her need one second more.

Her legs dropped to the floor, and she pushed against him while tugging at the hem of his T-shirt until he flung it off. The robe fell to the ground as they found their way to the couch. Her mouth went dry as he stripped off his boots and jeans, taking her hand as he sank onto the cushions.

She straddled his legs, feeling the evidence of his desire press against her. The realization his reaction was all for her gave Sara a feeling of power she savored, much as she did the warmth of his skin under her hands. She ran her fingers through the short hair on his chest and felt his stomach muscles contract when her tongue skimmed across his nipple.

His hands ravaged her hair, tugging gently until she looked up at him. "You're overdressed," he told her.

She stood and shimmied the pajama pants down past her hips. Then with a breath she lifted the tank top over her shoulders. Sara knew she had a decent figure—although in L.A. even the geriatric set had decent figures. She was well aware what a perfectly sculpted body looked like and just as aware that hers didn't fit the bill. She stood in front of him for a moment, hands held over her breasts in only her cotton panties, wishing she'd had the foresight and budget to buy something more worthy of the moment. But the way Josh's eyes darkened then sparked reminded her that this wasn't Hollywood.

Maybe a real guy wanted to be with a real woman after all.

The thought gave her confidence a boost at the same time as another layer of her heart's armor unfurled for this man.

She took a tentative step closer, and he moved forward to the edge of the sofa. He reached out and cupped her thighs, causing her to shuffle forward until her knees grazed the front of the couch. His mouth pressed against her stomach, drawing small circles of kisses as his fingertips mimicked the pattern on her legs.

Slowly, he gripped the sides of her underpants and

smoothed them down until they fell in a puddle on the floor. He pulled her closer until she was once again on his lap, this time only the thin fabric of his boxers separating them.

"You're the most beautiful thing I've ever seen," he whispered as he took her breast in his mouth, loving the sensitive tip with his tongue. Her back arched against the pleasure he was giving her. He lifted then gently lowered her onto her back on the couch.

Sara felt open and vulnerable, unable to resist her desire in the moment. But when she looked into his eyes, there was something more. An answering need that had nothing to do with a physical release. It was as if he was claiming her with every kiss, every touch. Marking her body and soul as his. She'd never belonged to anyone, and the thought of giving herself now in that way both terrified and exhilarated her.

"You've got a pretty darn good superhero impression going tonight," she said, trying to ground herself with humor.

But the light in his eyes only glowed deeper. "And we haven't even started to fly."

He kissed her again and his hand moved down her bare skin to the place where her body needed him the most. His fingers found her core, stroking her center until her legs would barely hold her. Slowly, he lowered her to the sofa. His mouth found hers as his fingers continued to drive her wild with pleasure.

When she was so close to the brink she wasn't sure she could take any more, she turned her head. "Inside me," she whispered on a tortured breath. "I want you inside."

He lifted away from her for a moment, time enough

to strip off his boxers and pull his wallet out of his jeans, yanking a condom wrapper from the side pocket. Sheathing himself, he covered her once more, his elbows resting above her shoulders as he cradled her face between his hands. "Open for me, Sara."

And she did, biting down on her lip as he filled her completely.

His lips found hers, soothing the place she'd just bitten with his tongue. Her arms wrapped around his shoulders, her fingernails grazing across the corded muscles in his back as he began to move. She moaned, or maybe it was him. Sara was so lost in the pleasure of how he made her feel she couldn't tell.

An intensity built in her body, a golden light filled every fiber of her being. He whispered her name over and over in a voice so full of reverence it made every inch of her tingle in response.

She gripped him tighter as the waves of pleasure washed over her and felt him shudder in response, his body releasing a desire that matched her own. After several minutes, they both stilled, Josh's face nuzzled into the crook of her neck. He kissed her softly, as if to soothe her fractured nerves and emotions.

"I've never felt…" she began, hardly able to put a sentence together. "That was…"

"Amazing, epic, mind-blowing, incredible," he supplied, kissing her once for each adjective he offered.

"All of the above," she admitted when she could form a coherent thought. "I don't know how else to describe it."

"No movie references do it justice?" He lifted his head to look into her eyes.

She saw a hint of amusement but also a question

there. "This is better than the movies," she answered simply. "It's real."

He kissed her deeply again, an exclamation point at the end of her sentence, then cradled her in his strong arms.

Josh used one finger to trace the beam of moonlight that made a sliver of Sara's back gleam in the darkness. She gave a contented sigh and turned her cheek on the pillow.

"How was round two? Better than the first?" she asked, her voice a husky growl that gave him a satisfied tug low in his chest.

"We're a good fit," he answered.

She lifted her head to look at him. "In the bedroom, we're a good fit," she amended for him.

"Not bad on the sofa, either." He tried to ignore the shadow that crossed her face. He knew what she meant but wasn't ready to let reality intrude on this night quite yet.

"I still want to sell the house," she said quietly.

He groaned. "Don't tell me you think we made love so I could convince you not to sell the house."

"I just mean…"

"Because that would make me a royal jerk and you a bit of a hussy. Neither one of those is the case." He propped himself up on his elbow, his hand stilling on the curve of her waist.

"I know you've got goals for the summer and I've got—"

He held one finger up to her lips. "You're trying to pick a fight and it won't work. Tonight was amazing. That's enough. Let me wallow in my undeniable sexual prowess for a few minutes more. It's been a while, you know?"

Her head flopped back down onto the pillow. "I don't want your expectations to change."

"Have you ever been with a guy who hasn't wanted something from you after?"

She squeezed her eyes shut tight.

"Sara, answer me," he prompted.

"My track record with men isn't exactly stellar. Most people I know live their lives wanting something from others. For a while, I couldn't tell if men were interested in me or the doors I could open to parties, premieres and the like. Let's just say I had a lot less offers once my star began to fade."

"Nothing about you is faded," he said, and placed a kiss on the inside of her elbow. He felt her gaze on him but didn't look up. He was too afraid of what his own eyes might reveal.

He didn't expect to change Sara's mind about selling her grandmother's property, but at the same time he still wanted…more. He wanted more for her and from her. He wanted her to see what he saw when he looked at her: a smart, beautiful woman who had so much to offer.

He knew what it was like to believe you were a one-trick pony. When he'd gotten hurt and realized he'd never ride competitively again, he figured he had nothing more to give anyone. The only thing he'd ever been good at in his life was bull riding. In the ring, nothing else mattered. Not his messed-up family, his sister's death, the tenuous relationship he had with his daughter. For those few seconds, his concentration had been completely focused on staying on the back of one thousand pounds of angry animal.

With that gone, he'd wondered what else he had in life. Then he'd gotten another chance with Claire and he'd realized that the time in the ring wasn't as important as he'd once thought.

What mattered was each tiny moment in life and how you lived it. He'd made up his mind to do better, both for Claire and himself. Slowly, he was coming to realize the accident had been an opportunity. A second chance to live life on his own terms.

He wanted Sara to realize that she was more than the on-screen persona created by Hollywood. She had choices and didn't have to prove her worth to anyone but herself.

"I got offered the audition."

He realized his hand had tightened on her hip when she fidgeted underneath it. His mind raced, then he remembered a moment from earlier in the night. "The bearded guy you were talking to at dinner?"

She nodded. "He's a hot director right now. Most of his work has been in television, but he's agreed to make Ryan's movie his first big-screen project."

"Congratulations," he said, unable to muster much enthusiasm for the word.

"Aren't you going to ask why he wants me to read?" Her eyes held a hint of accusation.

"I watched *Just the Two of Us*," Josh answered honestly. "Back when it was a network show and recently, too. Claire's been ordering each season online."

Sara swallowed and looked away. "I didn't know that."

"You were a good actress, Sara. You may be out of

practice, but I doubt that has changed. You had some bad luck, but it doesn't diminish your natural talent."

A lone tear dripped from the outside corner of her eye, and he brushed it away with his lips. "Why don't you seem happy about this?"

She blinked several times. "I stopped believing I had any talent," she told him. "The washed-up child star is such a familiar cliché in Hollywood. Why should I be any different?"

"Because you're an original." Josh took her chin in his fingers and turned her to face him. "You're better than they gave you credit for. You're more than Serena Wellens ever dreamed of being." He studied her for a minute, then added, "You know you don't have to prove anything to anyone? Not your mother, not the critics. Not Ryan or your former friends. Not even me."

"Thank you for saying that," she whispered. "How did you know Ryan is pushing me so hard?"

"That guy is full of bad ideas."

That coaxed a bit of a smile from her. "He knows the director, Jonathan Tramner, from a project they did a few years back. They reconnected because Jonathan has a place in Aspen. He was a fan of my show and, when he heard I was in Crimson, asked Ryan to set up a meeting."

"Which is why Ryan wanted to take us all out to dinner last night," Josh guessed.

"Yes." She shrugged. "The casting people will flip, but Jonathan wants me to read for the lead. He's only in Aspen through next week, so I'm supposed to get the script tomorrow." She glanced at the clock on the nightstand. "Later today, I guess. If I'm interested, I have to meet him at his place on Saturday."

"No way."

She drew back. "No way, what?"

"Even I've heard stories about what happens on casting couches. You're not going to his place alone."

That produced an actual laugh from her. "Trust me, I'm fairly long in the tooth by Hollywood standards. If Jonathan Tramner wanted to make a pass at an actress, he could find a more nubile victim than me."

"Trust me, you're plenty nubile." He scooped her up until she was pressed across the top of him, her long hair tickling his skin. "Are you sure this is what *you* want?"

She rested her arms across his chest, cradling her chin in her hands. "It's been so long since I had a chance to act, it's hard for me to know. But I loved it once. In the midst of all the other crazy in my life growing up, the actual work was good. I know you say I don't have anything to prove, but you're wrong. I have something to prove to myself."

He nodded, leaning up to kiss her on the tip of the nose. "I get that." His stomach burned at the thought of her back in Hollywood. Yet he couldn't blame her for taking another shot at the life she once loved.

Hell, what did he have to offer her here anyway? Running a guest ranch in a tiny mountain town couldn't compare with being on a movie set.

As if reading his thoughts, she said, "It's a long shot, and I'm still committed to making this summer work. To you and Claire."

"I'll drive you to the audition."

Her big eyes widened a fraction. "You don't have to do that."

"You're not alone here, Sara. I—"

Before he could say more, she kissed him sweetly on the mouth. "That's the nicest thing anyone has said to me in a long time."

He could hear the emotion in her voice and it pulled on his heart. He couldn't afford to give himself to this woman but couldn't seem to stop the tumult of emotions she created in him. Running his hands up her bare back, he deepened the kiss. "There's time before I need to go back to the main house," he whispered to her.

She wriggled her hips against his. "Let's make the most of it, then."

Chapter 12

"You're ready."

"I'll never be ready." Sara slumped her head onto the kitchen table and thumped it several times.

"I agree with April," Claire told her, scooping a spoonful of peanut butter from the jar. "We've been practicing every day for the past week. You're perfect for the part of Amelia. They'd be crazy not to hire you."

The more Sara thought about the audition, the more she was afraid Jonathan Tramner would be crazy if he actually did hire her. Yes, she'd rehearsed the lines, tapped into the emotion of the character, a single mother fighting for custody of her autistic son. Both April and Claire had read through pivotal scenes in the script with her dozens of times. But was she really ready to put herself out there in this way again?

Luckily, she hadn't had much time to ruminate over

her doubts. After Josh's friends had left, the family reunion checked in, and she'd been busy arranging activities and making sure the needs of guests ranging in age from three to seventy-eight were met.

The family members were lovely, especially the grandparents. They'd been thrilled to share stories of their courtship and fifty-plus years of marriage. Although it was clear their children had heard the tales many times, they gamely listened over and over, adding funny commentary about childhood antics, long-ago vacations and good-natured sibling rivalries.

Being on set during her childhood had been the closest Sara had ever come to feeling like she had a family. During her summer hiatuses, she'd count down the days until she could get back to filming, the only time her life seemed to make sense. As she glanced up to her grandmother's warm, welcoming kitchen and her friends here supporting her, she thought maybe she didn't need a set to give her that sense of normalcy any longer.

"Get a new spoon," she said automatically to Claire as the girl began to dip her used one back into the peanut-butter jar.

Claire pulled a face but tossed her spoon into the sink. "You'll be great at the part of the overprotective mother," Claire said as she pulled a clean spoon out of a drawer. "You already sound like one half the time."

Sara stood and claimed a spoon for herself then dipped into the jar over Claire's shoulder. "What if I do get it? What if I don't? I can't decide which is scarier."

"You'll know what was meant to be when it happens," April counseled as she dried dishes from breakfast and put them away in the cabinets.

"How are we friends when you're always so darn zen?"

"It's the yoga," Claire told her. "You should do it with us in the morning."

"I need my beauty rest more than I need to turn my body into a pretzel." She met April's gaze over Claire's head and felt a blush creep up her cheeks at her friend's raised eyebrows.

April had been leading 7:00 a.m. yoga sessions for the guests to start each day. Sara would normally be a part of each one. Now, thanks to Josh, the early mornings after he left her cabin were the only rest she was getting. Maybe he wasn't turning her body into a pretzel each night, but she was certainly moving in ways she hadn't for a long, long time. She thought they'd been discreet about their relationship, but from the look on April's face, her friend knew exactly what was going on.

"Have you and your dad made things right?" she asked Claire, wanting to turn the attention away from April's inquisitive gaze.

"I guess," Claire mumbled around a mouthful of peanut butter. "I'm mainly ignoring him. It's easy because he's so busy with the guests."

"You need to talk to him." She wrapped one arm around Claire's small shoulders. "He loves you, sweetie."

"Your mom came by the other day," Claire countered.

Sara heard April cough to cover a laugh. The girl was young but she was good. "Yes, I know. She texted me later."

"She said there's a photographer in Aspen who does

great head shots of models and actresses. She offered to drive me over."

"Your father isn't going to allow that."

Claire shrugged out of Sara's embrace. "What if I don't tell him?"

"Then I will," Sara said, her eyes narrowed. "Trust me, my mother is not someone you want in your life."

"She seems nice and she believes in me," Claire grumbled. "It's about time someone did."

"Your father believes in you. He wants to keep you safe so you have a decent future. You have choices, Claire. You can be whoever you want."

"As long as I do exactly what my dad says. How is that a choice?"

"Talk to him. Tell him how you feel."

Claire swiped a hand across her cheek. "He doesn't care about how I feel. He wants me to be the no-trouble little girl I used to be, playing quietly with my dolls in the corner. It stinks to get older."

"Amen, sister," Sara whispered, then caught herself. "You're barely a teenager. This is new territory for both of you. I know your dad loves you. Even if he's stumbling around how he shows it."

Buster galloped into the room and nudged his big head under Claire's arm. Her eyes widened and she shook her head. "I'm crying and Dad's here. I don't want him to see me like this."

Sara took hold of her arm. "He knows you're upset. He is, too, Claire. He's driving me to Aspen this morning for the audition. Why don't you come with us?"

"Not a chance," Claire said, shaking off Sara's grip. "I'm going to hang out with friends all day."

"What friends? Where will you be?"

"Friends," the girl repeated. "I'll be around town." She took a step toward the back door. "You're not my mother, Sara. You don't need to act like you really care."

Before Sara could argue, Claire had run out of the house, Buster following close on her heels.

Josh walked into the kitchen at that moment, his gaze swinging between Sara and April. "What's going on in here?" he asked, brow furrowed.

"Hormones," both women said at once.

Josh took a step back. "Should I wait for you in the car?"

Sara shook her head. "It's Claire. I pushed her to talk to you. Probably too far." She pointed a finger at Josh. "Why haven't you made things right with her yet?"

He threw up his hands. "I've tried. She locks herself in her room anytime she's in the house and tells me she has a headache. With guests coming and going, I've barely had time to take a breath, let alone pin her down."

"It's important, Josh."

"I know."

"Maybe you should stay here instead of going to Aspen with me. Rent a bunch of vintage John Hughes movies. Anything with Molly Ringwald. Might give you a sense of what you're dealing with."

"Your audition is important, too." His brows knit in frustration. "And there's no way in hell I'm watching teeny-bopper flicks from the eighties."

Sara bit down on her lip. "I can manage the audition." She didn't want to admit how embarrassed she'd be if she bombed the read-through. The thought of Josh seeing her at her most vulnerable made her chest tighten.

"Let him take you," April told her, sliding one arm around Sara's shoulders. "You're not alone, Sara."

Sara glanced at her friend, the one who'd been at her side through both her slow descent into obscurity and self-sabotaging attempts to ruin her own life. April had stayed with her no matter what. There was no one Sara trusted more.

"Am I good enough?" she whispered, too desperate for the answer to care that Josh could hear her pathetic question.

"You're better," April assured her. She turned to Josh. "I'll be at the house all day, so I can keep an eye on Claire. I'll suggest that her friends come here to hang out."

"Thanks," Josh said gruffly. "I have a van coming to pick up the family reunion for the airport later this morning. We have a couple of days until the next guests arrive." He glanced at Sara. "I'll take Claire out on the ATVs tomorrow, spend the whole day with her on the mountain." He took a breath, then added, "I'll make things right."

Sara nodded. "Good. Then let's get this over with."

With a last hug for April, she made her way to the front of the house and Josh's truck. She put her hand on the door but before she could open it, Josh spun her to face him.

His lips met hers, and he kissed her for several moments, his palms encircling her face. His touch helped to melt away the anxiety she'd felt since the morning, giving her a sense of delicious pleasure that curled her toes.

"Not here," she told him when she finally broke the connection. "Claire could see us. Anyone could see us."

"I don't care," he answered, and kissed her again. "We shouldn't have to hide." He dipped his head until his eyes were level with hers. "Never think for a minute that you're not good enough, Sara."

Her gaze dropped to the ground, but he tipped up her chin until she met his eyes again. "That director would be lucky to have you on his movie, just like we're lucky to have you at the ranch. You have a place here. No matter what happens. This is your grandmother's house and it belongs to you. You belong."

A light breeze blew in from the hills behind the ranch. The swirling gray clouds in the sky matched her tumultuous emotions. As much as she didn't appreciate it when she'd first come to Colorado, the crisp scent of pines in the air had become a salve to her frazzled nerves. In more ways than one, she was acclimating to life in this small town. The very thought scared her to her core. She'd never had a true home before and wondered if she was made to last in a place like Crimson.

She bit down on her lip and nodded. "Thank you" was all she could say in response.

He opened the door and she climbed into the truck, emotion welling in her throat. Raindrops began hitting the windshield, large drops of wetness that turned into a deluge by the time he was at the end of the driveway. He didn't say anything more as they pulled out onto the two-lane highway that led to Aspen. Sara was grateful. She wasn't sure she could manage a single word right now without bursting into tears.

The sound of the rain lulled her into a quiet trance. The sudden storm was so heavy, Sara could barely see beyond the rain-soaked windows to the valley beyond. Was this a good omen? Mother Nature washing away all the old gunk she harbored? Or a bad one, the mile-high version of *The Perfect Storm?*

"Are we going to make it?" she asked, only half kidding as the rain turned to hail. A ferocious rhythm pounded outside, echoing in the truck's interior.

"A normal summer storm, that's all," Josh answered with a wink. "To make sure I'm paying attention."

She closed her eyes as he took her hand in his, soothing her with his gentle touch. It was dangerous to have her emotions this close to the surface before she went into an audition. She needed to stay professional. She concentrated on breathing, pulling air in and out of her lungs as she thought about the character she was reading for, what made the single mother tick and how Sara could use her own experience to enhance the lines she read as Amelia.

After a few minutes, her mind cleared and all that was left was the character. This was the part she loved about acting, pushing off reality and turning herself into someone new.

By the time they wound their way into downtown Aspen a half hour later, she was in the zone, despite the continuing rain. Jonathan Tramner was staying at one of the upscale boutique hotels just off the town's center. Josh pulled the truck to a stop under the building's front canopy, ignoring the valet who came around the vehicle.

"I don't want to hover like a helicopter parent today," he said with a sheepish smile. "I'm learning something from my time with Claire."

Sara turned and gave him a small smile in return. "Thank you for bringing me here. I'll go up to the audition on my own. I need to do that. Dust off my Serena Wellens attitude in the elevator."

"Leave Serena behind, sweetheart. You don't need her anymore." Josh lifted the hand he still held to his mouth, grazing a long kiss across her knuckles. "I have some things to pick up at the hardware store just outside of town. I'll be back in thirty minutes and waiting in the lobby."

She grimaced. "Are you sure you want to come back so soon? These things can sometimes take a while."

"I'll be waiting," he assured her. "And don't forget, you've got this."

I've got this, Josh thought to himself more than an hour later as he shifted in the overstuffed chair at the side of the hotel's lobby, where he was out of the way but still able to see the bank of elevators in the back. He'd thought about heading to the bar, but since it was only noon and he still had to drive back to Crimson, that didn't seem like the best idea.

He picked up his cell phone and gave it a hard shake, but the screen remained dark. Thanks to his nerves, he'd spilled an entire cup of coffee on the damn thing shortly after dropping Sara off earlier. He wasn't sure whether he was more nervous that she'd get the part or she wouldn't. Either way, his heart hammered in his chest each time the elevator doors slid open.

He believed in Sara without question and hoped that whoever this *hot* Hollywood director was would be able to see what Josh did. He'd heard her rehearsing with both April and Claire over the past week, and the emotion in her voice had made a shiver roll down his spine. If she was as good as he thought, then in no time she'd have a better offer than anything he could give her. He wasn't sure what she wanted from her next chapter in life, doubted she knew herself. His heart couldn't help hoping it would somehow involve him.

His head lifted as the elevator dinged. Before the doors had opened fully, Sara bolted out. Her wild eyes scanned the room then landed on him.

"We need to go," she yelled, and motioned him toward the front entrance. "Now."

He sprang out of the chair and caught up to her within a few strides. "What happened up there? Did he do something to you?"

"Where's your phone? Why isn't it on?" she asked, not stopping to look him in the eye.

"Sara, what's the problem?" He swung her around to face him, trying to figure out why she looked so panicked. "How was the audition?"

She shook her head. "I left in the middle of it." Her hand squeezed his arm. "It's Claire. There's been an accident. We have to get to the hospital."

Josh's mind reeled like he'd taken a sucker punch to the jaw. Her words played through his head in slow motion.

Claire. Accident. Hospital.

He turned and ran through the sliding doors leading to the street. He'd parked his truck around the corner, not wanting to bother with the valet. He reached it in seconds and fumbled for his keys, his fingers shaking uncontrollably. He took a breath and steadied himself. He'd do his daughter no good if he was too crazy to get to her.

The rain had slowed to a light drizzle, and he hit the wipers to clear the windshield as he turned the key in the ignition. Sara climbed in next to him, breathing hard from following at his breakneck pace.

He pulled out onto the street, mentally calculating the route to the hospital in his head. The facility was located between the two towns, which would put him there in about twenty minutes. Fifteen without traffic. His mind saw the stretch of highway they'd drive in detail, from the tight curves to the areas where water was likely to pool after a storm. His focus was absolute, much like it had been during his bull-riding days. That had been Josh's gift in the ring. His ability to visualize the entire ride, anticipate how the animal was going to move before it did.

Control the situation.

His current life left him feeling more out of control by the day. All his well-crafted plans amounted to nothing when his daughter was in trouble.

"What happened?" he asked, his gaze remaining fixed on the road. "Is Claire okay?"

"I don't know," Sara answered, and his knuckles tightened on the steering wheel. "April said something happened at the creek. I had terrible reception in the hotel suite so the call dropped. Why didn't you pick up your phone?"

"Spilled coffee and fried it."

"She was trying to reach you for a while before she called me." He saw her glance at the phone held tightly between her fingers. "Do you want me to try her again?"

He shook his head. "We'll be there in minutes." If his head didn't explode from the pounding inside it first. Claire needed him and he couldn't be reached.

Wasn't the whole point of returning to Crimson so he'd be around to keep his daughter safe?

Now the one time she needed him, he'd failed her.

Like he'd failed his sister.

Sara reached out and placed a hand on his arm. "I'm sure she'll be fine. April would call back if there was anything else to report."

"I have to get to her," he whispered, not hiding the emotion that choked his voice. "I have to know."

Sara squeezed his arm but said nothing more. Josh knew how fast the creek on the far side of his property flowed after a heavy rainstorm. The water could go from a soft trickle to a raging current within minutes. That was how it was in the mountains. He hadn't expressly warned Claire to stay away from the creek because they hadn't been getting much rain this summer. She wasn't much inclined to be outside when she didn't have to be anyway. He should have thought of it, though. His job as her father was to think of everything he could. Josh knew all too well how losing your concentration for even a moment could cost a person. It was a lesson he didn't want his daughter to learn.

Within minutes, they pulled into the hospital parking lot. He threw the truck into Park, not caring that he'd stopped in the fire lane, and headed for the entrance.

"Claire Travers," he said to the receptionist behind the desk in the E.R. lobby. "I'm her father."

The woman barely glanced from her computer screen. "Exam Two, down the hall to your right."

Sara was beside him as he raced down the hall. At the room marked Two, Josh swung open the door. His heart skipped a year's worth of beats as he saw

Claire in the bed, her eyes closed. A white bandage wound around her head and her arm was casted up to the elbow.

He must have choked out a sound because she blinked and turned her head on the pillow. "Daddy," she whispered, her voice scratchy and slow.

But she'd said his name. Her eyes were focused on his. That had to be a good sign, right?

He took two steps toward the bed, then noticed April in the chair at the corner of the room. "She's okay," the woman told him, clearly reading the panic in his expression.

"I'm fine," Claire added groggily. "Just clumsy." She must be on some heavy painkillers.

As he got closer, Josh noticed the scratches all along her knuckles and a large bruise forming on one cheek. He clenched his jaw with a mix of worry, frustration and anger. He hadn't been there and she'd been hurt. He wanted to punch his fist into the wall, to feel a tenth of the pain she felt.

Even more, he wanted to know how to make it better. He'd not been around enough to kiss away boo-boos or mend scraped knees when she was younger. Maybe if he had, he wouldn't be so traumatized now.

He couldn't speak, couldn't move. She looked so fragile, her face pale against the white sheet. He lifted his hand then lowered it again, not sure what to do with his mixed-up emotions.

Sara took his arm and gently led him to the side of the bed, pushing him to sit next to Claire.

"What if I hurt her more?" he said through gritted teeth, making to stand again.

"You won't," Sara assured him. She moved to stand

next to him and took the hand from Claire's uninjured arm, wrapping Josh's fingers around his daughter's.

He swallowed around the lump in his throat. Claire's skin was cool to the touch, and instinctively he grasped her hand tighter, rubbing his fingers back and forth until warmth began to seep into her fingertips.

"You don't have to talk, sweetheart," Sara said, soothing her thumb across Claire's forehead below the bandage. "We're so happy you're okay."

Claire gave Sara a wobbly smile then her gaze turned to Josh. "I'm sorry I worried you. I knew it was stupid to go down to the creek after such a hard rain. Some of the kids thought it would be cool." She made a tiny sound that might have been a laugh. "I could hear your voice in my head telling me not to." She coughed, wincing from the effort.

"Don't talk," Josh told her, dragging in a shaky breath. "Rest now. I'm here. You're okay." He said the words as much for his own benefit as hers.

"She slipped on a rock and went down in the creek," April said, coming to stand at the foot of the bed. "The current was pretty strong, but she held on to a branch until one of the boys she was with could drag her out. She told me they were walking to a neighbor's house." April's breath hitched. "I'm sorry, Josh. You left me in charge and this happened. I'm so sorry."

April shook her head, then turned and left the room.

"It's not her fault," Claire said, squeezing Josh's fingers. "I lied about where I was going." She coughed again.

"Hush now," Josh told her softly. "I'm not mad at April." He lifted Claire's hand and kissed the inside of her wrist. "Or you, even though I probably should be." His voice caught as he added, "I'm just so damn glad it's not worse."

He watched as Sara bent to give Claire's cheek a gentle kiss. "I'm going to find April. You get some rest, and soon we'll take you home where you belong."

As she turned to leave, Josh caught her hand. "Thank you for taking that call," he said, and leaned up to kiss her quickly on the mouth. Her cheeks immediately turned a bright shade of pink as she glanced over her shoulder at Claire, who was now watching them with an interest that belied the effect of the painkillers.

"I'll be in the hall," Sara said, and left the room.

"So the two of you..." Claire began as Sara left the room.

Josh couldn't help but return his daughter's smile. "We'll talk about that later. We'll talk about a lot of things later. Right now, do as she said and rest. I want you out of here as soon as can be arranged."

Claire took a deep breath. "I love you, Daddy," she whispered as her eyes drifted shut.

"I love you, too, Claire-Bear," Josh answered, for the first time in years using the nickname he'd given her as a young girl.

One corner of her mouth kicked up, but within moments her breathing had slowed to an even rhythm that told him she was asleep.

He sat there for several more minutes, drinking in every one of her features. In sleep, she looked more the child than a girl on the cusp of becoming a woman. If only he could keep her small, maybe he'd be able to avoid the gray hairs he could imagine sprouting at the moment. How did any father of a teenage daughter ever sleep at night?

She'd said she could hear his voice in her head, but she'd made the bad choice anyway. That was exactly how he'd been as a teen, almost eager to thwart his mother's advice and his father's commands at every turn. He knew all about the trouble that could come from wanting to rebel against your parents. He'd seen it in each of his siblings, and had no doubt it had contributed to his sister's tragic death.

He wasn't kidding when he'd said he was going to talk to Claire later. About everything, just like Sara had originally advised. He couldn't stop Claire from making bad decisions, but if he was honest about his own feelings, maybe she'd feel freer to share hers and not act out. It was the exact opposite to the parenting strategy his own mom and dad had taken, which led him to believe it was far more sound than anything else he could try.

At this point, Josh would try anything to avoid his past from making trouble in his present life.

Chapter 13

Sara tucked the covers in tight around Claire, making the girl's slim body into a tiny cocoon, then adjusted the hot water bottle she'd placed near the bottom of the bed.

"Mmm," Claire mumbled. "Feels snug as a bug."

Hours earlier at the hospital, Sara had first comforted April, convincing her friend no one blamed her for the accident. Then she'd tracked down the doctor who'd treated Claire, making sure he discussed her injuries and treatment with Josh. The doctor reassured Josh that Claire's broken wrist was the worst of her condition and she'd recover without a problem.

Josh had been both overwhelmed and terrified at Claire being hurt. That was a normal reaction for any parent, but Sara knew that part of his anxiety had to do with memories of his sister's accident. She wanted to make sure the hospital staff didn't worry him any more than was necessary.

They'd brought Claire home just before dinnertime, and Josh had insisted on carrying her from the truck up to her bedroom. She'd been too tired to text her friends, but had begged Sara and Josh to watch part of season three of *Just the Two of Us* with her.

Unable to say no when Claire was clearly so out of it, Sara had climbed onto the bed with her while Josh hooked the iPad up to the television on the dresser. He'd positioned himself on the other side of Claire, her head resting against his strong shoulder. Sara had almost flinched when her younger self appeared on screen during the opening credits.

She'd pressed her head back against the headboard and remained resolutely still so Josh wouldn't see her reaction. They'd made it through three episodes before Claire admitted to being too tired to continue. She'd complained about a chill, and Sara'd felt almost frozen herself as she heated a water bottle and took an extra quilt from the linen closet in the hall.

Thankfully, Josh had disappeared by the time she returned to Claire's room. She bent to give Claire a kiss, surprised when the girl reached out to take her hand.

"You were a cute kid," Claire said sleepily.

"Cute only takes you so far," Sara answered.

"You're even prettier now," Claire continued as if Sara hadn't spoken. "Especially since you stopped wearing so much makeup and took the streaks out of your hair."

Sara rolled her eyes at this drug-induced critique of her beauty habits. She'd heard way worse. "I don't remember much about my gran, but I think she used to say, 'Pretty is as pretty does.' That makes more sense to me now than it used to."

"I'd like to be prettier," Claire answered around a yawn.

"You're beautiful, sweetheart."

"I haven't been much in the 'pretty does' category lately. I'm going to work on that." She tugged on Sara's sleeve until Sara sat on the edge of the bed.

"I like you with my dad," she whispered.

Sara felt her mouth drop open. "It's not serious. I mean, he's great. You know I'm only here for the summer and…"

She stopped as Claire's eyes closed. The girl's fingers dropped from her arm. Sara adjusted the pillow and blankets a bit more then straightened.

Tiptoeing out of the room, she flipped off the light and closed the door behind her.

"Not serious?" a voice asked next to her ear.

Sara jumped back, her palm landing with a thump on her chest. "Eavesdrop much?"

Josh laced his fingers in hers. "Only when it counts."

Too tired to argue, she let him lead her down the stairs. "We need to talk," he said quietly as they reached the bottom step.

"I'm tired, Josh." She huffed out a breath. "If *talk* is code for *argue,* I don't have the energy for it tonight."

"It's not," he assured her. When they stepped into the kitchen, she noticed the large trestle table was set for two, delicate china plates and beautiful crystal goblets. Candlelight danced from two pillars near the center of the table.

"What's this? Where's April?"

"April was tired. We talked and she went back to

her cabin." He held up his hands at her look. "It's fine, Sara. I don't blame your friend and she knows it."

"Good, because April would do anything to keep Claire safe."

"Sit down," Josh told her softly. "You haven't eaten since breakfast."

"Did April…"

"I ordered carryout from the Italian place in town. They delivered."

"I love meatballs," Sara said on a tiny sigh.

Josh smiled. "April told me they were your favorite."

She glanced at him, stunned for a moment that on a day when he'd been through so much, he'd think of her preferences. So much for her comment about not being serious. Her heart was seriously flipping in her chest.

"You didn't have to do this," she said casually, not wanting him to see how much the small gesture affected her. "I can—"

He leaned forward and kissed her before she could continue. "Let me take care of you," he said against her lips. "Just for tonight."

He held out a chair for her and she sat, biting on her lip as she looked at the spaghetti, salad and garlic bread in bowls on the table.

Josh scooped noodles, meatballs and the rest on her plate. She unfolded the delicate linen napkin before her and spread it on her lap.

"It smells delicious," she said, breathing in the tangy scent of the food.

"It tastes even better," Josh answered, serving himself generous portions of everything.

Sara cut off a chunk of meatball and brought it to her mouth. Josh was right; the food was divine. As soon as she swallowed the first bite, she realized how hungry she was. All she had at her little cabin was granola bars and an overripe banana, so she was especially grateful for this feast.

"Tell me about the audition," Josh said after a few minutes.

The meatball that had moments earlier tasted like a little piece of heaven turned dry in mouth. "I wasn't right for the part after all," she said simply.

"You left because of Claire." Josh studied her over the rim of his wineglass.

Sara didn't drink often, but she took a big gulp of her own wine to wash down the bite of food lodged in her throat. "It doesn't matter."

"You were up there for a while. Did you read at all?"

She nodded. "Jonathan was on a call for a long time when I got there. We talked about the character for a bit. I told him how I saw Amelia. We read a small piece from the script, but I couldn't concentrate because I could feel my phone vibrating in the purse at my feet. Finally, I took the call. Then I left." She lifted her hands and forced her lips into a smile. "End of story. Not a big deal."

"It is a big deal." Josh's gaze was sympathetic. "I know how hard you worked for this reading. How much you wanted it."

"Bad timing. Story of my life." Sara pushed away her plate, her stomach suddenly rolling precariously.

"Will you get another chance?" Josh leaned forward and tried to take her hand.

She folded her arms across her chest. "This *was* my other chance."

He shook his head. "That can't be the end of it. It wasn't your fault. I'll call. Ryan can call."

She tried to laugh. "Since when are you so ready to be rid of me? I didn't think you were excited about the audition in the first place."

"I'm not. But I want you to know that you're good. Whatever the future brings, you deserve it to be on your terms. You sacrificed a lot for Claire and me today."

"I told you it wasn't a big deal."

"I know it was a very big deal." His eyes turned dark as he watched her. "A serious deal."

"Why did you kiss me in front of Claire at the hospital?"

One broad shoulder lifted. "Because I wanted to kiss you."

"Oh" was all she could manage.

He stood, his face lit by the glow of the candles. "I want to kiss you now."

"Oh," she repeated.

"Do you want it, too?"

Her heart fluttered in her chest. She nodded, and he drew her out of her chair and into his arms, his mouth melding over hers as if his lips had been expressly formed for hers.

"I know you're not staying past the end of summer," he said, drawing back to look into her eyes.

Ask me to stay, a voice whispered inside her head.

"I can't give you the life you want here."

What if all I want is you? the voice asked silently.

She focused her gaze on his mouth, not wanting him to read the emotions she knew clouded her face.

"My priority has to be Claire."

She gave a brief nod. When would Sara ever be someone's number-one priority? His comment didn't surprise her; she couldn't blame him for it. Still, a tiny pit of despair opened in a corner of her heart. She made to turn away, but Josh held her close.

"Unless we could be enough for you."

Her gaze snapped to his. She saw a flame flickering behind his eyes that stoked a thunderous wildfire in her body.

"Would you consider making Crimson your home?" he asked softly. "I want you here. With Claire and me. It's not glamorous and there's still a long way to go before the ranch is set. But you make it better. Claire loves you and I…"

Sara held her breath as she waited for the words she hadn't known she longed to hear.

After a moment Josh continued, "I think we make a good team."

I love you. I love you. I love you. The voice in her head had gone from a whisper to a full-out yell. But she didn't say those three words. She wouldn't take the chance of scaring him away. She knew a good offer when she saw it. It was a perk of wading through bad ones for so many years.

"I think I might like that," she answered carefully. Which was only part of the truth. What she'd like was for Josh to drop to his knees and proclaim his undying love for her. She'd never ask for that. Sara tried never to ask for anything, too afraid of being disappointed.

Unaware of her inner turmoil, he bent and claimed her mouth once again. If he wasn't actually able to say the words, his touch certainly communicated the deep feeling she longed for from him.

This is enough, she counseled her inner voice. More than you ever expected.

Apparently her inner voice was a bit of a floozy, because it gave a small sigh then commanded her to concentrate on the kiss.

Which she did without hesitation.

Josh's touch was pure magic. He wrapped his arms around her waist as her hands twined through his thick hair. She loved being enveloped in his strength. The heat radiating from him warmed all the cold, lonely places in her soul.

"Upstairs," he said as his mouth grazed her ear.

She pushed against his shoulders with her palms. "We should clean up down here. If April comes in…"

"April won't be back tonight," he assured her as a devilish gleam lit his gaze. "Which gives me a better idea for right now."

He kissed her again, and at the same time lifted the hem of her blouse up over her head.

Sara's eyes widened. "We can't. Not here."

"Why not?" His grin turned wicked. "All the guests are gone. Claire is fast asleep and the pain meds will almost guarantee she stays that way through the night. It's only us. You own this house, Sara. You can do whatever you want with it and in it."

He stepped back, and she knew he was putting the power to decide where this night went next in her hands. Sara relished the feeling of being able to control something in her life, even if it was this one moment.

Her fingers reached behind her back and unclasped the strap of her bra. She let the satin fabric drop from her arms and smiled a bit as Josh sucked a breath. Slowly, she undid each button on her jeans, using her palms to slide the material over her hips and down her legs.

"You're going to kill me," Josh said, his voice ragged.

She straightened, wearing only her bright pink panties. "There are worse ways to die," she told him, making her tone sympathetic.

His hungry gaze rolled over her from her face to her toes then came to rest on her hips. "Put me out of my misery," he whispered. "Please."

The raw desire in his eyes made her want to run into his arms. Instead, she looped a finger through the thin waistband on either side of her underpants, bending forward a little as the small piece of fabric fell in a puddle at her feet.

"Is this what you want?" she asked, coyly placing her hands on her hips.

"You have no idea how much," he answered, and ate up the distance between them in two steps.

The moment he touched her, she realized she'd either been acting or fooling herself by thinking she was in control of this situation. Her whole body tingled in anticipation of being with him.

She tugged at his shirt but he circled her wrists in his fingers. "Not yet," he breathed against her breast before taking the puckered tip in his mouth.

Her head arched back with pleasure as he pushed her arms behind her, giving him better access to her sensitive flesh. An instant later, she let out a gasp as her bottom touched the cool granite counter.

"Right where I want you," he said, and dipped his head to place a line of kisses down her belly.

"Josh, this isn't..."

The protest died on her lips as he ran his tongue

along her inner thigh. "We need to be quiet," he whispered. "No noise."

Right. Claire upstairs sleeping. April in the nearest cabin. Quiet. She could do quiet.

But when he kissed the center of her being, Sara almost had to bite down on her arm to keep from crying out. The way he touched and tasted her was perfect, as if knew her body's needs better than she did. She felt the pressure build throughout her limbs, and when the release burst over her it was like the Fourth of July, New Year's and all the other holidays rolled into one. Fireworks exploded behind her eyes and a delicious tremor coursed the length of her body.

But it wasn't enough. "Need you," she said, gulping for air. "Now."

Immediately, Josh straightened and shed his shirt and cargo pants in an instant. He fumbled with the condom packet and gave a harsh laugh. "My fingers aren't working right at the moment."

She took the foil from his hands, then wrapped her fingers around his hard length, rolling the condom over his tip. When she glanced up and winked, he gathered her into his arms, lifting her to the edge of the granite as he sheathed himself in her. Her arms wound around his shoulders. She buried her face in the crook of his neck, biting down softly on his skin. He increased his rhythm, and she matched him stroke for glorious stroke until they dived off passion's cliff together. He murmured her name over and over, his warm, calloused palms stroking up and down her back.

After a few moments, they stilled, holding each other without moving. She wished she could give her heart the same release as her body, leave it blissfully content. Instead, the dumb thing continued to pound against her chest even after her breathing had slowed.

She knew the reason, even if she didn't want to admit it. She was in love. A litany of silly movie lines rang through her tormented mind: "You had me at hello," "You've consumed me body and soul," "You make me want to be a better…" Well, maybe she'd draw the line at Jack Nicholson.

Sappy chick flicks had been her favorite before this summer. She wondered if she'd even be able to watch one again. Because she suddenly understood the sentiment behind every tear-jerking scene. Hell, if she got the chance she should audition for one of those roles. She had a wellspring of lovelorn angst to tap.

He'd asked her to stay. Said they made a great team. Wasn't that enough?

But now that she'd really felt what it was like to be head over heels in love with someone, could she settle for anything less?

"Are you okay?" Josh drew back to look at her. He placed his hand across her chest. "Your heart's beating like crazy."

"Altitude adjustment," she said dismissively, scooting out of his grasp and bending to pick up her clothes. "That was quite a workout."

He took his own T-shirt from the chair where it had landed and pulled it over his head. "Stay with me tonight?"

Sara swallowed, then waved at the table. "We need to clean up."

"Clean up. Then stay," he told her. "At least for a few hours."

He looped his arms around her waist. "Please."

Knowing he couldn't see it, she squeezed her eyes shut tight. "You have good manners for a cowboy." She made her tone light. Perhaps she really was a decent actress.

"Is that a yes?"

She nodded, unable to resist. Was there anything he'd ask of her that she could say no to? April had always told Sara she needed to be better about guarding her heart. But when a person spent their life with little encouragement or true affection, it was hard to stand strong when a man offered her any little bit.

She'd gotten used to living on emotional crumbs. While Josh hadn't exactly baked her a cake, he was a good man. He was doing the best he could. She couldn't fault him for that.

Why not enjoy the ride, as long as it lasted?

Sara stepped into the Crimson visitors' center later that week. She'd just picked up the new brochures for the ranch from the printer and wanted to deliver them personally.

The latest guests had left for the airport that morning, and a new crop was arriving in a few days. She was taking this, her one off day, to run errands and arrange a few promotional things in town.

She tried to let April do most of the work with the locals, still not sure of the reception she'd receive. So far today, people had acted normal, no snide remarks about her career or how she didn't fit in here in the mountains. A few of the townies at the post office had asked about the ranch, appearing pleased when she told them their booking rate. Apparently, a lot of people had been rooting for Josh and her gran. It made Sara proud to be part of the ranch's success.

Ryan had been livid when she'd explained what had happened at the audition, but that wasn't her problem anymore. She'd done what she needed to in the situation. If she'd lost her best chance at regaining her career, so be it. Other than the cast on her arm, Claire had recovered nicely. Josh had taken her out for a picnic at one of the nearby waterfalls today. He'd invited Sara to come, but she knew that father and daughter needed time for themselves.

A slender woman with a severe ponytail looked up from a computer as the door jingled. Her mouth dropped open, and Sara recognized her as one of the women who'd been in the clothing store when the shopkeeper had been so rude.

"Hello," Sara said, stepping forward while ignoring the potential awkwardness of the situation. She could make a scene, but that wouldn't do anything to help the ranch. Despite her years in showbiz, Sara'd never been one to play the drama-queen card. "Who do I talk to about these brochures for Crimson Ranch?"

"I'm sorry," the woman answered immediately.

Sara waited for her to continue with, *I don't want to promote anything you're involved in.*

Instead, the woman said softly, "For that day in Feathers and Threads when you first came to town. I shouldn't have listened to Rita gossiping about you like that. I wanted to stand up to her but…"

"I'm not used to people standing up for me." *Josh had done just that,* her irritating inner voice piped up. "Don't worry about it."

"That doesn't make it right." The woman held out

a thin hand. "My name is Olivia Wilder, and I hope you'll accept my apology."

Sara's first reaction was to make a sharp comeback, probably aimed at herself. Josh had told Sara she was a difficult person to compliment. That was true, she realized. She also didn't take apologies well. It felt like letting her guard down. She'd learned long ago the negative consequences that came from that.

Olivia looked sincere, however, and Sara was growing tired of the energy it took to keep the walls built up around her. "Sara Wells," she answered. "Nice to meet you. I appreciate the apology."

Olivia's face broke into a wide smile, and Sara was amazed at the transformation. When Olivia Wilder stopped looking like she'd spent the day sitting on a large stick, she was quite lovely.

"We'd be happy to display your brochures here." She shuffled through some papers on the desk. "I also have a mailing of promotional materials going to several different cities around the state and the Midwest. A few to Texas as well, since they're a big part of our tourism business." She picked up a pen and did some quick calculations. "If you can get me an extra five hundred by the beginning of next week, I'll include you in what I send out."

"That would be fantastic," Sara said, doing a mental fist pump. "Do you manage the visitors' center?"

Olivia's mouth opened and shut a few times. "Not exactly." She tucked a stray strand of hair behind her ear. "I'm an artist, a painter. My husband is the mayor, and he likes me to stay busy with activities he deems appropriate and productive."

"Huh," Sara answered slowly. "That's funny, because you seem like a grown woman fully capable of deciding how you want to spend your own time."

"Yes, well…marriage is about compromise, I guess." Olivia flashed a smile that was anything but happy.

Sara placed a stack of brochures on the desk. "If it's what you want," she said, not believing for a minute that this woman was happy being her husband's puppet. Maybe it was because Sara had spent so many years doing other people's bidding with no concern for what she wanted from life. She could smell dissatisfaction like a bloodhound.

"I've convinced him to redo the community center," Olivia said by way of an answer. "Have you seen the building on the edge of downtown?"

"The one with scaffolding covering it?"

Olivia nodded. "It's going to be great. We'll have art classes, yoga, a camp for kids and…" she paused and pressed her lips together. "There will be an auditorium with a stage. I'd like to revive Crimson's community theater group."

"I didn't know this town had a theater group," Sara said, straightening the brochures. She looked up at Olivia and did a double take at the other woman's hopeful expression. "Oh, no. You don't expect me to get involved?"

"Craig thinks…" Olivia paused. "Of course not. Why would you give your time and talent to a small-town group? I'm sure you have more important ways to spend your time."

Sara cringed. She could tell Olivia was being sincere, but the truth was Sara didn't have anything more important to occupy her time. And nowhere to go at the end of the summer where she was really needed.

Claire needed her. Josh, too, even if he couldn't admit it. He wanted her to stay. If she could prove that she fit into his life, maybe they'd really have a chance.

Despite her fear, that was what she wanted more than anything.

"I don't have much experience in live theater."

"Most of us don't have any experience at all," Olivia answered with a smile. "I'd take any advice or help you're willing to give. There's a small improv group in town, but I think we could get a lot more people involved."

Sara nodded. "I'm not sure how long I'll be staying in Crimson," she said slowly, hating how hard those words were to choke out. "I'm happy to pitch in where I can."

Olivia's smile widened. "Craig would love to meet with you about his ideas—"

"I thought you were heading things up?"

"Well, I'm doing most of the work. But Craig likes to personally handle the VIPs."

Sara choked out a laugh. "I'm a VIP?"

"Of course."

"Do you only want me for the tiny bit of name recognition I have left?" she asked, raising her eyebrows. Better to know up front if she was being used or not.

Olivia shook her head. "You're a good actress. You have experience. I want the community center to be a success. I don't exactly understand what motivates my husband. But I'm not going to use you for publicity, if that's what you're asking. And I won't let him, either."

"You're tougher than you look," Sara observed.

"You're smarter than your reputation," Olivia shot

back, then clapped a hand over her mouth. "Sorry. Shouldn't have said that out loud."

"I take it as a compliment," Sara told her. "You don't strike me as a local."

"I'm from St. Louis. Craig and I met in college. This is his hometown. He has big political dreams and thought being mayor would be a good place to start." She paused, then added, "I'm not sure I fit into his plan the way he wants me to."

"I don't fit into anyone's plan," Sara answered. "I've gotten used to making my own way." She glanced at her watch. "I'm not expected back at the ranch for a few hours. Would you want to grab a bite to eat?" She bit down on her lip as she waited for Olivia to refuse. Sara didn't have any girlfriends outside of April. She'd found that once her fame died, so had her appeal as a friend.

"Really? You want to have lunch with me?" Olivia seemed shocked.

"I do." Sara realized she truly meant it. It was time to start living outside of her own doubts. "Then I think we should do a little shopping."

Olivia gave a knowing smile. "At Feathers and Threads?"

"Exactly," Sara agreed. She glanced around. "Can you leave for a bit?"

"Absolutely. It's a slow day."

"Great. It will be nice to know a friendly face in town."

They picked a Mexican place just off Main Street that Olivia said was the best. Sara noticed a few questioning looks as the mayor's wife walked in with her.

Olivia ignored them, choosing a table on the crowded patio out front.

"Are you sure you don't want something a little more secluded?" Sara asked as she slid into her seat.

"Are you embarrassed to be seen with me?"

"Very funny," Sara mumbled, but one corner of her mouth curved. She felt relaxed with Olivia, much like she did with April, and was grateful for the possibility of a new friendship.

"If you're thinking of staying in Crimson or spending any time here in the future, the town is going to have to get used to you being around. We've had our share of celebrities wander over from Aspen, so it's not too far out of the norm."

"It's silly," Sara admitted. "Being a celebrity has a way of creeping into every aspect of your life. A lot of stars claim they want their privacy but turn around and court the fame with the vacations and outings they choose. It gets to the point where you can't live with the recognition, but you don't know how to live without it."

Olivia nodded. "My father was a U.S. senator when I was younger. He loved the attention he received from everyone in our hometown when he was back there or on the campaign trail. I know it's not the same thing, but I have an idea of what you mean."

Sara breathed a little easier thinking there was someone else in town with whom she could be honest. That was a gift she hadn't received very often in recent years.

The waiter came and took their orders. Sara thought back to her last waitressing job, the latest in a long string of them. It had paid the bills, mostly, but she hadn't taken pleasure in it. She actually enjoyed the work she did on the ranch. She liked working with guests to pinpoint activities that would make their vacations perfect. She was good at coordinating and the customer-service part of it and wanted to make a difference for them. Most people who came to Crimson, Colorado, did it because they craved an adventure. Josh was well equipped to meet their needs. Sara balanced his resources by figuring out exactly what those needs were.

They made a good combination. She wondered if her gran would have been happy with Sara's contributions to the ranch and liked to think she would have been proud.

She and Olivia ate and talked. Olivia was a few years older than Sara, and her childhood had been very different from Sara's own: daughter of a prominent senator, private school then a prestigious Midwestern college. Still, they had an easy rapport, and Olivia had many kernels of wisdom to offer about fitting in in this small mountain community.

As their plates were cleared, a shadow fell over the table. "Olivia," an icy voice said. "You didn't tell me you'd be having lunch in town with Ms. Wellens today."

Sara looked up to see a thin, blond-haired man standing just on the other side of the gate surrounding the patio. He placed a hand on Olivia's shoulder and squeezed, but the gesture didn't look at all loving.

Sara disliked him on sight and even more when she noticed Richard Hamish, her mother's land-developer boyfriend, standing next to him.

The older man tipped his cowboy hat in her direction. "Afternoon, Serena. I've been meaning to pay a visit to Rose's family home to talk to you again about that offer."

"Her name is Sara Wells," Olivia told both men, shrugging out of her husband's grasp. "This lunch wasn't planned, Craig. Sara came into the visitors' center."

"You should have called me to join you," he said with a smile that didn't reach his eyes. "Or better yet, I could have taken her to lunch. It's not very responsible for the mayor's wife to leave her post unattended. What will visitors to our town think of that kind of welcome?"

Olivia cringed and Sara plastered a smile on her face. "They'll think whoever works at the visitors' center needs to eat and maybe the town should make arrangements for better coverage."

She turned her gaze to Richard. "Don't bother coming to the ranch. It's my home now. I own it."

"For now," the cowboy said with a smirk. "I'll send you my latest offer. I have another group of developers interested in the property. I can make you a good deal, Sara." He didn't try to hide his derision. "One that can get you out of the deep financial hole you're in."

Sara grabbed her wallet and took out a wad of bills. "It was lovely meeting you, Olivia. I hope we can schedule some girl time again." She gave Craig an icy stare. "I need to get back now."

The other woman quickly stood and gave her a quick hug. "I'm sorry," she whispered.

Sara returned the hug then turned to the two men. "I hope *not* to see either of you again anytime soon."

"I'm the mayor," Craig said coolly. "You'll see me everywhere if you have plans to stick around."

"Sara doesn't stick," the cowboy put in. "That's not the Hollywood way."

We'll see about that, Sara thought to herself. But that nagging voice inside her head suddenly sounded a lot like her mother.

If you'd only tried harder. You give up too quickly. Who are you if you're not on screen?

She glanced between the cowboy's knowing gaze, the mayor's smug smile and Olivia's sympathetic eyes.

The sympathy was the worst of it. Sympathy felt a lot like pity to Sara. She couldn't stand to be the object of anyone's pity.

She hooked her purse over her shoulder and headed for the exit, unwilling to make eye contact with anyone else. Needing to get to her car, to be alone.

When she finally did, the tears came fast and furious. Years ago, she'd vowed not to let anything make her cry, but she couldn't seem to help herself. She cried for the childhood she'd never had, for the lost innocence and all of the times she'd had to swallow her pride and self-respect. For all of the times one of her mother's boyfriends had made her feel less than who she wanted to be.

For all the times she'd made herself feel even worse.

Could this town really give her the second chance at the life she craved? It was different from the future she'd planned. Yet so far, all she'd gotten from her best-laid plans was a big pile of disappointment and failure.

She loved the acting part of the job, becoming a different character, bringing to life the words on the page. She might be just as fulfilled working in a tiny community theater as she was on a TV or movie set. She'd never know whether she was good enough to make a comeback in Hollywood, but she hoped that after a while that wouldn't matter to her any longer.

She hoped life in Crimson, Colorado, would be enough.

Chapter 14

A week later, Josh watched as Sara greeted each of the ranch's new guests with a warm hug. She had a way of making every person feel comfortable and welcome. It was a gift she shared with her grandmother. Part of why he'd wanted Trudy as a partner on the ranch from the beginning had been the way she put people at ease.

Josh could lead a trail ride or a hike or a four-wheeler drive over a mountain pass, but he was often awkward with casual conversation. He preferred doing to talking. Sara filled in the gaps naturally, both with the guests at the ranch and with Claire.

His relationship with Claire was on the mend, and a large part of the reason why was Sara's encouragement. Josh had some rough edges left over from his days on the circuit and Sara smoothed them, helping him to become the father his daughter needed him to be.

Tonight, Sara's blond hair hung in soft waves around her shoulders and the pale yellow shirt she wore made her eyes seem an even deeper blue. He was glad she remained mostly makeup-free. It was as if she was finally willing to let people see who she truly was instead of her carefully cultivated mask.

Josh would never admit it to her, but a small, selfish part of him was secretly relieved nothing had come of the audition. He didn't know how to compete with her former life. He understood a little bit about the lure of lights and fame. If Sara had to make a choice between her career and life on the ranch, he couldn't imagine she'd choose him. At least not yet. They needed more time for her to really see this was where she belonged.

She drew Claire forward and introduced her to the teenage son of one of the families checking in this week.

Their occupancy was full, and to celebrate, they'd decided to have a big cookout on the patio outside the main house. April had created one of her usual amazing feasts, and Sara and Claire had handled the decorations. Tiny lights glistened from strands wound through the wrought iron gate around the edge of the patio. They'd set the tables with colorful tablecloths and mason jars filled with wildflowers picked from the meadow near the pond. The mountains provided a commanding backdrop, especially now as the sky above them turned a dozen shades of orange and red. The sun was close to dipping behind the highest peak.

This was one of Josh's favorite times on the ranch. The moment when day slipped toward evening and all the colors softened while the sounds of nature became more pronounced in the shadows.

A soft country ballad played from the speakers on the porch. The lilting melody made Josh want to gather Sara in his arms and twirl her across the path from the main house to her cabin. He loved the feel of her in his arms, and though he'd given up dancing long before his knee injury, tonight seemed like the perfect time to make an exception.

As if reading his thoughts, her gaze found his through the groups of guests milling about. He watched as her breath hitched and a blush crept across her cheeks. He hoped she could read in his eyes all the wicked things he had planned for her later.

She took a step toward him, and he realized that he was happy. For the first time in…forever, Josh felt content with his life. The ache for his sister was still there, deep in his heart. His knee would never be as strong as it once was. Despite what it had taken him to get here, or maybe because of it, Josh was truly happy with his life.

Sara had a lot to do with that. He thought about the hope in her eyes when he'd asked her to stay in Crimson. She wanted more from him, more than he believed he was willing or able to give a woman.

There was no doubt in his mind that she deserved more than he could ever give her. But if she wanted him, what was holding him back from making her his? For real. Forever.

He had a sudden vision of the future. The image included a family: Claire, Sara and maybe even a baby. One with Sara's blond hair and dark eyes like his and Claire's.

As if she could sense the change in him, a shy smile lit up Sara's face as she stepped closer. Before she reached him, a loud honking had everyone at the cook-out turning toward the front of the house.

Josh could see a late-model sports car speeding up the long driveway that led to the main house, dust billowing behind it. Ryan's car.

A sliver of unease bracketed Josh's shoulders, but he ignored it. He didn't know what scheme Sara's former partner was cooking up tonight, but it didn't matter. Josh knew what he had to do.

He took the two steps to bring him to Sara's side. The scent of cinnamon and honey tantalized him, making his pulse stutter an erratic beat.

He wrapped his fingers around hers. "Sara, I need to talk to you."

"Sara!" Ryan's voice called from the front of the house.

She glanced up at Josh then to where Ryan was leaping onto the back patio.

"I have the most amazing news."

"Ryan, we have guests."

Ryan looked around for the first time, as if realizing there were other people at the house. Josh could sympathize. Sometimes when he looked at Sara everything else faded to nothing—that was how bright she glowed.

"Howdy, folks," Ryan said, then turned his attention back to Sara. "It's good there's a crowd. We're going to want to celebrate tonight. I talked to Jonathan Tramner today." He paused dramatically then raised his fists into the air. "He wants you," Ryan shouted. "He wants you for the part of Amelia!"

"That's impossible," Sara murmured.

Josh immediately released her hand and took a step back, feeling as though he was actually in a movie. He could see the scene in slow motion, him shouting an exaggerated no as the crowd looked on.

But this was real life and he kept his mouth shut, waiting to see how Sara would respond.

Ryan spoke before she could answer. "He loved your take on the character and said the short bit of the reading you did was fantastic." He glanced at Josh then back at Sara. "What made up his mind was the look on your face when you took the call about Claire. He said he saw Amelia in your face, all the motherly concern and love. He actually said it gave him chills."

Josh had chills right now. The bad kind, like right before you got sick to your stomach.

"I don't know what to say." Sara's hand fluttered to her chest as if to settle her breathing.

Josh kept his own breathing steady and even. Blood pumped through his veins, and he could have shot himself to the moon on pure adrenaline, but from the outside he knew he looked completely calm. It was a trick he'd mastered through decades of practice; whether it was his father coming after him as a kid or later when he was perched on the back of a bull, Josh earned a reputation for being cool under pressure.

The pressure on his heart right now threatened to overtake him.

"Say you'll accept the part. This is the kind of role that comes along once in a career, Sara. An award-winning kind of role." Ryan turned to the guests. "Give her some encouragement, everyone." Ryan's gaze met Josh's over her shoulder. "Our girl is going to be a star again."

Applause broke out around the small gathering, guests approaching Sara to offer their congratulations and words of encouragement. She might not get approval in L.A., but these people—strangers practically—were rooting for her. Josh guessed the rest of America would feel the same way. The country was built on comeback stories, and Sara would make a great one. She had talent but was smarter now. She wouldn't let anyone take advantage of her. She'd make career choices that would take her to the top.

Josh could see her future like a map and grew cold with the knowledge that it most likely didn't leave room for him.

He watched as April approached, taking Sara by the arms. "What are you going to do?" she asked softly.

"She's going to take the part," Ryan answered quickly. "She's wanted this for years. She deserves it."

"Let Sara decide," April told him sharply. "Think about it if you need to," she said to Sara in a gentler tone. "You don't have to give an answer right now."

Ryan tapped April on the shoulder. "Actually, she does. She reports to set next week."

"Next week?" Sara's gaze swung between April and Ryan. Josh felt himself sinking further into the background. Felt the walls he'd constructed for his own protection rebuilding, cutting off his heart. "Why so soon?" she asked. "I'm not ready to—"

Josh wanted to stop it, to swing her around and tell her everything he felt, all the plans he had for them. He wanted to beg her not to leave him. He couldn't, so he said nothing, stayed still as a statue while he watched her drift further away. The woman he hadn't believed would fit into his life only a month ago. Now he couldn't imagine living without her.

"Ready or not," Ryan answered. "They were already in preproduction when you met with Jonathan. He gave you a big break. The studio had a list of actresses they wanted. He fought for you, Sara. Do you know what that means?"

She nodded then turned to look at Josh as if to say, *Will you fight for me?*

Her eyes held a mix of hope, question and expectation. It was the last that did him in. After the accident, he'd felt broken and unfixable. He'd been given a second chance at life and with his daughter. But did he have enough to give to Sara, too?

He knew a life with her would mean revealing everything: his emotions, his heart. She'd want access to all the hidden crevices in his miserable soul. He could see it as he looked at her now, her gaze beginning to cloud as she read the doubt on his face. He was bound to disappoint her. He couldn't protect her, didn't have the guts to be the man she needed him to be. As much as he wished it was another way.

"Congratulations," he mumbled then forced a smile. "You deserve it."

Her breath hitched as she stared at him. All the people around them faded away as a single tear slid down her cheek. "So that's it?" she whispered.

He shrugged and ignored the pounding in his head. "Ryan's right. This is a once-in-a-lifetime chance. Take it." His throat felt like he'd swallowed a bucket of dust, but he didn't stop. "You don't belong here, Sara. I told you that from the start."

Sara clutched at her stomach, wondering if she might actually throw up. She didn't belong. Wasn't that the story of her life? Wasn't that what she thought she'd had here in Crimson with Josh? A place to call home for the first time.

Get a grip, her inner voice scolded and she bit down on her lip.

She turned to Ryan. "Make the call. I'll do it."

April reached for her hand, but she shrugged away, knowing if her friend touched her right now she might lose it completely. She'd gone soft this summer, let down her guard and her armor. That was the great thing about L.A., between the people and the traffic and the smog, she'd never questioned that every day would be a battle. She was used to it, ready to attack or go on the defensive no matter the situation.

Crimson Ranch and the mountains around it had lulled her into a false sense of security, made her believe she was safe in their shadow. She should have known better. She'd opened her heart and now she'd pay the price.

"You're crying." April handed Sara a napkin from a nearby table.

"Happy tears," she mumbled, praying she was a good enough actress to pull off this last scene. "Tears of joy for my dream come true." Her lips pulled into a wide smile. "I guess we have a real reason for a party now."

The guests cheered again, and Sara tried not to think about how much she'd miss meeting the vacationers who came to the ranch, hearing the stories of their lives. She'd already come to love the mornings when she walked across the property in the crisp mountain air to share a cup of coffee with April and any other early risers.

Yes, a part of her wanted her acting career back

on track. She wanted to prove she was more than a washed-up child star. She wanted to lose herself in bringing a character to life again, stretch her range and know she could connect with the audience in that way.

Was it too much to want it all?

"How can you leave us?" Claire's angry voice broke her out of her musings. "You're dumping us, just like my mom did, for a better offer. Why does everyone leave me like I don't matter? I thought you were different."

"It's not like that," Sara whispered in response. Her heart broke all over again for the pain in the girl's eyes. Pain she'd caused.

Claire stood in front of her, chin trembling. Her arms were crossed in front of her chest.

Josh stepped forward, his entire focus on his daughter. "Sara was never going to stay," he told her, his voice a cool murmur.

I want to stay, she wanted to scream in response.

Ask me to stay.

Give me a reason to stay.

Claire turned to Sara. "You're a liar. You used us when you had nothing. You made me think you really cared."

Sara shook her head. "I do care, sweetie."

"You're as bad as my mother." Claire's big eyes narrowed. "As bad as your mother. I hate you."

Bile rose in Sara's throat at the comparison to Rose Wells. She'd been disappointed by her mother for so many years, she felt like it had broken something fundamental inside of her. She didn't trust her own judgment, her ability to form lasting relationships, her capacity for love.

This summer had gone a long way to fix what was wrong in her life. Or so she'd thought. Now she realized this was just one more illusion, like a movie set that could be stripped away in days—or in a moment—leaving a vast emptiness in its place.

But she didn't want that for Claire. She'd only wanted to spare the girl the pain Sara had felt for so many years.

She took a step forward but Josh blocked her way, putting himself between her and Claire, his back to Sara. Just like that, he cut her off from the two people she'd come to think of as hers. Guests drifted to the far side of the patio, making her feel even more alone.

"*We're* going to make this place work, Claire. You and me." Sara watched as he put his large hands on each of the girl's thin shoulders. "This is our home now. I'm not going to leave you. We're a team."

Sara had to physically restrain herself from rushing forward and wrapping her arms around them both. She ached to be part of their "team," as Josh called it. But here she was, once again on the sidelines.

Claire threw herself against her father's chest and sobbed out loud. The irony of the embrace wasn't lost on Sara. It had taken the two of them having a common enemy—her—for Claire to lean on Josh the way he'd wanted. She took no comfort in pushing the two of them together at last. Her pain was too raw for that. There was too much hurt between them all for her to believe this was the best ending to their story.

With his arm around Claire's shoulder, Josh led her from the porch.

Sara whispered his name and he turned. Fool that she was, she still held out a glimmer of hope that he'd call her to him and they'd work together to make this right.

Instead, his eyes held only derision as he looked at her. "You need to be out of here by tomorrow. I'll handle the bookings for the rest of the summer."

Pride made her chin notch up an inch. "It's my house."

A muscle in his jaw knotted. "I'll find a way to buy it from you. Before the end of the season."

No, she wanted to scream. That wasn't what she meant. "Josh, I don't…"

Her voice faded as she realized she was talking to his back. He and Claire disappeared into the house. Sara turned to April, miserable and needing her own comfort.

Even her best friend looked disappointed, as if Sara could have done better. How? How was she supposed to fight for something that wasn't hers to begin with?

Ever the peacekeeper, April turned to the guests, who'd gone silent. "It's still a beautiful night," April said, making her tone encouraging. "And we're happy each of you is here. I've got dinner ready in the kitchen." She smiled, and only Sara could see it didn't reach her eyes. "Who wants to load up a plate?"

The guests smiled and clapped and Sara felt a palpable easing of the tension. If April happened to be an X-Men type mutant under her braids and patchouli-scented sundresses, Sara would guess her superpower was making people feel better. She'd blessed Sara with her gift too many times to count, but never had she needed it more than now.

So when her friend turned and enveloped Sara in

a hug, Sara sagged against her, wanting reassurance that she'd tried her best.

"What else could I do?" Sara asked, swallowing against the catch in her voice.

April pulled back and cupped Sara's face gently between her palms. Sara held her breath, waiting for the words of encouragement, the slant on the situation that would make Sara feel like a happy ending was still within reach.

"Make it right," April said simply, then turned and walked into the house to help the guests.

Sara whirled on Ryan. "What does she mean, make it right? I'm not the one who said I don't belong. I'm trying to make it right. I'm trying to resurrect my career, to pay her back the money you lost. I want the ranch to succeed. I want Claire to be okay. I want it all and I don't know how to get any of it. And she tells me to make it right?" She threw her hands in the air. "How do I do that, Ryan?"

He gave her a hug. "You start with what you should have done years ago. What I should have helped you accomplish. You take care of yourself."

The next morning, Sara folded her clothes and returned them to the suitcase she'd stowed in the back of the closet in her cabin.

She didn't go to the main house for breakfast, too emotionally drained to make small talk with the guests and too much of a coward to face April in the daylight.

As much of a nurturer as her friend was, April had made no secret last night that she thought Sara was making the wrong decision. Even if she hadn't said it out loud.

To Sara's surprise, April had told her she was going to stay on the ranch for the rest of the season. Apparently, Sara wasn't the only one who had experienced the healing power of the high mountain air. Sara had suggested that April contact Olivia Wilder to see about teaching yoga classes at the community center when it was complete.

Community.

It was a word that had held little meaning to Sara before this summer. With good reason, she realized now, since she clearly wasn't meant to be a part of this one.

Ryan was picking her up this morning to drive her to the airport, where she'd board a plane for the movie set. She was arriving a few days before shooting started, but an apartment had been rented for her and she wanted a chance to settle in before the rest of the cast and crew arrived. She also needed to get away from Colorado, from Josh and the dreams she'd been foolish enough to believe could come true for the two of them.

When a knock sounded on the door to the cabin, she called, "Come in," expecting to see Ryan. He was bringing by the contract and official paperwork for her to sign before they left.

Instead, her mother's voice rang out from the front room. "Serena, where are you? We need to talk."

Sara closed her eyes and took a steadying breath. The last person she wanted to speak to right now was her mother. But she walked from the bedroom into the main room of the cabin.

"Word travels fast," she said to Rose, who rushed forward to give her a hug.

"I'm thrilled for you, darling." Her mother smoothed

back her hair with a frown and slight tsk of dissatisfaction. "We're not going to let this opportunity go to
waste."

"*We're* not going to do anything," Sara replied, stepping out of her mother's embrace. "This has nothing
to do with you."

"It has everything to do with me." Although Rose's
voice was soft, Sara heard an edge of steel underneath.
Her stomach did a slow roll, the same visceral reaction she'd had to her mother's unspoken demands since
she was a girl.

"I'm your biggest fan," Rose continued. "Your first
manager, you'll remember." She combed her fingers
through her bangs. "It's time for me to get involved in
your life again."

Sara's head snapped back as if she'd been slapped.
"Not going to happen in a million years."

"Oh, yes. I think I may come to stay with you on
set, for moral support and to make sure no one takes
advantage of you. You're in a precarious place emotionally, since this is a chance you never thought you'd
get." Her mother leaned forward. "Truth be told, you
look quite ragged. Perhaps we could get you in for a
bit of Botox before filming begins?"

Sara threw her arms into the air. "Mom, what are
you talking about? I'm not getting Botox. You're not
coming to the set."

"I have nothing else to occupy myself right now,"
her mother said with a sigh. "I'd planned to help Richard with plans for the condo development. I've always
had an eye for interior design." She shrugged. "But
since you won't sell the house yet, his deal has stalled.
That leaves me free to focus my attention on you, my

darling daughter." She tapped her finger on her upper lip. "And maybe Josh's daughter. I really do see potential in her. She obviously needs some maternal guidance."

"Leave Claire alone," Sara said on an angry hiss of breath. Temper flared to life inside her. "And get out of my life while you're at it."

"Give me a reason to," Rose shot back, the smile never leaving her face.

"Really, Mom? You're going to try to blackmail me now. That's a new low. It doesn't matter. I'm not afraid of you anymore and I don't need your approval. I haven't needed you for a long time."

Rose had the gall to look offended. "You'll always need me. I gave you the career you had."

"I worked for my career," Sara told her. "I had the talent you never did, and I worked for all the success I had. Unfortunately, I was naive enough to listen to you back then, to think you had my best interests at heart. Trust me, I won't make that mistake again."

She brushed past her mother and opened the front door. "I'm not going to sell the house, and there isn't a damn thing you can do about it. Now get out. For good, Mother. I don't want to see you here again."

"Don't do this, Sara," Rose said. Her voice turned to a pitiful whine. "I love Richard, but things are rocky between us since the land deal isn't working. I need you to help me."

Sara squeezed her eyes shut. This was the first time since she'd been a girl that her mother had called her by her given name. But even that small concession was too little, too late. "Get out," she repeated, sweeping her hand toward the porch.

With a dramatic sob, Rose rushed forward. "You'll change your mind," her mother called over her shoulder. "You can't do it on your own. You're not strong enough. You never were."

Sara sank onto the edge of the sofa, not bothering to shut the door behind her mother.

Those last angry words echoed through her as her head dropped to her knees, tears spilling down her face, soaking her bare legs. All the emotions, the hurt and betrayal, the disappointment over what would never be poured out of her.

After minutes, she gulped in an unsteady breath and raised her face, wiping her hands to clear the wetness.

"She's wrong," a voice said softly from the porch. Claire stood in the doorway, clenching her fingers at her sides. "You're strong enough. I believe in you, Sara."

Tears came again as Sara propelled herself off the couch, wrapping her arms around the girl. "I'm so sorry, sweetie. I never wanted to hurt you in all of this. I do care about you, Claire. I promise. Just because—"

"I know," Claire interrupted. "I was mad last night. I'm pretty sure the therapist my mom made me see would tell you I have some wicked abandonment issues." She laughed softly.

"Join the club." Sara pulled back. "We should introduce my mother to yours. They could start a mutual narcissistic personality club."

"If it keeps them busy..." Claire started.

"And off our backs," Sara finished.

They both laughed and Sara hugged her again. "You can call me on set. And text. And tweet. And Facebook. And whatever other ways to communicate they invent in the next five minutes. I'm sorry this summer didn't work out the way any of us planned, but I'm still your friend."

Claire nodded and blinked several times. "My dad isn't great at relationships. He won't let himself be vulnerable," she said, sounding far more mature than her thirteen years.

"Your therapist talking?"

"My mom. She talked a lot about him, mostly complaining. I think that's part of why I'm so hard on him. Years of conditioning, you know?"

Sara knew all about years of conditioning. That might explain why she was so hard on herself.

"He's a good man, Claire." The words ripped open a fresh flash of pain across Sara's heart. It made her ache to think of Josh, which was hard not to do on the ranch, when every smell and sound was bound together by her time with him. "He loves you."

"He loves you, too," Claire said firmly. "I know he does. He's just too much of a…man…to admit it."

"Common problem," Sara answered. "There's practically a whole subgenre of movies based on unhappy endings—*Gone with the Wind, Shakespeare in Love, Casablanca.*" She waved her hand, trying to be flip, then realized her fingers were trembling. She tucked her arm behind her back. "Our lives are too different to make it work."

"What about *Notting Hill?*" Claire's chin jutted forward at a stubborn angle. "Julia Roberts and Hugh Grant made it work."

Sara couldn't help but smile. "I like the way your mind works, but this isn't the movies." She watched

Claire push the toe of one shoe into the floor. "I promise you'll be okay. Your dad will make sure of it."

"I wish you didn't have to go," Claire said, hugging her again.

Sara willed herself to remain strong when all she wanted to do was melt into a weepy puddle once again. "Maybe you can come to the movie premiere." She paused, then added, "If your dad agrees."

Claire smiled through a hiccup. "If I'm on my best behavior, maybe he will." Then she giggled. "Do you think you could introduce me to Justin Timberlake?"

Sara laughed in response. "If I ever meet him, you bet."

Chapter 15

"Can I go look at clothes?" Claire bounced on the tips of her toes as she smiled and nodded at Josh.

"At Feathers and Threads?" He arched a brow at her. "I thought you'd rather be seen in a potato sack."

"Don't be dramatic," his daughter answered, but her smile remained. "Sara told me they're carrying a couple of new lines." She bit her lip and glanced away.

Something that felt a lot like regret scraped across his insides at the mention of Sara's name. "I know you still talk to her and text. I monitor your phone even if I don't read them all, remember?"

"So annoying," Claire mumbled. "Can I go?"

"Sure." Josh glanced at his watch. "I need to load the rest of the wood into the truck, then I'll be down to pick you up."

"Thanks, Dad."

He watched his daughter cross the street toward the boutique on the corner. He felt a lightness fill his chest at the change in his relationship with Claire. It was followed quickly by the weight of knowing that Sara had a lot to do with the progress.

It had been three weeks since she'd left Crimson. Almost a month filled with emptiness and a constant longing to be with her again. He hoped it would fade soon, or he thought he might go mad from the pain of it. Pain he knew he'd caused himself.

He knew what she'd wanted that night on the patio. Her eyes had held a hope that he'd offer more. He'd wanted to, planned on it until Ryan had come in with his big announcement. How could Josh compete with the bright lights of Hollywood?

He cursed under his breath. When had he ever backed away from a fight? He knew it was a mistake, but in that moment he couldn't stop himself from making it.

He wouldn't ask her to give up another chance at her career. Yet he hadn't been able to offer her the relationship she deserved, because he was too afraid that when she was away filming, he couldn't protect her. It hadn't worked with his sister or with his relationship with Claire's mother. Here in Colorado, on the ranch, he could make sure everything was okay for the people he loved. He was in charge of his life and emotions. Things were simple, just the way he liked them. He was too afraid of losing her when she left him. Too scared she'd eventually choose her career over him.

As much as he knew now that he loved Sara with his whole heart, he'd tried to convince himself it was for the best. The whole reason he'd returned to Crimson was to protect Claire, to give her the normal life he'd always craved. Not to let the outside world seep in and destroy them.

It was irrational, he knew. Sara had been a positive influence on his daughter from the start. But he held on to his fear like an anchor and only now worried it might take him down, as well.

"You got a lot of posts there. Not sure you'll need that many."

Josh looked up into the face of Richard Hamish, partially shaded by the large Stetson on his head. "You have no idea what I need, Rich." Josh took a pair of work gloves from his back pocket and slipped them on. "Go play intimidating cowboy with someone else. It's wasted on me." He hefted several boards into the truck bed. "If you haven't heard, Crimson Ranch is having a great first season. I'm going to secure that loan and buy the house come fall."

"Not if she sells it to me first."

The older man sounded as if it were a done deal, confidence dripping from every syllable.

"You're bluffing." Josh kept working on loading fence posts into the truck, needing to keep his hands occupied so he wasn't tempted to wrap them around Richard's craggy neck. "Sara isn't going to sell you the house. Not now."

"Rose flew down there and is working on her as we speak."

Josh stilled. "On set with Sara?" He knew how much being near her mother upset Sara. She didn't need that kind of distraction when she was filming a movie.

"I sure as hell don't want Rose around me until this deal goes through." Richard spit a wad of tobacco into the street. "Dang woman talks my ear off. She meddles into every detail of a man's life. It's about time she uses her energy on someone other than me. She can wear that girl down. I'd bet my belt buckle on it."

"You think Rose will convince Sara to sell?"

"Her mom will head back here once Sara agrees."

"She won't do it." Josh wanted to be sure, but how could he? He'd given Sara no reason to believe in him. Why should she stick to their bargain at this point? If she wanted to get on with her life, the easiest path would be to sign the house over to her mother.

"If she wants to keep that fancy new movie role, she will."

"Sara earned that part. Even if her mother is an annoyance, she's not going to cost her the job."

Richard's smile was too confident. "Sara's had a bumpy few years. There's a lot of pressure trying to restart a life. You should understand that better than most. Who knows if she can handle it? She may crack, go back to using drugs—"

"She didn't use drugs and you know it."

"Doesn't matter what I know. The important thing is what the American people believe. One story in the tabloids and that production company will drop her in an instant."

Josh took a step forward, stripping off his gloves and grabbing Richard by the collar of his custom Western shirt. "You wouldn't…" His voice was a low growl.

"Who's going to stop me?" He pulled away from Josh's grasp. "Son, you've been outplayed."

Without thinking, Josh slammed his fist into the other man's jaw. Richard staggered back into the brick storefront. Several men rushed out of the hardware store to see what the commotion was.

"This isn't a game, you old coot." Josh shook out his hand, glancing at his knuckles where a few trickles of blood pooled.

"It's her life. And to answer the question of who's going to stop you?" He came close to Richard, who cradled his face in his palm. "That would be me."

Sara held her fingers to her ears, but even that couldn't drown out her mother's incessant rambling.

"I talked to craft services about your food allergies and exactly what they need to stock for you."

Sara's head shot up. "I don't have food allergies."

"Sensitivities, then."

"I'm only sensitive to your voice." She got up from the couch in her on-set trailer. "When is this going to end, Mother?"

When Rose had first arrived three days ago, Sara had refused to let her on set. But Rose took matters into her own hands, meeting with the director and one of the executive producers to spin a tale of Sara's fragile emotional state and how Rose wanted to make sure she didn't cost them money on the movie.

What Rose was going to cost Sara was her sanity.

Thanks to Sara's less-than-stellar reputation, the men had believed it. Rose had become a constant presence during filming. It was hard for Sara to stay connected with the character of a hardworking mom when all she wanted was for her own mother to leave her the hell alone.

"You know what it takes," Rose said simply, turning to the small bank of cabinets she was rearranging.

Rose had even gotten Jonathan Tramner, the director, to suggest to Sara that her mother stay with her in the studio apartment at the end of filming each day. Sara got no break, which was making her crazy.

"Why is Richard Hamish so important that you'll do anything to make me sell Gran's house to him?"

"I love him."

"It would be a revelation if you loved your own daughter half as much."

Rose didn't turn around, but her shoulders stiffened. "I do love you, Serena. I devoted my life to making your career a success. You owe me for that."

"I paid the bills for a decade." Resentment rose hot and strong in Sara. "I more than paid my debt to you." When her mother didn't turn around, Sara's gaze fell to the line of glass bottles on the small cabinet.

"Why is all that liquor in here?"

"One of the men helped me unload it." Her mother's voice was emotionless. "I explained to them that you might need a little something to calm your nerves."

"My nerves wouldn't be so shot if you'd leave. And you know I do yoga for…" Her voice trailed off as realization dawned. "You're going to make it seem like I'm a drunk?" She stood, pacing the small room. "Do you have needles stashed somewhere, too?"

"Sell the house." Rose spun around, her finger pointed in accusation. "Why are *you* so devoted to a man who doesn't want you? You're going to save his ranch and let my dream for a happy life be thrown in the trash. You shouldn't be protecting him. He doesn't care about you, Serena. You're not important to him. When are you going to stop being a doormat for people who are only using you?"

The air whooshed out of the room, and Sara thought her knees might buckle. Her mother was right. She was a doormat. No matter how tough she talked, how insolent her attitude, she let people take advantage of her. Her mother was first in that line.

Maybe that was what Josh had been doing, wooing her in Colorado to ensure her loyalty. It didn't matter anymore. Her time with him had given her the confidence to believe in herself again. Even if he didn't believe in the two of them, he'd given her a gift she could never repay.

"Good point, Mom." She pushed open the door to the trailer. "First I'm going to stop being a doormat for you."

"I didn't mean…"

"I don't care." She lifted her hands. "I don't care if you ruin my career. Again. If they fire me, I'll find another job, another path. Even if it isn't in Hollywood. I love acting, not being a celebrity." She thought about Olivia's offer to help with the community theater in Crimson. "I can make my life a success. I deserve happiness, and I'm not going to let you rob me of it for one second longer."

"You don't know what you're saying."

"She does."

Sara whirled as Josh filled the tiny doorway of the trailer. His gaze was fixed on Rose. "She should have said it a long time ago. I should have said it for her. To her." He turned to Sara. "You deserve happiness."

Rose stalked forward. "You only want the house. You don't care about her."

His eyes never left Sara's. "Sell the house."

She shook her head.

"I mean it," he said, and took her arms between his hands. Close enough that she could see the tiny flecks of gold in his dark eyes. Close enough that the smell of him wound through her senses like a drug. "Sell the house if it will make you happy."

"It's your future," she said softly.

"I'll make a different future," he answered. "With you, if you'll have me. No piece of property, no business is worth anything without you in my life to share it. I love you, Sara. I think I have since the moment you jumped on the counter and spun my world out of control."

She drew a shaky breath, unable to believe what she was hearing. "But you like control."

"I thought I needed it," he said, pushing a stray hair behind her ear. His touch made a shiver run through her. "I'm sorry for hurting you and letting you walk away." He dipped his head so he was looking directly into her eyes. "I was wrong about a lot of things. But one thing I'm definitely right about is that nothing is worth losing you."

She choked back a sob and tried to look away. He held her head steady. "Claire loves you. I love you. We both need you in our lives so damn much. Please give us another chance, Sara. Name the terms. Anything you want."

She shook her head. "I can't cook," she mumbled.

One side of his mouth kicked up. "We'll order takeout."

"I'm opinionated."

"I want to hear every thought in that beautiful mind."

Her eyes searched his. She saw the truth of his

words, of his love for her. Still, she was so scared to risk having her heart and dreams crushed once more. She didn't know if she could survive again.

"I want to act," she told him, wondering if it would be the nail in the coffin.

He leaned forward and ran his lips against hers. "I'll be at every premiere and production. I'll help you learn lines. I'll come to you wherever you are." His soft breath fell against her mouth. "Because I'm nothing without you, Sara. Wherever you are is where I want to be. Forever."

Her arms wrapped around his waist, and he pulled her to him, deepening the kiss until she was lost in sensation. "I love you, Josh," she said after a moment. "Forever."

"Well, that was a scene worthy of a Lifetime movie if I've ever seen one."

Her mother's sarcastic voice cut into Sara's bliss like a blade.

Josh held her to him, dropping a kiss on her forehead. "It's real, Rose. You wouldn't recognize real love, and I'm sorry for that." He met her mother's angry gaze. "I love your daughter and I won't let you hurt her anymore."

"Easy to say when you get what you want in the end."

"What I want is Sara's happiness."

"What you get is the house that should have been mine."

He looked down into Sara's eyes. "I meant what I said. Sell the house if it will make things easier for you. I'll find another property. We'll rebuild. As long as you're with me, I can make it right."

She shook her head. "It's right just the way it is."

Turning to Rose, she said, "I'm not selling, Mom. You can't blackmail me into it. You can't threaten. I'm not giving you power over me again."

"We'll see what happens when Richard takes control of this," her mother spit out, pulling out her cell phone and punching in numbers. "You always were ungrateful."

"I don't think you'll get a hold of him right now," Josh said casually. "He flew down to Houston this morning to see his wife."

Rose's hand stilled in midair. "Wife?"

"You didn't know? Yes, his wife of twenty-five years lives in Texas. Didn't you think it was odd how he never took you with him when he flew down there?"

"Those were business trips," Rose said woodenly.

"You were the one being used, Mom," Sara said. "I'm sorry."

Rose shook her head. "I don't need your pity."

"I don't pity you," Sara explained. "I'm sorry you think so little of yourself that you let a man treat you like that."

"That house should still be mine."

"It's not and it's never going to be. Move on, Mother."

Rose looked around the trailer as if not really seeing anything. "I need help. I need the house."

"Yes," Sara agreed. "You need to learn to stand on your own two feet. Trust me—that's the best help I can give you."

Rose's spine stiffened. "Once I walk out that door, you're dead to me, Serena. Be careful what you choose right now."

Sara didn't hesitate in her response. "I choose love," she whispered, and pressed her cheek against Josh's warm chest.

With a muttered curse, Rose fled from the trailer, slamming the door behind her.

Josh tipped her head up. "Forever?"

She nodded. "I choose you, Josh Travers. Forever."

* * * * *

We hope you enjoyed reading

Snowed In at the Ranch

by *New York Times* bestselling author

RAEANNE THAYNE

and

A Kiss on Crimson Ranch

by *USA TODAY* bestselling author

MICHELLE MAJOR.

Both were originally Harlequin® series stories!

From passionate, suspenseful and dramatic
love stories to inspirational or historical,
Harlequin offers different lines to
satisfy every romance reader.

New books in each line are available every month.

"I'm going to call my friend who's a nurse in the morning.
She's not working in that capacity now, but she grew up
in this town. She'll help get you with a good physical
therapist."

The warmth she'd seen in his eyes disappeared, and
she told herself it shouldn't matter. It was better they
remember who they were to each other—people who had
a troubled girl in common but nothing more.

She couldn't allow it to be anything more.

"You need a Christmas tree," he said as she started to
back away.

"I didn't see any decorations in your house."

He nodded. "Yeah, but Stella made me promise I would at least get a tree."

"I'll consider a tree," Madison told him. It felt like a small concession. "Although I'm not much for Christmas spirit."

"That makes two of us."

Once again, she wasn't sure how to feel about having something in common with Chase.

He cleared his throat. "I have more work to do— meetings and deadlines to reschedule. I can make it back to the bedroom."

"I'll see you tomorrow."

"I'll be here." He laughed without humor. "It's not like I can get anywhere else."

"Good night, Chase."

"Good night, Madison," he answered.

The words felt close to a caress, and she hurried to her bedroom before her knees started to melt.

Don't miss
Starlight and the Christmas Dare *by Michelle Major,*
available December 2022 wherever
Harlequin Special Edition books and ebooks are sold.

Harlequin.com

Love Harlequin romance?

DISCOVER.

Be the first to find out about promotions, news and exclusive content!

Facebook.com/HarlequinBooks

Twitter.com/HarlequinBooks

Instagram.com/HarlequinBooks

Pinterest.com/HarlequinBooks

YouTube.com/HarlequinBooks

ReaderService.com

EXPLORE.

Sign up for the Harlequin e-newsletter and download a free book from any series at
TryHarlequin.com

CONNECT.

Join our Harlequin community to share your thoughts and connect with other romance readers!
Facebook.com/groups/HarlequinConnection

HARLEQUIN

Heartfelt or thrilling, passionate or uplifting—Harlequin is more than just happily-ever-after.

With twelve different series to choose from and new books available every month, you are sure to find stories that will move you, uplift you, inspire and delight you.

SIGN UP FOR THE
HARLEQUIN NEWSLETTER
Be the first to hear about great new reads and exciting offers!

Harlequin.com/newsletters

HARLEQUIN
PLUS

Announcing a **BRAND-NEW** multimedia subscription service for romance fans like you!

Read, Watch and Play.

Experience the easiest way to get the romance content you crave.

Start your **FREE 7 DAY TRIAL** at www.harlequinplus.com/freetrial.